Gold Magic
Eggling

Lady Li Andre

Order this book online at www.trafford.com
or email orders@trafford.com

Most Trafford titles are also available at major online book retailers.

Printed in Victoria, BC, Canada.

ISBN: 978-1-4269-3145-1 (sc)
ISBN: 978-1-4269-3146-8 (e-book)

Library of Congress Control Number: 2010905020

*Our mission is to efficiently provide the world's finest, most comprehensive book publishing
service, enabling every author to experience success. To find out how to publish your book, your
way, and have it available worldwide, visit us online at www.trafford.com*

Trafford rev. 4/29/2010

 www.trafford.com

North America & international
toll-free: 1 888 232 4444 (USA & Canada)
phone: 250 383 6864 ♦ fax: 812 355 4082

Chapter 1

Dursdan readjusted his grip on the sack of flour as he started the last climb up the hill toward the house. The fresh cut hay from the fields smelled of the remnants of warm sunshine and the coming dew. Wisps of haze were already forming over the lower meadows. A few bees still lingered around the berry blossoms that crawled along the low rows of gathered rocks bordering the fields. The trees that had found shelter from the plow among the hedgerows shook their new green leaves in the gentle late afternoon breeze.

Dursdan whistled a stray tune, something he had picked up in the fields the other day, and tested the melody, keeping rhythm with his steps. Birds sang in the vines and he experimented with their variations. Maybe he would get out the flute after dinner and see how the tune played.

He glanced up at the house, its strong stone walls glazed with a reddish cast. A thin trail of smoke curled up from the chimney and drifted off with the breeze. He could almost smell his mother's cooking and his stomach rumbled in accord. The bag of flour didn't seem as heavy when he imagined all the wonderful delights his mother would concoct with it.

A flurry of chickens greeted him and scattered around his feet. He carefully stepped around them. "What are you still doing out? Silly birds. Hasn't Tolanar tucked you into your roost yet?" He chuckled. The chickens followed him up the path toward the house but stopped as he neared the main gate. They ran off helter skelter toward the hen house. "Very well trained. They're starting to put themselves away at night." He laughed as he unlatched the gate.

He stopped. The laugh died in his throat. The large rock in the opposite corner of the courtyard was occupied. Sinotio was perched there, vast wings outstretched to catch the last of the day's warmth, their shadow silhouetted on the front wall. Each silver scale of the mammoth body reflected the reddish glow of sunset as if tipped with blood. Long talons gripped the rock and his wide head rested on one claw.

Dursdan forced himself to move forward, pulling the gate shut quietly behind him. He glanced frantically around the courtyard hoping to see his father or brother. No one else was there. He was alone with the beast. A trickle of sweat dribbled into his eyes. Dursdan blinked to clear his vision. He swallowed and began creeping around the edge of the courtyard.

The dragon's eyelids were mostly closed but Dursdan could feel the Silver's gaze following him along the path. Tiny pinpricks ran down his spine. He tried to melt into the lengthening shadows of the inner wall. His throat tightened and a great inner drum pounded in his ears. He was almost to the door. Sinotio snorted. Dursdan jumped the last few steps and fled inside.

He stood for a moment in the dark front hall, pulling deep breaths of air back into his starved lungs. Finally he stopped shaking. Why couldn't Da find somewhere else to keep his dragon?

Muffled conversation came from the direction of the kitchen. Dursdan followed the sounds down the long main hall and peered around the doorway into the room. His father was seated at the heavy oaken table, with his feet crossed and propped on another chair, his deep blue jerkin open, its strings dangling down as if cut from a puppeteer's sticks. All he could see was his father's back but the smile on his mother's face was reassuring. Dursdan sighed with relief and paused in the shadows of the doorway, not wanting to intrude on their moment.

"You should have seen the trolls scatter. No, my love, they won't be a threat to us and ours any time soon." His father's hearty laughter filled the room. Mergadan drained the contents of his mug. "The house is so still. Where is everyone?"

"Your mum ate with Frecha so she won't be joining us for dinner. Tolanar came home frustrated with his lessons as usual. He's off studying." Dachia swung the large boiling black kettle out of the fireplace and dumped in the vegetables she'd been cleaning. "I haven't seen Dursdan yet." She pushed it back and added more wood to the fire. "From what I've heard, he may be over at the Miller's helping fix the stone. He has a knack for things like that."

Mergadan shook his head. "What he should be doing is preparing for his big day. You don't suppose he was off eyeing the Miller's pretty daughter?"

Dachia laughed. "I don't know that Dursdan thinks much of such things yet."

"Well, it's high time that he does. He'll be taking on new responsibilities in a couple of weeks. Hard to believe he's almost 16."

Dursdan's stomach tightened. Very little had been said about his upcoming Day Natal, at least not to him, not that he didn't know what was expected of him as the first son of a Lord.

"Speaking of that very thing, you'll never believe what I saw coming back from the northlands!"

Dachia sighed. "No, but I suppose you'll tell me."

"A Gold in mating flight."

Dursdan's mouth went dry. So Da had found one after all. He leaned closer to listen.

Dachia dropped the egg she'd been peeling. "For certain?"

"As certain as I'm sitting here. I really had to work to keep Sinotio from getting tangled up with the flock. You wouldn't believe all the colors chasing her."

"I didn't know there were any golden dragons left in these parts."

Mergadan refilled his mug from the pitcher on the table. "They're rare to be sure. Hasn't been a Dragon Lord with a Gold since the First Circle. Most of the wild Golds were destroyed during the Wizard Wars when my Da passed on."

Dachia leaned on the table in front of Mergadan and crossed her arms. "You're not."

"And why not? Shouldn't my son have the best that can be had? Why, our ancestry goes back to the very first Head of the Circle of Lords."

Dachia turned away from him and retrieved the egg, ripping the rest of the shell away and dropping it into the bowl. "It troubles me. Golds are the most dangerous and they hold the most magic." She smacked another egg against the table and started tearing at the shell.

Dursdan felt his skin prickle and he shuddered. He didn't want anything to do with magic. Vague images from distant dreams circled around his mind. He tried to back away but his body seemed locked in place.

"You needn't worry, my darling. I'll be cautious." Mergadan got up and stood behind her, putting his hands on her shoulders and massaging them gently. "She'll be tired after laying her brood, and hungry. I'll just wait until she goes out to hunt and sneak in and grab one." He took one of the eggs and rolled it around on the table to fracture the shell. He leaned closer to her ear. "Why, she'll probably not even miss it. One less mouth for her to feed." He slipped the egg from the peeling and added it to the bowl.

The nightmarish images in Dursdan's mind evolved into a mass of angry dragons, talons stretched out, looking for him.

"And if she sees you as a tasty morsel?" Dachia moved away from him and stood facing the fire.

The dragons were closing in on Dursdan. His chest tightened. He couldn't breathe. He could feel their breath on the back of his neck and hear the snap of their jaws.

Mergadan grinned. "Ah, don't be silly. Sinotio will easily be able to out fly her in her weakened condition."

The kitchen seemed distant, his parents' voices echoed across a great void. He was in a deep river gorge surrounded by high peaks as the dragons drew closer. This wasn't what he wanted his life to be. His stomach lurched as one of the great beasts dropped down on him.

Dachia turned back, finished the last egg and looked up at Mergadan, her red hair framing her face like a fiery mane. "I just wish you could take someone with you."

Dursdan leaned into the doorframe, trying to hide from the oncoming attack.

"This is something that a man has to do for his son. Alone." Mergadan gently cupped her face in both hands. "I don't expect you to understand, but trust me on this, wife, I've set my mind on it." His voice softened. "I just want Dursdan to have the best I can provide." He drew her toward him and kissed her on the forehead.

Dursdan was falling! He was going to die. His lungs refused to inhale. He could almost feel the talons sink into his shoulder. He tried to duck away. The flour sack fell to the floor at his feet.

Dachia looked over at him and stepped away from Mergadan. "Dursdan. I didn't hear you come in. What do you have there?"

Dursdan looked around, expecting a flight of angry dragons but it was only the kitchen and his parents. His heart still raced out of control but he managed to catch his breath. He hefted the sack back onto his shoulder and strode into the room.

Without glancing at his father, he plopped the bag down on the table sending a small cloud of flour dust across the wooden surface. "The miller sends his compliments."

Dachia smiled. "Well, that ought to keep me for awhile."

Mergadan cleared his throat.

Dursdan took a deep breath and turned to face his father. "Evening, Da. Noticed you were home. I trust all is quiet to the north?"

"The trolls are quiet enough but the wild dragons are all stirred up."

"Oh. I'm sure Tolanar would like to hear all about that." Did Da hear the quiver in his voice? "I've got to get this grime off of me. Ma's cooking smells too good to mix with axle grease and wheat dust."

"A moment, son." Mergadan put his hand on Dursdan's shoulder. For a brief instant, he again felt the dragon's talons, and then the feeling was gone. "You're less than a moon's cycle from your day of passage."

Dursdan managed to swallow. What was he suppose to say? He nodded.

Mergadan smiled at him. "It's time for me to fetch you an egg."

Dursdan looked down at the floor, studying the carefully joined floorboards, worn smooth by many pairs of feet. The words tumbled around in his head. He wanted to say them. No egg for me, thanks.

I'd rather just be a farmer. He again felt the pressure of his father's hand gripping his shoulder. If he could only get Da to understand. His tongue seemed glued to the roof of his mouth, trapping all the words behind it. His face felt as though it was burning.

The long metal bar squealed as Dachia pulled the kettle off the fire. "The food is fit for the table. Why don't you let the boy go wash up. We can talk about this later."

Mergadan released his shoulder and he escaped from the kitchen without meeting his father's eyes. He could hear his father grumble something about ungratefulness and his mother's reply. "He just needs time to get used to the idea."

Dursdan moved through the shadows of the back hallway and slipped into the washroom, lighting the candle. He grabbed the pump handle and pushed on it. Why couldn't he just tell Da no? Surely in the past there must have been some other first son of a Dragon Lord who didn't want to be a dragon rider. The very idea made him shudder.

The water splashed into the bowl and he let go of the handle. Leaning on the pump, he looked at his reflection in the glass - a stray piece of straw caught in his hair, smudges of old flour on his face, axle grime stains on his tunic. His was the face of a farmer, not the stern weathered face of a Dragon Lord.

He shook his head and dug his hands into the cold water. Bending over, he splashed it on his face, letting the cool droplets soothe his burning cheeks. He had to find a way to say it, before it was too late.

"What is wrong with you?" Tolanar slipped in from the shadows and planted himself in the doorway. "At least you could have thanked him. Think about the risk he'll be taking getting that egg for you."

Dursdan dried his face. He had already considered that. It wasn't worth it. "I don't want an egg. And maybe you should mind your own business anyway."

"You don't what?"

Dursdan looked over at his younger brother. "Leave it go, Tola. Ma will want us for dinner."

Tolanar smacked the doorframe with his hand. "You've got wheat dust between your ears! Do you want to embarrass Da in front of the Circle? It's your duty, you know."

"I said leave it go." Dursdan tried to push past him but Tolanar stood his ground.

"It's not fair. Rashir's right about you. You don't deserve to be the eldest."

Dursdan watched the hues of his brother's face darken. "It's not my fault that I was born a year before you. I didn't choose it."

"No, the fates chose you. You can't back away from your responsibilities."

"Maybe Da should give the egg to you."

Tolanar's fist shot out and caught Dursdan in the midsection. He doubled over. It wasn't so much the pain, but that his own brother would hit him. He let the spasms slip away and looked up at Tolanar. There was no sense of repentance in his brother's stance.

Footsteps echoed in the hall. "Boys, the food's on the table." Dachia appeared behind Tolanar. Her brow wrinkled. "Dursdan, are you all right?"

He tried to unfold but a tinge grabbed him. He grimaced. "Just a gut ache, Ma. I better pass on dinner."

She shook her head. "It's all the wheat dust you've been breathing."

"Ya, all shaken down from his rafters." Tolanar ducked past his mother in the direction of the dining room.

Dursdan managed to straighten up. "I think I'll live."

"And it might be your nerves as well." She touched his arm gently. "You've gone and grown up so fast. And here you are, nearly of age, and not quite ready for it, I'd imagine."

His cheeks were warming again. He desperately wanted her to understand. "I see things differently than Da does."

Dachia sighed and rubbed her hands on her apron. "Your Da is a proud man. He just wants the best for you."

Dursdan could see the concern in her eyes. "I don't want anything to happen to him because of me. From what I heard, it sounds very dangerous. Couldn't he look for a different one?"

Dachia shook her head. "He's been searching for months, Dursdan. This is the first female dragon he's found. And your Day Natal is almost here. You should have had an egg months ago. What will people think if you don't have an egg?" Dachia frowned. "It would be horrible."

Dursdan didn't think so but his mother seemed set on it. He rubbed his stomach. "Maybe I best go lay down a bit," he mumbled. "I'm not really hungry."

"Go on then. I'll tell Merg you ate elsewhere." She lightly touched the side of his face. "You will look handsome astride a dragon." She turned and melted into the shadows of the hallway.

Dursdan sighed and blew out the candle. The hall was dark with only the briefest illumination from the direction of the kitchen and dining room. He could hear his parents' voices. Da was still hot about it. He turned away from them. At least his room would be a quiet safe haven.

He rounded the corner and a basket caught him in his still tender midriff. There was a startled cry and the soft thumps of something hitting the floor. "I'm sorry, Gran." He shuffled around in the dark hall retrieving the dumped yarn balls.

"Shells, child. What are you doing creeping about in the darkness? Shouldn't you be at the dinner table?"

He grabbed at a stray ball, the rough yarn clinging to his still damp hands. "I wasn't feeling well." He dumped the balls back into the basket. "This isn't very good grade yarn. Are you working a rug?"

She chuckled softly. "You can't stave my curiosity by changing the subject." She found his hand in the darkness. "Only the experienced hands of a farmer could tell this is poor grade wool."

Dursdan was grateful his grandmother couldn't see him. The flush had crawled back to his cheeks. "It's what I'm best at. But somehow I just can't bring myself to tell Da that."

"This is not the place for that kind of talk." She handed him the basket. "Carry this into my room for me, will you Dur?"

She turned toward her room and he followed with the yarn. She held aside the heavy drape that served as a door and Dursdan ducked inside. "I just don't have the courage to tell him."

"Wouldn't hardly matter if you did. Nothing he could do about it." He handed her the basket and she set it on the table and turned up the wick of the lamp. "Old traditions are hard to break. And the Dragon Lords are one of the oldest traditions our people have."

"I know the stories, Gran." Dursdan sank down on her bed and studied the fading patterns of her floor tapestry.

"Tisk, my boy. You know what you've been told, and only that. You won't learn the real stories in school. I much doubt the Circle itself reveals the real stories anymore." She gently took his chin in her warm hands and pulled his face up. "You remind me much of your granddad. You're more like him than like your Da."

"But Granddad was a Dragon Lord, too."

Carala nodded and let him go then tucked herself into the rocking chair and picked up the blanket she'd been knitting. "Just so. But different." She picked through the basket and chose a new ball of yarn. "Those were different days as well, what with wars against wizards and all. Ah, his grand Red was truly a sight."

She rocked gently as new rows seemed to magically appear from her needles. Dursdan sat mesmerized by their clicking rhythm. Carala finished off a row and looked up at him. "There's more in you than you know."

He startled. Did she know about the dreams?

"Your bloodlines run deep and they carry some magic in them. Doesn't show itself often. Torgadan's mum passed it all on to me even as it had been passed on to her. All the old histories. That's the responsibility of the wife of a Dragon Lord. Best pick one who's got some brain. Not that your Ma was a bad choice but she doesn't keep it up like she should."

Dursdan felt the warmth creeping up his neck and was glad his half of the room was in shadows. He didn't want to think about a wife any more than becoming a Dragon Lord.

Carala chuckled. "Yes indeed. Much more like Torgadan."

Dursdan watched her gnarled fingers work the yarn onto the needle. He saw his own life being pulled like that strand, worked by someone else into a pattern that was beyond his control. "How do you choose which ball of yarn you'll work from next?"

"By feel. I touch the balls of yarn until I find one that feels right. That's the one I use." She paused and looked up at him. "But these balls of yarn don't feel right to you, do they?"

He shivered. Could she hear his thoughts? No, she was talking about the yarn. "Maybe I can find some better yarn for you in town."

"Perhaps." She put down her work and opened the large wooden trunk beside her chair. "You'll need something to barter with." She pulled out a beautiful knitted blanket. Carala shrugged and handed it to Dursdan. "I make them more to keep my hands busy than to stay warm. See if you can find someone who needs a new blanket."

He took it and got up to leave. "I'm sure I can find someone who will like it. It's a beautiful pattern."

Carala reached out and gently wrapped her hand around his. "There are many patterns in life. You have to make them with whatever yarn comes your way. Sometimes we don't get to choose the colors but we can control the pattern. It just takes patience." She nodded and let go of his hand.

Dursdan studied her face. It was softly lit by the oil lamp and showed the signs of age creeping around her eyes and mouth. She wasn't that old, really. Her white hair still had a touch of gold. It occurred to him that he was staring and looked away, his gaze falling on the open trunk. "Gran, what's that book?"

She looked down into the trunk and picked up the book, gently running her hands across the finely tooled leather cover. "Torgadan's Mum gave it to me. Armia was an amazing historian. She wrote it all down. Her Grandma was once a princess of a distant kingdom and her stories of the first war and the origins of the Dragon Lords are all recorded in this volume, as well as the entire history of this Valley up to her death. And I'm sure Korithiena encouraged her. She wrote much about Torg's Great Gran." Carala sighed. "I suppose I should have kept it all up to date but I'm afraid I'm not as good at things like that as she was."

Dursdan reached out to stroke the cover. "It's all there?" He still remembered Armia even though he was quite young when she had past on.

"Oh, yes. Armia loved to write." She opened the book and carefully turned the pages. She looked up at Dursdan. "You should have this. Read it. It will help you understand why it's your duty to be the next Dragon Lord of this family."

Dursdan took the book. "But isn't there any first son who didn't?"

Carala leaned back in her chair and shook her head. "None that I can recall."

Dursdan frowned. He could hear Tola laughing in the dining room. No doubt Da was recounting some adventure with the trolls.

He looked back at his Gran. "But what if something happens to Da? What if he gets hurt trying to get an egg, or worse?"

"It is a task of honor for a Lord to find his son the best egg he can." She looked toward her bedside table and Dursdan followed her gaze. There was a faded small painted portrait of a man. Dursdan studied the weathered face of his dead grandfather then looked back at Carala. Her features softened and her voice dropped to a whisper. "I still remember when Torg told me he'd seen a wild Silver. I was thrilled and terrified at the same time. But I was proud that he would go to such lengths for our son." She shook her head and patted Dursdan's hand. "Your Da loves you. I know he will do what ever it takes to procure you an egg. He's been searching for months, you know."

Dursdan sighed. "I know. Ma told me." Not that he hadn't already known. His father would be gone for days at a time and his mother would jump at every sound. His innards clenched. "I just couldn't bare it if something happened to him on my account. I'd rather go without."

"Nonsense. Your Da would never break with tradition. He will find you an egg if he must scour every mountain and valley." She picked her knitting up and began working the next row. "Best you not worry about it. Go get some sleep."

"Yes, Gran."

Dursdan retreated to his own room, dark but for the moonlight streaming through the open shutters. He draped the blanket over his chair and stared at the pattern in the dull glow. A few clouds drifted across the moon and for a moment, Dursdan thought he could see dragons flying in the pattern. He turned around and pulled the window shutters closed. He didn't want any dragons in his pattern.

He sat on his bed with the book in his lap, his fingers tracing the engraved design. He had a few faint memories of the stories Armia had told him when he was little. Now that he was older, he wanted to know these people of the past and demand answers from them. Why did he have to take a dragon and why did Da have to take this risk? If something happened to Da, he'd never forgive himself, and neither would Tola. There had to be a way to convince Da not to do this. Could the answer lie in this book?

His eyes felt heavy and he knew his mother would intrude if he lit a candle. He put the book down on the table beside his bed then undressed and slipped beneath the covers. He'd have chores to do in the morning. Dursdan took a deep breath and closed his eyes. Some nights were worse than others. Tonight he hoped for a dreamless sleep.

* * *

Aramel hummed softly as he examined the rugged walls of the canyon below in the last of the moonlight. It had taken him most of the night to hike to this remote valley. He couldn't risk using magic so close to her. He could see her cave still far below, its opening a darker crack in the shadowy rugged wall. It was going to be a rough climb but fortunately he'd have all day to make the descent. Strong north winds whipped down the narrow gorge. He pulled his thick fur-lined cloak closer. It was late in the season but the wind still held a hint of snow.

She was singing her birthing song. Not that anyone else would call it music. It rang with power and wildness, surged into reckless harmonies of magical creation, and wound down into the steady rhythm of a great beating heart. She was laying her brood.

He'd been waiting months for this moment. She was rare, this golden female, maybe even the last in the northern mountains. When he'd discovered her cavern in the dead of winter, a great plan had formed in his mind. He'd dug deep into his darkest libraries to find the book of calling. Not for her. He was no fool. But he watched and waited and when she was ready, he called them. And they came, male dragons of all colors. It had been like a rainbow chasing a golden sun around the sky.

A new sound was added to her song, a great trilling, as though a thousand small birds were being crushed all at once. Aramel smiled. She was finished laying. Now she would begin arranging her eggs in a manner that suited her. This would preoccupy her most of the day. Considering the length of her song, she had produced a considerable brood. At least one of those eggs would contain a golden dragon.

Aramel rubbed his hands together. This is what he had waited for all these long months. Soon he would have a golden dragon egg. It had cost him dearly but he had acquired all the necessary ingredients that he was going to need to test the eggs. With such a mixture of males, it was hard to tell which eggs might contain a pure golden dragon.

She would feed through the next night. He would be ready. There would be plenty of time for him to find what he was after. Aramel continued to study the steep slope. He wished for the hundredth time that he could just portal there but Golds were sensitive to magic. He patted the leather pouch containing a single portal spell. That was his way out.

Finally satisfied with his chosen route, he settled between some boulders, more to shelter from the wind than to hide. He listened to her singing to her new eggs. It was music to his ears. The sky was already moving from hues of pink to yellow and orange. Just a little longer to wait. It would be worth the risky climb. Very soon he'd have his own golden dragon egg, and not soon after that, his own golden dragon. Then he would have power. He'd open the Western Gate and those measly fools of the West who dared call themselves Wizards, would tremble before him. Aramel smiled.

Chapter 2

Dursdan woke with a start, his hands clasping the sides of his head with his ears still ringing. What was that awful sound? He drew back his hands slowly. Everything was quiet. The echoes of the dream faded away. He wasn't sure what was worse, the dreams he remembered, or those he didn't.

He looked around the room. Sunlight peeked in through the cracks of the window shutters and brightened the dancing dust motes. The beams fell across the colorful blanket and the book on the table beside him. They would both have to wait. He'd promised to help with the haying in the afternoon.

The rooster reminded him of the chores to be done and he scrambled out of bed and dressed quickly. There were eggs to be gathered and cows to milk. He slipped through the quiet house and grabbed a bread roll from the warmer. The water kettle was still hot from the night coals so he made a quick cup of tea.

The morning air held a hint of chill as Dursdan slipped out into the courtyard. The rock was in shadow and Sinotio was huddled in his wings for warmth, a huge living silvery tent dripping with dew. Dursdan tiptoed quietly around the edge of the wall and made it to the gate. As he lifted the latch, his back tingled. He looked over his shoulder. A pair of gleaming blue eyes peered at him from under one wing. He shuddered and hurried out toward the barn.

He finished his chores and grabbed up his books. There was activity in the courtyard. He could hear his father instructing Tolanar on the procedure for removing the dew from the dragon's wings. It was time. He had to convince him not to go. He was almost to the courtyard gate when Sinotio bugled. Dursdan stopped, his heart racing. He remembered his mother's concern and forced himself to move toward the gate. As he reached it, a huge silver form sprang out of the courtyard. Dursdan cringed and ducked against the wall, shielding his head with his arm. The dust from the down draft blinded and choked him.

When he could see again, he looked up and saw his father sitting in the harness on the Silver's back, waving down. The dragon made a broad circle over the Valley then turned northward. "No! Da, wait!" Dursdan groaned. He was too late!

Tolanar came rushing out the gate, almost colliding with him. The elation on his face turned into a scowl. "Where have you been? You should have been here to see Da away."

"I was coming to tell him not to go."

"What?"

"You said it yourself last night. He's placing himself in great danger to get this egg. It's crazy. I don't want an egg if it means loosing Da."

Tolanar's face seemed to crawl. "You're a disgrace to this family. How can Da call you his son?" He spit on Dursdan's boots then turned and ran down the hill toward the road.

Dursdan gave one final glance at the quickly vanishing speck in the sky. His stomach lurched as the dragon disappeared over the distant horizon. His cheeks burned. He squeezed his eyes shut to force the tears out of his vision and wiped his sleeve over his face. He looked down at his books dangling in their leather strap, sighed, and then followed his brother toward the town.

Men were already out in the fields, hitching work animals to plow and wagon. The winter wheat needed to be gathered so the fields could be prepared for summer crops. Dursdan usually enjoyed watching their progress but today he trotted down the road barely noticing the workers.

The town was a bustle of activity. He could hear the ring of the blacksmith's anvil and smelled fresh bread baking somewhere. Women chatted over quilt patterns while some men loaded sacks of seed onto carts by the granary. A few people pushed handcarts loaded with winter goods toward the mercantile, ready to trade for the things they needed. He passed through the crowd lost in his thoughts.

Dursdan crossed the bridge and headed up the hill, amid a flock of younger boys, toward the school. The Master was opening shutters and shouting reprimands from the windows. The school stood alone on a broad flat terrace. Its old stone walls were hung with ivy and pockets of moss. The red slate roof glowed in the morning sun.

Dursdan was distracted by a high-pitched wail and looked up. A small red dragon sat perched on the top plates, peering down at an older boy on the school steps. Morazan looked up at his hatchling. "Come down you silly goose. I'm not coming up there to get you."

The little red dragon cried mournfully then launched itself off the roof. The boy was forced to catch it and the weight knocked him off balance, sending him sprawling, the Red squawking his displeasure.

The other boys in the schoolyard laughed. Rashir almost fell off the branch he'd been perched on. "Hey Mora, looks like Shatsu needs more flying lessons!"

Morazan frowned. "He's just started using his wings. Give him a chance!" He patted the little Red's head affectionately. "But I sure will be glad when he can fly on his own. He's getting heavy." Morazan gently pushed Shatsu off his stomach and got up, straightening the crumpled mess of his deep green tunic. He turned and waved at his younger brother. "Hey, Def, Ma says to remind you to come home right away after school." The little boy waved back. "I have to get on to my own classes. See you later." He walked back down the hill, the tottering hatchling in his wake.

Dursdan looked across the town toward the large stone keep of the Circle and wondered what kind of classes Morazan and his hatchling were required to take.

"They sure grow fast."

Dursdan caught his breath. He hadn't heard the boy come up the path behind him. He turned and managed to smile at Borgan, glancing down at the bulk that rested on the boy's stomach, uncertain what to say. "How is it?"

Borgan patted his bulging egg pouch and smiled down at his burden. "I can't wait to see what he looks like. I took him to Frecha. She's the best at scrying eggs. She says he'll be a Black and his name is Daroth."

Anlahad joined them. "Do you suppose she's always right? She said my egg is a Bronze but Ma thinks it's a Brown."

Dursdan shivered. He looked toward the northern mountains. Even though he was standing in the sun, he felt cold.

Sormato struggled across the schoolyard lugging a bin of warmers as well as his egg pouch. "I'd go with Frecha on a bet. Don't know that she's ever been wrong." He set the bin down. "Anyone else need a change?"

Anlahad reached for the tongs and opened the bin. "Thanks, Sorm. Hey, what about you, Dur? What color egg do you think your Da will fetch you?"

Dursdan couldn't swallow. He shrugged, trying to look unconcerned, and finally managed enough spit to unstick his tongue. "I can't say." The bell began to ring. Dursdan gratefully slipped away from the egg-toting trio and into the school.

He sank into his seat beside Conor and began arranging his books for the daily lessons. Conor nudged him. "Are you okay?"

Dursdan shook his head. He managed a weak smile. "How did you guess?"

"Well for one, you're as pale as fresh milk." Conor grinned.

It took Dursdan a moment to catch the line. He chuckled. "Leave it to you to find the fun in everything." Dursdan sank deeper into his seat and heaved a sigh. "Everything's gone wrong."

"The stone didn't set?"

"The stone?" He'd almost forgot. "Oh, no that went well. Miller even gave me a fine sack of flour for my trouble. No, it was after that everything fell apart. Da was home. He's seen a dragon in mating flight."

Conor glanced over at the egg carriers. "Guess you'll be joining that crowd soon. Will you want a new seat mate?"

Dursdan looked over at him to see if he was joking but Conor's face looked serious. His throat tightened. What if Conor didn't want to sit next to him anymore? They'd been friends as far back as he could remember. He bit his lower lip to keep it from trembling. "I don't want an egg."

Conor's brows arched up. "What? But Dur, your Day Natal is almost here. That's what the first sons of Dragon Lords do, ain't it? Take on an egg. Why, my Pa would think I was daft if I didn't want to farm."

"I just wish I wasn't first son." He looked over to where Tolanar sat in vivid attention as Borgan explained the scrying process Frecha had used on his egg. "Tola's more into things like that than I am, and I'm a better farmer than he is."

Conor laughed behind his hand. "Oh, no doubt of that. Remember last fall when Master Damitrus had us in the fields? He called for a handful of wheat and Tola brought him oats!"

Dursdan was forced to smile. "But that is just my point. He knows nothing of farming. I do most of the work at our place. The cows run in terror if they see him with a bucket." Conor hid his laugh in a cough and nodded in agreement. "But it's more than that, Con. I've just never liked dragons much." The images from dreams swarmed around him. His mouth went dry and he quickly shook them away.

Conor put a hand on his arm. "Steady there, Dur."

Dursdan's vision cleared. He glanced over at Conor. The light brown mop of hair with a piece of straw caught in the disarray reminded him more of his own reflection. Conor's face, drawn with concern, was the same tan as his own. They wore similar rough tunics, tied round the waist with a cord, and leather pants with heavy soled boots. "I wish I'd been born your brother."

Conor grinned. "I dare say we wouldn't be as good of friends in that case." Conor squeezed his arm and let him go. "I can't say I understand it all, but whatever comes of it, I'm here with you."

Dursdan felt a weight lifted from his soul. "Conor, you'll always be my best friend. Even if I have to take an egg, that won't change."

Was Conor's lip trembling? "I believe you, Dur."

The Master called the classes together and Dursdan threw himself into his studies, trying to put everything else out of his mind. Conor had to shake him when lunch was called. They walked out into the schoolyard and found a spot under one of the large trees to share a lunch. He was comparing wheat growth rates with Conor when Rashir walked up. His neatly kept light green tunic with its bright yellow sash nicely accented his dark skin and hair.

He stood over them until Dursdan looked at him. "Is there something you need, Rash?"

Rashir puckered his face. "You disgust me. You're a disgrace to the Dragon Lords." He kicked dust on their books. "A first son doesn't study weeds, he learns about dragons." His thick voice rolled almost into a growl. "Useless nonsense, anyway."

Dursdan brushed the dirt off of the books. "Our family has a considerable acreage of farmland that needs to be kept up. Tola doesn't pay attention to his classes, therefore it falls on my shoulders, as first son, to learn all that I can so that the land doesn't go to waste."

Rashir sneered. "Ha, a fat answer! Tola would make a better Lord than you. Why don't you adopt yourself out to a farmer so Tola can take an egg."

Dursdan had never thought of that. Families did adopt out on occasion but he seriously doubted that the children made that decision. It usually only occurred in very large families and it was the younger siblings who were moved to other homes. "I doubt my Da would allow it."

"Your Da would probably be glad to be rid of you. You're nothing but a stupid farm hand. You even dress like one of them. You don't even wear your family colors." He made a big deal of sniffing the air. "Ha, and you smell like one of them, too."

Conor growled and started to rise but Dursdan put a hand on his shoulder. "Let it go, Con. He's not worth it." Dursdan slowly stood up and put himself between Rashir and Conor. He struggled to control his anger at the insult to his friend. "I think you should make better use of your time, Rashir. I heard you didn't do so well on your last exam. Maybe you should be off studying."

Rashir laughed. "This, coming from you? You're wasting your time on farming classes. Does your Da know that?"

Dursdan shrugged. He'd completed all his requirements a year ago. What else was he suppose to do in school? "Mind your own, Rash." He turned and pulled Conor to his feet. "Come on, Con, it seems to be getting a little breezy around here." He guided his friend away from the still laughing Rashir.

Conor looked back. "What's his issue?"

"He just likes to make a stir. He and Tola have always been friends and Tola's on my back for something I said to him last night." Dursdan rubbed his tender midsection and sighed. He looked up, scanning the sky. "I really wish Tola could take the egg."

Conor glanced around. "Your brother saw all that, I'd imagine."

"Tola probably put Rash up to it." He looked back in the direction Conor had pointed. Tolanar was sitting on the fence next to Ragan, both staring coldly at him. They were a study in contrast. Tolanar wore a well-fitting blue jerkin over a white shirt tied with a sliver sash, similar to their father's, with fine linen leggings dyed a rich blue. He even wore a pair of tall black leather boots that Da had given him last wintertide. Ragan wore a rough cotton tunic, leather trousers, and mid-calf rough boots, much as Dursdan did. His dark tanned face and black hair contrasted Tola's lighter complexion and sandy mop. "Now there's an interesting pair." Dursdan shook his head. He wondered what had brought those two together. "Wonder how long that's been going on?"

Conor turned in the direction he was staring. "A bit of an unmatched set, wouldn't you say?"

Dursdan nodded. "Tola I understand. He has teased me ever since we were little. I've always been terrified of Sinotio. Tola helps Da with him, not me. Rash is right about that. Da would be better off giving Tola the egg."

"But does your Pa agree with that?"

The bell rang, calling them back for afternoon classes. Dursdan shrugged and led the way back toward the school. Tolanar and Ragan entered as they reached the steps. Conor shook his head. "I wonder how much of this is Ragan's doing."

"What do you mean?"

"Ragan hates you, you know. His whole family hates your family. That's why I could never figure why he took up with Tola. Doesn't make sense."

"What does he have against my family?"

"Just because, I guess. His Pa, Doran, sometimes helps my Pa with things and they talk. I listen. Doran says really bad things about the Dragon Lords, your Pa especially. Calls them all cattle thieves."

"That's crazy. We have our own herd. Da wouldn't take from others."

"You forget about the tax. Your family doesn't have to pay it because your Pa is a Lord. We pay it, usually without a grumble, because my Pa knows the Lords keep the trolls away, but others aren't as willing."

During afternoon classes, Dursdan pulled out a law book from the shelf and sat down to review it. He had forgotten about the tax. It made him wonder what else he might have let slip. Some of the laws bothered him because they seemed to ask more of the farmers than of the Lord's families. He put it back on the shelf as the closing bell rang.

As he returned to the desk, Conor grinned at him. "Thanks for letting me use your notes. I finally got my calculations to work right." He handed Dursdan back his book. "Where are you headed?"

Dursdan tied his stack, swung it over his shoulder, and walked toward the door. "Aber's place. I'm helping with his haying. He's already cut our fields for us."

"That's grand. Did you have a good crop come in?"

"One of the best. It's already spread in the lower crib." Dursdan went out the schoolhouse door and ran straight into Tolanar. "Whoa, Tola. Doors are for passing through, not standing in front of."

"I don't believe you."

Dursdan forced a laugh and patted the doorframe. "Sorry, Tola, that's just the way it is."

Tolanar scowled. "Rash mocked you and you did nothing."

Dursdan frowned. "What was I suppose to do? Rash is full of hot air." He blew into his fist. "Hot air rises. Just let it go." He opened his hand and pushed it up for emphasis.

"He challenged you."

Dursdan pushed past Tolanar. He and Conor parted company and Dursdan started walking away.

Tolanar called after him. "You should have fought him."

Dursdan stopped, wheeled around and marched back to his brother until they were face to face. He felt the frustration welling up inside. He lowered his voice so the gathering crowd wouldn't overhear. "You're worried about me embarrassing Da because I don't want an egg and yet you're encouraging me to fight the son of another Lord. Don't you think that might also embarrass him? You'd better think on that, Tola."

"The only thing I think is that my older brother is a coward."

Dursdan could hear the snickers from the kids around them. "Too bad. If I were you, I'd head home and do the chores. I promised Aber I'd help put up his hay this afternoon. He's fixing the wheel of our cart for us." Dursdan swung his tied stack of books over his shoulder. "Tell Ma not to wait on dinner. We'll work until it's too dark to see, and the moon's full bright tonight, so that may be pretty late."

He turned to go but Tolanar grabbed his shoulder. "I don't understand you. Why do you bust your back working with these farmers?"

Dursdan pushed his hand away. "Aber hays our fields for us before he hays his own so that our stock has food to eat so we can feed Da's big fat beast. I feel it's only fair that someone from our family should be helping with the work. Since I've never seen you offer to help and Da's always off doing whatever it is he does, that leaves me." Tolanar stared, eyes wide. Dursdan turned and walked away from his brother.

Dursdan moved through the village, a dark mood swirling around him. The people blended into a mass of moving colors. Dragon Lords, with their respective rainbows, moved among the earth tone farmers and merchants. Even the women reflected the colorful patterns. Lady Rayina, dressed in a flowing red gown trimmed in deep purple, waved at him from a doorway. He nodded absently at his mother's friend.

The miller's wife, in a soft light brown dress and white apron, smiled at him from her bread stand. She beckoned him over. "There ye be, Dursdan! I have a fresh roll for ye." She handed him a warm package that smelled of fresh bread, warm butter, and honey. "My Redis is quite happy with your work and old Norgas is beside himself with relief. He was a feared they might have to cut a whole new stone."

"I'm glad I could help. And thank you." He held up the parcel. "This smells wonderful."

"Ah, you're too sweet." A blush came to her cheeks that almost matched the flame of her hair. "Are you headed home then?"

"I'm off to help put hay up at Aber's."

"Seems that's the common ground this afternoon. Jac is off there, too, somewhere. If you see him, will you let him know I'll keep his dinner in the night oven?"

"I'll do that, Tishoma. Good afternoon to you!"

He left the village, crossed the main bridge, and paused to listen to the millstone's soft rumble. There was no more creaking or moaning. The pin he'd placed yesterday was indeed holding. He leaned his arms on the rail of the bridge and watched the water splash around the wheel. The river seemed to grow for a moment; the water tumbling over the wheel became a massive waterfall. Spray dappled his face and a chilly wind raced down his back. He glided through the river valley, exhilarated by the rush of the powerful water.

A dragon bugled and Dursdan grabbed the rail for balance. He looked down and saw the reflection of a great bronze dragon in the water flowing under the bridge. He glanced up as the Second of the Circle flew off toward the Keep. He shuddered. Why was it so important for his father to get an egg? And if it was, why couldn't Tolanar take it instead? Why did it have to be him?

Dursdan sighed and pushed away from the railing. He glanced at the sky again. Its rich azure cast held neither clouds nor any sign of his father. What would he do if Da didn't return? He didn't want to think about it. He absently opened the honey roll and began tearing the still-steaming bread. The sweet warmth eased away some of his dark mood. Carts drawn by cattle passed by, the drivers waving. Dursdan knew all of them. Everyone knew everyone else in the Valley.

He glanced around the snowcapped mountains that framed his world. He'd heard some riders talking. The only things beyond the mountains were the wastes filled with trolls. It seemed the only purpose for the dragons was protecting the farmers and their crops. So where had they come from? He thought about the book his grandmother had given him the night before. Maybe the answers were in it.

Dursdan was distracted by a shout. He looked around and noticed a tall, red-haired youth waving at him from a nearby field. Much of the fresh cut hay was neatly piled in long rows waiting to be gathered. Farther down the field, other men were still cutting and raking. The sun-warmed grasses filled the air with a sweet aroma.

Dursdan grinned and jumped the fence and strolled toward his friend. He missed the older boy's company in school but Jacobi had passed his Day Natal and completed his finals. He now helped his father in the mill.

"Well met, Dur. How goes it?"

Dursdan held the rake while Jacobi took a drink of water. "I hear the stone is working well."

"Who told you that?"

"The stone did. No more creaks or groans." They both laughed. "I also bring news from your Ma."

"Oh?"

"You'll find your dinner in the night oven."

"Many thanks for that news." He ran a hand through his rust colored hair. "It's hot and hungry work out here." He took a final swig from the water jug, capped it, and slung it back over his shoulder. "I was just thinking about you."

"I hope it's nothing bad."

Jacobi chuckled. "None of it. Your Day Natal is almost here, isn't it?"

Dursdan's innards solidified and the bread he'd eaten seemed heavy. "Yes, it's a couple of weeks away."

"I can hardly wait! I have something special for you. I think you'll like it."

He relaxed again and smiled. "Do I get a hint?"

Jacobi bit his lip. "I don't want to spoil the surprise, but it has something to do with a fishing adventure we had a couple of years ago."

"Just as long as it isn't a dead fish." They laughed again. Dursdan looked around. "Have you seen Aber?"

"You just missed him. He's headed up to the barn with a full load." Jacobi took the rake back. "You might want to go up and help unload. We've got plenty of hands here in the field."

Dursdan jogged toward the barn and caught sight of the hay wagon. He picked up his pace, took a shortcut across the field, and arrived at the hayloft at the same time as the wagon. He was out of breath and sank back against the open door, gulping down air.

Aber chuckled. "Never met a lad in such a hurry for a day's work." He relaxed the reins and the yoked cattle shuffled. "Here there, you lot, stand still."

Dursdan grabbed their collar and quieted them. He peered into the shadows of the hayloft. "Looks like these boys have been busy today."

Aber climbed down from the wagon. "That they have. This will be the eighth load. Mirana went off to fetch some grain bags for them."

"I'll pump a bucket of water and grab a rake."

"Good lad. I'll get started here."

Dursdan walked around the barn to the lower side and grabbed a bucket and rake. He stopped at the pump and began filling the bucket.

Something soft thumbed him on the back. "Thought that was you racing across the field."

"Best not spill any of that grain or two hungry cattle will be after you!"

Mirana laughed. "Good to see you, Dur. How goes it?"

He let go of the pump and grabbed the bucket. "Well enough. Lead on, there are hungry and thirsty cattle waiting on us."

They served the cattle then dug into the hay with the wide rakes. It was warm in the loft and the work soon had them sweating. The hay dust clung to the moisture. By the time they had finished the load, they were all covered in fine golden particles. Aber dumped the last of the pile and took the wagon back to the fields while Dursdan and Mirana finished spreading.

When they were done, Mirana sat down and offered a water jug to Dursdan. He sat next to her and gratefully accepted it. The cool water relieved his dry throat.

Mirana pulled at a few loose straws and began braiding them. "Tambo told me what happened in school today between you and Rash."

Dursdan shrugged and handed her the jug. "It was nothing. Rash was just letting off some steam. He keeps looking at all the other boys carrying eggs and he's just jealous. His own Da hasn't found him an egg yet. I don't know what his fuss is all about. He won't be sixteen until the fall."

"But you'll be sixteen soon." She took a drink and set the jug down. "You'll have to carry an egg around just like those other boys."

Dursdan clenched his teeth and shook his head. "I don't want to."

She gasped. "But Dursdan, you're the eldest son. It's your responsibility to one day become a Dragon Lord."

Dursdan stared at her. "My responsibility? I think it's a foolish tradition, one that has maybe outlived its time." He thought of his father, off facing a dangerous beast because of some stupid tradition and shook his head. "You're just a girl. You wouldn't understand."

The color came to her cheeks. "Just because I don't get to go to school doesn't mean I don't know anything. I've read all the old histories."

"You can read?"

Mirana smiled. "Not all farm girls are silly and empty headed. My Mum taught me. Her brother used to be a Dragon Lord, you know."

"No, I didn't. Who's your uncle?"

"His name was Lenadon. I don't remember him. He was older than Ma. He and my grandpa were both killed during the Wizard Wars."

Dursdan wasn't sure what to say. He tried to brush some of the dust off his pants. "My granddad was, too." He studied the calluses on his hands.

"But don't you see, that's why it's so important for you to have a dragon."

He shook his head. "I'm afraid I'm not following your logic."

"There are only a handful of Dragon Lords left. What will our people do when there are none?"

Dursdan wrinkled his brow. "Farm? Besides, how could there ever be no more Dragon Lords? There are twenty-two Lords in the Circle. There are at least ten, maybe more, older men who aren't Lords yet but they already have dragons. I've lost count of how many winglings and hatchlings there are and there are three boys in school carrying eggs around. And how many younger boys who are sons of Dragon Lords who will eventually have eggs? I don't see how I would be missed."

"The Circle has a fraction of what it started out with. Some lines ended during the Wizard War and many wild dragons were killed. There are hardly any left now. Why do you think Rash's Pa is having such a hard time finding an egg? Or maybe you didn't hear that little tidbit. And what about your Pa? You're almost 16 and you don't have one yet. From what I heard, Borgan's Pa had to fly a whole week's journey from the Valley just to find one. Someday, there may be no more wild dragons at all."

Dursdan wished it would all happen tomorrow. He looked out the large doors of the hayloft at the bright blue sky. Where was Da looking? Was he all right? He kicked at the straw with the toe of his boot. "If there were no wild dragons then we wouldn't need Dragon Lords to protect the stock."

She punched him on the shoulder. "Don't tease. You know the wild dragons don't go after the stock. If it weren't for the Dragon Lords, the trolls would have destroyed this Valley years ago."

"From what my Da said, the trolls aren't much of a threat anymore."

"Yes, because the Dragon Lords patrol the northern wastelands. The trolls aren't blind and they're not stupid. As long as they remember what happened the last time they attacked us, they won't do it again. And seeing dragons fly over them is a good reminder."

Dursdan looked at her and searched for a safe way to change the subject. "Which histories have you read?"

"All the ones that Tambo has brought home from school."

Dursdan nodded. "I've read those, too. Gran says it's not all there. That's only what they want you to know. She gave me a book last night. My Great Gran wrote it."

"What's in it?"

"I don't know. Haven't had time to look at it yet. Everything. Gran said that Armia loved to write. I'll have to read it and let you know."

"I'd love to see it."

Dursdan studied her face. She was serious. He nodded. "I'll bring it over when I can."

Aber called up to them. "There's another load waiting in the field."

"Coming, Pa."

Dursdan helped her up and brushed off his trousers. "More work for the weary." He smiled and followed her down the ladder. They walked with Aber out to the fields. Dursdan picked up a rake and began tossing the hay into the wagon as Jacobi and Mirana pulled it into long rows down the field.

The afternoon began to fade. Large shadows swept across the field and a shout from above startled Dursdan. He looked up, blocking the sun with his hand, and saw a group of dragon riders flying in formation.

All but one. He couldn't tell the color of the dragon because of the angle. The larger dragon in the lead swerved around and Dursdan could see the worn face of Lord Crastrom. The distance was great but he could just make out the orders the Lord was shouting at the rider. "Hey there, Satolam! Get your dragon back into the formation! This is no time for games."

Dursdan shook his head as the formation turned and flew over the field toward the east. The lone dragon, a gleam of blue shining off its wings, took its place and the large Red returned to the front of the V-shaped group. The five dragons continued across the Valley and Dursdan went back to pitching hay. He sighed. Surely they could do without him. There were plenty of dragons in the Valley already.

The moon was just rising full at the eastern horizon while the sun sank at the other when Aber's wife, Kalista came to the fields with heavily laden baskets. All the workers gathered around her as she and Mirana passed out the food. Dursdan gratefully accepted the meat roll and cup of tea. He and Mirana sat back-to-back, leaning on each other for support, as they ate the warm food. Dursdan surveyed the fields. There was still more hay on the ground but the full moon shed plenty of light to work by. When they had finished eating, Dursdan helped Mirana to her feet and gave his cup back to Kalista.

They worked well into the night. The moon was directly above them as they finished the last load. Dursdan helped unhitch the team, said goodnight to the other weary workers, and pushed the repaired cartwheel down Aber's lane toward the road. The night was still, with only a slight breeze and the occasional cricket or frog. His body was sore but all the hay was in. The eastern horizon was still dark but it would only be a matter of hours before that changed. And he had chores to look forward to in the morning.

He followed the road then turned up their own lane, pushing harder at the uphill climb. The house on the hill was dark. He looked across the shadowy fields surrounding the house and knew what each one would contain. He'd made plans for planting and reserved seed last fall. Tolanar had looked confused last harvest-tide when Dursdan had carefully walked through the fields gleaning, by hand, the best for the next year. How was Tola ever going to manage? He was far more interested in helping with Sinotio. Why couldn't Da see that?

He rolled the wheel into the barn and leaned it against the wagon. It would have to be greased before it was placed back on the axle. Another thing on his list for the morning. At least there were no classes to attend.

He carefully lifted the latch of the courtyard gate and slipped in. He didn't want to wake the Silver. But as his eyes adjusted, he realized the rock in the corner was empty. His father had not returned. A shiver ran through him and settled in his stomach.

The house smelled of a good dinner, one his stomach regretted missing. A dim light emanated from the kitchen. He peered around the corner. A single candle stood sputtering on the table. Carala was making a cup of tea. He cleared his throat so as not to startle her. She turned around, blinking in the dim light. "Is that you, Merg?"

"No, Gran, just me."

"Oh, Dursdan. You're finally home. Dachia left some dinner for you and your Da in the warmer. Come in and sit and I'll dish you out some."

"Da hasn't come back?"

"No." She busied herself with a platter and spoon then placed the food on the table in front of him. "I was hoping he'd be back before I was. I've been over to see Avanta. Rad was worried about her. And you know your Mum. If her little brother is worried about his wife, everyone should worry about her." Carala chucked dryly. "But she seems fine."

Dursdan was relieved. He deeply loved his Aunt and Uncle. The thought of her being ill made him worry. "Were the little ones giving her much fuss?"

"I dare say Adachi isn't that little anymore. He's in his eleventh year now. And he might benefit from an older boy's company."

The hint wasn't lost. Dursdan choose to ignore it. Adachi had a tendency to be annoying, especially at school. "And the girls, are they well?"

Carala smiled. "Lusica was tending her Mum as if she were grown. What a sweet child. As for Cluyesa, She was tucked in next to Avanta. She's really too little to understand much."

Dursdan hid a grin behind his fork. Clu was just three but she understood more than most gave her credit for. She was definitely his favorite of his little cousins. She was his shadow whenever he stopped in for a visit.

Carala sat down across the table from him. Her face seemed even more wrinkled in the dim light. Dursdan put down his fork. "Are you feeling all right, Gran?"

She smiled. "Just tired. Rad brought me home on Osiral. It's been awhile since I've flown a dragon back. Even though I was wrapped from head to toe, I still managed a chill. Spring is fresh and still has a bite to it."

Dursdan shivered for a different reason. Just the thought of being on a dragon was enough to give him a chill. He changed the subject. "We got all the hay in tonight."

"Hmm. Good of you to help with that but I wonder at how you spend your time. Tola regaled us at dinner with an interesting tale. Perhaps you'd like to share your version with me?"

Dursdan could only imagine what his brother had said. "It was nothing. Just some cocky show from one of the boys in the class."

Her brows went up. "Indeed. Tola said you insulted the son of a Lord."

"Was that his version? Well, if it's an insult not to fight another for a stupid reason, then I guess I'll just have to continue to be insulting." He got up and took his platter to the wash pan, rinsed it, and added it to the others drying in the rack over the night coals.

Carala grabbed his hand as he turned to go. "You are the first son of the House of Dan. That is not a responsibility to be taken lightly."

Dursdan studied his grandmother's face. He'd heard quite enough about responsibility for one day. He shook his head, squeezed her hand gently, and kissed her on the forehead. "Good night, Gran."

His own room was a mass of strange starlit shadows. He stared out the window at the quite barns and henhouse. All was well there. He contemplated whether to leave the shutters open or to close them. There was too much to do on the morrow. He left them open so the sun would wake him. The bed welcomed his tired body. He closed his eyes and drifted into sleep.

* * *

The egg shimmered briefly then cracked, a swirl of blue leaked from the shell. Aramel growled with frustration and looked back at the scattered remains of the eggs. Were there no golden dragons at all?

The moon was setting and the shadows deepened in the vale. It had been a long night. He'd found many blues, a handful of yellows, a green here and there, even a red but not one golden dragon in the whole brood. He kicked aside the broken remains of the eggs and stepped around the oozing puddles, their colors already fading. He held up his staff so that its light reached all the corners of the cavern. All that remained were broken shards.

A strong breeze blew into the cavern. She was returning! He moved deeper into the recess and quickly set up a portal spell. As he laid the last piece, his eye caught the glint of gold tucked far back in a crevasse. Was there one more egg?

He reached up and pulled it off the shelf of rock. Its surface gleamed in the mage light from his staff. His hands shook as he quickly pulled out the ingredients to test the egg. He could hear the golden female as she landed on the ledge outside. He sprinkled the last ingredient on the egg and sealed the spell with a chant. The egg glowed gold! He had found his golden dragon!

The female screamed her defiance and rushed into the cave. Aramel grabbed up his staff and began the portal chant. The golden female reached out a powerful forelimb and just missed the Wizard. The portal spell was scattered across the floor. Aramel flung himself backward to escape her second swipe. He tripped over a protruding rock and fell back. The egg rolled out of his hand. He reached for it. The female dragon stomped a heavy foot down between his hand and the egg. Aramel looked up at the gleaming teeth and darted away from their snap. He swung his staff, sending sparks flying around the cavern. She backed off a little but was not fully deterred.

He could see the first hues of morning lighting the entrance of the cavern and made a dash for it. Her scales scraped the floor as she followed. He ran for the ledge and began scrambling up the steep side. She burst out of the cavern and extended her wings, turned and dove toward him. He continued to scramble through the narrow passages between broken boulders. She pursued him fiercely.

He topped a narrow ridge and spotted the crevasse he had noticed during his descent. Aramel worked his way from one rock to the next, fending off her attacks with his staff. He was almost there. She reached for him again, her sharp talons gouging the rock beside him. On her upbeat, he raced across the distance and squeezed into the narrow opening.

She attacked the cliff face, sending a shower of dust and small pieces down on top of him. Then she wheeled around and disappeared. Everything was quiet. Aramel crept toward the opening. There was no sign of the golden female. He sighed. Well, at least he knew the egg was there. He'd just portal in and grab it. He'd need more ingredients. He crawled out of the crevasse and began the long journey back to his stronghold.

Chapter 3

He was flying along a steep gorge, following the river toward the mountains. The chill of the early morning air exhilarated him. A golden shadow swept across the canyon below him. He tracked back toward the origin of the flight and noticed a darker place in the side of the canyon and dove toward it. An opening appeared, a deep cave. He flew in.

The floor was littered with fragments that crunched under his feet. Slippery goo oozed up through his toes. The smell turned his stomach. He shook his head to clear his nose. Something gleamed in the dark recesses at the very back of the cave. Something golden.

A loud scream filled the cavern. He turned to see teeth and claws reaching for him. The golden prize was tucked away. His own teeth and claws ripped at his attacker. He felt his skin being slashed, ripped, shredded. He screamed in anger and pain.

Dursdan gasped for air. Something had him by the shoulders. He fought back.

"Dursdan, wake up!" He opened his eyes. Gran sat on his bed, holding him. Her eyes were wide. "What is it child? You screamed so, I thought for sure something had broken into the house and attacked you."

His mouth was dry and his body ached. He looked down at himself and was surprised not to see any blood. "It was just a dream." He said it more to convince himself than relieve his grandmother.

Dachia ducked past the drape into his room. "Is he all right?" Her voice shook.

"He'll live but a cup of tea might do him good."

His mother disappeared. He could hear Tolanar grumbling in the hallway. "Another one of his stupid dreams." Then feet stomped away.

Dursdan looked up at Carala. Her face was pale in the early light of dawn. "Has Da come home yet?"

She shook her head.

Dachia returned with a steaming cup and handed it to him. "Here, this will make you feel better."

He sipped at the hot tea, uncomfortably aware that they were staring at him. "I'm sorry I woke you."

"It's just been such a long time since you've had a dream like that." Dachia came and sat on his bed next to Carala. She pushed the hair back from his eyes. "I'd thought you'd grown out of such things."

"I'm okay, really." He finished off the tea and handed the cup to his mother. "I've just had a lot on my mind lately."

Dachia nodded and got up. "Try to get a little more sleep. Tola can do the milking this morning." She pushed back his drape. "I won't say anything about this to your Da." She went out and the drape fell closed.

Carala sighed. "I know she means well but I can see you won't get anymore sleep. The sun's nearly risen. Just lay here a bit and rest. Let her close her eyes again."

He nodded and lay back down. "Thanks, Gran."

Carala nodded. "I doubt I'll get anymore sleep myself." She got up and left the room.

Dursdan watched the colors of the sky change. Early sunlight lit up his room. He tried to let go of the dream but the images still haunted him. The echoes of the nightmare rang in his ears. For a moment he could taste blood and feel the gash marks in his body. He shuddered. What if Da were lying somewhere wounded and dying? It was all his fault. He pulled up his knees and buried his face in his arms. Hot silent tears welled in his eyes. He could feel the edge of the dream threatening to sweep him away again.

Dursdan shook his head to clear the images away. He needed something to distract his mind. He looked around the room, his gaze falling on the book. He reached over and took it, running his hands across the finely tooled cover. He looked closely at the design. It was a great battle scene with trolls swarming around a mighty dragon and an angry looking man. Other dragons with riders were attacking and being attacked by the horde.

He closed his eyes. The images from the dream threatened again. Dursdan looked back at the book. He wanted to put it down but curiosity won and he opened it. He paged through it carefully, noting the fine script and occasional sketch. It was divided into sections. The first was titled "Memories of a Princess," the next was "Words of a Wizard's Daughter," the third, "My Memories", and the fourth, "The Families of the Dragon Lords." That section was more of a list with many names that covered the last half of the book. He ran his fingers down the lists, looking at all the names of people who had been born, lived, and died in the Valley. He finally found his own. There were many notations that made no sense to him, little quips about events that he'd never heard about.

What he was most interested in were the lists of the Dragon Lords and their dragons. He noticed that in the very first generation, all the sons had dragons! He found a note written in a margin that referred him to a different section. He turned to that page and was immediately drawn to a sketch at the center. It was a man with a huge dragon curled around him. Dursdan couldn't take his eyes off the man's face. It looked much like his own.

Below the image he read, "*I begged Korithiena the other day for a sketch of Zaradan and his golden dragon, Malthia. This is her work, spring of 55.*" He looked at the name again then went back to the lists and found it. It was the first Lord of his own family. This was his heritage.

He turned back to the sketch and stared at it. It seemed to come alive before him. From somewhere deep in his mind came a remembered voice. Great Gran Armia sat in the heavy wooden rocker with him in her lap. She was telling him the story of Lord Zaradan. "*He had great strength, not just physically. He had the ability to lead men. If it had not been for his skillful leadership and great sacrifice, we of the Valley would have all been destroyed by the trolls."*

A warmth filled Dursdan, and a profound sense of loss. He hugged the book closely and shut his eyes. He could still smell the strange shawl that Armia used to wear and feel her arms around him. This book was a link to that lost piece of his past.

The knock startled him and he almost dropped the book. He opened his eyes and looked around the room. He was alone. He closed the book carefully and set it back on the table. The knock came again. "I'm awake."

Dachia came in with a tray of fresh bread and tea. Her face turned to worry when she saw him. "Dursdan, you're as pale as a sheet. Are you still ill?"

He shook his head. "No, Ma. I'll be all right." He took the tray.

She sat on the edge of his bed. "This is a new recipe that I got from Rayina. She and Ashandra have been working on some new ideas for rolls and breads. That young lady will make a fine cook someday."

"Well, Lodaki is still alive." Dursdan picked up the small round loaf and took a bite. It had an odd taste, slightly sweet but also salty. The texture was smooth, almost sticky. He managed to swallow it. "Interesting." He gulped some tea and burned his throat. "I still think your bread and rolls are the best." That made her smile. "Ma, do you remember Great Gran Armia?"

Dachia frowned. "I suppose that dream made you think of her." She looked down at her hands. "Gran Armia was quite a lady. She used to tell such stories of the old days. Some of them sounded a little fluffed but they were fun to listen to."

"Why do think the dream reminded me of her?"

"She used to sing you to sleep again after you'd had a bad dream." Dachia looked out the window. "She was much better at comforting you than I was."

Dursdan shook his head. "I barely remember her." A shadow passed across the window. Dursdan jumped forward. "Is it Da?"

Dachia shook her head. "No, just Rad, leaving for home. He came by this morning to get a tea for Avanta. She's still not feeling well." Dachia continued to scan the sky. "Merg may be a few days yet. I talked to Darita, Sangan's wife. She said it took him a whole week to get back with Borgan's egg."

Dursdan sank back down into his pillow. A whole week! But what if he never came home? The images from the dream returned and he blinked them away. "I wish I'd told Da not to go."

Dachia turned and stared at him. "What?"

"I wanted to, before he left. It's too dangerous. I don't really need an egg."

"Don't be ridiculous! You're the first son of this family. Of course you need an egg." She stood up and moved toward the door. "Your Da will be fine. He's a seasoned warrior who fought in the Last Wizard War and has killed many trolls." She was wringing her hands and her voice seemed to tremble. "He'll have no problem getting you an egg."

Dursdan sighed. "Don't fret, Ma. I'm sure you're right."

She let her hands drop. "Tola's finished the chores and is off somewhere. I'm headed over to help Rayina tie a quilt. I'll tell Ashandra you liked the roll." She gave a final glance out the window. "Will you be all right?"

Dursdan was shaking. "I'll be fine. Don't worry about me."

She nodded and left. Dursdan finished his tea and set the rest of the roll aside. Maybe the chickens would eat it. He got dressed, choosing a fine white linen shirt and soft black leather trousers. He looked at the colorful blanket draped over his chair. It was a beautiful pattern, finely knitted with tight stitches. Surely he could find someone in town who would take it in trade for some good yarn.

It took him a little longer to ready the cart as Tolanar had tried, but failed, to grease the wheel before putting it on the axle. He had to yank it off, apply more grease, and reset the wheel. Then he chose a good pulling steer and hitched the wagon. He shook his head as he loaded the trade items. How was Tola going to manage a farm if he couldn't set a wheel?

Dursdan tapped the steer and jogged off down the road toward the town. The nightmarish dream images still haunted his thoughts. He shuddered. That was one dream he wouldn't have minded forgetting.

Dursdan led the steer across the bridge and into the village. Market day was always busy. There were no classes so the streets were filled with children. He smiled at the games they were playing but declined to join in when asked. He had fresh milk and eggs to barter.

It was a festive atmosphere amid the shops as well. Colorful tents had been erected between the regular buildings to cover the stalls of market day sellers. Wonderful wares of every description crowed tables. Many of the wares were winter goods, made during the cold months when snow kept all but necessary outings to a minimum. Dursdan let his eyes rove the tables. Fine wooden utensils and bowls were displayed in one stall while another was draped with colorful tied quilts. He eyed a pair of well-tooled boots but decided his had not worn through enough to warrant the cost of a new pair.

As he walked, he mentally reviewed his list of all the things the family needed. He was startled to overhead his father's name and stopped to listen. Humatsu, Second Lord of the Circle, stood talking to Molahad and Thorazan. They were sitting on high stools at one of the many food booths. Humatsu shook his head. "I had expected him back by now. From the way he described the location to Dors and me, it wasn't all that far. I just hope he hasn't run into trouble."

Molahad slapped his knee and chuckled. "Mergadan doesn't believe in doing anything small, especially when it comes to his first born. My Da said he caused quite a stir in the Circle when he announced his intention the other day." He nudged the other rider with an elbow. "Do you think he's found a stray Silver?"

Thorazan grinned. "I've heard rumors of another Bronze in flight. Maybe he's after one of her eggs." He shook his head. "Personally, I found a Red to be challenging enough for me. I still have the scars to prove it. My Da wouldn't tell me all the details about the meeting, but it sounds quite impressive."

Molahad rubbed his own shoulder. "Thieving from a Bronze is no easy task. I was lucky to come away intact."

Humatsu rubbed his chin. "I'm not allowed to say what color he's after and neither are Lord Sorazan or Lord Falahad. We are bound by oath. But I do agree on one thing, he'll go to all lengths for his son. He's a brave man."

Dursdan shuddered. What if Lord Humatsu was right? What if something had gone wrong and Da was laying somewhere injured, or worse?

The men turned to other topics and Dursdan moved on. He kept glancing at the sky, straining to see all the dragons as they flew here and there. His thoughts were elsewhere but he managed to barter the milk for a bolt of fine linen for his mother. The eggs were exchanged for a jar of good fresh lard. After a final glance skyward, he moved toward the yarn sellers.

"Hey, Dur, wait up."

Dursdan turned to find Steban jogging toward him. He grinned. "Where have you been? Haven't seen you around in a while."

"My Pa and I were up in the mountains gathering special woods. He's teaching me how to make flutes." He produced a small reed from his pocket and handed it to Dursdan. "I remembered how well you play. I thought you'd like to test my very first one."

Dursdan bowed and set down his burdens. "I'd be glad to, Steban. Everyone knows Saldor is the best flute maker in the Valley. You couldn't have a better teacher." He put the flute to his lips and played a short tune. The notes were crisp and on key. Several people nearby applauded.

Steban joined them. "I don't know, Dur. Your playing could make even the worst flute sound rich."

Dursdan handed it back. "Don't be so hard on yourself. That's a grand way to start. Someday you may be a better flute maker than your Da."

Steban smiled. "Well, I'm sure you'll be as good a Lord as your Pa. Will you ride a Silver beside him or maybe a Bronze?"

"Does everyone know?"

A harsh laugh startled Dursdan and he turned to see his brother leaning on a nearby post. "So it seems." Tolanar shook his head and joined them. "Da told the Circle he was going after the egg so now everyone knows. Not all of it, just that's he's gone. The Lords are sworn to secrecy about the color."

Steban looked puzzled. "Is that in case he fails?"

Tolanar frowned and stared at Dursdan. "I'm sure Dursdan hopes he does."

"I just don't want anything to happen to Da. Is that so wrong?"

Tolanar scowled. "Face it, Dur. You're terrified of dragons. I've seen you duck for cover when they fly over and you make a habit of avoiding Sinotio. Wouldn't Da be hard pressed if he knew that!"

Steban put a hand on Tolanar's shoulder. "Don't take so much out on your brother. It's no secret that you'd rather take the egg. But it's Dursdan's place as eldest."

Tolanar pushed his hand away. "Ha! Tell him that!"

"I'm afraid Tola is right, Steb. I don't like dragons. Never have as far as I can remember. And I don't really know why." He was afraid to tell them it was because of the dreams. He didn't want anyone to know about that.

Steban shook his head. "Well, we all do what we have to when the time comes. For example, do you remember the girl I chose on my Day Natal?"

Dursdan remembered all too well. "I really felt bad about that. It's a shame they wouldn't let you keep Narisha as your chosen."

"But I couldn't. We were too closely related. That's why Frecha checks the records for each Choice. So instead, I had to choose Litka. At first, I thought it would be terrible. But as I got to know her better, we found we really liked each other. As a matter of fact, we're sealing the bond next week and you're both invited."

Dursdan held out his hand. "Congratulations. You know I'll be there."

Steban shook it. Tolanar clapped the young flute apprentice on the back. "Good for you. You can count on me, too."

A dragon flew over and Dursdan looked up. It was Trusumo, the Red of Dorsadram, Head of the Circle. He landed in the large square, attracting several Lords who had been in the village for market day. "I hope that doesn't mean trouble."

Tolanar shook his head. "Probably not, but I'll wander over and see what's up." He shuffled off to join the gathering crowd. Dursdan noticed Conor and Mirana moving toward the square. What had brought them to town?

"Your brother is really something, Dur."

Dursdan turned back to his friend. "I'm just not sure what."

Steban laughed. "Oh, I almost forgot. Do you know who Pa and I found in the mountains?"

Dursdan grinned. "I bet you'll tell me."

"The dragonless rider."

"I thought that was just a story."

Steban shrugged. "He lives out there by himself. Pa says his wife died before the war and his only son died in it. He's got no reason left to be here so he doesn't come back."

"Who is he?"

"His name is Terarimi. He's a strange man. But he knows the trees up there and showed us some of the finest mountain maple my Pa had ever seen."

Dursdan thought about the book and wondered if this man was on the list. He'd look it up later. The Red departed and the crowd dispersed. He lost track of Conor and Mirana. "Well, I promised my Gran that I'd get her some better yarn to work with. I'd best go find it."

"Stop and see Tresel. He's been experimenting with some new dyes. My Ma couldn't stop singing his praises. I think it made Pa jealous!" Steban gripped his arm. "Good luck, Dur." He winked and moved back toward his father's shop.

Dursdan found Tresel's stall and looked over the yarn. Some was better grade than others but the colors were as amazing as Steban had said.

Tresel came over when he finished with an exchange. "So, the newest eggling carrier-to-be has come to my humble stall."

Dursdan ignored the greeting and held up a ball of yarn. "This is good quality."

Tresel brightened. "Ah, a man with the gift of touch. That is the finest spring wool. How do you like the color?"

"The colors are brilliant. Have you found a new dye source?"

"Indeed I have. And a new technique for the color setting. You can wash it and the color will hold. The wool may shrink, talk to the sheep, but the color won't fade."

Dursdan chuckled and held up the blanket. "How many balls of your wonderful new yarn is this worth to you?"

Tresel took the blanket and studied it. "The stitches are prefect and the pattern is beautiful. I bet Carala made this. I'd recognize her work anywhere. For her, pick your 20 favorite balls of yarn and we'll call it a good exchange."

Dursdan was impressed. "Done. Gran will be pleased to know that her work is so appreciated."

"Any time she wants more, bring by another. I bet this will go fast. Your grandmum probably has at least one blanket in every house in this Valley. Everyone loves them." He smiled and handed Dursdan a sack for the yarn. "Give her my regards." Dursdan picked out the best balls and tucked them into the sack. Tresel whistled. "No wonder her blankets are so good. She has you to pick out her yarn! I hope your Pa is as good at picking out eggs. What color do you think he'll bring you?"

Dursdan groaned. "I don't know. Thanks for the yarn, Tresel."

He took his goods and went back to the cart to load them. A group of girls moved to intercept him. Soricha, Ashandra, Jazia, Masola, and Tracina encircled him before he could reach it. "I'm sorry, but these things are getting heavy and I'd really like to get them on the cart."

Soricha giggled. "We'll help you, Dur." She took the bag of yarn, Tracina took the lard, and Masola grabbed the linen. Everything was put on the cart and the girls returned.

Dursdan was puzzled. "That was very nice of you. What's this all about?"

Jazia smiled. "Your Day Natal. You have to choose a girl, remember?"

Tracina winked. "We thought you'd like to see your choices up close."

Dursdan groaned. He looked at the girls crowding around him. He'd known all of them his whole life but he'd never really known any of them. Were they really expecting him to choose right now? "I still have time to decide."

"My Da thinks your Da found a Silver or Bronze." Ashandra came closer. "Those colors have much higher status in the Circle. A higher status is also translated to the wife."

Dursdan stared at them. "That's what this is all about? A status contest?" He turned to walk away and almost collided with Rashir.

"Well, Dur, you certainly have drawn a lot of attention today."

He realized Rashir wasn't really looking at him. Dursdan glanced back, following his line of sight. He should have known. Rashir was staring at Ashandra. "I was just leaving. Maybe you'd like to entertain them for awhile."

"I can't imagine why any of them would be interested in you. You're nothing but a stupid farm hand."

Tracina stepped behind Dursdan. "Oh, be quiet, Rash. You'll have your chance when the time comes. Dursdan has first pick."

Rashir sneered. "Why would you want a husband that reeks of stock dung?"

Dursdan side steeped out from between them. "Why don't all of you go have a lovely little chat without me. I really need to get these things back home."

Ashandra stepped forward. "I'll walk with you, Dur."

A crowd had begun to gather around them. Dursdan noticed Mirana as well as Conor and Anlahad. All the faces seemed to blur at once. Rashir was challenging him but his head began to scream. Dursdan put his hands over his ears trying to block out the sound.

Jazia hurried toward Dursdan with a look of concern. "What's is it? What's wrong?"

Rashir pushed him. "You're a coward."

The sound grew louder. Dursdan turned toward the north. It felt as though he was on fire.

Conor was beside him calling his name. He turned on Rashir. "What did you do to him?"

"Nothing! What's his problem, anyway?"

"Make it stop!" Dursdan felt as if his head was going to explode.

Anlahad pointed north. "There's a dragon coming in. By the sound of it, he's not well."

Dursdan knew. He stumbled away from the crowd toward the bridge. It was Sinotio screaming in his head.

Mirana was beside him. She called back. "Conor, bring the wagon. We have to get Dursdan home."

He didn't remember much of that trip. It got to a point where he could no longer hear or see beyond the scream in his mind. He felt arms around him and knew Conor and Mirana were there.

He was vaguely aware of pushing through the courtyard gate, of Radachi demanding answers from his stunned friends, but what he was most aware of was that he'd found the source of the scream. "Make it stop!" His own words echoed painfully in his head and dragon cries went up from all over the Valley. Suddenly, the noise was gone. It was so quiet that Dursdan could hear his own heartbeat. He opened his eyes.

Three very stunned dragons were staring at him. Radachi's white Osiral had his wings wrapped around Sinotio, supporting his weight. Red Natalo had the injured dragon's head on his shoulder. He looked quizzically down at his rider, Lord Crastrom. The Silver was in bad shape. Blood oozed from numerous wounds and a section of his wing was crumpled at an odd angle, but his eyes looked straight at Dursdan. Osiral and Natalo seemed to bow. Sinotio blinked.

Radachi swiveled back and forth between the dragons and Dursdan. "Shards! What just happened? Dur? Are you all right?"

Crastrom stared at him, wide eyed.

Dursdan was looking at the angry wounds on Sinotio. A sickening thought came to his mind and forced him into motion. "Da!" He ran to the house and yanked open the door. He could hear his mother crying. His knees almost buckled. "This is all my fault." He ran toward his parents' room.

Mergadan lay in the bed. Avanta was helping Carala bind his wounds while Dachia sat weeping in the corner. Mergadan fought against the bindings. "Where is Dursdan? Where is my son?"

His knees felt weak but he managed to move forward. Carala saw him and drew him into the room. "Your Da needs you. Come."

He allowed her to pull him closer. He swallowed hard. "Da, I'm here."

Mergadan tried to sit up but Avanta held him down. "No, Merg, save your strength. Dur, come here so your Da doesn't have to move."

Dursdan stood beside the bed. "It's all right, Da, I'm here. Just stay still."

Mergadan struggled to move and pulled a sack from the blankets beside him. Its rounded bulge dwarfed his large hands. Avanta looked at Carala and drew back. Dachia came forward and stood behind Dursdan. Mergadan opened the sack, withdrew the contents, and shakily held the egg out to his son.

Dursdan stared at the object in his father's hands. It was larger than he had expected from what he'd seen of the others, bigger than any melon he'd ever grown. Its surface swirled as though liquid gold lay just below the solid shell. His father's blood smeared some of the swirling design and reflected a reddish cast on the golden pattern. Dursdan shivered, the fleeting whips of last night's dream haunted his mind.

"Take it," whispered his father.

Dursdan couldn't move. He felt his mother's hand on his shoulder. "It's all right."

He managed to reach out toward the egg. The swirls seemed to increase, the patterns shifting as though anticipating his touch. His fingers brushed the surface. For a moment he saw the face of a fierce golden female dragon reflected in the turbulent swirls, heard her scream of defiance, felt her anger at the theft, smelled her anguish, tasted his father's blood, fresh on her tongue. He jerked back.

The grip of his mother's hand tightened. Her breath softly tickled his ear. "Dursdan, your Da has risked much for this. Take the egg."

Dursdan looked up and met his father's eyes. A gaping wound seeped blood across his forehead. In his mind, he again felt the dragon's talons rake Mergadan's face. His father tried to smile. "I wanted you to have the best."

Dursdan wanted to scream. What did Da know of what was really best for him? Had he ever asked? Did he once ever consider that maybe his son had other dreams for his future?

Dursdan's gaze shifted. Tolanar's face evolved out of the shadows of the doorway. Dursdan watched the anger play across his brother's strong features. If only he could convince Da to give Tola the egg instead. How could he do it? He tried to find the words. He looked toward Tolanar but his brother drew back into the shadows.

Mergadan groaned. "Dursdan." His voice was low and wispy.

Dursdan turned, feeling as if time had somehow slowed, and watched the color draining from his father's face. Trembling hands pushed the egg closer. Dursdan swallowed hard. It was his fault. Da had come to this because of him. He hadn't had the courage to tell him not to go. The egg began to slip from Mergadan's grasp.

As if from a distance, Dursdan watched his own hands catch the egg. He felt his mother's sigh of relief on the back of his neck; heard his brother stomp down the hall and the slam of the outer door. His father shrunk into the pillows, a strained smile on his face.

Dursdan tasted salt at the edge of his mouth and glanced down at the egg in his shaking hands as one of his tears slipped from a cheek. It splashed on the surface, causing ripples in the swirling golden pattern.

Carala moved forward. "Mergadan needs rest. Dachia, didn't you tell me you had made a special warming pouch for Dursdan's new charge?"

Dursdan let his mother lead him away from his father's bedside. He continued to stare at the egg. She led him into the sitting room and held out the new pouch. He let the egg slip into its waiting opening and watched his mother pack the warming pads around it and fasten the lid. She put the strap over his head and wrapped the waist ties around and through the loops. He could feel the warmth of the heating pads seep through the material to his abdomen. The weight rested heavily on his shoulders. It might as well have been a stone around his neck.

* * *

Aramel moved the jars and boxes around on his shelves. He was certain there should have been another box of bane leaves. He sighed and gave up his hunt. He was also short on yarrow powder. Bother. It meant a trip down into the valley to trade with the farmers, foolish peasants. He'd have to make up some quick spells to barter with, a few fast grow spells and maybe a cattle-healing spell. But it couldn't be helped.

The lack of ingredients also meant he couldn't just portal down to the town, he'd have to use alternative means. How could he have let his supplies get so low? It was true that the golden dragon had occupied most of his time lately. He didn't want to wait too long before making another attempt. She might decide to move her last egg. He'd make certain that he had enough on hand for a search spell, just in case.

He looked up at the raven sitting on its perch. A note would be in order. He hastily scribbled a list of ingredients and tucked the scroll into a leather roll and bound it to the bird's leg. With a few words of instruction, he took the raven to the roof and released it.

Then the Wizard began assembling the ingredients he'd need for the quick spells. He also pondered his route of travel. He searched the shelves to see what he had left. Ah, callaberry seeds. Well, he'd ride to town in style. After preparing his barter spells, he rolled up his favorite rug and went back up to the ramparts. The sky was strewn with stars and the moon reflected pale light from the snow capped peaks around him. Surely the miserable farmer would be asleep. His messenger would have to wait until morning. It would do him no good to leave now. Besides, the callaberry seeds usually worked better when they had time to germinate before use. He sprinkled them over the rolled up carpet, pulled his thick cloak around himself, and sat down to wait out the night.

Chapter 4

The dream was unlike any he'd ever had before. He heard
someone calling and went to find whom it was. He walked
through strange halls hung with sheer drapery. She came
out from behind a veil and seemed startled. "Was it you who called?"

He stared at her. She was very tall with long flowing white hair,
seemingly ageless. She was dressed in a flowing white gown and mist
swirled around her when she moved. "You did call."

"Me? I didn't call anyone. I was looking for someone who was
calling."

She laughed and it sounded like a thousand tiny bells. "I only
returned your call. But I see that you are not what I expected." She
reached out and touched him. "But the one I seek is very near to you.
He is young but he is strong. I like that. He will do."

"Who are you?"

"I am Timotha. I am very far away but I will find you." She looked
closer at him. "What have we here?"

Dursdan looked down and found his stomach was glowing. He
began to panic. "What is it? What's wrong with me?"

She laughed. "What a delight! But I should have seen that you are a man." She touched his face. "A man like I have never encountered before."

He shuddered. The glow in his stomach increased and began to radiate heat.

Timotha laughed again. "Oh do not fuss so, little one. I have no designs on your human. It is not his kind I seek. I need my own kind." She seemed to swell.

Dursdan backed away and found himself falling. The glow of his stomach became a golden light that encircled him. He struggled to breathe. A weight threatened to crush him. He pushed forward and sat up. The egg pouch rolled uncomfortably across his stomach. Gray shrouds from his dream still lingered. He shook his head to clear them. It had only been a dream.

Dursdan laid back in his bed, listening to the activity in the house. There had been a constant stream of visitors all night, some coming to help tend his father and others coming to support Dachia through this terrible tragedy. The house seemed quieter but Dursdan was still afraid to leave his room.

The egg lay on his stomach like a weight. He felt cold next to the warmth of the heating pads. He heard Tolanar grumble about doing chores and realized it was morning.

The day was overcast as if responding to the mood in the house. Someone tapped at his doorframe. "Dursdan, are you up? I've made some fresh tea."

Dursdan sat up. "Yes, Gran, I'm awake."

She slipped into his room barely disturbing the curtain and handed him a streaming cup. "Your Da is doing much better. He will need a great deal of rest but he will survive. Radachi assures me that Sinotio is also out of danger. Crastrom tended him all through the night." She paused and looked at him. "Rad told me something odd happened yesterday when you came home."

Dursdan sipped at the hot tea. He hadn't given the event any more thought. He'd been far too concerned about Da. What had happened? The dragons had stared at him. What had that awful noise been?

Carala rubbed the cover of the book. "Did you have a chance to read any of this?"

"A little. There's a huge list in the back with everyone's name in it. And I found a sketch of the first Lord of our family."

Carala nodded. "I remember it. Interesting that you found him first." She glanced at the egg pouch. "How does it feel?"

Dursdan wasn't sure what she was asking. "I guess I'll have to change the pads soon." She looked at him and he knew that wasn't what she had meant. He sighed. "I've been so worried about Da that I haven't thought much about it." He tried not to. It was his fault that Da lay in the other room critically wounded. He would bear the egg.

"Think on this. You have abilities within that are untested. You did something yesterday that no rider has been able to do before. Read the words of your ancestors and consider your heritage." She got up. "I have to go relieve your Mum so she can get some sleep."

Dursdan looked at the volume. "Is the story of Terarimi in this book?"

Her face wrinkled. "Where did you hear that name?"

"Steban said he was a dragonless man."

Carala nodded. "So he is. I suppose you will find it there toward the end." She sighed and looked down at her hands. "He blamed Torgadan for saving his life."

"I don't understand."

"Terarimi rode a blue dragon, Asdroth. The dragon was struck during battle and Terarimi fell. Torg managed to catch him but Asdroth fell to his death. Terarimi was never the same. And he never forgave Torgadan for saving him."

Dursdan shook his head. It sounded crazy. "What happened to him?"

"No one knows. He just disappeared. Everyone was too busy trying to survive to wonder about him." Voices echoed in the hall. "It sounds like Avanta has returned. I'd best go help." She ducked out the door.

Dursdan picked up the book and stared at the cover. That's what it was to be a Dragon Lord, killing things or being killed by things. He wanted to cry. He dressed and went into the dining room. Radachi was sitting at the table with Dorsadram. Dursdan stopped in the doorway, reluctant to enter with the Head of the Circle sitting in the room.

Radachi looked up. "Ah, here he is now. Come in Dursdan."

Dursdan stared at his uncle but did as he was asked. He seated himself at the table. Dorsadram watched him. Avanta hurried past, dropping a plate of fresh sweet bread on the table then moved off toward the bedrooms. Dursdan hid his discomfort behind a steaming hot roll.

"Are you ready for fresh warmers?" Radachi held up a pair of tongs.

Dursdan nodded and managed to swallow. "They feel a little cool."

His uncle chuckled. "I'm sure you've seen other boys do this a thousand times but this will be your first. Watch carefully how I do it so you don't get burnt." Dursdan pulled back the pouch cover and Radachi whistled. "That's a beauty. Let's hope it was worth it."

Dursdan felt his gut tighten. The bite of roll felt like a rock. He stared down as the swirling gold surface and had a momentary flash of memory from the dream. His mouth went dry and refused to swallow.

Dorsadram shook his head. "I still can't believe that Merg was crazy enough to go after a Gold egg." He looked at Dursdan. "You be careful with that egg, son. It almost cost your Da his life."

Dursdan was well aware of that. He watched carefully as his uncle removed the cool pads and added warm ones. Then Dursdan resealed the pouch. "Thanks, Rad."

"Not a problem. Now, on to other things. Dors is just as curious as I am about what happened yesterday." Radachi swung the chair around backwards and straddled it. "What did you do, Dur?"

Dursdan shook his head. "I don't know. There was a loud sound in my head. It got to the point that I couldn't see or hear anything else. I remember saying 'make it stop' and then it was all quiet and everyone was staring at me."

Dorsadram leaned forward. "Not just the dragons here were staring, but every dragon, even the hatchlings, were suddenly quiet and looking in this direction."

All the dragons in the Valley? Dursdan didn't know what to say. "In all honesty, sir, I don't know what I did."

"It's not just what you did, boy, that I have some clue to, it's how you did it that I'm more interested in."

Dursdan felt the droplets beginning to form on his forehead. His insides shuddered. "I really don't know."

Radachi put up his hands. "Okay, Dors, you've asked your question and gotten as much answer as there is to be had. Now leave the boy alone. He has to be off to school."

"Do I really have to go?" He dreaded the thought of being seen with the pouch.

Dachia came bustling through the dining room on the way to the kitchen. "Yes." She paused at the door. "Your Da is doing much better this morning and you need to continue on with your studies. The house will be full of people all day and you'll just be underfoot." She turned and went into the kitchen.

Dorsadram chucked. "Ah, a true Lord's wife."

Radachi leaned over to Dursdan and whispered behind his hand. "It's a good thing he didn't see her yesterday." Then he winked at Dursdan and sat up. "Sinotio will be fine in a week or two. He's as tough as iron. You go on with your studies and don't worry." He got up and Dorsadram followed suit.

Dachia came back from the kitchen and handed both of them more sweet bread and shooed them out the door. She paused beside Dursdan. "Your Day Natal celebration is only a couple weeks away." She pushed the hair out of his eyes. "You've grown up so fast. The next thing you know I'll be holding my first grand baby." Dursdan stared at her. "You must be so excited. You'll be choosing a girl to court at your Day Natal. I still remember when your Da chose me." She looked down the hall in the direction of their room then back at egg sack Dursdan wore. "You have a wonderful future ahead of you." Then she hurried off down the hallway.

Dursdan shook his head as if coming out of some strange dream. Or was it a nightmare? He went back to his room to get his books, stopping in the door of his parents' room on the way out. Mergadan was propped up in bed with Dachia, Carala, Avanta, and Rayina hovering over him. His father was scowling. "Quit pestering me, I'm fine. Where's Dursdan?"

Dursdan cleared his throat. "I'm here, Da."

Mergadan looked up and motioned for him to enter. He managed to squeeze into the crowded room. Mergadan shoed the women out.

"I'm not going to fade away in the next few minutes." They reluctantly left. Then he motioned for Dursdan to sit.

"I've sworn everyone to secrecy. Only the close family and Dorsadram know for sure it's a Gold egg. He's decided not to announce it to the rest of the Circle yet, even though they knew my intentions. Keep a lid on it for the time being. Sometimes it's okay to brag but in this case, it's not a good idea." Dursdan had no intentions of telling anyway. His father's voice dropped to a low whisper. "Something was amiss with the Gold's clutch. All the other eggs were cracked."

Dursdan had a flash from a dream, the cracked eggs with colored goo oozing from them. He wobbled slightly. The touch of his father's bandaged hand made him focus on the present.

"Are you all right, Dur?"

"Just a little tired yet, but I'll be okay."

"Good." Mergadan leaned back into the pillows and sighed. "We will live through this. Off with you now. Your Ma said you were going to school. That's good. Knowing her, this house will be a busy place today." He sighed. "If I survived the claws of a Gold queen, I should be able to survive the ministrations of my own wife."

Dursdan left his father to rest and slipped out of the house before any of the women could detain him further. The clouds had lifted and the sun fought to burn off the last remnants. The chatter of birds and the drone of bees merged with the shouts of men working in the fields. He passed over the bridge and into the village. The schoolyard was swarming with running screaming children. Soon, only a handful of younger students would attend as the older children helped in the fields through the summer. They played as if they would never play again.

Dursdan noticed Conor sitting on the fence and went over. "Hey, Con. How goes it?"

"Better than yesterday, I'm thinking." He looked down at the pouch. "So your Pa came through. Will he live to see it?"

Dursdan nodded. "I never had the chance to thank you yesterday. I'm not sure I could have made it home without your help."

"In all fairness, Mirana helped, too. But you're welcome all the same." He grinned. "That was a really cool trick you did with the dragons. Where did you learn that, your Pa?"

Dursdan shrugged. "I don't know. Everyone keeps asking me but

I really don't know. I just did it because I had to. It was like they were making all this noise in my head. Or maybe it was just Sinotio. But I just said 'stop it' and they did, or he did." Dursdan felt confused trying to explain something he didn't understand himself.

Conor patted him on the back. "I guess farm boys aren't suppose to understand things like that anyway." They both laughed.

"Well, it looks like the farmers club is in session. Are you going to use your dragon to plow your fields?"

Dursdan groaned. "Leave off, Rash, and go away. I'm too tired to deal with you."

Rashir sneered. "It must be tiring almost getting your Da killed. So what is it, Silver or Bronze? Or maybe your Da is so weak that a Green or Blue flayed his hide."

Dursdan slid off the fence. "Back off, Rash. My Da paid a serious price for this egg and I'm not doing anything to endanger it."

"Listen to those big words." Tolanar advanced behind Rashir. "Considering he almost dropped it yesterday when Da gave it to him. I'm surprised you took it at all."

Conor tried to intervene but Rashir pushed him away. "Go find some dung to play in. This is between Dur and his brother."

Conor glanced at Dursdan, and then backed away. All of the frustration suddenly came to a head. Dursdan advanced on Tolanar. "Do you think I wanted this? I'd much rather that Da had given the egg to you!" He felt his eyes burning and fought to keep the tears away. The last think he wanted to do was to cry in front of everyone.

Tolanar's face was dark red. "Then give me the egg."

"I can't!" Dursdan felt a tear forming in the corner of his eye. He refused to blink. "Because of the risk that Da took to get this egg. I won't make that sacrifice meaningless. He gave me this responsibility and I'll carry it." He turned away from all of them and started walking.

"Where are you going? What about school?"

Dursdan didn't answer his brother. The tears choked him and he didn't trust his voice. He just kept going. Once he was out of sight of the schoolyard, he wiped his face on his sleeve.

He didn't care where he went as long as Rashir and Tolanar weren't there. He found himself walking toward the marketplace. It was still busy, even when it wasn't an official Market Day. People hurried by, glancing in his direction. Some waved and smiled, others stared and gave him space. He could only imagine the rumors that were circulating now.

He saw a familiar wagon and team standing by the granary. Aber walked out talking to a strange old man that Dursdan had never seen before. That was odd enough. But the man himself was peculiar. He was dressed in a long flowing dark blue robe with a hood that covered most of him from head to toe. Dursdan assumed he had toes even though he hadn't seen any feet. Occasionally as he walked the robe revealed a deep crimson garment beneath. Dursdan would have considered it a dress but it was on a man. His hair was white and long, as was his beard, which seemed to be braided at the tip.

A flash of movement caught his attention. Mirana was standing on the porch of the granary waving to him. He walked over. "I should thank you. Conor said you helped get me home yesterday."

"It was nothing. Are you better?"

He nodded. "I'll live, and so will my Da and Sinotio."

"I'm so glad to hear that." The school bell rang in the distance and she gave him a puzzled look. "Shouldn't you be headed for school?"

Dursdan sighed. "Rash and Tola started in on me, so I left. I learned in one of my classes that it isn't good to expose an egg to heated emotional debates."

"Oh, I guess that makes sense." She glanced down at his burden. "How is your egg? It wasn't hurt during your Pa's escape, was it?"

Dursdan hadn't considered that. "I don't think it was. Radachi looked it over this morning as he showed me how to change the pads. I'm sure he would have said something if he'd noticed a problem."

Aber walked past them grumbling something about ungratefulness and disappeared into the mercantile. Dursdan and Mirana watched the old man lift a sack off the cart. "What does your Da trade with him?"

"Some strange plants that he grows. Aramel is the only one who buys them. My Pa says he's a Wizard."

Dursdan gasped. "But I thought there were no more Wizards."

She shrugged. "Most of the Western Wizards left after the war. Pa says that Aramel stayed behind. He's keeper of some gate, or something like that. He doesn't come around much. Pa was surprised when the raven showed up with the note this morning saying that he'd meet us in town."

The Wizard walked past them then stopped and turned around. "Good morning to you, my young Lord."

Dursdan felt a chill crawl over him. There was something about the old man's voice. It was a mixture of mockery and almost hatred. He had to remind himself to be polite. He bowed awkwardly. "Good day to you, sir."

"And how is your egg faring?"

Dursdan's arms curved protectively around the pouch. "Well enough, thank you."

"Let me see it and I'll tell you if it will be male or female."

Dursdan took a step back and hit the support of the overhang. His breath caught in his throat. There was no way this strange old man was going to see his egg. He stumbled for an excuse. "The warmer pad is cooling. I don't want to open the lid until I'm ready to replace it."

The Wizard cackled. "I can heat it for you easily. That's a simple bit of magic."

Dursdan's eyes went wide. "No thank you, sir. I don't much care for magic."

This time Aramel's laugh was harsh and loud. "A Dragon Lordling who doesn't care for magic. What a complication! What do you think you harbor in that pouch, boy? Dragons are all about magic. They were created by it."

Dursdan managed to slide around the post. "Thank you very much but no thank you, sir." He turned and ducked into the mercantile. He could hear the Wizard laughing as he turned and walked away up the street.

Marx looked over the counter at Dursdan. "I don't blame you. He gives me the creeps, too."

Dursdan leaned against a barrel. He realized he was shaking. Mirana came in and touched his arm and he looked up at her. "I'm sorry. I supposed that really looked dumb."

She shook her head. "I don't much care for him. He gives Pa some little spells that help out some times. Other than that, I wouldn't want anything to do with him either."

Marx brought Dursdan a dipper of water. "If you ask me, that old mite should have packed off with the rest of his kind."

Aber came out of the back room with Soren. "He's getting stingier every time." Soren looked at Dursdan and scowled. "But it takes all kinds I suppose. What are you hauling about?"

"An egg."

Soren snorted. "That's stating the obvious. I may be just a woodsmith but I've been around long enough to have seen my share of egg pouches. I meant what color."

Dursdan shrugged. "It's too early to tell. I just got it yesterday."

Soren stared at him. "Let me give you a hint. Look at it. Bah, useless creatures." He took his packages and stomped out the door.

Marx leaned on the counter. "He leaves the impression that he doesn't much care for Lords or their dragons."

Aber nodded. "There's a fool around every corner. Wait until the trolls raid his wood storage this fall and see who's first in line begging the Lords for protection. Ha!" Aber picked up his own parcels. "Do you need a ride, Dur?"

Dursdan thought of the reception he'd get at home and winced. What would his Da say when he found out that Dursdan hadn't gone to school. He wasn't going to rat on Tola, even if his brother was being a pain. And he certainly couldn't walk into school late. "Do you have any work that needs to be done?"

Aber laughed. "Have you ever seen such a lad? He's jumping to work at the slightest notice. Not today, Dur. Can't imagine you'd be much good with that thing dangling about your middle anyway."

Mirana put a hand on his arm. "Maybe you could join us for lunch, if you don't have other plans, that is."

Marx and Aber chuckled but said nothing. Dursdan looked at them but Marx only winked. Aber shook his head. "Well, best be going. Good day to you, Marx."

Dursdan and Mirana hopped on the back of the wagon while Aber climbed into the seat. He snapped the reins lightly across the steers and they started jogging for home. Dursdan let his feet swing in rhythm to the cattle's trot. He noticed Mirana was smiling.

At the farm, Dursdan offered to help unhitch the cattle while Mirana went in to help her mother make lunch. The steers took an interest in the egg pouch. Aber pushed their noses away. "Silly beasts. Someday you might end up on that thing's menu."

Dursdan chuckled. "I doubt that unless you trade them to me. Da only feeds Sinotio from our own herd."

"That's true. Merg is a fair man, unlike some."

Dursdan stared at Aber. "Aren't all the Lords fair?"

"Some are more fair than others." He hung the harness on the wall. "Your grandpa, now there was a fair man. He always kept his word and made straight deals. He was honest and truthful. It was a sad day when he passed on."

Dursdan thought of his granddad but no image surfaced. "I was pretty young when he died. I don't remember him." He looked down at the stack of books in his hands and realized that he had grabbed Armia's book with the rest. "But I bet Armia wrote about him. She was his Ma."

"That she was, and a fine lady, too. I remember the days when we'd all sit and listen to her story telling." He sighed and looked at Dursdan. "You're a good lad and you come from good roots. You'll be a fine man someday."

Mirana returned carrying a basket. "Pa, Mum says you should come in and help her put up the loom. She's got weaving to do." Aber headed for the house and Mirana held up the basket. "I brought lunch out. The kitchen is covered in yarn. Shall we go to the loft?"

"Sure." It was actually one of Dursdan's favorite places on Aber's farm. He wished his small barn had a loft. Maybe he'd build one someday.

He was trying to get used to the weight of the egg but it was challenging climbing the ladder without banging the pouch on the next rung. Mirana helped him up the last step. "That looks awkward. Maybe I could adjust the straps to make it easier to carry."

Dursdan struggled to catch his breath. "If you think it will help. I wasn't expecting it to be so heavy."

She moved the straps and made some adjustments to the knots. "It's an interesting pouch. Where did you get it?"

"I guess my Ma made it."

"Do you suppose she'd mind if I made a few small alterations? It would make it more comfortable to wear and it wouldn't hurt your back as much."

"How did you know it was hurting my back?"

She grinned. "Let's see, the way you're standing, along with the look of pain on your face."

Dursdan laughed. "I get the idea. But can it wait until after lunch? I have something to show you."

"The egg?"

"Maybe later." He sat down in the straw and patted the patch next to him. "I brought the book with me."

"Oh, Dur, that's wonderful!" She brought the basket and split the lunch between them.

Dursdan showed her the list of names. "These are all the people that have ever lived in this Valley. I want you to look at the beginning of the list. There's something I noticed."

He took a bite of the sandwich and pointed at the first families. He watched her reading. He knew when she found it because she began reading faster.

Mirana looked up. "They were all Dragon Lords."

Dursdan nodded. "I haven't had time to read all the history sections yet but look at the numbers. It took me forever to figure out what they meant. I think those are the years from when they first came to this valley. Now look at the sons. Do you see how every son in the first generation was a dragon rider, too?"

"But what happened?"

"I'm not sure but what ever it was, it happened in the 27th year. Look at these numbers. If I'm not mistaken, those are the dates of their deaths."

Mirana looked down the list again. She frowned. "But that would mean that all these men died in just that one year."

He nodded. "I want to read the histories and see what happened but now look at the sons after that year."

She studied the book. "Now it's only one son from each family."

"The firstborn." Dursdan looked down at the egg pouch. "Like me."

She put her hand on his arm. "I'm sorry, Dur. I know you don't want this but you have it." She pointed at the pouch. "Right there in your lap, as they say. Maybe some good will come of it."

"Yes, maybe I could use my dragon to plow my fields."

"What?"

"Nothing, just something Rash said to me this morning."

Mirana closed the book and looked at the cover. "This is so beautiful. Someone really spent a lot of time and added in all these little details. And just think of all the time that Armia spent writing it."

"I just wish I had the time to read it." He looked at her cradling the book. "Why don't you read it first? I've kind of got my hands full with this egg. Maybe I can come over now and then and you can show me the really good parts."

She turned and looked at him. "Are you certain? This is an important family treasure."

"I know you'll keep it safe."

She looked down at the book. "Dur, I just had a thought. If only Dragon Lords came to this Valley, then where did the farmers come from?"

Dursdan laughed. "Where do you think they came from? We all came from the same place. Look at the list. All our names are there, yours, mine, your parents, my parents. We all came from the Dragon Lords."

"Then why do they act as if there is a difference? Some Lords treat farmers as if they were less than human and some farmers act as if the Lords were different creatures."

Dursdan shook his head. "I've noticed that, too. Hopefully the answers are in that book. But I can tell you, only 36 men and their wives came to this valley. Their names are recorded on those pages along with their children - all their descendants, right down to us."

"Where did they come from? I've never heard anyone speak about anything outside of our Valley except trolls and wizards. The Dragon Lords were men. There must be other people somewhere."

Dursdan nodded. He'd been pondering the same thought. "Maybe the answers are there. I wish I had the time to find them myself but I have the feeling I'm going to pay for today's absence, if not from the Master, than from my Da. And he'll take it out of my hide."

"Dur, he wouldn't do anything to endanger that egg, not after what he's been through to get it. Just tell him the truth, or part of it. There were some strong emotions in school today and you didn't want to expose the egg to them."

He nodded. "That might work for today but what about tomorrow? Rash and Tola aren't going anywhere."

She chewed on a piece of straw. "I'm sure there must be a way." She looked over at him. "Dur, can I see it?"

Dursdan shrugged. "All right. But you have to promise not to tell anyone."

Mirana's forehead wrinkled. "Everyone already knows you have an egg. What's the point?"

He undid the latch and moved the warmer pads aside. The egg caught the stray beams of light filtering in through the walls and seemed to glow by itself.

Mirana gasped. "Oh, Dursdan, it's so beautiful!" She gently touched the surface. The swirling colors danced around her finger as if trying to catch it. She giggled. "It's playing tag with my finger."

Dursdan watched the swirling colors rotate and collide then reform into new swirls. They circled around Mirana's touch. Maybe the egg was playing. "It does seem to like you." He glanced at her and felt a warming sensation he'd never experienced before. It made him uncomfortable. "I have to cover it back up so it stays warm."

Mirana nodded and removed her hand. "I think you're very lucky."

Dursdan stared at her. "I'm only doing this because it seems I don't have a choice." He looked down and latched the lid.

"There are some things that we don't get to choose in life. I didn't choose to be the daughter of a farmer, I just am. And you didn't choose to be the first son of a Dragon Lord but you are one. And you will carry that egg because of who you are."

Dursdan scowled. "That's not why I'm carrying this stupid egg! I'm carrying it because my Da was crazy enough to steal from a Gold Queen and it almost cost him his life. He dropped this burden on me without considering what I wanted for my future. I'll carry that burden because I don't want him to feel he almost killed himself for nothing."

Mirana stared at him wide-eyed for a moment then looked down at her hands. "Will your Pa live?" Her voice was quite and trembled slightly.

Dursdan looked down at the egg pouch. His face burned and tears threatened to blur his vision. He blinked them away. "He'll live." Dursdan was afraid to look up at her. He hadn't meant to sound so harsh. She probably hated him now. "I'd best go help your Da bring in the cows." He got up and glanced in her direction. Were her shoulders shaking? He hadn't meant to make her cry. He sighed and went down the ladder. She didn't follow.

He kicked at the loose straw on the floor and looked up at the hayloft. He could hear her pitching the hay down the chute. Dursdan shook his head. He'd never understand girls. Something inside of him hurt. What was it? He looked down at the egg. It was already causing him grief. He wished he'd given it to Tola but what would he say to Da? He frowned and went out to find Aber.

* * *

Aramel tucked the rug back into its corner and dumped the contents of the sack out on his table. Clumps of dried plants, tied together with ribbon, and small cloth pouches tumbled out. He should have plenty to keep him.

He pulled out what he needed for a location spell and set the ingredients in their positions. The chant ignited a ring of vision on the surface of the table. He easily found the dragon's cave but she was not there. As he'd feared, she'd moved her remaining egg to some other location.

He modified the spell slightly and began searching for the female dragon. He grabbed a pinch of eggshell dust made from a fragment that had clung to his cloak. After almost an hour of searching, he finally found her. She was wrapped around a tall rock spire, warming herself in the fading sunlight.

Aramel wrinkled his brow. But where was the egg? He looked at her closely. The dragon's head drooped and her eyes appeared glazed. Had the egg been smashed during their final confrontation in the cavern? No, it couldn't have been!

He added more shell dust to the spell and scrawled a symbol in the powder with his finger. The image changed abruptly. Aramel grabbed the table for support. The search spell raced far away from the golden dragon on her lonely perch. It went reeling down the mountain toward the valley. But how could this be?

It slowed to show a boy plodding up a hill toward a house where smoke curled from a chimney and a silver dragon rested outside. It was the same boy he had seen in town. He must have scribed the mark wrong. But then Aramel stopped. The boy was carrying an egg. It couldn't be! He pushed the spell closer, even tighter, so that it focused inside the sack. It was there!

In a rage, Aramel pushed over the table, scattering everything across the room. The stupid little boy who didn't like magic had his golden egg! He grabbed up his staff and banged it on the floor. Sparks sizzled from it and scorched the stone. He flung his power around the room and it spun out of control, knocking things off the shelves. He danced about, unleashing his fury, smashing things with the power of his staff. The room was a dazzling display of sparks and exploding vials. A bolt of energy hit a shelf of glass bottles, scattering shards in all directions. Some of them sprayed across the Wizard's exposed bare arms. He cursed in a language foreign to human ears.

Aramel breathed hard and collapsed into his chair, fully spent. His mind gradually calmed and he began to think. There had to be a way to get his egg back. The boy had said he didn't like magic. He sat up. But that golden egg represented far more magic than that ignorant whelp had ever dreamed of! Maybe he could convince the boy to trade the egg for something less magical. Aramel began to scheme.

Chapter 5

Dursdan pushed the food around in his bowl and glanced over at Dachia. Her eyed were half closed but she managed to take a bite of the stew. The big dining room table seemed empty with just the two of them sharing it.

The outer door opened and closed. Dursdan looked up. Tolanar stood in the shadows of the doorway. Dachia brightened. "Tola, come sit and I'll dish you out some food."

Tolanar sank farther into the shadows and stared coldly at Dursdan. "I'm not really hungry, Ma."

Dursdan looked closer. His brother's voice had a strange quality to it. His clothing seemed dirty and out of place. "Are you all right?"

"As if you would care!" Tolanar turned away and stomped down the dark hallway.

Dachia looked over at Dursdan. "What's wrong? Did something happen at school today?"

He swallowed hard. "I don't know." He studied the potatoes and pushed the corn kernels around them.

Dachia sighed. "Your Da has been beside himself with worry today. I suppose that means he's on the mend but I just know there's more to it than that."

Had Da told her about the other eggs? He found one of the sweet brown beans hidden under a piece of meat. It was usually his favorite part of the stew. He sighed and buried it again. The egg felt heavy on his stomach.

The outer door squeaked, footsteps echoed in the front hall, and Carala came into the dining room with Radachi in her wake. He helped her take off the heavy shawl. "Are you sure you don't want me to stay in case they need you again tonight?"

She patted his arm. "No, no. Go home to Avanta. Samila with be fine. There are plenty of women there attending her. Kalista and Mirana are there. Someday that young lady will be as good a midwife as her Ma."

Dursdan sighed. So that's where she had disappeared to in such a hurry. Mirana had gone to the birthing. He felt bad that he hadn't been able to apologize for his rudeness to her in the loft.

Radachi looked over at him. "And how do you fare tonight? Adachi was worried about you."

Dachia's face wrinkled. "Dursdan?"

He felt the flush on his cheeks and didn't dare look up. "It's nothing, Ma."

He felt Radachi's hand on his shoulder. "Dur, I know this is a tough adjustment for you. I don't think your Da realizes what kind of burden he's placed on your shoulders. Being a Lord of the Circle, I've heard more than is common knowledge. If you need to talk, you know where to find me."

Dursdan felt his eyes burning. "Thanks, Rad." He continued to study the contents of his bowl, hoping to control his eyes.

"Rad, why was Ada worried?" Dachia pushed her chair back and came to Dursdan's side. "I've known there was something wrong since he got home tonight."

Dursdan wished he could slide under the table and disappear. Radachi patted his back then took his sister by the shoulders and kissed her on the forehead. "Don't fret so, my little Dachy. The boy will be fine. Just give him some space to grow into the responsibility he must carry. Now, I must be home to my responsibilities. Avanta is feeling much better tonight. Thank you, Gran, for that. But I want to tuck the little ones in." He tapped Dursdan on the shoulder. "Walk me out, will you, Dur?"

"Of course." Dursdan was grateful for the excuse to leave the table. He turned away before his mother could see his face but Carala cast him a worried look. He shook his head and followed his uncle down the hall toward the main door. "Thanks, Rad."

Radachi chuckled. "I still remember what it was like for me when they told me that my Da had passed on and I was a Lord. It was like the world itself was coming down and crushing me." He took Dursdan's arm in a firm grasp and shook it. "I meant what I said. If you need to talk, come and find me."

Radachi opened the door and a soft cool breeze scented with night jasmine bathed Dursdan. The dragons were quietly murmuring in the corner of the courtyard. Dursdan stopped in the doorway. Sinotio, covered in bandages, was almost as white as Osiral in the moonlight. Both dragons turned and looked at him. He shuddered.

Radachi chuckled. "Sometimes I wonder if dragons can talk to each other. I know they're smarter than some given them credit." He whistled softly and the smaller white dragon bounded across the courtyard. Radachi held up his hand and Osiral nuzzled it gently. The dragon's eyes seemed to glow in the moonlight. "There are times when I'm certain that Osi understands what I'm saying." The dragon seemed to coo in response.

Dursdan backed away and remembered to breathe. Sinotio snorted from his corner. Dursdan's heart drummed in his ears. His uncle climbed onto the White's back and waved. Dursdan waved back then quickly shut the door so the dust from the dragon's down beats didn't get in.

The hallway was quiet. He could hear his mother and grandmother talking softly but decided not to rejoin them. The few bites of dinner he had managed to swallow, sat heavy in his stomach. He slipped past the dining room door and into the kitchen. He carefully changed the pads and made sure the egg was secure in the pouch, sealed it up, and retreated to his room. He was tired and easily sank into a deep sleep.

His dream began with a hazy sort of awareness. Timotha, dressed in a flowing white gown with beaded trim came again. She appeared tired but happy. "Men are such easy creatures. It's a shame my current burden is not like you. I would have gotten much farther today. But I can see this is going to be a long journey." She sighed and sank down on a pile of mist that supported her form as if it were a chair. "And how do you fare?"

Dursdan had no clue how to answer. Instead, he was filled with questions. "Where do you come from?"

She spun her hand around in the mist and a window seemed to appear. Through it, a vast body of water was visible. Large areas of sand accented by oddly shaped tall rock formations met the water, which stretched to the curved horizon. White birds danced across the waves and occasionally dove into the water, reappearing moments later with a wiggling fish. A small village nudged the water's edge in the distance. "This is where my home has been for many long seasons now. And how does your home appear?"

"How did you make that window?"

She laughed. "It is not a window but a picture from my mind. May I show you?"

Dursdan nodded. She reached out her hand and gently touched his forehead. The mist swirled around in front of him and his view of the Valley began to emerge. He thought of all the places he knew and they appeared before him in the mist. Then he thought of his own home. "This is where I live."

She had been staring at the images intently. "I know this place." Her voice was very soft, barely a whisper. "I remember." She drew back and covered her face with her hands. "Oh, I remember." She began to cry.

Dursdan went to her side and put his arms around her. His stomach began to glow, not the intense burning that had occurred the first time, but more of a soft warmth that radiated comfort.

"Please don't cry." The voice came out of the Mists and startled Dursdan.

He looked around for its source. "Where are you?"

The Mists swirled and parted and a young man stepped out. He wore a dark purple shirt, short leggings, and tall black boots. His hair was a deep brown but it was his eyes that drew Dursdan's attention. They were a bright green. He came forward and stood on the other side of Timotha. "What makes you cry, fair lady?"

Timotha looked up. "Just old memories, my lord. Things from long ago."

Dursdan straightened and held out his hand. "I'm Dursdan."

The young man looked at him. "That's an odd name for a dragon."

Dursdan was startled. "I'm no dragon. I'm human." He put his hand down and looked the newcomer.

The young man stared back at him. "I've never dreamed a human before. Mostly just Lady Timotha, and sometimes Lord Trusumo."

It was Dursdan's turn to stare. "Lord Trusumo?" He recognized the name. "That's Dorsadram's dragon!"

The other became excited. "You know him then! How grand! I wish I could see him. I mean the real him, not just the way he appears to me in this dream world." His face seemed to soften. "I've always wanted to see the sky filled with dragons."

Timotha cleared her throat. "My lord, have you forgotten your manners? Lord Dursdan did ask for your name."

His cheeks reddened and he bowed. "Forgive me, my name is Menatash."

Dursdan bowed then looked up. "Of the house of Tash?"

"I suppose so. I've never thought of it that way. My father is Elatash, and my grandfather is Jaritash, Emperor of the Three Kingdoms."

"The Three Kingdoms? Then you're not from the Valley." It was Dursdan's turn to become excited. "Tell me more about your kingdoms."

Menatash shrugged. "What's to tell? They are filled with people who have never even dreamed of dragons, to say nothing of knowing them personally. I'd much rather be where you are."

Dursdan felt a growing heaviness in his stomach and realized he was feeling cold. He put his hand there and it was cool to the touch. He frowned. "Something is wrong."

Timotha stood. "It is time for you to go." She kissed his head. "All will be well."

Menatash came around and held out his hand. "Perhaps someday we will meet again. Until then, fly well."

"I don't fly. I usually just walk." But he shook the offered hand strongly. "Until we meet again."

The dreamy mist began to swirl and fade. He tossed restlessly and tried to turn, but the egg was in the way. He opened his eyes and blinked. Warm sunlight streamed in the open window. His dreams were becoming quite strange. His hand rested on the egg pouch. It felt cooler than it should.

Dursdan rubbed his eyes and swung out of bed. He dressed quickly and went out to the kitchen to change the pads. Carala was cooking the morning meal. "Are you feeling all right? You look pale." When he'd finished with the pads, she handed him a bowl of warm mash.

He took it gratefully, adding its warmth to that of the fresh pads. "I'm all right, Gran. I was just worried that the egg was getting cold." He sat down at the heavy oaken kitchen table.

She smiled and put a cup of tea down in front of him. "I told Dachia there was nothing to worry about."

A shadow slipped around the corner headed for the main door. Carala leaned out the kitchen doorway. "Tola, don't you want some breakfast? Dachia said you didn't eat dinner last night."

"I'm kind of in a hurry, Gran. Is it something I can take with me?"

"Let me see if the morning rolls are done." She came back to the fireplace and opened the heavy oven door. "I think they'll do." Tolanar stayed just beyond the doorframe. Carala wrapped the roll in a napkin and brought it to him. She gasped. "Shell, my boy! What has happened to you? Come into the light and let me have a look."

"It's nothing, Gran, really." But Carala grabbed his hand and pulled him into the kitchen.

Dursdan stared. "Tola! What happened? Are you all right?" Dursdan got up and went to his brother's side.

Tolanar snarled. "Get away from me!" He glared down at the egg pouch. "You don't deserve it."

Dursdan backed away. The food turned in his stomach. His brother's face was wrapped in a snarl heavily accented by the dark blotch radiating from his left eye socket. "Tola?"

"Don't speak to me! You're not worthy to be the first son of the House of Dan!"

Dursdan backed away, shook his head, grabbed his tied stack of books, and left the kitchen. He went out the main door, not even glancing at the Silver. He stood outside the gate and leaned on. What had happened to Tola? He sighed and headed for the barn.

He fed the cows and cleaned their stalls. The egg pouch was constantly in the way and his back had begun to trouble him. He wished he'd let Mirana make those alterations before he'd made her mad. He was hoping she'd still speak to him.

He was almost done with the milking when Mergadan staggered out into the barn. Dursdan was so surprised he almost spilled the milk. "Da, what are you doing out of bed? Is there something wrong?"

"Is there something wrong, he asks. First you fight with your brother and then you pass on school, and you ask if something is wrong?"

Dursdan could see Tolanar in the doorway, his darkened socket more pronounced in the daylight. "Tola and I did have a verbal disagreement but I never touched him." He pointed at the pouch. "I'm carrying this thing around, remember? That would make it very hard to fight anything."

Mergadan advanced on him. "I do remember that you're carrying it, believe me. I paid dearly for it." He brought his fist down on Dursdan's stack of schoolbooks. They slid to the ground. Mergadan looked down at them. "What are these?"

"My school books. I figured I'd try to get into the school without being verbally attacked this morning."

Mergadan looked up at him. "These are farming texts. Why are you studying farming?"

Dursdan pushed the cow over and brought the pail of milk with him and set it at his father's feet. "It could have something to do with living on a farm." He picked up the books and dusted them off.

"You are the first son of a Dragon Lord. You have more important things to be studying."

"I have already finished all of my other requirements, so if you want me to go to school, you'll have to let me study farming. Besides," he looked over his father's shoulder at his brother, "someone in this family has to know how to keep this farm going or we, and our dragons, will starve."

Mergadan stared at him. Dursdan couldn't believe he had just said that to Da. He waited for his father to strike him but the blow never came.

"What are you doing up?" Carala stood in the barn door with a basket of eggs in her hand.

Mergadan shook his head. "Trying to figure out my sons."

She chuckled. "Better late than never."

Dursdan picked up the pail of milk and walked past his father. He handed it to Carala. "I'd put it in the house myself but I don't want to be late for school." He looked back over his shoulder at his father. "That is assuming Da still wants me to go."

Mergadan turned around. "Study what you will but mind that egg."

Carala shook her head. "Go back to bed, Merg, and don't fret about the egg. Dur is taking good care of it. He's not like you. The boy has to find his own path." She turned to Dursdan. "I'm glad I caught you before you left. I have a special project I'm working on and I need a set of needles made. Please stop by the blacksmith shop on your way to school and drop off the order. These eggs should do as barter."

Dursdan took the eggs and left. He walked down the lane without looking back. The fields and the town went by in a haze. Why had Tola accused him of fighting? Was he hoping that Da would take the egg away and give it to him instead? Maybe he should have taken the blame. It might have been better in the long run.

The smithy doors were open and the heavy clang of metal against metal echoed from the dark recesses of the blacksmith shop. Arazan was singing a merry tune while he worked and keeping time with the strikes of the hammer. Dursdan peered into the shadows, letting his eyes adjust.

Arazan changed the words of his tune slightly. "Now there's a lad, standing at my door, I know not what he comes here for. But I see he's got a basket in his hand, so come show me, lad, what you've brought this man!" Arazan set his hammer down, laughed deeply and opened his arms. "Come, come, Dur! You're never a stranger here!"

Dursdan grinned and entered the shop. "I've brought you a basket of eggs from Gran. She needs some special needles made. Here's the order."

He took the paper and the eggs. "Ah, my sister has a new project in mind. How grand! And how goes it with you, my boy?"

Dursdan looked down at the egg pouch. "Da found an egg."

Arazan roared out a great laugh. "My boy, you make it sound like the end of the world. Why I can still remember when my brother, Itogan, got his egg. I had but six years to my name but I admired that shiny black beauty. And what a fine beasty it has produced. Why Samita is one of the biggest Blacks ever hatched in the Valley." He patted Dursdan's head with one of his huge hands. "I'm sure you'll do just as well with your egg." He read through the order. "Ah, these will be no problem. I'll have them ready for you this afternoon. Stop by and see me after school. They'll be just as Carala ordered!"

"Thanks, Ara. I'd better get headed up the hill. I have some catching up to do." He left the smithy and made his way to school.

Dursdan ignored Rashir and Tolanar all morning. He sat next to Conor and caught up on the things he'd missed the previous day. At lunch, Conor pulled him aside. "How do you like Tola's pretty eye?"

Dursdan frowned. "He managed to convince Da that I gave it to him."

"Ha! That's a laugh. Ragan showed his true colors yesterday and belted Tola good."

"What for?"

Conor looked around and lowered his voice. "Tola wouldn't tell him what color the egg was. I didn't know things like that were kept a secret. The other carriers never stop bragging over their egg colors. Why, you'd think Borgan was next in line for Head of the Circle just because his egg is a Black!"

"There are some unusual circumstances with this egg. Something about how my Da found the nest. I hope you won't be angry but I promised my Da that I wouldn't tell."

Conor clapped him on the back. "Don't worry yourself about it. Considering Ragan's mood, I think I'd rather not know. I'm sure now that Ragan has been fueling both Tola and Rash. Don't know to what end. Maybe just to make your life miserable."

Dursdan sighed and rubbed his sore back. "As if it isn't enough." He caught movement out of the corner of his eye. Tolanar was coming toward them. "I figure the best way to keep out of a fight is to avoid one all together." He pulled Conor back toward the school. "Tola isn't likely to cause trouble with Master Damitrus in sight."

He slipped away as soon as classes were over and headed for the smithy. Arazan had finished the project as promised. He admired the man's work, looking down the straight long needles. "You are truly a master of your craft, Ara. Gran should have made those eggs into a fine custard first."

Arazan laughed. "While it's true, I do love a good custard, my sister knows how much I love hard boiled eggs." He pointed at a large cast iron pot sitting by the forge. "Always hot!"

Dursdan nodded and held up the needles. "Thank you. I'm sure these are exactly what she needs." He looked out across the street and noticed Kalista and Mirana loading something into a wagon. Would she still talk to him? He hoped so. They had been friends for a long time. He hoped she'd accept his apology. He waved at the blacksmith. "Good day to you, Arazan."

The smith glanced across the road and winked. "And good luck to you, Dur." He chuckled and went back to his forge.

Dursdan walked across the road and tapped Mirana on the shoulder. He managed to duck in time to prevent a collision with the loom board in her hand.

She gasped. "Oh, Dur. My goodness, are you all right?" She put the piece down on the wagon and helped him stand.

"My back's a little sore but you missed me. Not that I didn't deserve it."

She laughed. "Don't be silly. I was hoping to see you. You have to come and see what I've found in the book. It's amazing."

Kalista came out with another piece. "What will truly be amazing is if we get this loom loaded before dark."

"I'll help."

She looked down at the pouch. "Not with that egg you don't. You're already sore. Who designed that pouch? No let me guess, Dachia. She was never much good at things like that. Mirana, will you help this poor boy before his back gives out?"

Mirana giggled. "I started to yesterday but it needs some serious alterations."

Kalista nodded. "No doubt. Well, you be sure and stop by on your way home so we can have a look at that for you. You're going to be carrying that egg around for several months. You want to be able to stand after it hatches." She went back into the shop for another loom board.

"I really do need to help Ma with this loom, but please do stop by later."

"I will." He was a little confused but also relieved, and he did want to know what she'd found that was so exciting. He watched her disappear into the shop. Was his heart beating faster?

"Now why am I not surprised."

Dursdan turned around to find Tolanar behind him. He sighed. "What is it now, Tola? Must you always find some fault?" He walked toward the mercantile.

Tolanar followed. "You're the son of a Dragon Lord. Do you want to disgrace our family by choosing the daughter of a farmer?"

It took every bit of will power Dursdan had to keep him from turning around and giving him a matched set of blackies. He took a deep breath. "Tola, go home and leave me in peace."

Wagon wheels creaked behind him and Dursdan glanced over his shoulder. Mirana waved as the wagon rolled past, and he waved back.

"Good day to you, sir."

Dursdan almost jumped. The strange old Wizard was standing in front of him. This wasn't his day. But he managed a smile and stiff bow. "And what can I do for you?"

"Ah, my young Lordling, it is I who can do for you."

Dursdan took a step back and bumped into Tolanar. "I already told you I didn't need anything you had to offer."

The Wizard smiled. "But you also said you didn't like magic. I'm here to solve your problem, you see. That golden egg is very strong magic. I can exchange it for a less magical one."

Dursdan stared at the Wizard for a moment while the words sunk in. How had the old man known that he had a golden egg? Only close family knew. He turned on Tolanar. "Did you tell this man about the egg?"

Tolanar's eyes went wide. "I didn't Dur, honest."

"Then how does he know?"

Tolanar shook his head.

The old man cleared his throat. "Magic calls to magic. I am a

Wizard. I understand these things. Now, I am prepared to offer you a much more mundane egg in exchange for this very magical one."

Tolanar looked at Dursdan. "If you trade your egg, Da will have your hide."

"And if you keep interrupting our barter, I'll turn you into a frog." The Wizard dug into his robe and produced a strangely bent stick.

Tolanar's eyes went even wider and he fled.

Dursdan sighed and faced the Wizard. "I already told you, I don't want anything you have to offer. So just leave me, and my egg, alone."

A sizable crowd had begun to gather. The Wizard looked around. "You don't know what you're dealing with, boy. You'll be sorry!" He pulled a strange ball from a pocket, mumbled some odd words, and threw it at the ground. The air around him shimmered and he was gone.

Dursdan stared at the empty space where the Wizard had been a moment before. He grimaced. There was a strange metallic tang in the air. The crowd murmured amongst themselves. He heard familiar voices behind and turned to see Balashir and Humatsu moving through the crowd. Balashir pushed the crowd back while Humatsu approached. "Are you all right, Dur? Marx said you were in some kind of trouble."

Dursdan shivered. "It was a Wizard. He wanted my egg, said he'd trade me for a different one."

Humatsu looked concerned. "A Wizard. Did he say what his name was?"

Dursdan shook his head. "Aber trades with him some times. I remember Mirana saying something about him guarding a gate."

Balashir joined them. "All the Wizards left, didn't they?"

Humatsu shook his head. "All but one, Aramel of the West was left behind. Was he an old man in a dark blue robe?"

Dursdan nodded. "I still want to know how he knew about the egg. Tolanar swore he didn't tell."

"Who's to say? He's a Wizard." Humatsu looked toward the northern mountains. "What concerns me more is why. What's that old skunk up to?"

Balashir looked puzzled. "I thought you said he was a Western Wizard. Weren't they on our side?"

"They were. But after the war they decided to leave. They felt that their presence endangered us. They all went through a great Portal called the Western Gate. They left Aramel behind, told him he was the guardian. I think it was because they couldn't stand him. He had, shall we say, some issues. He was a very low-grade Wizard. They probably figured he'd be harmless."

Balashir looked at Dursdan's egg pouch. "I guess they were wrong. But why would he have such an interest in Dursdan's egg?"

Humatsu looked at him then around at the crowd. They were all whispering amongst themselves.

Dursdan could hear various snippets of conversation but the one that troubled him most was the mention of the golden color of his egg. He turned to Humatsu. "They know."

"So it would seem." Humatsu guided Dursdan through the crowd while Balashir worked to disperse it. He led Dursdan toward the main square where his large bronze sat watching. "If you want, Dozi and I can take you home."

Dursdan looked up at the large Bronze and backed away a step. "Ah, no thanks. I think I'll walk."

The old Lord laughed. "It won't be so bad, Dur. Your dragon will grow with you." He patted Dursdan on the shoulder and mounted Dozi. "I want to report all this to Dorsadram. You'd best head home."

He had much the same idea, with one stop in between. He headed for the mill bridge that led toward home. Half way to Aber's farm, a shadow flew over him. He looked up to see Osiral circling to land. He jumped off the road to give the White plenty of room to set down.

Even before the dragon touched the ground, Mergadan jumped down and stomped toward Dursdan. Radachi sat on the dragon's back, shaking his head.

"Dursdan, get on right now."

His father's tone was angry but no amount of anger would get Dursdan anywhere near that dragon. He backed up farther. "I'd rather walk."

"And I suppose you'd rather trade the egg I worked so hard to get, for a lesser one?"

Dursdan stared at his father. It took him a moment to put all the pieces together. Tolanar must have run all the way home. He felt something snapping deep inside him. He squared his shoulders and looked Mergadan straight in the eyes. "First you dump this egg on me without even considering that maybe, just maybe, I might want to do something different with my life. You do have a son who would rather be like you. But will you let me give him the egg? No, of course not. It would damage your pride if your first-born didn't hold with tradition. That's all it is - tradition. There's no law written in stone."

Mergadan tried to say something but Dursdan cut him off. "So now that you've dumped this responsibility on me, now you're saying that I'm not worthy of it? Make up your mind. I didn't give the egg to my own brother when that would have made both of us happier. What makes you believe that I'd barter it away to some stranger?"

Mergadan backed away a step. Osiral cocked his head and gazed at Dursdan. Was the dragon laughing at him? Dursdan stared back, for the first time in his life, looking a dragon in the eyes. Osiral pulled his head back and snorted. Radachi began to laugh. "Spoken like a true Lord."

Mergadan turned and stared at his wife's brother and Dursdan walked away. He didn't look back, even when he heard the other dragons. He knew it was Trusumo and Dozi bringing the Head of the Circle and the Second. Let them talk behind his back.

He took the short cut through the fields and walked up to farmhouse. Aber was sitting on the steps whittling pins for the new loom. "Some advice, Dur. When you're wife gets mad at her loom, don't offer to get her a new one. There's more work in it for you than if you'd just fixed the old one."

Dursdan smiled. "Is Mirana about?"

"She's out in the barn, finishing the evening milking. If you ask me, it's a great place to hide from Kalista and her new loom. I wish I'd thought of it first."

Dursdan found her sitting on a stool chatting with a cow. "Oh, Annabelle, you're lucky you get to stay out here in the barn. I just know there won't be any peace in the house until that loom is fully threaded to Mum's satisfaction."

Dursdan leaned over the cow's back. "And all she can say is 'moo.' Cows aren't much for conversation."

Mirana laughed and squirted a milk stream in his direction. "You scared me half to death. I'm almost done. She's the last."

Dursdan helped her carry the milk to the creamery and turn the cows out. Then she pulled him toward the hayloft. "Now come see what I've found." She pulled the book from a soft bag that she had hidden in the straw. "I keep it here so Tambo doesn't find it. I'm not sure he's ready to read all this yet." She paused and looked at Dursdan. "I'm not sure I was."

"Is it that bad?" He sat back in the hay trying to get comfortable.

She nodded and opened the book. "There are so many wars. That's why the Dragon Lords were created in the first place. There was a huge war. It didn't really have anything to do with people to begin with. It was between elves and wizards and trolls, and lots of other things I've never heard of before." She opened the book to the section about the Wizard's Daughter.

Dursdan saw the first sketch and frowned. It looked like a violent storm gone wrong. "These look like people to me."

Mirana nodded. "Eventually the war spilled over to the Kingdoms of Men. We weren't really part of it but thousands of people died. The Wizards of the West took pity on us and chose 36 of the bravest men to become the Dragon Lords. They were given dragons and trained how to fight. It was the Dragon Lords who eventually turned the tide of the war and destroyed the troll armies."

"So there are other people outside this Valley." Dursdan pointed at the map in the book. "The Kingdoms of Men." He thought back to his dream and shivered.

Mirana sighed. "For awhile, the Dragon Lords were great heroes." She flipped to the first section of the book. "They were given wives from the finest houses. Armia's grandmother, Corinda, was a princess. But it didn't last. Dragons do eat a lot and I guess the farmers of the Kingdoms were afraid the dragons would eat all of their stock and then start on them."

"That's crazy. Dragons don't eat people."

"We know that because we live with dragons. They are part of our lives." She reached out and gently touched the egg pouch. "But those people in the Kingdoms were afraid because they didn't understand the dragons. They told the Dragon Lords to let their dragons go."

Dursdan laughed. "How crazy is that? A dragon is a life long commitment." He looked down at the pouch and sighed. "One that I'm about to make, whether I like it or not."

The loft had fallen into shadows. It was becoming difficult to see the book. "There's so much more I want to show you."

Dursdan wanted to touch her but he was afraid she might still be mad. He didn't want to upset her again. "Another day. There were some names I wanted to look up. Thank you for your help with this. I would have never had time to read so much so quickly." He thought he saw her blush.

She carefully wrapped the book back in its cover and tucked it under the hay. "I'm grateful that you asked me. I've always wanted to know more but girls aren't suppose to think about such things."

"Ha! Don't forget it was a girl who wrote that book in the first place."

"But she was the wife of a Dragon Lord. I'm just a farm girl."

Dursdan shook his head. "We all come from the same roots, good roots." He managed to stand then helped her to her feet. "Nothing else matters."

She smiled. "Who did you want me to look for?"

He felt a little foolish. "A dragon named Timotha and a rider named Menatash."

* * *

Aramel pushed the bottles around on the shelf. Stupid boy! He didn't know whom he was dealing with. He dug deeper into to the back of the shelf. Where was that cursed bottle?

Aramel was still thinking about the obvious argument he'd witnessed between the boy and his father. Perhaps the father was having second thoughts about giving such a priceless treasure to that ignorant whelp. Maybe he could do a trade with the Lord himself! No, he'd met those types before. Self-righteous lot, all of them. Ah, there was the bottle of thrush toes.

No, he wouldn't waste time with that. There were other ways. Aramel set the bottle on the workbench. He'd have to watch the boy carefully, find the most likely time and place to make it all work. If the boy wouldn't give him the egg, he'd take it. He went back to the old dusty volume and began reading the rest of the ingredients. It would be simple enough.

Aramel carefully measured the items and placed them in the spell. What annoyed him most was that the egg was rightfully his in the first place. He had called the male dragons and he had tested the eggs but now some foolish brat who didn't like magic had his egg!

The last thing was a thin thread of glistening silver, the vein of a fairy wing. It was hard to come by as most of the little beasts had disappeared long ago. The wizard carefully placed it in the spell. It made a slight popping sound and the entire mass glowed. Aramel smiled. All it would take was a little patience. Soon the golden egg would be back in his hands, where it belonged.

Chapter 6

Dursdan reluctantly turned toward home. The alterations that Kalista and Mirana had made to the pouch made his burden a little easier to carry. The courtyard was in shadows by the time he arrived. Sinotio sat curled on his rock, his injured wing carefully wrapped. Dursdan glanced at him and shuddered. He kept to the wall and went inside.

His mother was in the front hall. She looked at him but said nothing and retreated back into the kitchen. Dursdan swallowed. How was he going to face Da?

Mergadan appeared in the doorway of the dining room. "Food is on the table. Best come eat it before it gets cold." He disappeared back into the room.

Dursdan stood in the hallway for a moment, uncertain what to do. Tolanar came in the front door and almost ran into him. He looked at Dursdan and scowled. "Are you going to stand there all night? Get moving. I'm hungry."

Carala came out of the kitchen with a heavy pot. "Dur, set this on the table, will you?"

Dursdan took the pot and went into the dining room. Mergadan was seated at his place at the head of the table. Dursdan set the pot down on a trivet and moved toward his own chair. Mergadan cleared his throat. "That's no longer your place."

Dursdan froze. He looked down at his chair and struggled to swallow. Mergadan tapped his knife on the edge of his plate to get his attention. Dursdan looked up. His father pointed at the chair opposite his at the other end of the long table. Dursdan gasped. That was the seat normally reserved for guests!

Tolanar came in with a large platter loaded with steaming roast. "Since you're still standing, will you help me get this on the table?"

Dursdan moved the trivets to accommodate the platter and helped his brother set it down. Then he slowly moved toward the chair and stood looking at it.

The women entered and took their seats without saying anything. Tolanar mumbled something but slipped into his own chair. Mergadan looked up at Dursdan. "Well, are you going to sit so we can eat?" Dursdan managed to pull the chair out and seat himself. Mergadan cut into the roast and looked up at Dursdan expectantly. Dursdan stared at him. Mergadan shook his head. "Hold out your plate. I realize you were too young to remember what it's like to have a Lord and rider in the family at the same time. You best get used to it. That's how it is." Dursdan lifted his plate and Mergadan loaded it with food. Then he served Dachia and Carala, and finally Tolanar.

After everyone was served, Mergadan filled his own plate and began to eat. Dursdan picked up his own fork and stabbed at the roast. Everyone ate in silence for several long minutes.

Carala looked around the table then cleared her throat. "Well, Medoris is a happy man tonight. Samila has given him his first son. He's named him Yadoris."

Dachia smiled. "Osiris must be pleased as well. Especially after two granddaughters."

"Oh, to be certain. He came around this afternoon, strutting about as if it was his and not his son's child. What a man."

Mergadan chuckled. "Medoris will do more than enough strutting of his own, have no fear of that. But I know for a fact that Osiris was worried that it might be another girl." He held up his glass. "Health to the House of Ris." He looked at Dursdan.

Dursdan awkwardly picked up his own goblet. "To the House of Ris." Everyone else joined in the toast.

Dachia and Carala began discussing the arrangements for the new baby's welcoming feast and Dursdan concentrated on his own plate. Soon it was empty. He waited quietly. Mergadan cleared his throat to interrupt the women. Dursdan looked up. Mergadan pointed at the roast. "Do you need more food?"

"No, Da."

"Then you don't need to wait on the rest of us. You are a man of this house now."

Dursdan felt his cheeks warm. He got up, picked up his plate, and fled into the kitchen. As he was changing the warmers, Tolanar brought his own plate in. He set it in the pan, paused, and then turned to Dursdan. "So, can I at least see it?"

For a moment, a surge of protectiveness went through him but he shook it off and held the pouch cover aside. Tolanar came closer and looked down at the egg. Dursdan watched his brother's face soften. His eyes burned. This should have been Tola's egg, not his.

Mergadan came in with his plate. "Is the egg all right?" He too came over to see it.

Dursdan tucked the last warmer around it. "Yes, Da." Tolanar turned away and Dursdan resealed the pouch.

Mergadan nodded. "Good. I want to go see how Sinotio is faring." He left the kitchen.

Dursdan stood for a moment, the hot coals from the fireplace warming him. He still couldn't grasp the changes in his life. They were coming too quickly. He heard his mother clearing away the dishes and realized they would need the space in the kitchen. He went to his room and picked up the book he needed to read for class. He struggled to focus on the text.

The words kept blurring and vague images swirled in his mind. He gave up trying to study and blew out the light. It was difficult for him to get the egg pouch off and on again by himself but he was self-conscious about it and preferred to do it alone in the dark. Once he had his clothes changed and the egg pouch retied, he slumped into bed. The moon had not risen yet and it was dark except for the stars. He closed his shutters most of the way.

Sleep finally came and he drifted off into the dreamy mist. He could hear Timotha singing before he saw her. She was sitting on the edge of a mist pool, draping her fingers in the swirling fog. She looked up and stopped singing as he approached. She smiled at him. "I am grateful to have good company tonight. Varimato is not pleased with me."

Dursdan sat down beside her, amazed that the mist held his weight. "Who is Varimato?"

She laughed and the sound of small bells echoed through the Mists. "Why, he is my current rider."

"Your current rider? You've had more than one?"

She nodded and swirled the fog some more. She seemed sad. "He is my sixth. I suppose I should be used to it by now. Humans are such short lived creatures."

Dursdan was puzzled. "I thought that dragons died when their riders did. I didn't know they could take another."

"I do not know much about other dragons. I have been away from them for a very long time. I left that Valley long ago. Is that so with the dragons that live there?"

Dursdan tried to remember the last time a Dragon Lord had died but couldn't. He'd never heard of a dragon being passed on and there were no riderless dragons around. "I think that's the case. Menatash mentioned Trusumo. He's an old dragon and his rider is very old but I remember Dorsadram talking about receiving Trusumo as an egg."

"How odd. Do I seem old to you?"

He looked at her. Her face was soft and unwrinkled, as were her hands. It's true that her hair was white but she didn't feel old. "No, you seem timeless."

"Ah, as it should be." Dursdan looked up at the unfamiliar voice. Menatash was walking toward them with a distinguished gentleman. He had flaming red hair and a slightly darker complexion. His face was lined with wrinkles but he still had a sense of energy about him.

Timotha got up and greeted him with a kiss on his forehead. "Greetings, Trusumo. How are you?"

"As well as can be." He looked at Dursdan and bowed. "And greetings to you, young Lord. How fares your charge?"

Dursdan swallowed and looked down at his stomach. It glowed softly. "It seems to be fine."

"Very good." He took Timotha with his other arm and dragged Menatash along with them. "What Lord Dursdan says is correct. I age with my rider."

As they passed, Dursdan got up and followed in their wake. Menatash freed his hand from Trusumo's arm and fell back to join Dursdan. "I was hoping you'd tell me more about your Valley."

Dursdan shrugged. "What do you want to know?"

"Are there many dragon there? And what colors are they?"

Dursdan had to stop and think. "I guess it depends on how you define 'many.' And they come in all colors, red, blue, green, brown, yellow, white, bronze, and silver."

Trusumo cleared his throat. "As to the number, I could best answer that. There are 22 in the first circle, 13 junior dragons, 4 winglings, 3 hatchlings, and 4 egglings for a full flock of 46."

"That's quite impressive." Menatash's voice held a hint of disappointment.

"Oh, there used to be more in the good old days. But the last war took a terrible toll on us." Trusumo shook his head. "And old Natalo is quite worried. His rider has no heir. His line may very well end with this generation."

Menatash frowned. "That's terrible. I wished I lived in your Valley. I would gladly give up these kingdoms to become his heir."

Dursdan looked down at his glowing stomach and sighed. It seemed everyone else wanted to be a Dragon Lord but him. "I'm not sure if that would work."

Trusumo chuckled. "It has been done before. When I was young, one of the houses was in similar straights so the Lord took the husband of his eldest daughter and made him heir." A slight breeze rippled the draperies. "Oh, shards. He has been getting up early these days. I must go." The Red bowed formally and released Timotha's arm. He walked away through the swaying Mists and was gone.

Dursdan stared wide-eyed at the retreating form until he disappeared completely. Menatash sighed. "He's a grand dragon. I've been dreaming with him for many years now."

Dursdan became curious. "How old are you?"

"I've just turned 16."

"Did you have to...?" Dursdan hesitated, not sure how to ask it. "Pick someone to be your wife?"

Menatash shook his head. "I don't think I'll have much say in that process. My parents will probably arrange it. That's just how Royals are, I guess."

Dursdan sank down onto a cloud chair. "Oh." He wasn't sure what was worse. He remembered the girls swarming around him in town and shook his head.

Menatash seemed to look over his shoulder. "Oh, bother. I guess I have to go."

Timotha lightly touched both of them. "We should all go now. The sun will be rising soon. Until we meet again."

The Mists swirled and Dursdan found himself floating. Around him, he could hear voices singing morning songs. He rolled over and his head made contact with the wall. He sat up rubbing the spot. Early morning light was visible through the cracks of the shutters. He opened them. The sun had not yet risen and the world outside was fresh and renewed. He breathed in deeply. The air was heavy with the scent of fruit blossoms. It pushed the last lingering fragments of the dream away.

He heard Tolanar stumbling down the hall, grumbling. His footsteps stopped at Dursdan's door. "Dur, are you up?"

"I am. What is it, Tola?"

"Da wants me to do the chores but the cows don't like me as well as they like you. I'll do the rest if you do the milking."

"Done." Tolanar walked away and Dursdan rolled out of bed. He changed, retied the pouch, and went to the kitchen for a new set of warming pads. His mother was pulling fresh baked bread from the night oven. He waited in the doorway until she set the heavy pans down and released the handle.

Dachia looked up at him. "Are you well this morning?"

He shrugged. "I'll survive. That bread sure smells good."

"Give it time to cool." She looked past him down the hall. "And your Da as well. Radachi told me what happened, but from what he said, you'd already done the right thing. I told Merg that he had no right to be angry with you." She pulled the kettle out and poured him some tea. "He's still recovering. He just needs to get busy again and he'll be back to himself."

Dursdan took the cup. "Speaking of it, I'll be plenty busy today. I'm planting the vegetable seedlings after school."

"It will be good to have fresh vegetable close at hand." She smiled and brushed the stray hairs out of his eyes. "I don't know what we'll do when you marry. This house isn't very big. It won't be a problem at first, until the children come."

Dursdan choked on his tea.

"Are you okay?"

He nodded as he tried to cough the hot liquid out of his lungs. "Just went down wrong." He managed to catch his breath. "The bread will have to wait." He grabbed fresh pads for the egg and headed for the door. "I promised Tola I'd handle the cows."

"But your Da wanted him to do the chores."

"Yes, that's all well and good, but Gran likes a little milk in the morning and the cows don't like giving it up for Tola."

He finished the milking and left the pail on the table, grabbed up his books and some bread, and headed for school. He found Conor there already. They went in to the school and sat down before anyone else arrived.

"My Pa came in early for a load of seed. Something got into the storage bins over winter. My Pa thinks it was rats but I think it was something else."

"Why do you say that?" Dursdan handed his friend a piece of bread.

"I saw the tracks. They don't look like rat tracks. There were shaped like human feet but smaller, and the footsteps were paired."

"That doesn't sound like rats, or swamp trolls, if that's what you were thinking." Dursdan went to the shelf and pulled out a book. He sat back down and began paging through it as Conor looked over the pictures.

Conor put his hand down on a page. "There, that one."

Dursdan looked at it carefully. "Are you sure? Those are wood gnome tracks. There haven't been any of those around for a very long time."

Master Damitrus entered the classroom. "Ah, you two are here early."

"Sir, I think you should see this. Conor found some tracks outside his Da's seed bins and they seem to match these."

The Master came around and took the book. He looked at it for a moment then peered over the edge of the page at them. "Conor, are you sure these are what you saw?" Conor nodded. "This is serious. I have to report this to the Circle right away. And you'll need to come along, Conor, so you can show the Lords where you found the tracks."

"Yes, sir." He got up and looked back at Dursdan. "Sorry."

Dursdan shook his head. "For what? Your early warning may save us a load of grief."

Master Damitrus nodded. "Quite right. Dursdan, you'll have to tell the class to get started on their studies when they come in. I'll return shortly." He rushed Conor out the door.

Dursdan sat back down. Anlahad came in moments later. "Where are Master Damitrus and Conor going?"

"Conor thinks he found wood gnome tracks and the Master felt the Circle needed to hear about it right away."

Anlahad nodded. "Yes, that probably would be urgent." He came and sat across from Dursdan. "How's it going?"

Dursdan shrugged. "My back hurts and I can't find a comfortable way to sleep."

Anlahad laughed softly. "I know the feeling." He ran his hands around his egg. "He feels heavier everyday."

"When is he due to hatch?"

"Soon."

Other students began filing into the school. They bustled about, creating enough rumors to last a year. When they had taken their seats, Dursdan stood up. "Master Damitrus has been delayed. We are to all begin our daily lessons on our own and he will return shortly."

Most of the students obediently got out their books and began, but Ragan stood up in the back of the room. "Well, and why should we listen to you? Just because your Pa was crazy enough to bring you a Gold egg, it doesn't make you second master in school."

Dursdan shook his head and ignored the comment. He got out his own books and began to study.

Rashir came up beside him. "So, why don't you let us have a look at this amazing golden egg?" He pulled at the straps that held the pouch.

Dursdan was up before Rashir could pull back. He slapped Rashir's fingers away. "Don't touch!"

Rashir began to howl. Dursdan rolled his eyes. "What is your problem?"

"You broke my fingers!"

Sormato laughed. "You're full of fluff. Dursdan didn't hit you that hard, and if they had broken, we would have heard them snap."

Ragan had come up behind them during the commotion. "It figures that one carrier would stand up for another. You're all that way."

Brogan stood up. "Listen to the cheeky little farm boy. You forget, Rashir will be carrying soon enough. If you're so against us, why are you standing up for one of us."

"That's enough!" Dursdan moved away from the confrontation. "There is no 'us' or 'them.' We are all the same."

Everyone turned and stared at him. Ragan pushed forward. "That's dung. How can we all be the same? It's the Dragon Lords who have the dragons."

"Where do you think we all came from? Long ago, when our people first came to this place, we were all dragon riders and farmers and whatever else it took to survive and turn this Valley from a wilderness into what it is today."

Most looked at him in amazement. Even Tolanar was quiet for a change. But Ragan slapped his hand on his shin and began to laugh. "What a load! Do you really expect us to believe that?"

"Since it is the truth, it should be believed." Master Damitrus shut the door and moved to the front of the classroom. Conor came and took his seat and all of the students returned to their own places. Dursdan sat down next to Conor.

Conor handed him something under the desk. "Thought you might like to see this." Dursdan opened the cloth and found a small arrow inside. "Lord Dors says it's wood gnomes for sure." Conor looked around. "So what did I miss?"

Rashir was already coming to the front to face the master. "Sir, Dursdan has broken my fingers."

"Well, let's see them." Master Damitrus took Rashir's hand and tested each finger. Rashir made a grand show of agony at each touch. Master Damitrus scowled. "Your fingers are perfectly fine. Return to your seat."

The Master called the classes together and the students fell into the daily rhythm. Lunch break was called in time and Conor followed Dursdan out into the schoolyard. Dursdan was surprised to see Mirana waiting by the fence. She waved when she saw him. Conor waved back before Dursdan could. She walked over and joined them. Dursdan noticed that Conor was blushing.

Mirana smiled. "I hope I'm not disturbing you at school."

Conor cleared his throat. "Of course not. It's lunchtime. And how are you today?"

"Quite well, thank you Conor." She looked over at Dursdan. "I was hoping to have a word with you."

Dursdan looked over at Conor and shrugged. "Excuse me a moment, Conor. I'm sure I'll just be a minute. You go ahead and start eating."

Dursdan followed Mirana away from the school grounds to a row of low trees by the river and pulled the bag from under some low branches. She sat down on the ground and motioned for Dursdan to do the same. She pulled out the book. " I found her."

Dursdan stared for a moment. "Who?"

"The dragon you asked me to look up."

"You found Timotha?"

Mirana sighed. "Well, you asked me to look, didn't you? Anyway, this is really important." She pointed to a section of text. "Timotha was the dragon of Voramato. It seems he had a twin sister named Zamisha. When he was seriously wounded in that first big war, his sister took Timotha and destroyed the leader of the other army, essentially ending the war."

"What happened to her?"

"That's the best part, no one knows. Zamisha took Timotha and left the Valley."

"Why did she leave?"

Mirana looked down at the book. "Because she didn't want to give Timotha up and the First Circle wouldn't let her keep the dragon."

Dursdan's cheeks began to burn. "And what exactly was she suppose to do. It's amazing enough that Timotha survived after Voramato died. She obviously bonded with the dragon along with her brother. Surely the Circle should have known that."

"Dursdan, why are you so angry? This happened a long time ago. It's not like we can find them and apologize."

"I'm sorry. I've just been dealing with a lot of stuff." He looked at the book then up at her. "What about Menatash?"

She shook her head. "I did find the house of Tash and looked through the entire line. There's never been a Menatash."

"Not here in the Valley, maybe."

"Why do you say that? Wait a minute. There was a member of the house of Tash who left the Valley. I'm afraid it's not a very pretty story." She closed the book and pointed to the figure on the cover surrounded by trolls. "He's not fighting them, he's leading them."

"What?"

"Do you remember the great war in 27? After that, the Circle decided that only the firstborn son of the family should be a dragon rider. Well, not everyone agreed with that. Lord Kolitash wanted his grandson, Romitash, to become the heir but his younger son, Moretash already had his egg. So Kolitash secretly got an egg for Romitash and trained him himself. When the Circle found out about it, Romitash was banished, Kolitash was kicked out of the Circle, and Moretash took his place."

"Wow, so Romitash left the Valley and who knows what happened to him."

She sighed. "Unfortunately, there's more. You see, he came back." She turned to the mural of the first Wizard War. "It happened back in 69. Armia writes a lot about it. Your grandpa had just received his egg, he hadn't even turned 16 yet. Romitash came back with an army of trolls all backed by the Eastern Wizards. Your Great Grandpa, Salgadan, was killed in that war. Moretash, had to kill his own nephew, Romitash, to end it all."

Dursdan shook his head. How had Menatash ended up in his dreams? Had he somehow created the name after reading the list? He didn't know. The school bell rang for afternoon classes. "I have to get back to class. I just hope Ragan has settled down."

"Why, what happened?"

"He caused problems for me this morning. It seems he's bent on making my life miserable. Conor says he's heard that Ragan's Da hates our family." He got up and helped her up. She slipped the book back into the bag. "I need to plant the vegetable garden today so I'll be busy after school."

"I can come and help. Now that Pa has the winter hay in, he's been doing most of the evening chores and it will give me an excuse to stay away from Mum and her loom. I'll watch for you on the road."

Dursdan watched her walk away then returned to school. The students were settling into the afternoon classes as Dursdan slipped into his seat. Conor looked over at him. "What was that all about?"

The tone of his friend's voice startled Dursdan. He looked over at Conor. There was a hard edge to his features he'd never seen before. He wondered what Conor was thinking. He wasn't sure what to say. Would Conor be offended because he had shared the book with Mirana instead of him? "She was offering to help me plant the vegetable starts. She wanted an excuse to stay away from her Ma's loom for awhile."

Conor nodded. "She's a good farmer's daughter, isn't she."

Conor went to work on his lesson and Dursdan sat puzzling over what had just happened. What was wrong with Conor? Was Mirana still mad at him? What was a dragon from the past doing in his dreams? He shook his head and began work on the afternoon lesson.

* * *

Aramel coughed. His workroom was awash in thick gray smoke. So much for that spell. He slammed the book closed, went to the shelf, took the ingredients he needed and made a hole spell. Soon the smog was gone. With a flick of his hand he closed the hole.

He went back to his workbench and reactivated the search pool. The boy was still in school. What a silly waste of time. Aramel remembered all the useless hours of drivel they had tortured him with. He wanted to learn real magic, not simple grow or heal spells. Curse his bothersome fellows who had left him in this stronghold. He'd decided long ago that the Portal didn't really need to be guarded. The Elder Wizards had set up such powerful shields around the stronghold that nothing could get in. It wasn't even detectable to anything less than a mage. Just another waste of his time.

He readjusted the spell to see what the father was up to. The old fool was messing about with his dragon. The creature looked as though it had been attacked by a horde of trolls. But he knew all too well what that angry golden queen was capable of. He shuddered and closed the spell.

He went back to the book and tried to figure out what had gone wrong. It should have been a simple matter to do a replacement spell. He looked at the false egg he'd created. It wasn't half bad. The boy probably wouldn't even notice the swap. If he could get the spell to work, that is.

Then he would have his own golden dragon and when it was old enough, he would harness its power and open the Portal and escape this dreadful place. And those who had left him here would pay dearly!

Chapter 7

Mirana met him on the road and they walked the rest of the way together. She kept pointing out all the wonders of early summer, the flowers, the butterflies, the fresh new leaves. Dursdan watched her with mild amusement. "You seem so happy."

A light blush came to her cheeks. "I'm just glad for an excuse to get away from the farm." She pulled the book out of the bag. "Besides, I've been busy reading this afternoon and I think you might be interested in some of the things I've found."

They arrived at his place and Dursdan went into the barn for the starts and tools. "I've been waiting for just the right day to plant these. We haven't seen frost for two weeks now. It should be safe."

"My Pa planted his this morning, too. I guess good farmers think alike." She giggled. "But Pa is envious of your starts. He says yours are always better than his."

Dursdan took the tray out to the prepared garden. He'd been working the soil since the snows had melted and it was ready. "A couple of years ago, I picked up a piece of broken glass that Mikel had been experimenting with and made a real window in the south wall of the barn. It's not very big but it's enough to warm and brighten a small corner." He began setting the starts in little holes.

Mirana sat down on the grass near the plot with the book in her lap and opened it to a section. "I found a case where the firstborn wasn't the heir."

Dursdan stopped and looked up at her. "You did?"

"But I'm afraid it's not going to help you much."

"Why?" He set the plants down and came over to see the book.

She pointed at the section. "Well, there was a good reason. There were two sons born to Sormishir back before the first big war. The eldest was only 4 when the war happened. Corinda remembered the whole thing. When Sormishir was hit in battle, he tried to land his dragon. His little son saw him coming and ran out to help but the dragon faltered and crashed. Dragon and rider were both killed and little Samashir was terribly crippled. His younger brother, Remashir, was given the egg when he was old enough. It turned out to be a good thing. Samashir was only 24 when he died."

Dursdan shook his head. "So much sadness." He sat down beside her and cradled the egg in his lap. "I can't imagine living in those times."

She touched his arm softly. "Our ancestors paid dearly for the peace we have today." She turned to another section she'd been reading. "The wars took many. Think on this. We only have 22 Lords left in the Circle. There were once 36. Five of those houses were lost during the first war. Another house was almost lost during the war in 69."

"How was it saved?"

She pointed at the book. "Badetro had only one son, Vandetro. He was only 20 when he died, leaving just an infant daughter. Badetro's elder daughter, Rakisha, was 16 at the time. Lord Lomotri had a young son, Willan, who was just turning 16. So Badetro asked Willan to marry Rakisha and he made Willan his heir. He even changed his name to Wiletro."

"Lord Wiletro?"

She gave him a puzzled look but continued. "Both he and his son, Dasetro were killed in the last Wizard War. I don't know what will become of that house. Dasetro did have a son but he's still too young. No one from that house sits in the Circle."

Dursdan nodded. "That must be Ranestro. I should have realized he was related to Lord Wiletro." He'd read about the bravery of Lord Wiletro in the last days of the war. "He fought a mighty battle. We were required to read about it in school. Without his sacrifice, we might have lost the war and all that we know would have been destroyed."

"A total of nine houses were lost from the Circle in the last war. And we'll probably be loosing another after Crastrom passes on. I'm surprised he hasn't asked you to consider Drasia."

"She's younger than me." Dursdan pulled himself up and went back to his planting. "She's Tola's age." He stopped and looked up at Mirana. "Wait a minute. If Badetro could do it, why not Crastrom?"

"I don't follow."

"Well, it's quite simple. Tola wants to be a rider and Crastrom's line is in danger of ending. Crastrom asks Tola to marry Drasia and Crastrom adopts Tola and makes him his heir!"

She closed the book. "That's all well and good, Dursdan. But how are you going to get Crastrom, Drasia, and Tolanar to go along with all of this?"

He dropped in another plant. "I'll find a way."

He finished the row, lost in thought. Mirana put the book down and began planting with him. They finished the garden before the sun set. Mirana dusted off her hands and picked up the book bag. "I'd best be getting home before they worry." She looked back at the garden. "It will be beautiful this fall."

Dursdan looked at her in the ruddy light of the sunset. She looked beautiful right now. "I'll walk you home."

She laughed. "It's not dark yet and I surely know the way." She reached out and touched the pouch. "Besides, I think someone is getting chilly."

Dursdan glanced down, concerned. He placed his hand next to Mirana's on the egg. "I think your right. I'm sorry, I'd better get some fresh pads. Are you sure you'll be all right?"

"Oh really!" She pushed him gently toward the house.

He paused by the courtyard gate and watched her walk away. Gran had told him to pick a good one. He couldn't think of anyone better.

His mother set a platter of small doves on the table and smiled at

Mergadan. "Your Da hasn't had an excuse to ground hunt in awhile. I've missed it."

He smiled back. "It did me some good to get out. But I will be glad when Sinotio is back to full strength." He spooned a serving of yams on Carala's plate. "There's been a report of wood gnomes vandalizing some seed bins. It seems whenever they start coming down to the Valley it usually signals larger troubles."

Carala shook her head. "Dirty little things. I can still remember when they got into the house. They killed all the cats in the Valley that year. The rats have been a pestilence ever since."

Tolanar sat pushing the food around on his plate and occasionally glaring down the table at Dursdan. When a pause came in the conversation, he looked up. "I saw you playing in the dirt with Aber's daughter this afternoon."

All eyes turned toward Dursdan. "Mirana helped me plant the starts for the garden. With her help, it was done before sunset." He took a drink of water. "We should have plenty to keep us though next winter."

Mergadan took a swig of his ale. "You shouldn't be wasting your time planting with a farmer's daughter. You should be out spending time getting to know the eligible Lord's daughters."

Dursdan looked up to see Tolanar smirking. "I'm sorry, Da, but I can't seem to find one who's willing to get her dainty hands dirty. The vegetables needed to get into the ground." He looked purposefully at Tolanar, who looked away.

The conversation died down at the table and Dursdan was glad to escape to the sanctuary of his room. He opened the egg pouch and glanced down at the egg. The golden pattern swirled in rainbow eddies. It felt heavier as it lay on his stomach. He wondered about the tiny creature forming inside. He repositioned the warming pad and closed the lid.

Sleep came easily after the hard work in the garden. He drifted through the Mists, floating on a semi-solid cloud. He heard someone crying. He began swimming through the mist toward the sound.

Timotha was curled on a cloud couch, weeping. He pushed away the misty draperies and came and put an arm around her shoulder. "What's wrong?"

She looked up. "Oh, Dursdan. I am so worried about Varimato. He is not well. We had a run in with some creature I have never seen before. It bit him on the arm before Vari could kill it. He treated the wound as best he could but it has gone black and is oozing dark red puss."

"Please show me what the creature looked like." She waved a window into existence and a small bristling beast appeared. Dursdan gasped. "It's a basher hound! I've seen pictures but I thought they were all gone. Where are you?"

The image changed to a strange swampy forest. "We have been flying many hours a day to the north but I must stop and rest occasionally. We came down in a small clearing by a river in this forest and that thing came out of the bushes and attacked. We had done nothing to provoke it."

"Basher hounds aren't intelligent." He thought about the dragons. "At least not that we know of. You may have just intruded on its territory." He sat down next to her. "Now let's see. I know I've read something about the bite they inflict. If I can only remember."

"Why do you not just window the memory?"

"I can do that?"

She nodded. "May I?"

"Yes, of course."

She touched his head lightly and the mist swirled. "Now think of what you are trying to remember."

He pictured the beast in his mind and a vague image of the book he'd read. Words on a page shimmered in the window. "And there it is! I've got to learn how to do that." He scanned the words carefully, learning quickly how to move through the text. "Ah, here it is. If you're bitten, you need to boil the flower of an angel lily, cut open the wound, and pour the hot liquid on it. But I've never seen a real angel lily."

"And you have never seen a real basher hound but it exists. So must this flower."

Dursdan thought of a plant book he'd discovered on Master Damitrus' personal shelves. He slowly paged through the volume. "Here, this is an angel lily."

Timotha studied it. "I have seen flowers like that around here." She looked down at her hands. "I wish I had hands like yours. My claws are big and awkward." She sighed. "And Vari does not understand me."

"Maybe if you brought some of the flowers to him and dropped them in a pot, he might get the idea."

Her eyes shed tears again. "He is so very ill. I am not sure I can rouse him."

Dursdan shook his head. "I wish I could do more to help you but you must still be very far away. I've never seen trees like that anywhere."

She nodded. "You do feel very far." The Mists seemed to darken in an area. "He stirs. Perhaps there is still hope!" She got up and kissed Dursdan on his forehead. "Bless you, wise one. We may yet meet in the light of day." She moved toward the darker Mists and disappeared.

Dursdan walked on along for some time. There was no sign of Menatash, or anyone else for that matter. His stomach glow brightened and he looked down at it. "What are you?" But there was no answer.

A darkness appeared in the mist in front of him. He thought he heard someone calling his name. He moved toward the darkness. "Are you getting up or not?"

Dursdan opened his eyes. Tolanar was leaning over him. He glanced up at the shuttered windows. Sunlight streamed through the cracks and made him blink. These dreams were becoming a problem. "How long has the sun been up?"

Tolanar snorted. "Some time now. It's seems you're the only one allowed to sleep in these days. I had to do all the chores. Da was red hot at me when he found out you'd done the milking. Even he is up and gone, off with Lodaki to do more hunting. I think he liked Ma's praise last night."

Dursdan could hear his mother and grandmother in the kitchen. The house smelled of fresh rolls and bread. "Why didn't you wake me sooner?"

"Da wouldn't let me. Said you needed more sleep because you carry the egg. If you ask me, you're using it to make an excuse to be lazy!"

Dursdan rolled out of bed. "I've never been lazy. I've always done my share around here, and then some."

Tolanar leaned against the doorframe. "Is that why you had the little farm girl over?"

"Mirana offered to help. And we got the job done, the vegetables are in the ground."

Tolanar laughed coldly. "A farmer's daughter! Well, no Lord's daughter would want you anyway. Rashir is right; you stink of dung. I guess that's all you can get, a farmer's daughter."

Dursdan stood and faced his brother. "Mirana is better than any Lord's daughter. She's smarter, prettier, and isn't afraid of a day's work. If I could get her to accept me, I'd be the luckiest man in the Valley!"

The drape opened behind Tolanar and Carala peered in. "Boys, is everything all right?"

Tolanar glared at Dursdan than shook his head. "We'll see what she thinks of you when you fail your classes because you overslept!" He ducked out the drape past Carala and disappeared down the hall.

Dursdan frowned. "Is it that late already?"

"I'm afraid it is. I was coming to see if you were up. I have a fresh roll and tea for you."

Dursdan swung open the shutters and glanced at the sun. "Oh, I'd better pass on the tea but I'll gladly take the roll with me. Thanks, Gran."

She let the drape fall back and he quickly dressed and grabbed his books. He paused long enough in the kitchen to change the pads and grab the offered roll, and then he was out the door and off at a fast jog down the hill.

The school bell was still ringing as he jogged through the empty schoolyard. He made his way to his seat. The morning lessons went quickly.

At lunch break, Dursdan noticed Natalo lounging on the roof of the smithy, his red scales gleaming under the noonday sun. He excused himself and headed toward the center of the village.

Arazan and Crastrom were looking over a pair of handles when Dursdan entered. Crastrom pointed at the crack. "Do you really think it can be fixed so they still match?"

Arazan laughed. "Of course, my friend. I'll have it done before Market Day."

Crastrom smiled. "Thank you, Ara, and I'll have a keg of my best honey for you then. I know Dra will be happy to have her favorite chest fixed by her celebration day." The Lord looked at Dursdan. "And how's our golden egg carrier today?"

Dursdan suddenly realized he had no idea how to propose his solution. He bit his lip. "Well enough I suppose." He looked around the smithy at all the various projects and desperately tried to think of something. He glanced at the handles. "I was wondering, I mean, Drasia's celebration day is coming up and Tola is hard pressed to come up with the right gift for her."

"Tolanar? I had no idea your brother had taken an interest in my daughter."

Dursdan took a breath. "Oh yes, for some time now. He's just too shy to approach her. Being the second son of a Lord has its draw backs." Dursdan wrinkled his nose. That hadn't sounded right. "I mean, it's a shame he wasn't first son. He's so much better at helping Da with Sinotio than I am." The truth was easier to say.

Crastrom nodded his head. "Your Da is lucky he has two fine sons." He sighed. "If only I'd had a son to help me with Natalo."

It was the prefect in! "Why don't you ask Tola?" Dursdan swallowed hard. "I know Da wants me to take more of the responsibilities with Sinotio as I'll have my own dragon to look after soon." The words felt heavy in his mouth.

Crastrom brightened. "What a splendid idea! If he were helping me with Natalo, he'd be closer to Drasia. They'd get to know each other better and maybe when his Day Natal comes, he'll choose her." Crastrom paused and looked at him. "Not that I'd mind you choosing her but I understand that there are girls your age to choose from."

Arazan chuckled. "And dragon's breath, that boy has a good eye!" He winked at Dursdan. "As for a gift, I might make a suggestion. The last time Drasia was in here with her Mum, she took a fancy to this little box. Now, if Tola brings me a dozen fine fresh eggs, I'd consider it a good trade."

"I'll let him know."

Crastrom put an arm around Dursdan's shoulder. "Don't mention our little conversation to him. I want to speak with your Da first. But I'm sure Merg will be more than happy with the arrangement."

Dursdan waved to both men and hurried back to school. He could hardly concentrate on afternoon lessons. He rushed toward the door as soon as the end bell rang. Master Damitrus called out as the students fled the schoolyard, "Remember, exams tomorrow!" Dursdan had not really thought about it, but tomorrow would be his last day in that school.

He jogged most of the way to Aber's farm but eventually had to slow to catch his breath. He was sure now it wasn't his imagination. The egg was getting heavier.

Mirana was hanging wash on the line when he arrived. "I need your help."

"Dursdan, what's wrong? You look like you've run all the way here."

He collapsed next to the laundry basket. "As much as I could." He looked up at her. "I found a way to get Crastrom to ask Tola."

"That's wonderful." She pinned up a shirt. "But what do you need from me?"

"Crastrom is going to ask my Da first. I need to figure out a way to get my Da to suggest to Crastrom that he adopt Tola as his heir."

She took the wooden pins from her mouth. "What's Crastrom going to ask your Da first?"

"For Tola to come and help with Natalo. I just need a way to get Da to make the next move."

"That's a considerable challenge." She pinned a pair of pants to the line. "My Pa mentioned seeing Mergadan and Lodaki out in the back fields today."

"They were hunting. Da brought home a brace of doves yesterday and Ma couldn't stop singing his praises."

She giggled. "I wonder what your Mum would think of nice fat goose. Pa's been complaining that the geese have been eating all the seeds he's planted. I could mention the fact that your Da is a good bird hunter."

"How would that help?"

She struggled with a large sheet. Dursdan got up to help her. She pinned her end. "I've been telling Pa about the things I've been finding in the book. Maybe I could drop a hint about Tola really wanting an egg and Crastrom really needing an heir. My Pa's pretty smart when it comes to things like that."

Dursdan laughed. "It must be where you get it from."

Her cheeks turned pink. Dursdan didn't think it had anything to do with the warm afternoon sun. "I do what I can." Kalista called for Mirana. "Wash day. I'd best go." She smiled at him and waved as she went back into the house.

Dursdan walked down the road toward home whistling a tune, something he hadn't done in days. Now all he needed to do was get Tola to take a dozen eggs into Arazan so he could get the box. He looked up the hill and saw activity around the house. His mother was also doing wash and had several lines of clothes out to dry.

As he drew closer, he noticed Carala feeding the chickens. He took the grain sack from her shoulder and helped finish spreading the seed. The chickens danced around their feet. Carala smiled at him. "Where have you been? Tola said you couldn't wait to get out the door at school."

"I had to stop and see someone." He wondered what else Tola had said. "Do you suppose we'll have enough eggs to spare a dozen tomorrow?"

Carala frowned. "Perhaps. Your Ma and I did finish the baking this afternoon and since your Da brought home half a stag, I dare say we won't be needing eggs for dinner. What do you need them for?"

"Arazan would like another dozen. He has something for Tola if he brings them in."

Carala looked at him. "Oh, I know my brother has a love of eggs but there must be something more. I suppose you can take then. I won't deny him a dozen eggs. But I wonder, what do you have cooking, boy?"

Dursdan shrugged. "I'm just trying to help my younger brother."

"Then you should be in the courtyard." Mergadan put a hand on his shoulder. "It's high time you learned how to take care of a dragon. And it seems your brother is quite good at it."

Dursdan turned to look at his father. "Well, he had a good teacher."

"Crastrom wants Tola to help him with Natalo. If that works out, I'll need you to help me with Sinotio."

Dursdan swallowed. He hadn't considered that. Well, it was working, for better or worse. "Yes, sir." Dursdan forced himself to walk through the open gate and into the courtyard.

Tolanar was scrubbing the Silver with a long handled brush. The dragon was purring. Dursdan didn't know dragons could do that. He made himself walk forward and stared up at Sinotio. The dragon moved his head so Tolanar could get at a particular spot. Dursdan was afraid to interrupt but the Silver opened his eyes and swung his head down to return the stare.

Dursdan stood shaking, afraid to move. Tolanar laughed. "What a joke. And to think Da wants me to go help old Crastrom so you can learn about dragon care. You're too scared to even touch him!"

Dursdan couldn't remember ever touching a dragon in his life. Sinotio moved his head closer. Dursdan swallowed hard and backed up. "Nice dragon."

Tolanar doubled over, slapping his leg and howling with laughter. He whacked Sinotio on the rump. "Go eat him, Sino."

Unbalanced by the shove, the Silver lunged forward, trying to regain his purchase on the rock. Dursdan shrieked in panic as the large beast came forward. Sinotio's eyes went wide and he reared back his head and began to bugle. Dursdan went over backward and hit the ground hard.

Mergadan was at his side. "Sinotio, enough!" He looked down at Dursdan. "What happened? Is the egg all right?" All Dursdan could do was nod. Mergadan looked over at Tolanar. "What's all this about?"

Tolanar controlled his face. "He tripped and startled Sinotio. The dragon lost his balance and almost fell on him."

Sinotio snorted and glared at Tolanar. Mergadan shook his head and sighed. "Maybe this arrangement with Crastrom is a good idea. I've been slack in my duties." He helped Dursdan to his feet. "Go in and get cleaned up. Tola and I will finish up today. But in a couple of days, Tola will be off helping tend Natalo and you will have to learn how to take care of a dragon."

Dursdan nodded and escaped into the house.

* * *

Aramel cursed the Others for the hundredth time that day as he watched the confrontation. He had no idea what was being said but it seemed that the younger brother had no love for the older. He hit the table scattering the spell. Of course! The younger was jealous. He obviously had more skills with the Silver and probably felt he should have had the egg.

Now how could he turn all this to his advantage? He looked through a stack of books until he came to one that held his attention. He could plant an idea in the younger brother's dreams! He flipped through the pages to find the exact spell. It seemed simple enough.

Aramel went into his pantry and dug out the ingredients. Everything he needed was there! He took the items back to the worktable and laid the spell. All he had to do now was wait until the boy went to sleep.

He sat in his chair and conjured up some dinner. No use waiting on an empty stomach. The pheasant was divine, as always, and the wine had a perfect aroma. Magic was the only way to live!

It was growing late. Surely the lad would be asleep by now. He whisked the empty plates into oblivion and went to work. He opened the dream box and began chanting. By morning, the golden egg would be his.

Chapter 8

For the first time in days, Dursdan was completely alone in the Mists. He wandered about for a while looking for Timotha but there was no sign of her. What if her rider had died because of the basher hound's bite, would she have died too?

He gave up looking and made himself a misty chair. He really wanted to learn to make a window on his own. His first couple of attempts did nothing but then he was able to make the clouds swirl. It took him awhile to realize that he hadn't been thinking about anything in particular.

His thoughts drifted to Mirana. A window materialized from the mist and there was her face with the last rays of sunset falling on it. Dursdan sat and stared at it for a long time. He was certain she was the one.

He woke with the rooster, dressed, and went out for warm pads. Tolanar was in the kitchen dishing out eggs and venison strips. It was one of the benefits of his father's half stag. Tolanar watched silently as he changed the warmers. He followed Dursdan to the table. "Exams are today."

Dursdan shrugged. He'd already completed the required exams that Lord's sons needed. Farming came naturally to him. "I doubt I'll have a problem."

"It's a good thing it's not a hands on test!" Tolanar laughed. "You'd probably pass out instead of pass the test."

Dursdan didn't miss the emphasis on the word pass. "Since I'm taking the farm exam, I wouldn't mind a hands on. I'm quite good with crops and cattle."

His brother's jaw dropped. "Da will have your hide!"

"Why? I passed the Lord's exam last year. Top marks." Dursdan left the table with Tolanar staring at him.

Mergadan was in the courtyard with Aber when Dursdan entered. Dursdan stayed back in the shadows and watched. Aber seemed quite sincere. "I'd really appreciate it, Merg. If I don't get rid of some of those geese, I won't have any crops come summer. I'll gladly come along and show you where they are."

"Thanks, Aber. It's been awhile since I've been back there and I'll appreciate the company. Maybe we could stop by your place. I wanted to thank your daughter for helping Dur with the garden the other day."

"It's nothing. Dur helps a great deal around the farm. I'll certainly miss his help once that egg hatches. No doubt he'll be too busy to think about farming after that."

"And I'm afraid Tola won't be around to help, either. I'm sending him over to help Lord Crastrom. Old man's not getting any younger. Dragon care is hard work."

"Oh, you're a smart man making good use of that old custom. And Tola is the perfect lad for it, what with his natural abilities with the beasts."

Mergadan looked puzzled. "What do you mean?"

"Well, Crastrom has a daughter Tola's age, doesn't he? And the man has no sons. I've heard it's an old custom that when a Lord has no male heirs, he marries a daughter off to an eligible lad and makes that boy his heir."

"Really?" Mergadan picked up the bow and quiver of arrows that had been leaning against the wall and put his other arm around Aber's shoulders. "You'll have to tell me more about it while we go get rid of your goose problem."

After the men left the courtyard, Dursdan emerged from the shadows. "Yes!" Sinotio snorted. Dursdan eyed the Silver and walked quickly through the courtyard and out the gate. He wanted to run all the way to school but the egg was feeling particularly heavy. He did jog occasionally, for the sheer joy of it. It was going to work!

The schoolyard was bustling with boys running, climbing, and playing games. This would be the last day of school until fall for all except the youngest. He noticed Anlahad sitting on the fence. He didn't look well. Dursdan went over. "Are you okay, Anla?"

"I'm well enough, I suppose." He looked down at his pouch. "But I think there's something wrong with my egg."

Dursdan wrinkled his brows. "What makes you say that?"

He undid the flap. "Have a look."

Dursdan peered at the egg. It was a beautiful creamy bronze color that swirled and danced much like his golden egg did. He gently felt it. The egg was warm but the shell seemed a little soft. "That's odd." He prodded it gently. The bronze swirls danced around his fingers. At one point he left a dent. The swirling pattern changed. It focused around the dent and the entire surface seemed to ripple.

"Oh, it's definitely never done that before."

Tolanar was coming toward them. Before his brother could speak, Dursdan reached out and grabbed his arm. "Quick, go find Master Damitrus!"

Tolanar was off running. Dursdan looked at Anlahad's panic stricken face. "Don't worry. Everything will be all right." He looked around. "Why don't you come sit over here in the shade of the tree."

Anlahad followed Dursdan. "Oh, Dur, what if I've done something wrong and hurt the egg."

Dursdan shook his head. "I don't think you've done anything wrong." He looked down at the egg again. Something appeared to be sticking out of the dent. He touched it. "Ouch! It bit me!" Dursdan held up his finger and examined the puncture wound then looked at Anlahad and laughed. "Your egg is hatching!"

This made the boy panic even more. Borgan was walking in their direction. Dursdan called to him. "Go find Molahad or Lord Falahad. His egg is hatching!"

Borgan grabbed several other boys, gave them quick directions, and they all ran off. Dursdan focused on the egg. A sharp beak now protruded. The dent was swelling and the rippling increased its speed. The little dragon chirped pitifully. Anlahad grabbed Dursdan's arm. "Please help him. I just know something's wrong."

Dursdan had never seen a baby dragon hatch before. He had no clue what was supposed to happen or how. "I think we should just wait for someone who knows what they're doing."

"But he might die! Please, Dur, help him!"

Uncertain what to do, Dursdan reached into the pouch and put his finger next to the baby's head and inside the shell. It did have some hardness. The baby struggled as if entangled in something. It appeared that it was fighting to breathe. He pushed his other finger though the shell on the other side and began pulling it apart. With a resounding crack, the egg shattered into hundreds of pieces. The little baby bronze shivered in the egg goo. "Pick him up, Anlahad, and hold him close."

The mystified boy reached into the sack and picked up the little dragon. It nuzzled his neck and curled into a ball in his arms and began to purr.

There was a collective cheer from the crowd that had gathered around them. Dursdan had been too preoccupied to even notice. Shouts from the rear announced the arrival of Master Damitrus. He knelt down next to them. "Is everything all right?"

Anlahad parted his fingers to let the little bronze head peek out. "Dursdan saved him." Then he cuddled the baby closer, his tears washing the goo from its body.

The cry of dragons made everyone turn. Red Latofu bearing Lord Falahad and White Nasila with Molahad landed gracefully in the schoolyard. Both men jumped down and ran toward them. The crowd parted to let them through. Molahad sank down beside his son. "Are you all right?"

"I'm fine, and so is he." He looked down at the little dragon curled up and sleeping on his chest. "I'm going to name him Durdansi, because Dursdan saved his life."

Lord Falahad's brows went up. "What?"

Master Damitrus showed them a handful of the shells. They were still gooey. "Anlahad may be right. It doesn't happen often but there was an odd deformity in the shell. It didn't fully harden. Under those conditions, unless the shell is broken from the outside, the baby strangles to death before it can ever get out."

"And Dur pulled apart the shell." Anlahad looked gratefully toward Dursdan. "Thank you."

Dursdan didn't know what to say. He shrugged and backed out of the group so Lord Falahad could sit next to his grandson. "I'm just glad he's all right." He worked through the crowd and out into the schoolyard. Latofu and Nasila were looking at him. Latofu seemed to bow. Dursdan shivered and ran to the schoolhouse.

The exams were delayed to allow everyone to meet the new baby Bronze. It took some time for the students to settle down and the tests to be administered. Dursdan had no difficulty completing his. He finished and placed his exam on the Master's desk.

Damitrus held his hand and pulled him closer so he could whisper in his ear. "Good work today, Dursdan. I know you'll do well with your own when the time comes. Good luck to you."

"Thank you, sir." He shook his hand warmly. "It's been an honor to study under you." He paused at the door and looked back at the classroom. He was finished here. He went down the steps into the schoolyard.

Dorsadram was sitting under one of the trees. He rose and came over to Dursdan. He extended his hand and Dursdan shook it. "Good job this morning, Dur. I'm proud of you, as I'm sure your Da will be when he hears the news. How did you know what to do?"

"I don't know, sir, I just did what seemed right."

The Head of the Circle looked down at the egg pouch. "They say there's a lot of magic in a golden egg." Dursdan swallowed hard. "And your family has strong bloodlines tied to magic. I remember Korithiena well. She was a daughter of the greatest Western Wizard of all times. It's a shame she decided to pass on with the Others. I doubt you saw her much although I believe she watched over you when you were very young. Many believed that she could talk to dragons."

Dursdan felt a chill run through his body. He should have known all this. After all, one section of the book was all about her. He was determined to learn more. "I don't think I can do that, sir."

The old man shook his head. "I wouldn't be so sure of that." He touched the egg pouch gently. "Merg was right to get you this egg." He looked back at Dursdan. "There are things in our history that you won't find on the shelves of the school, or even in the halls of the Circle. Things not spoken of. But you should know the name Zaradan. My great granddad, Meladram often spoke of him. Zaradan was the only Dragon Lord to have a golden dragon. Come by some time and I'll share with you a special book Sorendram wrote. I find it very inspiring. It talks a great deal about Zaradan, the First Head of the Circle." Dorsadram patted him on the shoulder. "Be well, Dur."

"Until we meet again, sir."

He nodded and whistled. Trusumo circled and landed in the schoolyard. He looked at Dursdan and seemed to bow. The Head of the Circle looked back at Dursdan then mounted the Red and they leapt into the sky.

"Wow, that was something."

Dursdan turned to see Conor standing on the steps. "How did your exam go?"

Conor came down to join him. "Easy. Thanks for showing me the trick to those calculations last week. I don't think I could have passed without it."

Dursdan smiled. "Glad to help."

"Say, Dur, I'm planning on going to your Day Natal. Are you coming to mine?"

Dursdan stared at his friend. "Your Day Natal?"

Conor laughed. "I have one, too, you know. Fortunately I don't have to lug a plow around with me for months before the event."

Dursdan looked down at the egg pouch. "Lucky you." But he wasn't laughing. The jibe hurt coming from Conor.

Conor whistled softly and Dursdan looked up. "And there's the girl I'd like to ask."

Dursdan followed his gaze and gasped. "Mirana?" She was walking up the hill toward the schoolyard.

"Of course. She's great. And she has a lot of experience on her father's farm. Remember last Midsummer's Dance? She danced with me."

"Once." Dursdan knew because she had danced the rest with him. Apparently Conor hadn't noticed that.

"And her Pa and mine are good friends. I'm sure her family will be pleased."

The words choked in Dursdan's throat. Rather than say the wrong thing, he walked away. He could hear Conor calling behind him but he couldn't turn around. What if she accepted Conor's offer to please her family? He didn't want to think about it.

He could hear Conor jogging behind him. "Hey, Dursdan? What's up with you?"

Dursdan groaned. "Not now, Conor." He choked on his words. "Just let me be."

"Don't tell me you were going to ask her. Dursdan, you're the first son of a Lord. You're supposed to marry a Lord's daughter."

"Who says? I should be able to choose who I want, regardless of what her Da does for a living."

"But that's what everyone expects, that you pick a Lord's daughter. That's how it's always been."

Dursdan stopped and faced him. "No, it hasn't. We've only lived in this Valley a little over a hundred seasons. It's maybe only the past couple of generations that we have been so divided." Dursdan shook his head. He watched Mirana walk into the schoolyard, a warm smile on her face.

Conor put a hand on his arm and dropped his voice. "Mirana would be a good wife for me. She's smarter than most farm girls. I need someone who can work beside me and keep the farm going."

"I'm sorry, Conor. I can't marry you." Both turned and looked at Mirana. She laughed. 'We're too closely related."

Conor went pale. "But how?"

"Your Ma and my Pa are practically cousins. The proposal would never be accepted."

Dursdan remembered Steban's rejected first choice. It hadn't occurred to him that he and Mirana might be too closely related to marry. Obviously, Conor hadn't thought about it either.

Conor studied the dirt. "Oh."

"But I happen to know someone who's quite gone on you and isn't related. I think she was hoping you'd notice her. She tried to get you attention at the Midwinter Festival."

"She did?"

"If I remember correctly, she gave you a gift. But I think she was too shy to give it to you in person."

Conor brightened. "Yes! I did find a gift under the Sharing Tree! It was a beautiful blue pot. I'm using it to grow herbs on my windowsill. But I just thought it was from my parents."

Mirana grinned. "She asked me what your favorite color was. That's how I know where the pot came from."

"But who is she?"

"She made the pot for you on her Pa's wheel."

Conor's face grew a big grin. "I see! Well, I should go and thank my secret gift giver!" He turned to Dursdan. "I'm sorry I said what I did. I hope you'll forgive me and still come to my Day Natal."

He shrugged. "You know I'll be there. Speaking of celebrations, are you going to Steban's wedding tomorrow?"

"Of course!"

"Then I'll see you there as well." He held out his hand and Conor shook it.

They stood together watching Conor jog toward the potter's shop. Dursdan turned and looked at Mirana. "How is it that you looked up your relationship to Conor? Where you hoping he might ask you?"

"Not at all. I had actually looked it up for Daltrica. She really has been gone on him for a long time. Besides, I overheard Conor's Pa say something to my Pa. I think the world of Conor but I have someone else in mind."

"Oh." Dursdan started walking toward the bridge. The world around him seemed to darken. Who did Mirana hope would choose her? He remembered the glow of her hair in the setting sun and couldn't swallow. He stopped in the middle and absently listened to the mill wheel turning. She came and stood beside him. He looked down at their rippled reflections in the river, very much aware of her presence.

She touched his arm gently. "Are you all right?"

Dursdan sighed. "It's been quite a day. Anlahad's egg hatched this morning."

"I've heard." She giggled. "Durdansi is a cute name for a baby Bronze."

He groaned. "I guess that's all over town now."

"Don't fret over it."

"It just gives Ragan and Rashir more fuel to throw at me."

"That reminds me, I was coming to find you. I figured out what the issue is with Ragan's family. You should see it. It will explain a lot."

Dursdan nodded. There were other things he wanted to look up in the book as well. They walked down the road in silence most of the way. Dursdan saw his father crossing the road in the distance and grinned. "I almost forgot to tell you. I overheard your Da talking to mine this morning. Aber's a genius! My Da took it straight. I think this is going to work."

"It's good of you to do this for Tola, considering he's been such a beast to you."

He shrugged. "He's my brother."

They arrived at the farm and climbed up into the loft. Mirana pulled the book bag from under the straw and drew out the volume. "It amazes me how so many things that happened long ago have made such an impact on things happening right now." She opened the book and set it on his lap. "It goes back to the time right after the first war, when the firstborn son decision was made. There were a few extra conditions back then. Armia wrote down the actual ruling."

Dursdan picked up reading where she pointed. "In that generation, if the original Lord didn't survive, the eldest living son already with an egg or the firstborn son of the eldest became the heir." He looked up at her. "So many died. What if the heir didn't have an egg yet because he was too young? Like Ranestro. How would he get one?"

"It seems a member of the Circle was chosen by lot if there were no close kin who could get an egg for them. And that's still the case, I think. I've found a couple of instances in later years where the Pa died before his son's time and someone else fetched an egg for him. I'm sure it will be the same for Ranestro."

"So what does all of this have to do with Ragan?"

"He and his family are part of the House of Dan."

Dursdan was speechless. They were related? Finally he managed to breathe. "Where in the book?"

She turned the pages. "Zaradan and Korithiena had three sons, Sitrodan, Haladan, and Aradan. Zaradan and his two eldest were all killed in the war. Aradan was only 14 at the time."

"So he didn't have an egg yet."

"Exactly. When the ruling came down, Sitrodan's nine-year-old son became the heir and Aradan was furious. He felt cheated. But the ruling couldn't be changed or it wouldn't have been fair to everyone else."

Dursdan nodded. "And it was the opposite problem in the house of Tash because Moretash has already received his egg making Romitash ineligible to be the heir."

"Yes. In the case of Aradan, he went on to become a farmer and have sons of his own. Doran is one of his grandsons."

"And all that resentment has been passed down through the generations. I wonder if they even remember the real reason."

"I doubt it." She pulled some loose straws out and began braiding them together. "I wish we could solve this problem as easily as we solved Tola's."

Dursdan sighed. "We don't know if it's solved yet. I was thinking about that on the way here. I didn't stop to consider this relationship thing. Is Tola too closely related to Drasia?"

Mirana bit her lip. "I didn't think about that either." She took the book back and began reading.

Dursdan laid back and closed his eyes, listening to the sounds of the barn. A slight breeze whistled through the cracks of the loft. How could he find out whom Mirana was interested in? The cows jostled together as they were let in for milking. It must be getting late. He opened his eyes and glanced over at Mirana. Thin beams of light illuminated her face as she studied the book. His stomach tightened. He couldn't imagine choosing anyone else but her. He sat up. "I'm sorry, I have to go. I'm sure Da will be wondering where I've been."

"Well, to relieve your mind, I can't find any relationships between the two families so it should be a good match."

"As long as Tola and Drasia think so."

He climbed down from the loft and started home. The sun was setting and the air glowed red. The warmth of the day made the berry blossoms sweeter in the hedgerow. As he got to the top of the hill, Mergadan emerged from the courtyard. "Where have you been? I don't know what's gotten into you boys. There are cows to be milked and fed."

"I'm sorry, Da. I didn't realize how late it was. I'll get started right away."

Mergadan caught his shoulder. "I hope it was time well spent. I heard you were looking the girls over in town the other day. Has one caught your fancy?"

Dursdan had a brief flash of memory of the girls swarming around him and groaned. How had Da found out about that? "I don't know, Da. I may have one in mind." But what if she said no?

Mergadan chuckled. "I had a couple of pretty girls chasing me when I was your age." He looked toward the house. "Your Ma was really something."

Tolanar came up the hill and Dursdan made it an excuse to pull away from his father. He noted the puzzled look on his brother's face. "What's up, Tola?"

Tolanar shook his head. "Talk about a strange trade. I don't like to argue with Arazan but look what he gave me for that dozen eggs I took in to him." He opened a package he had been carrying and held up a little metal box. "What am I supposed to do with this?"

Dursdan admired the beautifully crafted tin. "It's very pretty. It might make a good gift."

Mergadan came over to see it. "I bet I know who might like it if you're going to give it away. I think Cras mentioned his daughter's celebration day was coming up."

Dursdan grinned. "You could give it to her and maybe you'll win some points with the old man."

Mergadan chuckled. "Not that he needs them. Cras can't wait for you to come over and get started."

"And Drasia is cute. Maybe you'll catch her attention."

Tolanar nodded. "That's a good idea." He looked up at Dursdan. "You weren't thinking of asking her, were you?"

"Drasia? No. She's younger than me."

Mergadan laughed. "I'd sure like a hint, Dur, but the cows are getting restless and I need to finish rebandaging Sinotio's wing."

Tolanar tucked the box back into the wrapping. "I'll help Dur with the feeding then come give you a hand, Da."

Mergadan nodded and went back into the courtyard. Dursdan walked to the barn with Tolanar. He picked up the bucket but Tolanar grabbed his arm. "I'm sorry about yesterday. I know you've always been touchy about Sinotio. But the way you saved Anlahad's little Bronze." He sighed. "I guess you'll do."

"Thanks, Tola." Dursdan turned away and smiled. He was glad to have gone through all that trouble for his brother.

That night, Dursdan tossed and turned, struggling to fall asleep.

Finally he found a comfortable position and drifted off into the Mists. Much to his relief, he found Timotha there. She looked very tired. "I was worried about you last night."

She patted the cloud beside where she sat. "I am very grateful to you, my Lord. Because of you, my rider yet lives. He is still very weak and it may be some days before we can resume our journey, but we will fly again."

"I'm glad to hear that. Have you seen Menatash?"

She shook her head. "Not for some time. But that is not unusual. There are times when I do not see him for weeks on end. I think perhaps he may sleep during the day."

"How odd."

She laughed. "He is a prince. I would imagine he can do whatever he wants whenever he wants." She looked down at his stomach. "Your little one grows."

"The glow does seem brighter."

"Will you tell me about the dragon near you?"

Her change of topic threw him off. "Near me?"

"I can sense him. What is he like?"

Dursdan thought for a moment. "Do you mean Sinotio?"

The mist began to swirl. Had he summoned a window without thinking about it? But the misty drapes parted and a handsome man stepped through. He had shiny silver hair and brilliant blue eyes. He wore gleaming silver chain mail over a shiny gray tunic and breeches. "Good evening, my Lord Dursdan." He laughed and it sounded like a bubbling brook overflowing.

Timotha got up and clapped her hands. "Oh, how grand." She turned to Dursdan. "Why did not you tell me he was so handsome!"

"Sinotio?" Dursdan stared at the silver-haired man.

"You called, did you not? Now if you would be so kind as to make proper introductions, I am dying to know who this beautiful one is."

"Uh, okay." Dursdan stood up. "Timotha, this is Sinotio."

Sinotio laughed. "I am afraid he is not well cultured. Please forgive him."

Timotha joined his laugher and it was like a rack of tiny bells caught in a current. They went off together in the Mists and Dursdan stood staring for some time. When they didn't show any signs of returning, he wandered alone until the rooster called to him.

He retrieved fresh warmers and some breakfast from the kitchen and went into the dining room. Tola was seated at the table. "How did you sleep, Tola?"

"Never better." He shoved another bite of food in his mouth. "Lord Crastrom was here this morning. I'm going over to help with Natalo tomorrow."

"That's great." He started at his place at the table for a moment then sighed and went to it. He sank down into his chair and picked at breakfast.

Tolanar glanced up at him. "You look awful. Did you have another one of your bad dreams?"

"You could say that. Maybe it's just nerves." His dreams were certainly becoming strange. Now he was dreaming Da's dragon! What next? He wasn't sure he wanted to know. He looked over at Tolanar, busily downing his porridge. "Don't you ever have bad dreams?"

"Don't know. I don't think I dream at all, at least not that I can remember when I wake up." He shrugged. "I'm to do chores this morning. Da said he had something else for you to do."

"I hope it doesn't take too long. Steban's wedding is today."

"Shells! I almost forgot. Thanks for reminding me." He grabbed up his dishes and disappeared in the direction of the kitchen. The next moment he raced past the dining room entry down the main hall. Dursdan heard the big door slam shut a heartbeat later. He shook his head. And Aber thought he was in a hurry to do chores. What would he think of Tola? He had to chuckle.

Dursdan finished his food and rinsed his dishes then went outside. Mergadan was in the courtyard helping Sinotio stretch his wing. The dragon looked at him and seemed to smile. Dursdan felt cold.

"There you are. Dur, what's gotten into you? You're as pale as a sheet. Are you ill?"

He swallowed. Maybe he was. "No, Da." He focused on his father and tried to ignore the large beast grinning at him from the rock. "Tola said you needed something."

"Sinotio needs to eat again. He's still not fit enough to fly so you need to drive a steer up here for him."

"But the steers are all the way out in the west pasture where he normally hunts. I was hoping to get to Steban's wedding today."

"Ah, I'd forgotten about that. You and he were good friends in school. Well, why don't you just drive the herd up to the near pasture while Sino's recovering? Then you won't have to go so far to fetch one."

He felt Da was missing the point but he knew better than to argue. "Well, I guess it won't take me too long. I should still be able to make the ceremony."

"At least get them started. I'll send Tola down to help you."

Dursdan sighed and resigned himself to the task.

* * *

Aramel watched the younger brother carefully. Something had gone wrong. The boys seemed to be getting along better, not worse. He stomped his foot. Stupid spells. Or maybe the ingredients were inferior. Who knew if these peasant farmers could really raise the plants he needed with the proper potency.

He looked back at the younger and watched him doing his chores. Bother, it might be the boy didn't even remember the dream. Useless waif. He tuned the spell to watch the egg carrier. He'd moved out into the fields and was herding a pack of cattle. What a foolish thing to do with an egg about his middle!

Aramel watched the cattle. They were stupid beasts but the boy seemed to have no trouble with them. Ah, but there was one still on the far side of the field and the boy was obviously not getting its attention. Aramel quickly pulled a volume from the stack and paged through it.

He gathered the ingredients from the workbench and began the chant, adding each item in carefully measured increments. The beast began to move away from the boy. He continued his chant. It bucked and began jogging across the field. The boy was running now. It reached the fence and crashed through it. The boy paused only a moment to survey the damage then took off after the wayward cow.

Aramel laughed. This was too simple! He began gathering the ingredients for a portal spell. He'd wait until the boy was far enough from the cultivated lands, then just portal down and grab the egg. Herding cattle was dangerous business.

Chapter 9

Dursdan shook his head as he thought about the damaged fence, yet another chore for him to tend to. It was a good thing the steers were being moved. He hoped Tolanar would be able to get them up the lane and into the other pasture by himself.

Dursdan looked back toward the house. He could make out the form of his brother coming down the lane. The steers were wandering in his direction. Another form moved beside him. Dursdan strained his eyes to see who it was. Red hair flashed in the sunlight. It was Mirana! Part of him wanted to turn back and forget the lost steer but what would he tell Da? The way Sinotio was eating, they'd need every steer they had. And what would he say to Mirana?

A heaviness settled in his gut. Dursdan shook his head and moved off into the thickets away from the managed land. Who did Mirana want to be with? He tried to think of all the eligible boys their age and sighed. It could be any number of them. An image of her, with her hair framed by the setting sun, floated in his mind.

He pushed his way through the brush, following the path of mangled branches. What had gotten into the crazy animal? Dursdan had never seen a steer act like that before. The day was becoming warm and the egg seemed even heavier than it had when he woke up.

An odd sound startled him. It seemed to be slightly to the left of the crushed path. The thickets wiggled in that direction. Could the steer have tried to double back and become tangled? He moved off the path and struck out through the brambles. Everything was over his head and the ground was rough, covered with hidden rocks and holes that created a serious obstacle course. The egg pouch caught on the protruding twigs. Dursdan wrapped his arms around it to protect the egg. Soon his arms were covered in tiny scratches.

The noise was definitely becoming more urgent. Had the steer found a bog? He spotted movement up ahead and hurried the last few steps. He crashed out into a tiny clearing and found not the steer, but a small, agitated blue dragon. It was mewing pitifully and pawing at something on the ground.

"What are you doing out here?"

The dragon whirled around and jumped at him. Dursdan tried to back away but the branches behind him caught on the straps of the egg pouch and held him fast. The Blue continued making the strange sounds and looked back over its shoulder.

Dursdan tried to see around its bulk but the area was too small. He swallowed and began edging around the Blue. "Nice dragon, it's all right. Just back up a little."

The Blue swung back to its goal and Dursdan could see something lying on the ground. He slowly moved closer. It was a body! He thought he could glimpse a light blue shirt and deep purple pants under the dirt and brush that covered him. It must be Satolam!

The Blue looked up at him, its large eyes swirling. It swung its head back and forth between Dursdan and form on the ground. Dursdan swallowed. "Back up a little, will you?" He tried to get closer. The dragon whimpered but slowly retreated. Dursdan went forward cautiously and felt the young man's chest. It was moving. "Well, that's a relief. At least he's alive." The Blue tried to move closer. Dursdan gasped. "Don't get so close! You might step on him!"

The little Blue recoiled as if it had been slapped. It cowered in the brushes, moaning. "I'm sorry. I didn't mean to yell at you." He looked down at Satolam and gently brushed the twigs and leaves away. "He looks like he's hurt pretty bad." Dursdan was most concerned by the odd angle of one arm. It might be broken. "I have to find a way to get help."

The little Blue slowly pushed its head forward and nuzzled the hand of the fallen rider. It hiccupped and let out a loud high-pitched cry. Dursdan though he could hear a dragon bugle in response. He stood up and scanned the sky. A Red circled in the distance. Dursdan waved his arms and shouted. "Over here!"

The Red changed course and flew in his direction. Dursdan could see a flash of dark blue and red on the dragon's back. It was Lord Crastrom. The Red circled around the small clearing, the Lord looking down. Dursdan pointed to the form on the ground. "It's Satolam. He's hurt bad!"

The large Red circled one more time then landed with an indignant stomp on the brushy foliage. Lord Crastrom jumped down. "What happened?"

"I don't know. I came this way looking for a loose steer and heard his Blue making a ruckus." Dursdan backed away as the large Red moved his head in closer to see the little Blue. It gurgled at the other dragon and Natalo wrapped a wing protectively around the little Blue.

Crastrom shook his head. "He just couldn't wait! He had to come out and try it on his own." The Lord knelt beside Satolam and gently felt along his arms and legs. "At least one arm broken and who knows what else." He whistled and the Red crushed down more bushes to get closer.

Dursdan's knees felt weak. He wanted to back away but there was nowhere to go. The Red seemed to look at him. Dursdan shuddered.

Crastrom grabbed his arm. "Here, pay attention!" He handed Dursdan a bundle. "Help me roll out this stretcher. We need to get him back quickly."

Dursdan did the best he could to help move Satolam carefully onto the stretcher. "Will he be okay?"

"He'd have been better if he'd waited for the rest of his class before trying to fly more advanced patterns with his dragon. Blues are tricky. They turn sharper."

Dursdan glanced up at the little dragon. It wasn't much bigger than a steer. "I wouldn't think it was old enough to be ridden."

Crastrom laughed. "Don't you pay attention? Sudo is almost 3 years old. He's full-grown. Of course he's old enough. Satolam has been practicing with his class for several months already. But it seems he wanted to get on to the more advanced maneuvers." Crastrom shook his head. "It's a good thing Merg sent me out to look for you."

"He did?"

"He was worried when you didn't come up with the steers. I told him he was crazy to send you out with that egg anyway." He glanced at Dursdan's arms. "Are you all right?"

"I'll be fine. Just get Satolam back safely. I'll find the steer and head back home."

"You should come back with me. Sudo could easily carry you."

Dursdan looked over at the little Blue. Its eyes were still swirling but it leaned toward him. He shivered. "No, that's okay. I need to find the steer. Sinotio's been eating like a pig with his injured wing."

Crastrom chuckled dryly. "They usually do." He bound the straps of the stretcher to Natalo's harness. "All right but be careful. I'll let your Da know what happened." He climbed up onto the Red's back and settled into the saddle. "If you don't find it soon, let it go. I'm guessing Petolam will make it up to you for finding his son." He patted Natalo's neck. "Come on, my beauty, let's get this reckless lad home."

Dursdan backed up to give the dragons space to take off. The Red bound into the sky, his strong back drafts whipping the broken brambles around in the small clearing. Dursdan shielded his face with his arms. The little Blue followed. It hovered for a moment, seemingly still in one place, and chirped at Dursdan. He looked up and waved at the little Blue. It darted around like a honeybee! Then it turned and followed the large Red back toward town.

Dursdan stood in silent amazement. Tricky indeed! He'd never realized blue dragons could fly like that. He shook his head and forced his way back to the steer's original path.

The path led to a larger opening at the edge of the forested foothills. He began tracking around the edge of the clearing, looking for signs of passage. The air seemed to hum and he got a strange taste in his mouth. It made the tiny hairs on the back of his neck stand up. He looked around. The silence was heavy, as if a blanket had been thrown over the small meadow. He drew the egg closer.

Something that was almost a sound made him turn around. He spotted the old Wizard walking through the forest headed in his direction. Now what was he doing up here? He stopped at the edge of the clearing, his cape swirling around his body. "Well, what have we here?"

Dursdan shrugged. He had no idea where the Wizard came from. Maybe he lived nearby. "Hello there. Have you seen a loose steer?"

Was the old man laughing? "I haven't seen any such beast." He looked at Dursdan from under heavy brows. "And how is your egg faring today?"

Dursdan looked around and realized how far he'd come. He had no idea where he was. There were no dragons in the sky. A feeling began to form in the pit of his stomach. He held the pouch tighter. "Well enough. But I've already told you, I'm not interested in a trade."

"So you did. Therefore, I'm not going to ask you to trade." He came closer and seemed to grow. His face darkened. "Give me that egg!"

For a moment, fear held him in a tight grip. Then from somewhere deep inside his mind, an inner power melted fear's grip. He turned and ran. He could hear the Wizard cursing behind him. Dursdan crashed into the forest, the lower branches whipping at his face. He cradled the egg in his arms. It made running a challenge.

Tree branches and ground thorns reached out for him as he ran. The ground under the trees was carpeted with a thick layer of needles and leaves from last year. They were damp and decaying from lying under the snow all winter. It slowed him ever more.

The land began to tilt downward. He must be near the edge of the woodlands.

Dursdan burst out of the forest and caught himself at the last moment, skidding to a stop so fast that he sat down hard. In front of him was the edge of a cliff. It fell steeply down into a misty valley far below. He looked up at the rugged mountains beyond the valley. There was nowhere to go. He could hear the sounds of crashing branches behind him. Dursdan looked back over his shoulder.

The Wizard emerged from the forest cackling. "It seems you've found the edge of the world. There is no place left to run, boy. Give me the egg and you might live to see tomorrow."

Dursdan glanced over the edge. It was a straight drop for a considerable distance. He might survive it but the egg surely wouldn't.

The Wizard shifted behind him. "Think of how much easier your life will be after you rid yourself of that magical burden."

Burden indeed. A stray thought caught his mind. He could throw it over the edge and it would be gone. The Wizard would leave him alone and his life would be his own again. But how would his Da feel? He looked down at the egg. And what about the baby dragon? No, he'd been dumped with this responsibility. Enough people would be happy to see him fail and disgrace his family.

"Quit dawdling, boy, and hand over the egg. My patience is dwindling." The Wizard edged closer.

Dursdan looked at the edge and followed its jagged line back toward the forest. He felt the dirt under his hands and grasped two handfuls. The back of his neck twitched from the Wizard's husky breath. Dursdan pushed himself up with his knuckles, spun round and threw the dirt in the old man's face. He didn't wait to see his handiwork but dashed along the edge toward the forest.

The old man spit and coughed. "You worthless brat! You'll get no mercy from me!"

Dursdan forced his way through the branches. He could hear the Wizard mumbling something. He felt a strange tingling and smelled something similar to Arazan's hot forge. The taste was strong in his mouth. He paused and looked around. There was no sign of the Wizard.

One of the trees beside him began to sway. He tried to move away but a branch reached out and grabbed him. Dursdan struggled, breaking off small twigs but was still held in its grasp. Another large branch reached out to grab him. He twisted, trying to block it. The smaller branches became entangled in the straps of the egg pouch.

The Wizard cackled, his voice seeming to come from all directions at once. "You can't run from me, boy. My magic controls this forest."

More branches reached for him. Dursdan felt the twigs entwining in his hair and clothing. He could hear the Wizard moving closer. He fought frantically but the branches held him fast.

Dursdan could hear his own heart pounding in his ears. He couldn't let the Wizard get the egg! As crazy as the old man seemed, there was no telling what he'd do with it. He could see the swirl of dark blue moving through the trees.

Dursdan felt something building deep inside himself. He drew a sense of calm from its presence. He stopped squirming, focused, and concentrated on the tiny twigs that surrounded him. The Wizard strolled into the clearing, chuckling to himself.

Dursdan felt the grasp weakening and with a loud shout, wretched himself around. The rest of the branches snapped. He was free! He pulled out of the embrace of the tree and stumbled forward.

This time Dursdan didn't stop to look back. He could hear the Wizard howling in frustration. The foliage brightened and he burst out into another clearing. The air hummed.

The Wizard emerged out of the forest from the other direction and turned to face him. "I gave you enough chances. Your life is nothing to me." He drew a twisted stick from his sleeve. "Give me the egg!"

"Never!" Dursdan surged forward hoping that a moving target would be harder for the Wizard to hit. He felt a searing heat graze his forehead. He stumbled but caught himself before he hit the ground and landed on his hands and knees.

The Wizard was on him. "It's mine!" He tugged at the pouch straps. Dursdan heard the whoosh over his head and thunk of something hard connecting. There was a sharp crack of splintering bone. "Yeow!" The Wizard screamed in his ear. Then the weight was gone.

"Since when do Wizards attack egg carriers?"

Dursdan looked up at the source of the unfamiliar voice. A well-muscled man, weathered face drawn into a snarl, leaned over the Wizard, who sat curled into a ball, grasping his own shoulder.

The Wizard scowled up at the man. "Curse your interference! This isn't your affair, Ghost. Go back to your haunting and keep out of it."

"Blast Fundermeth for leaving you behind! You're nothing but a troublesome meddling rodent."

The Wizard cowered. "You wouldn't hurt an old Wizard, would you?" Then he grinned wickedly and reached into his robe.

Dursdan rolled over to protect the egg. There was a loud pop and the air was filled with blinding smoke. The man coughed and cursed the Wizard. "Measly little coward!"

Dursdan looked around. The smoke lifted. The Wizard was gone.

The man waved the last of the smoke away and looked at Dursdan. "Are you all right?"

Dursdan looked down at the egg pouch. It seemed intact. Trickles of blood oozed down his face. He brushed it away. "I think I'll live." He looked up at the man. "Who are you?"

"Time enough for that later." He held out a hand. "Can you rise?"

Dursdan took the offered hand and was pulled to his feet. "How did you find me?"

"You can thank your steer for that. He blundered into my camp, bawling like a frightened calf." He pointed toward the edge of the clearing. The steer was tethered to a shrub. "Don't see those up here, as a general rule. I figured someone must be looking for him."

"Thanks. For both me and the steer." Dursdan took note of the rough clothes the man wore, tanned hides sewn together and accented with animal furs. His beard was scruffy and streaked with gray as was his hair. The wrinkles of age framed his features but his bare arms spoke of strength born of hard work.

"Do you live up here?"

"Not here, in particular. I was out fishing in the river. The best rapids are not far from here. You can spear the fish as they struggle over the rocks heading upstream." He gave Dursdan a once over. "Curious." He looked back at the steer then at Dursdan again. "Are they giving eggs to farm boys now?"

Dursdan felt the warmth rising to his cheeks. "My Da is a Lord but we have our own lands. That beast was supposed to feed my Da's dragon."

The man laughed. "No wonder he ran."

Dursdan looked around. He vaguely remembered something Steban had said and looked back at the man. "Are you Terarimi?"

His face hardened. "I don't use that name anymore. If you must call me something, call me Terar." He looked down at the pouch. "Why was old Aramel so hot to get his hands on your egg?"

Dursdan swallowed hard. It was no longer a secret, everyone in that valley knew about it. "It's golden."

His brows went up. "Shells! Your Da managed to find a Gold queen and snatch an egg from her? Does he still live?"

"He survived but he'll bare the scars the rest of his life." Dursdan looked down at the pouch. "And I'll bare the egg."

The man snorted. "You sound so forlorn. Do you realize what it means to be the companion of a golden dragon? They hold powerful magic. Some say they keep you from aging as fast as other men. Though I can't say for sure if that's true. The only Lord to ever have one, died before his time in a terrible war."

Dursdan nodded. "Zaradan."

"Yes, well, it's good to see that they still teach history these days." He looked away in the direction of the Valley. "So, you know who I am, now do I have the honor of knowing the name of the golden egg carrier?"

"Forgive me, my name is Dursdan, son of Mergadan."

The man stared at him. "Dursdan? You are of the house of Dan?" The man seemed both amazed and angry. "I can't believe it." His face curled with disgust. "I just saved the kin of the man I hate most."

* * *

Aramel paced back and forth in the depths of the forest, batting at the branches that reached out to snag his clothing. Curse that boy's luck! Why had that old hermit decided to meddle in his affairs? His shoulder ached where the staff had fractured the bone. He applied a quick spell from his pocket to dull the pain. It would have to do until he got back to his workroom.

He continued tracing his steps, waiting for the spell to fully take effect. After all the months of planning with the wild Gold, why was his prize eluding him? That egg was his! He stomped his feet. There had to be a way!

He wouldn't be able to move against the boy directly again now that the whelp knew to what lengths he was willing to go to get the egg. And he might not receive the best welcome in town if he needed something from the farmer. Bother! He resumed his pacing. He had stacks of books filled with spells. Surely in that arsenal there had to be a solution.

The pain in his arm had begun to lessen. He reviewed his previous failures. The dream box had proved ineffective and although he'd made a beautiful replica, he couldn't get the swap spell to work. That had been a shame. He'd already have his egg by now. The boy would never know the difference. He kicked at the debris on the ground. Bats teeth! What had gone wrong with that spell? What was he missing?

A flock of birds took to flight from the branches above and interrupted his meditation. He shook his head. How glad he would be to remove himself from this place! He sighed and resigned himself to abandon the swap spell. He'd have to find a different approach. He prepared a portal spell and went back to his stronghold.

Chapter 10

Terarimi turned away and began walking back into the forest. Dursdan forced his shaking legs to move. "Wait, I wanted to thank you."

Terarimi turned around snarling. "Thank me! Yes, I suppose that's what Torgadan wanted. My thanks." His dark eyes glared from under heavy gray brows. "Perhaps I should go back and tell him how grateful I am."

Dursdan shrugged. "You can't."

"And why not?"

"Because he's dead. He died in the last great war when I was very young. I don't remember him."

Terarimi stood and stared at him again. He shook his head. "How old are you, boy?"

"I'm almost 16."

The man laughed coldly and pointed at the egg pouch. "Guess I should have known that." He turned and looked down toward the Valley. "And how old were you when Torg died?"

"I'm not sure. Maybe three or four." Dursdan thought a moment. "I could look it up to be sure."

Terarimi looked back at him. "Look it up? What, did you start journaling as a babe in arms?"

"No, but my Great Gran wrote down everything in her book. I'd imagine you're in it, too, though I haven't had time to find your story yet."

He snorted. "A story? Do you think that's all life is, one big story?" He studied the clouds rolling across they sky for a moment. "Your Great Gran. Of whom do you speak?"

"Her name was Armia. She was Torgadan's Ma."

His face seemed to soften. "Ah, Little Ari. She was always so good at telling tales. And how does she fair?"

"She's passed on, too, about ten years ago now."

Terarimi's face seemed to fade. "I remember when I was a child, she would pretend I was her magical doll. My Da always doted on his youngest sister." He shook his head and looked up at Dursdan. "I suppose that's why Torg did it. He was a fool."

"My Granddad was a great man. He saved your life. You should at least be grateful for that."

His face hardened and he turned back into the woods and strode away. "You know nothing."

Dursdan followed him, forgetting about the steer. It had pulled the tether line free and by the sound of it, was headed back toward home. He followed Terarimi through the woods until it opened out into another meadow clearing.

Terarimi stopped and turned around. "Why are you following me? You've thanked me enough. Now go back to your own and leave me in peace, what little I have."

"Why do you stay up here?"

Terarimi snarled. "Why would I go back?" His words bit hard. "To be pitied by everyone who saw me? I think not. I have no purpose there. My Az is gone. But you wouldn't understand." The old man shook his head. "A dragon is more than a flying steer, more than just a way to get around. Some of his life energy joins with your own; you become bonded. Why do you think a dragon dies when his rider does? I should have passed on when my Az did. There is nothing for a rider who has lost his dragon." He bowed his head. "Nothing."

Dursdan looked down at the egg he carried. He'd had it for only a week and had spent all that time wishing he didn't have it. He looked back as Terarimi walked away. Was this egg bonding with him now, even as he carried it? Was that why he couldn't toss it off the cliff or give it to the Wizard? Dursdan shuddered.

He didn't try to follow this time but just let the old man fade back into the forest. Dursdan blinked. Terarimi was his kin! He stood a moment longer in that quite glen trying to absorb everything that had just happened.

A distant bawl of a steer broke him out of his ruminating. Dursdan made his way back down the foothills and caught up with the animal. It had stopped to graze in a clearing. He broke off a sapling and lightly tapped its rump to remind it to move. It was hard moving through the think brush but he eventually found the path the animal had made. Traveling was easier and the steer jogged along.

Dursdan glanced back toward the forested foothills quickly loosing their detail behind him. Why did the old Wizard want the egg so bad? He thought about what Terarimi had said about the Gold extending the life of its rider and shuddered. More magic! He looked down at the pouch, feeling it drag on his shoulders.

He almost walked into the tail of the steer. It was standing by the fallen rails. Dursdan gave the steer a slap on its rear and it hopped back into the field over the broken rails. He had to tap it again to get it across the field and through the far gate.

Dursdan guided it down the lane, looking for the other steers. What had Tolanar done with them? They weren't in the empty field he had planned for them. He looked across the other pastures and groaned. There were too many steers in the puller pen. He sighed and tapped the rump of the steer. It jogged in through the gate where the others grazed quietly. Dursdan took note of which steer was missing and frowned. One of the best pullers had been culled from the herd. He shook his head and turned up the lane toward the house. He would have to separate them later.

Tolanar was hauling bones in a wheelbarrow from the courtyard. "I'll be glad when his wing is fully mended and he can go off and feed in the field again. This is a pain."

Dursdan looked down at the bones. "Who picked this animal?"

"I did. You took off and disappeared somewhere and Sinotio was getting impatient. You don't leave a hungry dragon waiting. And I wanted to get on to the wedding, too."

"As a general rule, you don't feed that hungry animal our best pulling steer. Don't you ever pay attention to what's going on around here? Maybe I should let you train the next one."

Mergadan came through the gate. "What's all the fuss? Sinotio is trying to digest his meal."

Dursdan shook his head. "I'm sure he'll have a tough time of it. Sully was all sinew and muscle, very little fat. Steers get that way when they pull all the time." He walked past his father and into the courtyard. He gave the Silver a disapproving glance. Sinotio hid his head behind one wing and gurgled apologetically.

Mergadan entered the courtyard and shut the gate. He looked ready to say something but a dragon shadow crossed the courtyard. Dursdan looked up as Natalo circled to land. He instinctively ducked back against the wall as the large Red back-winged and landed gracefully in the center of the shrinking space.

Carala climbed down with the help of Crastrom and Mergadan rushed forward to help her the rest of the way. She let him lift her down from Natalo's foreleg. "Thank you, Merg." She patted the dragon's leg. "And thank you, Natalo, for your ride. You take good care of Cras now."

The Red purred and gently rubbed his head against her. Crastrom chuckled. "This old boy certainly likes you. I just hope that Satolam realizes how luck he was. Not just because Dur found him, but because he has such a good healer."

"Ah, listen to the flattery. Will you come in and have some tea? I seem to recall Dachia was having guests over. I'm sure she has a fresh pot."

Crastrom grinned. "Not that I wouldn't enjoy some of Dachia's cooking but I need to get back and report to the Circle on Satolam's condition."

The Lord hopped back into the Red's saddle. "Say, has Dur returned yet? He was having some trouble locating a stray steer."

Natalo swung his head and looked over at Dursdan but he shrunk farther back into the shadow of the wall, hoping not to be noticed.

Mergadan looked over at him. "Yes, he's just returned. I was wondering what had taken him so long."

Crastrom leaned in the saddle and looked down at Dursdan. "Looks like you should let your Gran tend you. That scrape on the forehead could get infected." He patted the dragon on the shoulder. "Alright, Nata, let's go."

The dragon snorted, shook his head, and sprung into flight. They circled once, and then flew westward across the Valley.

Mergadan came over to Dursdan. "What happened? Is everything all right?"

All the frustration over the steers drained out of him and he leaned back against the wall. "I'll live."

Carala was looking at the scratches on his arms and the gash on his forehead. "We'd best get those cleaned up right away."

Dursdan followed his grandmother into the house. He didn't have the energy to explain everything to his father at that moment. He heard voices coming from the dining room. Carala continued into the kitchen but he paused and peered around the corner. Dachia, Rayina, and Ashandra were sitting at the table having tea. They all looked up at him. Dachia frowned. "Dursdan, where have you been?" She put down her cup and came toward him. She brushed at the dried blood on his forehead and examined the scratches on his arms. "You're hurt. What happened?" Carala came from the kitchen carrying a bowl and Rayina got up to help her. Ashandra looked pale. Dursdan pushed his mother's hands away. "It's nothing, Ma. Just a few scratches." He didn't want her to worry. "I had to chase down a steer. He got up into the forest and I guess the trees don't like being disturbed." Carala drew out a cloth from the bowl and applied the warm water to the injury on his forehead. Rayina worked on the scratches on his arms. She frowned. "That's not something you should be doing, Dur. You might hurt the egg."

He pushed himself away from the women. "Thanks for your concern but the egg is fine." He went into the kitchen and replaced the warmers.

Dachia came in with the bowl. "You shouldn't be so rude, Dur. She was only concerned for your safety."

Dursdan sighed. Everyone was concerned for the safety of the egg, it seemed. He tucked a fresh warmer in and shut the lid. "We can't afford to lose any steers right now. That beast has been eating double while it's mending and Tola managed to feed it our best puller today. I'll have to train another now."

"Why don't you let your brother do that?"

"That depends." He turned and looked at her. "Do you want to actually get somewhere safely or do you want to take a joy ride across country while the steer decides where it wants to go."

Dachia shook her head. "Your brother will be in charge of this farm after you go into training."

"That's one possibility but he might have other plans." He left the kitchen and went to his room. The fresh pads seeped through the sack and warmed him as well. He looked down at his clothes. They were stained and torn. He couldn't go to Steban's wedding like this.

The soft tap on his doorframe startled him. "Dursdan, may I come in?"

He groaned. "No." The last thing he wanted was to have Ashandra pestering him. "Why don't you stick to tea?"

"I was hoping to see you today."

"You saw me as I came in. Congratulations on achieving your goal. Now let me be. I've had a long day already."

She pushed past the curtain and into his room. "Maybe I could tend your hurts."

He scowled. "This is my room and I didn't invite you in. Get out!"

Her eyes went wide and she put her hands to her face. A sharp rap on the doorpost made her jump.

"Dursdan? Is everything all right?"

Dursdan pulled back the curtain and let Carala in. "Gran, could you please explain to this girl that it isn't proper for her to come barging in to someone's personal room without permission."

Gran frowned but Dursdan could tell she was hiding a laugh under it. "I think you should leave, my dear."

Ashandra nodded and fled out the door. Dursdan could hear her muffled crying and her mother's offended voice. More muffled voices, doors closing, then the house was quiet.

Dursdan sank down onto his bed and closed his eyes. "I've done it now. Ma will have a fit over this for sure."

Footsteps in the hall gave him a moments warning before his mother burst into his room. "That was extremely rude!"

Carala shook her head. "Dachia! Pay attention to your son. He's tired and sore and could stand a change of clothes. Do you think he wants a girl bursting in on him without his say?"

"But they were guests in our house."

Dursdan clenched his jaw to keep his voice under control. "In your part of the house, maybe, but not in my room."

Dachia frowned. "I'm sure she just wanted to help."

Carala's eyebrows arched and she pursed her lips. "And what exactly was she planning to help with? That doesn't seem very proper for a young lady of her upbringing."

"Oh, I suppose not." Dachia's face reddened and she ducked out of the room.

Carala pulled a small tin of salve out of her apron pocket and motioned for him to sit on the bed. She sat next to him and began applying the salve to his forehead. "Will you tell me what happened?"

Dursdan sighed. "I don't know, Gran. I've never seen a steer act like that. I had to chase it all the way into the foothills. And then the Wizard showed up."

"What Wizard?"

"I guess his name is Aramel. Everyone else seems to know him but me." Dursdan looked out the window and groaned. It was late afternoon. There was no way he'd make it to Steban's wedding.

Carala grabbed his hand. "What did the Wizard want?"

"He wanted the egg."

"What!" Carala jumped to her feet. "Did you tell your Da of this?"

"No. I was too mad about the puller to ever think of it."

"Dursdan! Go now! Find your Da and tell him what happened. This is important."

He didn't want to tell Da anything at the moment. Heavy footsteps echoed in the hall. The curtain was pushed aside and Mergadan stood in the doorway. "Did you upset your Ma on purpose? Where have your manners gone to?"

It was too much. Dursdan jumped up and pushed past his father. He could hear Carala chiding Mergadan for the intrusion but he kept on walking. Mergadan's voice echoed in the narrow hall. "Dursdan, where are you going?"

He didn't bother to turn around. "To find someplace I can be without being walked in on." He went out into the courtyard, ignoring the stare of the Silver, and went through the gate. He started to run. It didn't matter the direction. His eyes stung from the tears and his vision blurred. He just kept running.

Eventually his burning lungs and stinging legs forced him to stop. He doubled over, drawing in huge gulps of air. His face was damp with sweat and salty from his tears of frustration.

He finally looked up. The river was just below. It churned around a bend where large rocks had hung up a collection of logs from the spring floods. The water growled its way through the obstacles. Dursdan picked up a handful of stones and made his way down to the riverbank.

He had just yelled at Da. He threw a stone and hit one of the partially submerged logs. He had embarrassed Ma's guests. Another stone found its target. And he'd probably hear more about it when he returned. He sighed. Why couldn't they let him lead his own life? He wasn't stupid. He knew what his Ma had been trying to do. He threw the rest of the stones and they scattered across the surface to be swallowed by the hungry current. Would Gran tell Da about the Wizard? Surely he'd hear an earful on that subject as well.

He stuck his thumbs in the pouch ties and started walking down the shore. The willow saplings and cattails forced him farther up the bank. In the distance, he could see his favorite tree. How many times as a child had he gone to that spot?

He wandered over to it and leaned against the old willow. The river was quieter here. The water spun lazily around splash-shined rocks and the old tree's branches dipped into the current, briefly teasing its flow.

Dursdan sank down between two roots, finding the niche, laid his head back on the gnarled bark and closed his eyes. A few birds chattered in the branches overhead, but he didn't mind. They weren't talking to him.

A light breeze stirred through sighing leaves and a bee zoomed by, hovered briefly, drawn by the sticky sweet smell of a water lily. The river chuckled at the foolish insect then took up a conversation with the frogs. A cricket and a grasshopper began to quarrel. A duck scolded her brood somewhere in the cattails on the opposite shore. A rush of wings whirled around Dursdan's head and weight rested on his bent knee. He propped one eye open and discovered a butterfly had perched there.

It tested his breeches for nourishment but rolled up its tongue in disgust. The colorful wings flapped gently, catching stray rays of the fading light that seeped through the leaves. It washed its face then turned a crystalline eye in his direction and laid its wings flat so that he might study their intricate patterns. What had once seemed just a jumble of yellow and brown became a detailed tapestry. The butterfly gave a final bow and twitched back into the breeze.

Dursdan watched the delicate wings flutter away. He was startled by the hues of color surrounding him. The river laughed and the frogs chuckled in chorus. A fat bullfrog pulled itself onto one of the glistening rocks and blinked at Dursdan. He smelled of loam and rich mud. A fly mistakenly journeyed too close. The bullfrog stretched out his tongue and snatched it out of the air. It winked at Dursdan again, smiled, and slipped back into the water.

The river began to sing. Dursdan could feel the mist on his face. It was like the mist of the waterfall a day's journey upstream. Could it have snuck down the river to spill over the bank these many miles from its source? He could smell the wet stones that the sun and water argued over, taste the earthiness that the currents washed down from the mountains. For a moment, he was caught up in the sweeping flow.

Something much closer caught his attention. He pulled his focus back to see the tiny spider dangling a hands breadth in front of his nose. Its thin silken line reflected the filtered light of the sunset giving it a reddish tinge. Eight arms danced before him. Dursdan was afraid to breathe but he had to exhale at last and his burst sent the tiny spider sailing outward.

Something began to laugh inside of him. It was not his own laughter. It resonated and echoed the river, the frogs, even the birds who were giggling at the frantic spider as it spun wildly out of control back toward Dursdan's face. The spider regained some dignity as it landed all eight feet on the tip of his nose. It waved two front legs at him in reprimand then began climbing back up its line, back into the safety of the leaves away from silly boys with windy breath.

The childish laughter continued, a pure delight for the experience of life. A rainbow of hues and shades, a symphony of sounds, a wealth of smells and tastes, the tickling of touch, this was what it was to be alive, to be experiencing it all for the first time.

Dursdan looked down at the bulge in his lap and the breath caught in his throat. It was in his head! It was touching his mind! He wanted to scream but no sound would escape his tightened throat. Something snapped. The world of rainbows and symphonies shattered around him. He found his voice. "Don't touch me! Leave me alone!"

He could feel the confusion and the sadness at his rejection. He loathed this creature that had been forced on him. It was bad enough that his dreams were filled with such intrusions but he wouldn't stand for his conscious thoughts to be attacked.

Dursdan heaved himself up and started to run again. He angrily pushed the alien thoughts away from his own mind. Everyone and everything seemed bent on determining his destiny. It was his life. He wanted to make the choices. At that moment, he wished that he'd thrown the egg over the cliff.

His body forced him to slow his pace. He jogged along and finally took note of his surroundings. He'd come a considerable distance. He was out in the far fields almost to the foothills. The river was forced into a narrow canyon and he could hear the churning rapids not far off. The sun was sinking over the western mountains and the sky was painted with a warm palette. So much for Steban's wedding dance.

He felt the dragon before he heard the whoosh of its wings. Osiral circled and landed not far from him. Radachi jumped down and approached. "Dur, are you all right?"

"I suppose my Da sent you to find me."

His uncle shook his head. "I haven't seen Merg today." He looked back at his White with a puzzled expression. "It was Osiral, actually. He started acting strange. I went to comfort him and he nudged me to get on then flew straight here."

"*She is sad. I was worried.*"

"Don't do that!" His shout startled the dragon, who pulled back in alarm. Other dragons called from the valley.

Radachi spun around. "Shells, what's going on?"

"Tell your dragon to leave me alone." His voice was so low it was almost a growl. "The egg is fine. I wish everyone would leave me alone!"

Dozi and Trusumo appeared overhead. Radachi gasped. "What's this? Where's Dors and Huma? Dragons don't fly alone!"

They landed and slowly approached. Trusumo bowed his head and turned it so that he could focus one eye on Dursdan. Dursdan stared back. "Don't even start."

Trusumo shook his head, turned away and bounded back into flight but Dozi remained. She and Osiral seemed to exchange glances. Dursdan heard a soft whispering like the rustle of dried leaves, in the back of his mind. "*Is everything well?*"

Osiral shrugged. He heard the whispering again. "*As well as can be. She is sad. He is angry. But they live.*" Dozi turned as if to address him but Osiral shook his head. "*I would not do it. It hurts.*"

The bronze lowered her head and backed away. She turned and sprang into the air, circled once, then headed back toward the village.

Radachi stood staring at Dursdan. "I don't suppose you could tell me what just happened."

Dursdan shook his head, trying to clear the strange wispy sounds from his mind. He stared up at the White. "Why don't you ask him?"

"Dragons can't talk."

Dursdan turned and began walking away. "Don't make a bet on that." He readjusted the weight of the sack and started off toward home.

* * *

Aramel stood peering into the pool on the surface of his worktable. He watched the Lord tending the Silver. There was no sign of the brother. Where was the young lordling? He was puzzled. He sprinkled some powder in one corner and a new image formed. Ah, there he was. Striding down the road toward the house, no worse for the wear from their earlier confrontation.

Aramel rubbed his shoulder. He'd used a quick spell to dull the pain but the effects were beginning to wear off. He'd have to use a mending spell on it soon. Curse the interference of the old hermit!

He turned back to the puddle as the lordling entered the courtyard. There was a brief exchange between them. The Lord seemed agitated. Aramel was frustrated that he couldn't hear their words. Someday he'd find a way to enhance the spell.

The image stayed focused on the courtyard as the lordling entered the house. The father returned to his ministrations on the Silver. Eventually the dragon settled into a comfortable position. The color faded from the clouds as sunset became night. The Lord stood watching his dragon for a time then went into the house himself.

Aramel grew tired of his vigil and wiped the pool off the table. This was getting him nowhere. There had to be a way to get his hands on that egg. He slumped into his chair and grabbed a volume off the shelf. Maybe he could find a more useful spell. His arm stung from the weight of the book. Bother! He laid it back down and went to prepare a mending spell.

Chapter 11

Dursdan struggled to fall asleep. He had chosen not to eat to avoid any confrontation at dinner. Now he laid tossing and turning, his empty stomach grumbling, unable to find a comfortable position with the egg pouch wrapped around him. If only he could take it off at night. But he knew better than to even think it. He was sure his parents looked in on him while he slept. It made Da nervous enough when he removed it to change his clothes.

Dursdan sighed. Why did he have to do this? He thought back on the one instance that was different. But did he have the courage to seriously injure himself? Sinotio grumbled in the courtyard. "Oh, get out my thoughts, you awful beast. Mind your own business."

"Dursdan, are you all right?" Carala's voice was tense with concern.

He had become accustomed to the question. "I'm fine, Gran, just having trouble falling asleep with that noisy creature outside."

She peered in around the curtain shedding flickering candlelight across his dark room. "I think he's worried about you. He tried to get up and fly somewhere this afternoon. Mergadan had to hold him down lest he do more damage to his mending wing."

Dursdan felt a tinge of guilt, especially remembering Osiral's thought that his outburst had hurt the White. He looked down at the egg. Had he hurt her, too? And why suddenly was it a she?

"Dursdan?" She had stepped into his room, letting the curtain fall behind her.

"Sorry, Gran, I just have a lot on my mind."

"I have no doubt of that. I take it you didn't tell your Da about the Wizard. You need to. That's important."

"You didn't tell him?"

"No, Dursdan. That is your responsibility. Do you understand?"

He didn't. "Yes, Gran." Dursdan rolled onto his back and let the weight rest on his stomach. He glanced up at her in the doorway. She had a basket of yarn. It looked like some of the yarn he'd gotten from Tresel. "What are you working on?"

"A special project for your chosen one."

Dursdan cringed. That was the last thing he wanted to think about. "I suppose that's why Ma dragged Ashandra here this afternoon."

Carala chuckled. "Dursdan, there aren't that many girls in the Valley. Your Ma has tried to guess, based on her ideas, who you might choose."

"What if I wanted to choose someone else?" A certain farm girl, for instance. But his mind went farther. "Maybe someone from outside the valley?"

Carala gasped and stared at him with a look of astonishment. "Outside the valley?"

Dursdan propped himself up on one arm. "You do realize there's more to the world than this little valley. There are kingdoms of men all around us. I could leave the Valley and find a girl somewhere else."

Carala was speechless. She continued to stare at him. Finally, she managed to find her voice. "What ever gave you such an idea?"

Dursdan shrugged. "Just something I thought about after reading part of the book. We didn't always live in this valley. If I've calculated it right, we've only been here a little over a hundred years."

"And did you read why we came here?" Her voice grew cold. "We are Dragon Lords as our ancestors were. Our people will not give up the dragons. We were given them by the Wizards to protect and serve."

"We were given them to fight a war that ended more than a century ago."

"The wars weren't over. Your granddad died in a terrible war."

Dursdan swung his legs around and sat up. "One that we probably caused." She tried to speak but he continued. "The only reason the Eastern Wizards attacked the Western Wizards was in retaliation because the Westerners were harboring us. If the Old Lords had just left well enough alone,"

She stepped forward and slapped his face. "Curb your tongue!"

Dursdan stood up, towering over her. Anger burned in his stinging face. "Get out of my room." His voice was low and dangerous.

Her eyes went wide and she backed out, letting the curtain fall and cover her retreat. Dursdan shook his head. What was wrong with him? He looked down at the egg pouch. Before he'd gotten that thing he would have never dreamt of speaking to her in such a way.

He sank back down on his bed and curled into a ball. What was he becoming? His eyes filled with tears. He didn't want this, never had. Why couldn't anyone understand that? All they talked about was his responsibility as first son. Sobs shook him. And here he was, threatening Gran. It wasn't right.

He cried himself to sleep. Through the Mists, Timotha came. He tried to turn away but she followed. "You are angry."

"Leave me alone." Even his dreams pestered him. She continued to follow. "Can't you hear? Why do you bother me?"

She bowed her head. "I heard your call. I answered."

His stomach glowed softly. "And this thing, what is it doing to me?"

She turned her head to look at him, ready to reply.

"Be careful, dear one." Sinotio walked through the mist toward them. "His anger is mighty." He bowed to Dursdan. "My Lord. Forgive me for not coming when you needed assistance."

Timotha turned on him. "What happened? Is that why the little one is in such a state? Was she injured?"

Sinotio held up his hands and chuckled. "Peace! The Little One mourns because he yelled at her. She will live. As will the others." He turned and looked at Dursdan. "I am afraid he was mad at several of us today. I am sorry about the steer but I was hungry and it was brought before me."

"Enough!" Dursdan had to slap his hands over his ears to keep the echoes from deafening him. Timotha and Sinotio both backed away, alarmed. The golden glow retreated. Once the echoed died down he removed his hands and looked at the dragons. "I don't know why I have these dreams. Maybe the stress of all this is getting to me."

A laugh echoed from the mist. Menatash joined them. "You really don't understand do you? These aren't ordinary dreams."

"Why should I believe the figment of one of them?"

Menatash shook his head. "I asked my Great Grandmother about you, about the Dragon Lords and their Valley. She was surprised that I knew of it. She was sure that my father had no knowledge of such things. My Grandfather's father was once one of you."

"Romitash."

Menatash looked shocked. "You know him?"

Dursdan looked away. "No, but I know of him. He died long before I was born." He remembered the terrible battle scene on the cover of the book. "He betrayed the Valley and led an army that nearly destroyed us."

"Oh." Menatash studied his hands. "She didn't mention that part."

Timotha came and stood next to Menatash and put a hand on his shoulder. "You are not your ancestor."

The words echoed around in Dursdan's head. He wasn't his ancestor, either. He looked down at his dimly glowing stomach. Then turned to Menatash. "Do you know what burden I carry?" The other shook his head. "I bear an egg. Against my will this responsibility was thrust on me because of tradition. I didn't ask for it nor do I want it." The glow faded completely.

Timotha shook her head. "Poor little one."

"I am not little!"

"I was not referring to you, my Lord, but to her. She needs your love and support to grow properly." She looked off into the Mists. "She was taken from her mother against her will. She had no choice either."

Dursdan had not considered that. He'd been so focused on his own issues, he hadn't given any thought to the egg.

Timotha looked lost in thought. "I do not remember my mother. I dreamed her once long ago but she frightened me. Voramato and Zamisha were my world. They were everything to me. When Voramato passed beyond the edge, I thought I was lost but Zamisha held me. She took me away from the Valley."

Menatash looked up at her. "You're from his valley, too?"

"Of course, as is Trusumo. The Outer dragons are all wild. They have no use for men." She looked down and her voice became very quiet. "No use for dragons touched by men."

Sinotio came and encircled her with his arms. "Hush, my love. Do not fret. I am here and I too am touched by men. I will cherish you."

She leaned against him and Menatash backed away to avoid getting crushed. "What a pair." He looked over at Dursdan. "So how do you know Sinotio?"

Dursdan stared at the Silver man holding the White lady. "He's my Da's dragon."

Menatash whistled. "That's something." He pointed at Dursdan. "And you, what's your dragon?"

Dursdan looked down at his stomach and winced. "She's... cold!"

Dursdan sat up so quickly he fell out of bed. He cradled the egg to protect it and rolled, hitting his arm hard. It was still dark. He sat up and felt the pouch. It was cool. But he had changed the pads before coming to bed.

He got up and ran to the kitchen. The lamp was turned down and the night coals glowed softly giving the room a ruddy cast. He slowly opened the pouch. The swirling patterns were very slow. He touched the egg. They ignored his fingers. He quickly pulled the cooled pads out and replaced them with warm ones, then resealed the pouch to keep the heat in.

"What is it, Dur? I heard the noise."

Dursdan was startled. "I'm sorry, Da. I got up so fast that I must have tripped on the bed sheets." He looked up at his father. "The pads got cool. She was cold."

Mergadan came forward and placed his hand on Dursdan's shoulder. "Are you all right?"

Dursdan tucked the warmers around the egg and closed the lid. "I'm sure it's fine."

"That's not what I asked." Mergadan sighed. "Carala was right. I had no right to jump on you like that this evening. Your room is your space. It's just your Ma. She gets so upset I can't think straight sometimes."

"I know that feeling."

Mergadan grinned. "I knew you'd do well." He felt the pouch. "Seems warm enough now. Why don't you try to get a little more sleep. Aber said he'd be planting the lower field in the morning and I know you well enough, you'll want to be out there helping."

Dursdan nodded. "Thanks, Da." He turned to go.

Mergadan cleared his throat. "That was a brave thing you did today, helping Satolam. Cras said he was hurt bad."

"Gran took good care of him. I'm sure he'll be okay." Dursdan paused, remembering his grandmother's words, and turned back to his father. "Da, what do you know of the Wizard Aramel?"

Mergadan frowned. "Dors and I have spoken some concerning this Wizard. He was left behind by the Western Wizards when they departed."

Dursdan noted the stiffness in his father's words. "Have you ever met him?"

"No. Why do you ask?"

"I saw him in the forest today while I was looking for the steer." He swallowed hard. "He wanted me to give him the egg and when I refused, he attacked me."

"What! Why didn't you speak of this earlier?" Mergadan took his shoulders. "Did he harm you?"

Dursdan touched the scratch on his forehead. "It's nothing. Terarimi came along and scared him away before he could do much."

"Tera? You've seen him? I've heard rumors that he still lived. Did he seem well?"

Dursdan didn't know what to say. "He looked fit." Dursdan stared at the burning coals. "He didn't want to be disturbed."

"I see." Mergadan let go of him and turned toward the fireplace. "It was a sad case. I remember. My Da saved him but his dragon... well, there was nothing that could be done. It hurt my Gran something terrible."

"Well, I best get some sleep if I'm to help plant a field tomorrow." His father said nothing. "Good night, Da." He left his father standing in the kitchen and went back to his room. The pouch was warm against him. He lay back down but was afraid to go back to sleep. The dreams had become far too real. What if they really were real? He had heard the dragons in his head. What if, out there somewhere, there really was a White and her rider struggling to get to the Valley?

He'd heard his father's footsteps some time ago, and brief murmured words between his parents but the house was quiet now. He got up, slung a heavy robe around his shoulders and crept down the hallway. He paused for a moment at the front door. Perhaps he'd lost his mind. He sighed and opened the door.

Sinotio sat at full attention on his rock in the courtyard. Starlight gleamed off of his shining sliver scales and bright blue eyes. He was watching Dursdan. Pulling the robe tightly around him and the egg pouch, Dursdan approached the Silver and their eyes met. "You can understand me, can't you."

Sinotio nodded.

"Can you understand everything people say?"

Sinotio shrugged.

"Can you talk to any other human?"

Sinotio shook his head.

"Why can you talk to me?"

Sinotio lowered his head and leaned forward until his right eye was only a few inches from Dursdan's face. A whisper formed in the back of his mind. "*You will not shout?*"

Dursdan sighed. "No, I won't shout. I need to understand this. Why me?"

"*You are special.*"

"Because of this egg?"

"*No, we have always dreamed together, you and I. I remember. You were with me when we found the egg.*"

Dursdan closed his eyes remembering the dream. He shuddered. "And you've been dreaming with me now? With Timotha and Menatash?"

Sinotio seemed to smile. "*Timotha. Is she not beautiful? And she has chosen me!*" The Silver pulled his head back and extended his wings. "*I must be able to fly when she arrives.*"

"Do you know where she is?"

Sinotio shook his head. "*Still very far away.*" He lowered it sadly.

"What are you doing?"

Dursdan jumped. Sinotio came up in defensive posture. "Tola, you almost scared me to death." He whirled around to face his brother. "What are you doing sneaking around at this time of the night?"

"I could ask the same of you. I thought you were afraid of Da's dragon."

"Maybe I'm getting over it now that I'm toting one of my own."

Sinotio leaned forward and looked at Tolanar. "*He is angry.*"

"I know that."

"What do you know?"

Dursdan sighed. "Just talking out loud. Go back to bed, Tola."

"I think you've gone off your rocker." Tolanar gave them one final glance then disappeared inside the house.

Dursdan turned back to the Silver. "And all the dragons can talk to each other?"

"*Of course.*"

"Yes, of course. It's just us stupid humans that can't hear."

"*You are not stupid. You can hear.*"

Dursdan looked down at the egg pouch. "Is she okay?"

Sinotio brought his head down and nuzzled the pouch. Dursdan held his breath. Sinotio looked up at him. "*She is afraid.*"

"Me too."

He returned to the house and crawled back into bed. He didn't want to sleep. He laid awake listening to the night sounds. Somewhere in the distance, an owl hooted. The crickets chirped in chorus outside his window. He could even hear the cows stamping in their stalls. He wondered if they dreamed, too.

At some point his eyes closed and he drifted back into the Mists. He didn't see anyone else nor did he go looking. He walking among the sheer white draperies thinking about what Timotha had said. He looked down at his stomach. The glow was barely noticeable.

"I'm sorry. I shouldn't have yelled at you. It's not really your fault. You didn't choose this either." He rubbed the dull spot gently and it glowed a little stronger. He sat down on a pile of clouds and began humming to her.

Timotha found him and sat down next to him, draping an arm

around his shoulders. "What choice do any of us really have? Only one really."

Dursdan looked up at her. "And what is that?"

"Only how we act upon what destiny sets before us."

* * *

Aramel had dozed off with the volume in his lap. He stirred in his sleep and it crashed to the floor. The Wizard woke with a start and looked around. All was as he'd left it. He bent down to pick up the book. It lay open to a spell he'd never paid much attention to before. It gave him an idea. He picked up the book and brought it to his workbench.

He spent the better part of an hour searching for the ingredients for the spell. He never seemed to have what he needed when he needed it. Finally it was all assembled. He began the search spell, carefully laying out the scry sticks in the right pattern. The pool appeared on the table. The image was misty at first but as he added more items and chanted the incantations, the image cleared.

Bathed in moonlight, a lone troll sat on a boulder eating the leg of some unfortunate beast. Its strong teeth crushed the bone and it growled as the meat fed its belly. Thick arms covered with dirty hair, matted in places, held the flank. It occasionally looked up as if expecting to be attacked.

Aramel wrinkled his nose. He didn't much care for the creatures. They could be temperamental and difficult to control. He glanced over at the handler spell and began the first line of incantation as he carefully placed a black feather into the pool.

The troll looked up and scented the air. It looked down at the remains of the leg and shrugged, flung it aside, and jumped down from the boulder. Another line of the spell and a silver ring was added to the pool. The troll began walking to the south.

Aramel smiled. If all went well, it should be there by mid-afternoon.

Chapter 12

Aber was in the field shortly after dawn. Dursdan brought his own planting wedge and they began to plant the summer corn. They easily kept up with each other. Aber worked the row next to him. "I'm sure going to miss your help. I get the feeling that Tola's going off to Crastrom's."

Dursdan finished a row and paused to take a drink. "It will be good for Tola. He's better with dragons than I am." He looked down at the egg. "I just hope I can manage this when the time comes."

Aber laughed. "Lad, I've seen your talent with animals. You're one of the best at training pulling steers. Why, many a farmer in this Valley has one of your pullers at his plow or wagon. And I seem to recall you trained Nub, didn't you?"

"I did. Is he working well for you?"

"Better than any I've ever had."

Dursdan started the next row. "But dragons are more complicated than steers." He looked back toward the house and he briefly felt Sinotio dozing on his rock. "And this is a Gold."

"They do make quite a fuss over the color, don't they." He paused to switch to the next sack. "Your Day Natal is coming up, isn't it?"

Dursdan leaned on his planting wedge and looked over at Aber, wondering where the conversation was going. "It's next week."

"Your family and mine go way back, though, as Mirana informed me, there have never been any marriages between them." He chuckled. "She was very certain of that."

Dursdan swallowed hard. "She was?"

"She looked it up in a book and showed it to me."

Dursdan's mind was racing. "I gave her Great Gran Armia's book to read. She's had more time lately than I have."

Aber nodded. "That's a grand thing for you to do. It was hard on Kalista when her brother and Pa died. There were some who thought our marriage was odd, she being the daughter of a Lord, and all."

"Kalista seems to be quite at home on the farm." He looked across the fields. "If Tola goes off with Crastrom, this farm will be mine someday. I'm going to need a wife much like her."

Aber nodded. "You're a man of many talents and a Pa would be proud to have his daughter be your wife."

Dursdan looked over at Aber. "I thought Mirana had someone else in mind?"

Aber chuckled. "Don't know what ever gave you that idea but you're all she talks about."

Dursdan felt his heart jump. "Then you don't think she'd mind if a certain son of a Lord asked her?"

Aber smiled. "I dare say she wouldn't mind a bit."

"I know my new studies will take up some of my time, but you know you'll have my help in the fields whenever I have time to spare. This little dragon will just have to get used to that idea." Dursdan began to whistle as he resumed planting. They worked on through the rest of the morning and finished the field by lunch.

Mergadan came down to meet them at the field gate. He carried a basket of food and a jug of cider. "My thanks to you, Aber, for your help with this. Come and sit awhile and have some lunch. Dachia was quite pleased with the geese and has made an amazing lunch mix from the leftovers."

"Far be it from me to turn down her cooking. How are things faring with Tola?"

Mergadan laughed. "He and Natalo hit it off quite well. Cras is impressed and overjoyed. And it seems his daughter, Drasia has taken a shine to him." He winked. "Maybe all this will work out in the long run. Cras and I talked on the subject for some time. He's off to ask Dors his opinion."

Dursdan listened quietly, trying not to smile. He munched on his sandwich in great satisfaction. "*Natalo says Tola is fine.*" Dursdan jumped as the soft voice tickled through the back of his mind.

"You all right, Dur?" Mergadan touched his son's arm. "Did something bite you?"

"I'm okay. I just got a chill."

Mergadan looked around, a concerned expression on his face. Aber watched. "Is something up, Merg?"

"I don't know. Egg carriers tend to be sensitive to certain things." He looked over at Dursdan. "Was it anything specific?"

Dursdan groaned. Great, now he had his Da jumping at figments. "It was probably nothing, just a stray breeze. I've been working in the sun all morning and now that I'm sitting in the shade, the sweat feels cool." In his mind he chided Sinotio. *Don't do that!*

"*I am sorry.*"

Mergadan accepted his son's explanation but the look of concern didn't fade. "I think I'll walk into town and see how Tola is getting on." He looked over at Dursdan. "And I need to speak with Dorsadram on certain matters."

Aber chuckled. "Bet you've been using those leg muscles more than you have in some time."

Mergadan grinned and slapped Aber on the shoulder. "You're right about that. I've gotten used to just jumping on Sino when I want to go somewhere. Perhaps this is a good lesson for me."

"Can I come with you into the Village, Da? I wanted to find Steban and apologize for missing his wedding celebration yesterday."

"Certainly, I'll be glad for the company."

Aber walked with them as far as his own lane. Mirana was near the house, hanging laundry. Dursdan wished he had a good excuse to go and talk to her. Aber shook his head. "Don't know what's gotten into Kalista lately that every linen in the house has to be cleaned."

Mergadan chuckled. "Spring does that. Dachia and my Ma have

been up to the same thing." The men shook hands. "Good day to you, Aber."

Dursdan walked down the road with his father, watching their neighbors tending their fields. It was probably the first time in his life that he'd been with his father longer than a meal lasted. They had never really had anything in common. He could feel a soft tickle in the back of his mind. *What is it now?*

"*You have things in common.*"

Dursdan sighed. *Like what?*

"*You like to fish. He likes to fish.*"

"He likes to fish?"

"Who does?"

Dursdan could hear Sinotio chuckling in the background. He had forgotten himself and spoken out loud. "Ah, that is, do you like fish?"

Mergadan looked over at his son. "Why, yes I do."

"So do I."

His father stared and him then shook his head. "Are you suggesting we go fishing some time?"

"That would be great. I know a fine fishing hole." They walked on in silence for a while. "Da?"

"Yes?"

"I'm sorry about how I acted at first. I guess I just wasn't ready. But I know you risked everything to get this egg."

Mergadan put his arm around his son's shoulders and smiled. "Well, your Gran said you had to find your own way. I guess I should have given you a little more warning."

They crossed the bridge into town and Dursdan noticed Steban walking out of his father's flute shop. "I hope he'll still speak to me." He looked at his father. "See you back at home."

"Try to make it back by supper." Mergadan cleared his throat. "I might be able to use a hand with evening chores."

Dursdan smiled. "I'll see you then." They parted and Dursdan moved off in the direction Steban had gone.

The apprentice flute maker had headed out of town in the other direction. Dursdan had to jog to catch up with him. He whistled when his friend was in sight. Steban turned and stopped to wait.

Dursdan caught up. "I've always envied your long legs." He had to pant to catch his breath. "Where are you bound?"

"Just out to Lord Lodaki's place. He ordered a special flute from my Pa. Joram has a celebration day coming up and he's almost as good as you are with the flute."

Dursdan groaned. He just hoped that Ashandra wasn't about. He could feel the light whispers. "*Dormaro says the women are gone.*"

Dursdan breathed a sigh of relief. *Thanks.* "Maybe I could walk out that way with you. I had no idea Joram played."

Steban grinned. "Walk with me, then. I dare say Joram was too shy to let on in your presence. Your abilities are well known." He pulled out the flute and held it up. "Do you think he'll like it?"

Dursdan took the instrument, admiring the colorful inlays of patterned wood. "It's beautiful." He played a small piece. The sound was rich with a hint of undertone. "And the sound is amazing." He handed it back.

Steban carefully slipped it back into the case. "Someday I hope to be able to make flutes so well." He looked over at Dursdan. "And how do things fare with you?"

"I wanted to apologize for missing your wedding. By the way Tola talked at breakfast, it was pretty grand."

Steban shrugged. "Word is you had some trouble yesterday. That's a sweet scratch you're carrying around on your noggin."

"It was nothing. Just had to go after a loopy steer that took off into the foothills." He felt the strange metallic taste on his tongue again. Why did he remember that so vividly? "So was your wedding everything you dreamed it would be?"

"All that and more. Litka was so beautiful. The ceremony was perfect and the dance was grand."

"I'm happy for you." Dursdan looked down at the egg and sighed.

"Dursdan, I know you feel you're not cut out to be a Dragon Rider but I really think there's more in you then you know."

Dursdan looked over at his friend. "It's just been hard for me to accept. Everyone and everything around me seems to be controlling my life. I have no choice but to go along."

Steban stopped. "There are always choices, just maybe not the ones you want. We can choose how we accept the things we can't change.

I have learned to love Litka because I chose to accept her. Maybe you can't change some things. You have the egg and that's simply the way it is. Now your choice lies in how well you will tend it and how good of a rider you will be."

Timotha's words echoed in his head. "We can only choose how we act."

"Exactly." Steban slapped him on the back. "You've heard about Satolam?"

Dursdan nodded. "Thankfully he should recover. My Gran's been tending him."

"He's lucky indeed. From what I've heard, he made a bad choice. He decided to go ahead of the lessons because he thought he could do more than he really knew. He not only jeopardized himself, but also his dragon. That would be a hard loss for the Valley. There are rumors around the village that dragon eggs are hard to come by these days. Rashir's Pa still hasn't found a nest and he's been searching for some time now. Your Pa was lucky to find you one."

Dursdan held the egg sack close. "He was lucky to survive. It seems so foolish to risk so much. Maybe it's time to change. If there are no more dragon eggs to be found, that may be the end of the Dragon Lords."

"What a sad day that will be." Steban shook his head. "My Pa has been working on some old ballads from the time of the First Circle. Our ancestors had great courage to protect the dragons by leaving behind everything they knew and loved to come to this remote place. It must have been a difficult choice for them to make."

Dursdan wondered what Zaradan had left behind to come here. He couldn't imagine the Valley without its village, farms, and fields. 36 desperate men and their wives had come to a wilderness and forged a new life for themselves to protect their dragons. Dursdan ran his hands over the egg pouch. Would he have had that kind of courage?

They had paused by a small stream to take a drink. Dursdan felt a strange tingle of unease and looked around. The forest seemed still and heavy. "Maybe we should continue."

"Indeed." Steban began walking and Dursdan fell into step beside him. The flute maker looked over at him and grinned. "Speaking of choices, I noticed that Tola spent a lot of time with Crastrom's youngest daughter. What's up with that?"

Dursdan laughed. "It's for Tola's own good, a little gift for him from me."

"You arranged a marriage?"

"Not exactly. But hopefully it will work out that way. Tola is good with dragons and Crastrom has no son."

"Ah, I see. And you're hoping that if Tola and Drasia marry, Crastrom with get Tola an egg."

"Something like that." Dursdan was beginning to feel queasy. "So the dance went well? I'm truly sorry I missed it."

"I bet Ashandra was, too. She'd been bragging to everyone all evening that she was going to dance with you. But as it turned out, she danced almost every dance with Rashir last night."

"That's not surprising. Rashir's been gone on her forever." Dursdan stiffened. Something was not right.

Steban stopped and surveyed the forest along the road. "Do you smell something? It could be a dead animal."

Dursdan sniffed. It was a putrid smell as if a something had lain in the bushes for several weeks. The metallic taste grew stronger. "I can't imagine Lodaki leaving something that awful lay about for very long. Smells like it's been dead for a month."

"Something's up, Dur. The birds are quiet."

The small hairs on the back of his neck began to itch. He instinctively cradled the egg. "I don't think we should stop. We're not far from Lodaki's. Let's hurry."

Steban nodded. They began to jog down the road. The metallic taste became so strong that Dursdan thought he might retch. Or was it the smell doing that? The pressure tightened in his chest. A dark shadow seemed to loom, even though there were no clouds in the sky. "Run, Steban!"

A deep growl echoed from the undergrowth behind them. Dursdan risked a quick glance over his shoulder. A large form burst from cover and charged up the road toward them. "We'll never out run that!"

"What is it?"

Long hairy arms, a twisted pig-like face, ragged matted fur that served for a basic covering, Dursdan recognized the troll from his studies. "Are you sure you want to know?" *Sinotio? What do I do?*

"*Dormaro comes! As do others. Keep running!*"

Dursdan pushed himself to the limit. "Keep going as long as you can. Help is on the way. I can hear dragon wings."

The black form of Dormaro whooshed over them a heartbeat later. Lodaki had a battle spear in hand. Dursdan stopped and turned to watch. The dragon came at the troll, claws extended. The troll lashed out, forcing Dormaro to back wing. Lodaki struck with his long spear. It caught the troll just under the shoulder. The beast grabbed the spear from Lodaki's hands and snapped it as if it was a mere splinter.

Dursdan gasped. He hadn't realized how large the creature was until that moment. It stood almost as tall as the large Black, more than twice the size of a man. He felt a dragon in the back of his mind. "*Fear not, my Lord, we have come.*" Trusumo led a pack of Dragon Lords down toward the troll.

Sadaki, on his Brown, Mercia, placed himself between Dursdan and the battle. Mercia bent her head down to look at him. "*You are safe. We would never let such a dirty beast harm you.*" She turned back to the battle and raised her wings as a shield.

Sadaki sat in readiness, a long sword poised in battle stance. "Catch you breath, Dur. And you, Steban. All is well."

Dursdan watched from behind Mercia's wing as the Dragon Lords fought the troll. Trusumo, with Dorsadram, worked to distract the creature while Jasorad, on his great Red, Azu, used a heavy metal spike to spear it through. The two smaller white dragons, Lutaza, with Nasadal, and Osiral, with Radachi, grasped the metal rod in their claws and together, pulled the troll off the ground.

It screamed and lashed out, catching Obodo, Dormato's Brown, on the wing. The dragon screamed with pain. Dursdan covered his ears with his hands and fell across Mercia's front leg. The sound reverberated in his head. It threatened to crush him. He could hear Obodo sobbing. "*It burns, oh, it burns!*"

Arms were around his shoulders. He managed to squint and looked up. Sadaki was beside him. The young rider was talking but Dursdan couldn't hear his words. His mind was filled with dragons, all working to coordinate the destruction of the troll. He watched from under the Brown's wing.

"*Bring it around so I can get a grab.*" Trusumo circled as the Whites swung the creature on the pole. The large Red dove, and at the last minute, turned in flight and hit the troll, claws out. The beast fell to the ground under the dragon's massive weight.

Dozi landed near the troll's head and took it in her claws, squeezing down. "*Vile creature. It disgusts me to touch it.*"

"*Ha! Then let me at him. I will tear it to shreds.*" Red Moroto, with Vomitri astride, touched down gracefully and pranced over. He sniffed at it. "*No fair. It is dead. I wanted a turn at it.*"

Trusumo backed off the limp form and looked at Moroto. "*You know your rider would not approve.*"

With their leader's signal, all the dragons backed away so the Lords could get a better view of the dead troll. Dorsadram whistled. "Haven't seen one of those in awhile."

Another dragon circled around the battle zone. "*May I land now, Tru? My Lord and Lord Merg are impatient.*"

The Red looked up and signaled for the others to make a space for Natalo to land. He touched down beside Trusumo. "*Wish I could have joined the fun.*"

Trusumo shook his head. "*Lord Merg is still on the mend. It was best to keep him out of the battle.*"

Mergadan was beside his son, demanding of Sadaki an explanation. Obodo was still whimpering in the background. Dursdan could feel his pain. "Will someone please help Obo?"

The other Lords all looked at each other. Dormato looked up. "Don't worry, Dur. It's just a scratch. He'll be fine."

Crastrom moved toward the Brown. "Best let me have a look at that, Dor. These marsh trolls are a nasty lot. They carry all sorts of wicked germs on their claws. We don't want a bad infection."

Trusumo moved toward Dursdan with his Lord. He came up and leaned his head down to touch Dursdan's shoulder. "*You feel his pain?*" He sounded surprised. Then he pulled up and turned to Dozi. "*Comfort Obodo.*"

The large Bronze moved forward and allowed the injured Brown to put his head on her shoulder. "*Hush now, dear one. All will be well. Lord Cras will tend you and you will heal.*"

Obodo looked over at Dursdan. "*Forgive me, my Lord. I did not mean to distress you.*"

"I'll be all right." Dursdan sat up and looked at all the Lords staring at him. Some were swinging between him and their dragons, with looks of wonder on their faces.

Dorsadram knelt beside him and put an arm on his shoulder. "It's all right, Dur. Crastrom is one of the best healers of dragon kind to be found. He pulled Sinotio through. Obodo will recover." He looked over at Trusumo, hovering at his shoulder. "If you could back up a bit, Tru, we don't want to crush the boy."

The Red shrugged apologetically. "*You will be well?*" Dursdan nodded. "*Then I will go help dispose of the mess before Moroto embarrasses his rider.*" Trusumo bowed and backed away.

Dursdan couldn't see past the circle of Lords that had gathered around him but he could hear Dozi mumbling. "*How am I ever going to get the stench off of my claws? No amount of washing will make it go away.*"

"Can you stand?"

Dursdan looked at his father. "Yes, Da, I can manage." He allowed Mergadan to help him to his feet. He looked up at Mercia, her brown head gleaming in the sunlight. *I didn't hurt you when I fell on you, did I?*

She pulled her head back and snorted. Her merry laughter echoed in his mind. "*Have no fear, Lord Dursdan. Your mere weight caused me no anguish.*" She leaned down to touch the egg pouch and the Lords all gasped. She looked up at them, focused on her rider a moment, then on Dursdan. "*Your little one is frightened. I tried to comfort her but she will not listen to me. She is hiding.*"

Dursdan looked down with concern at the pouch and felt it. The pads were still warm. Sadaki tapped Mercia's nose and she backed up. "I'm sorry, Dur. I'm sure she didn't mean any harm."

Dursdan looked up at the wingling rider. "Don't punish her, Sad, she was just concerned about the egg." He held it close. "But she's all right. Just scared."

The Lords mumbled amongst themselves. Mergadan tugged at

Dursdan. "Come, it's getting dark." He looked back at the battle site. "Where there's one troll there could be more. I should have realized this afternoon when you tensed that trouble was about. You just haven't been trained to recognized it yet." He looked up at Dorsadram. "With your permission, Sir."

The old man looked lost in thought. He glanced at Dursdan then over his shoulder at his large Red, then back to Dursdan. "I still have questions, but I suppose they can wait until the morrow." He bowed to them. "Good Even Tide, Lord Mergadan, Dursdan."

Dursdan looked over at Steban. "Will you be all right?"

"I will. Lodaki has offered to fly me back to the shop." He smiled. "I've never flown on a dragon before. But you best go with your Pa."

Mergadan pulled his son away. "I'm sure that Lord Humatsu would gladly bear you home."

The Lord bowed in acknowledgment. Dursdan looked up at the large bronze dragon and shivered. "I'm sorry, Sir. I think I'd rather walk."

Mergadan stiffened. His face grew dark. Osiral nosed forward, bowing at Dozi. "*Forgive, darling, but you are so wonderfully large. I do believe our little Lord is just a bit timid to climb up on your tall back.*" He swung to look at Dursdan. "*I am much smaller than Dozi. I would gladly bear you home. I promise, I will let no harm come to you.*"

Dursdan swallowed and slowly reached out to touch the White's nose. Radachi chuckled. "No offense, Huma, but it seems Osi has won the privilege of conveying the egg carrier home."

Lord Humatsu laughed and looked up at his dragon. "At least she doesn't seem too put out. You never want to offend a Bronze."

Dursdan was horrified. *I didn't offend you, Dozi, did I?*

She turned her head to look at him with one eye. "*No, my Lord, I understand.*" She preened her wing delicately. "*Some are just too taken with my beauty to wish to spoil it.*"

There was general laughter among the dragons. Trusumo snorted. "*That is quite enough. Lord Merg is right. There could be more trolls about.*" All the dragons stopped and peered into the darkening shadows.

The Lords followed their dragon's example. Humatsu mounted Dozi. "Best get the lad home. I have the feeling more trouble could be about." She backed up for a clear space then sprang into the sky.

Dursdan shielded his eyes from the dust as he watched her circle the area then turn to the north. Osiral nudged him again. *"She will make sure no danger lies before us."* He knelt and curved his wing back. *"We shall fly."* The White grinned.

Dursdan swallowed. His uncle put an arm around his shoulder. "Well, he's ready to go. Mount up then."

Dursdan gingerly touched the White's leg and carefully crawled to the neck ridge. Osiral looked back at him. Dursdan was shaking. He looked back at the White. "I didn't hurt you, did I?"

Radachi laughed. "Don't worry, Dur. He's got a tough hide." He climbed up and sat behind Dursdan. Crastrom and Mergadan were already in the air on Natalo. "Looks like they're waiting on us." He patted Osiral's neck. "Well, let's make Dursdan's first ride a good one, shall we?"

Osiral gathered himself to spring. *"Do not worry. You are not heavy. I am honored to carry you. I will get you home safely."*

Dursdan closed his eyes as the dragon launched into the sky.

* * *

Aramel stamped his feet in frustration. He banged his staff on the floor and sparks flew around the room. Curse those blasted Dragon Lords! How had they found the troll so quickly? He slammed the book shut and scattered the pool across the workbench. The dragons were searching the Valley as the last drops of liquid faded.

Rat tails! This would make it even harder to get at him! There had to be another way. He glanced down at the waiting portal spell and screamed. He would have that egg and leave the boy's body to rot!

Pacing back and forth, he stomped at each turn. The entire room shook. At one turn, a book fell off the shelf. Aramel stomped over to pick it up. No use treading on them. He glanced at the cover and stopped. Of course. Why hadn't he thought of that before?

He found the spell and read through the ingredients. He'd have to dig through his pantry but he was certain he had everything he needed. He closed the book with a snap. Soon, the egg would be in his hands. He laughed at the parody. His hands!

Chapter 13

Dursdan clung to Osiral's neck, afraid to open his eyes. Osiral laughed. *"But you are missing the most beautiful sight! Oh, please look, Dur. It is so grand."*

Dursdan squinted against the wind but managed to open his eyes. He gasped. The setting sun was reflected on the snowcaps of the surrounding mountains and painted them an array of shades and hues from yellows to reds to deep purple. "It's incredible."

"That it is, Dur. The Valley must be the most grand place anywhere." Radachi readjusted his grip around Dursdan's waist slightly. "You've never seen it all, have you?"

Dursdan looked down and instantly regretted it. He sank back into Radachi's arms. "No, but it's nice, too. Can we land now?"

His uncle laughed. "Do you hear that, Osi? Dur wants to miss out on this spectacular sight. Oh well, you'll have plenty of opportunities once your Gold is ready to fly."

Osiral turned toward the house on the hill, circled once, then lightly touched down in the courtyard. He greeted Sinotio as Radachi helped Dursdan dismount. Sinotio grinned. *"So, our boy has finally gotten airborne, has he? About time!"* He turned his head to look at Dursdan. *"And was it as bad as you feared?"*

Dursdan was having trouble getting his legs to hold his weight. *Yes. And I don't plan to do it again any time soon.* He looked at the White. *No offense, Osiral.*

The White bowed. *"None taken. I can see that Rad wants to be off with the others, searching for more trolls. Sleep well."*

Radachi kissed his sister on the cheek and jumped back up on Osiral. "Don't fear. Merg is safe enough. They're just scouting. Dorsadram won't let him get to close to battle yet." He patted the White on the neck. "Come on, Osiral, there's still a half moon to help us. Let's see what we can find." The dragon sprang back into flight.

Dachia stood in the doorway staring at her son. Dursdan wondered what was going through her mind. "I'm all right, Ma, honest."

She nodded. The courtyard gate creaked and Dursdan turned. Tolanar entered carrying the milk bucket. "Good, you're back. There's something wrong with Old Red."

"Is she ill?"

Tolanar looked down in the bucket. "I don't know. I just didn't get much milk from her."

Dursdan chuckled. "She's fine. I've been drying her for the past week now. I've made a deal with Gelnar to breed her. He wants the calf." He looked at Tolanar's confused expression and realized that he used to pay as little attention to dragons as his brother did to cows.

Dachia cleared her throat. "Well, your Da may be gone awhile. Why don't you boys come in and wash for dinner."

"Where's Da?" Tolanar handed the bucket to his mother.

"He's off with Crastrom. I'll tell you about it over food." Dursdan felt his stomach rumble. "For some reason, I'm hungry." He gave a final nod to Sinotio and followed his mother and brother into the house.

Dinner was eventful with everyone asking questions so quickly that Dursdan could hardly keep up and eat at the same time. Carala was concerned with the type of troll, Dachia was worried there might be more, and Tolanar wanted the play-by-play of the battle.

Mergadan joined them as they were finishing a sweet berry cobbler that Carala had made. He slumped into his seat at the table. 'Well, there doesn't seem to be any more around."

"If it was a marsh troll, as Dursdan says, then it's unlikely that there are." Carala took the used plates from the table. "They are loners, don't travel in packs like the rock trolls do."

Dachia sighed. "Thank goodness."

"Dorsadram has posted a watch just to be safe but I'm still out until Sino can fly again." He poured a tankard of cider and smiled at Tolanar. "Crastrom is quite impressed with your work. He couldn't stop singing your praises."

"I really like Natalo. And Crastrom has been grand. He's promised to take me flying tomorrow."

"And how was your flight home, Dur?"

Tolanar started at him. "You came home dragonback? How did they get you up there? Where you unconscious?"

Mergadan gave Tolanar a stern look. "Dursdan needed to get home quickly. Radachi brought him."

Dursdan swallowed and looked at his brother. "Well enough." Then he studied his father's face. "I'm sorry I didn't want to fly with Lord Humatsu."

Mergadan shrugged. "A White is smaller, better for a first run than a Bronze. Besides, it gave Rad an excuse to stop and see your Ma."

Mergadan and Tolanar began a discussion on Natalo's flight characteristics compared to Sinotio's and Dursdan excused himself. He was tired from the day's activities and had talked more than enough about flying.

Dursdan decided not to light a candle and changed in the dark. He lay down and felt the warmth of the pads seeping through the pouch. It was comforting and he drifted off to sleep quickly. The Mists formed around him but they were loud and filled with people tonight. Sinotio greeted him immediately. "We have been waiting for you."

"Who are all these?" Dursdan paused and looked at the Silver. "I mean, are they all dragons?"

Sinotio chuckled. "Of course. After today, everyone wanted to meet you."

A small boy chased another through the misty tendrils. The boys raced around Dursdan and Sinotio. The little boy stopped and grabbed Dursdan around the legs. He almost lost his balance but

Sinotio steadied him. Dursdan looked down at the boy. He had bright bronze hair and intense green eyes. Where had he seen him before?

The boy reached up and patted Dursdan's arm. "Thanks." Then he was off running after the older red headed boy.

"Who was that?"

"That was Durdansi, I believe. I heard you had something to do with his arrival."

Dursdan stared at the boy. "That's Anlahad's hatchling?"

A man in blue with striking light blue hair joined them. "I say, it is quite a ruckus with the young ones about. Why were they included in this meeting?"

"My dear, Kazar. They are members of this community. Trusumo thought they should be here as well." Sinotio waved at an approaching form. A young lady in a stylish long brown dress and braided brown hair approached. Sinotio turned to Dursdan. "I am told you quite fell for her today."

She stopped and bowed to Dursdan. "Greeting, my Lord. I hope you are recovered from your adventures this afternoon."

Dursdan couldn't stop staring. She was the most beautiful girl he'd ever seen. Sinotio jabbed him in the ribs and Dursdan gasped. Had he been holding his breath since she walked up? "I'm sorry, but may I ask who you are?"

She laughed lightly. "But of course you see me differently than I am, just as I see you differently. I am Marcia, the Brown of Sadaki."

Dursdan was stunned. Something she said had caught his attention. "You see me differently than I am?"

"Why, of course. I am sure we all do. I have seen you in the day and you appear as a young boy, not unlike my Sadaki when I first knew him. But here, in the Dream Mist, you appear to me as a great white warrior, dressed in golden mail."

Dursdan shook his head. What a silly notion. "But that's not me at all."

The dragons all looked at each other. Sinotio shushed everyone. "Here is Trusumo, finally. I wonder what took him so long."

The Red entered the Mists and all the dragons came forward and bowed to him. He returned their bow. "Good Dreams to all. Forgive my lateness but Lord Dorsadram did extra rounds well into the night.

We found no other trolls in the area. Samita, Eziki, and Dormaro are all out on patrol. A good choice from Dors, since Blacks have exceptional night vision and are hard to see in the darkness of night." He turned to Dursdan and bowed. "They send their apologies for missing this meeting and hope that they will pass you in the Mists in the future."

Dursdan wasn't sure what to say. "Um, pass my thanks to them for their help in the fight against the troll."

"This I will do." He turned as a radiant lady came to stand beside him. By her flowing bronze hair, Dursdan guessed she must be Dozi.

She put a hand on the Red's arm. "I believe this was not a random encounter."

There was a general murmur through the group. Dursdan found Durdansi tugging at his sleeve. "What is a troll?"

Kazar rolled his eyes. "Ah, and they just had to be included."

Durdansi shrunk around behind Dursdan. Mercia shook her head. "Do not be mean. Come here, Durdansi. Let us go off a ways and I will tell you all about trolls." She took the little boy's hand and led him away.

Trusumo cleared his throat. Everyone quieted. "On this, Dozi and I are in agreement." He looked at Dursdan. "Many things have been kept from you. Things that the Lords should have said but were afraid to, perhaps."

Dozi parted the crowd and walked back to Dursdan. "We listen to what they say. We understand them even if they do not understand us." She took his hand. "You are different. Do you understand this?"

"Because of these dreams and that I can hear you in my head?"

"It is much more than that." She looked at Trusumo and he nodded. She turned back to Dursdan. "How do you see us here?"

Dursdan looked around the group. "As people, very colorful people in some cases."

There were some chuckles from the assembly. Dozi smiled. "It is how your mind perceives us. We all know you. We have all seen you in the day at one time or another, but to us, you do not appear as that boy or even as a dragon in the Mists, but as a warrior." There were sounds of agreement from many. "And we all see you the same way. Trusumo and Sinotio commented on this. At first I thought it was strange. But on their description, I have gone back through the memories that were passed to me by Bacana, Bronze to Kalmatsu, second elder of my house. She carried the memories of first elder as well, back to the very beginning of the calling."

Natalo banged his red tipped cane. "Oh shards, do get on with it. All of us carry the memories of our elders." He turned to Dursdan. "What she is trying to say, is that we all see the image of Zaradan when we look at you here."

Dursdan thought back to the sketch in Armia's book. "That's how you see me?"

Sinotio shook his head. "Well done, Nata, scare the lad some more. Have you forgotten what you owe him?"

Natalo bowed his head. "Forgive, Lord Dursdan. I am grateful that you pushed your brother into the keeping of my Lord."

Dursdan was puzzled by the Red's tone. "I thought you liked Tola?"

"Oh, I do. He is a grand lad, to be sure. A gentle hand, a soft voice, knows all the spots a dragon likes to be scratched."

Sinotio sighed. "Yes, so well I know. I will miss him for all that. But you must also realize what Dur hoped to achieve."

Trusumo raised an eyebrow. "I was impressed that he pulled it off so well."

Dursdan grinned. "I'm trying to save the House of Trom, as well as my brother." He looked at the Sliver beside him. "You know that Tola has always been better with you than I. He deserves to be a Lord someday." He turned to Natalo. "Lord Crastrom has no male heir. If the house of Trom is to continue, he must appoint one. In the past, another Lord faced this same problem. He appointed the man who married his daughter."

There was a general rumble of approval. Dozi patted him on the arm. "I knew you had great potential. Rathan always said so. It is a shame he did not live to see this day."

Dursdan hadn't heard that name in a long time. He looked over at Sinotio. "That was Torg's Red, wasn't it?"

Sinotio nodded. "Even when you were very little, you would dream with us. This worried Rathan to no end." He looked away. "I still remember the night he died. You screamed his name for hours." A tear fell from the Silver's eyes. Dozi pulled out her hanky and handed it to him.

Trusumo called everyone to order. "Now that all this has been unraveled, we must move along. It will be morning soon enough." He came through the crowd and put an arm around Dursdan. "As we have said, we listen as the Lords talk. There was a great deal of concern when Lord Mergadan reported in after the incident. It seems the egg you carry was the only one left in one piece."

Dursdan remembered the dream. "Yes, all the broken shards with oozing goo." He looked at Sinotio and thought harder. "But I think I dreamed the egg before you and Da left, too."

Dozi looked at Trusumo. "How could that have been?" The Red shrugged.

Dursdan tried to think back, and then he remembered the trick Timotha had taught him. He thought hard and formed a window in the Mists. At first, it was just a golden haze, but then an image began to form, the face of the golden queen appeared. She was angry! Someone was endangering her brood. The image faltered.

Trusumo gasped. "The wild Gold! You could see her?"

Sinotio was touching the mist where the window had been. "How did you do that?"

Dursdan shook his head. "I don't know how I saw the Gold. As for the window, Timotha taught me."

Dozi's eyebrows went up. "Timotha?"

Trusumo cleared his throat. "Ah, yes. I was going to mention that at some point, since it seems she is on her way back."

All eyes turned to the Red. Kazar frowned. "And how long have you know about this?"

Trusumo shrugged. "I have chatted with her for some time now. As far as her returning, that is a recent development."

Dozi shook her head. "I do not understand how she can still be alive."

Dursdan had a sudden flash of a memory - something Terarimi had said. "I know." Everyone stared at him. "There's a reason that the Lords have to find a freshly laid nest. They can't just go out and catch a baby dragon." He looked down at the faint glow in his stomach.

She was still hiding. "Even before a baby dragon hatches, she bonds with the carrier of her egg." He looked up at them. "You are all bound to the men you serve. Your life is bound to theirs. Timotha said that when Voramato died, her bond with Zamisha held her. And Zamisha passed that bond to her son, and so on, so that she was not just attached to one life, but to a succession of lives. She lives on through her riders."

Trusumo formed a cloud chair and sat down. "How complicated it all seems."

Natalo grabbed Dursdan's arm. "Are you saying that if I form a bond with another, I will not die when Crastrom dies?"

"I don't know. You and Crastrom have been together a long time. Voramato was very young when he died and Zamisha was his twin."

Dozi nodded. "I remember from the memories. The Wizards made the Lords agree not to let Zamisha keep Timotha. Bacana warned Timo and she made sure Zamisha found out. And they left."

"But why did the Wizards object? Timotha would have died!" Natalo began to pace. "It just does not make sense."

"Oh, but it does." Everyone gasped as Timotha parted the Mists and entered the group. Many bowed to her. She smiled at Dursdan. "Sorry I am late tonight but we had a run in with some very small but very nasty creatures."

"What did they look like?" Dursdan was curious about the things beyond their Valley.

Timotha opened a window and a swarm of angry creatures with wings took shape. Kazar looked closely "Ugh! Pixies! What a nasty lot."

"I thought we got rid of the last nest a long time ago."

"But, Dozi, my dear, Timotha is still a long ways off. Obviously, there are still pixies about. Just not around here." Trusumo patted her on the arm to reassure her.

Latofu stepped forward, adjusting his red vest. "Let us keep it that way. I seem to recall those little brutes do devastating damage to the crops and cattle. We certainly do not want to bring that down on our Lords. Along with the return of a renegade."

A loud wave raced through the assembly. "Enough! We will have no more of that! Timotha is one of us, though she has been gone a long time."

"I still want to know what she meant." Dozi took Timotha's hand. "Tell us, please, why the Wizards did not want you to live."

Timotha shook her head. "It is complicated. It was Zamisha that caused the stir. She was a woman, already carrying her firstborn. As he grew inside her, I bonded with him, too."

Natalo whistled. "I bet the Wizards knew it would happen."

"I believe the Wizards wanted to limit the dragons." She released Dozi's hand and came to stand in front of Sinotio. "A male dragon is fertile as soon as he can fly." She smiled and touched his face. "But a female dragon does not reach maturity until her 80th year."

Dozi gasped. "I had never considered why the wild dragons laid eggs and we did not."

"Of course." Trusumo shook his head. "Because we are bonded to our riders, we die as they die and so the female dragons never grow old enough to clutch."

"But to what end? I do not understand!" Natalo paced back and forth. "What would it matter if our females did lay eggs?"

Dursdan remembered the dream. He looked around the room then at Natalo. "How many female dragons are in the valley?"

Natalo looked baffled. Trusumo stepped up. "Fifteen, including yours. Timotha will make sixteen."

"Yes, and how many eggs does a female clutch? From what I remember of the dream, there must have been 20 or 30 eggs in the Gold's brood."

Trusumo bowed his head. "Although I believe that to be a unique circumstance, I think I understand. Our females, being touched by men, would raise highly intelligent young, very much unlike our wild relatives." He looked around the room. "I believe the Wizards feared that we would one day, with enough numbers, become a threat. They could not risk this so they found a way to limit our life spans."

Natalo's reddish skin turned violet. "But that is just not right!"

"Right or wrong, is had been done." He looked at Dursdan. "What do you say, my Lord?"

Dursdan was still trying to work through all the information. He shook his head, formed up a cloud chair, and sank into it. "I doubt the Lords had any such knowledge." He looked up at Sinotio. "I know Da would lay down his life for you." He thought of Terarimi. "And I know what it does to a man who lives beyond the life span of his dragon. I agree with Natalo that is doesn't seem right but I also understand what you're saying, Trusumo. We can't change what has already been done."

Natalo snarled. "Then we shall all die before our times!"

"You aren't dead yet." Dursdan closed his eyes. "I know all these things now, but how am I ever going to get the other Lords to understand? They would think me crazy!"

Trusumo looked around the group. "And we have the problem that Lord Dursdan was originally pointing out. If all the females laid broods, what would happen to all the babes? Even in that amount of time, there would not be enough humans in the valley to pair with. And how would they feed us all? There are years when they struggle as it is."

Dozi looked at Trusumo. "What you say is true. But what if some of us chose not to clutch."

Timotha laughed darkly. "You can not choose! You either answer the calling or you die trying. Why do you think I am returning now? The few wild brutes that I have found in the Mists are uncivilized. They want nothing to do with me because I smell like humans." She looked at Dursdan, her eyes wide. "But I can feel the burning inside me. If I do not mate soon, I will die."

"Oh, bother." Rath shook his bronze crowned head. "A warning to you, my friends. My Lord calls for me. We must return to the day world."

Dursdan could already see some of them fading into the Mists. He looked up at Trusumo. "I will think on all this."

The Red nodded. "As will I." Then he faded away.

Now only he, Sinotio, and Timotha remained. The Silver embraced his chosen one. "I do not care what the others say. Do not be deterred, my love."

She fell into his arms and wept. Dursdan felt himself sliding out of the Mists. He could still hear her weeping as he opened his eyes.

He lay still, letting his eyes adjust. He heard voices in the outer rooms. One of them was Mergadan's. He couldn't tell who the other was. He rose. The pads needed to be replaced. The hallway was dark. He paused at the kitchen door, listening to the conversation. He could hear the fear and concern in the men's voices and peered around the corner of the dining room door.

Mergadan had his hands planted on the table in front of him. Lord Falahad sat facing him. "I'm telling you, Merg, something is up. It's not just Sinotio. Latofu was also difficult to rouse. Others as well, have reported the same. Tamtrax said he had to shake Rath's head for some time just to get a response."

Mergadan shook his head. "If it were just Sinotio, who is still on the mend, and maybe a few others who flew late patrols last night, I wouldn't be concerned. But this is serious."

"Anlahad was terrified when he couldn't rouse his hatchling for early feeding. That's what first drew me to the problem. But then I couldn't wake Latofu either." He sat forward and dropped his voice to a whisper. "You don't think that old crazy Wizard is messing with our dragons, do you?"

Dursdan had to bite his lip to keep from laughing. How was he ever going to explain anything to people with such foolish ideas? *"Maybe you should start."* Dursdan jumped and rammed his elbow into the wall. "Sinotio!"

Mergadan was at his side in an instant. "Dursdan, are you all right? What's happened? What's wrong with Sinotio?"

Dursdan sighed and rubbed his elbow. "I'm sure he's fine. He just startled me."

Falahad raised his eyebrows and looked at Dursdan. "I didn't hear a thing. Surely if you heard it from the hallway, we should have heard it here."

Dursdan pulled loose from Mergadan and moved to the door. "Come with me."

He went out into the courtyard where the Silver was waiting on the rock. Latofu also sat staring at Dursdan. Falahad looked up at his dragon. "What is going on?"

Dursdan turned and looked at his father. "Are you going to believe me if I tell you?"

Mergadan placed his hands on his son's shoulders. "I will."

A dragon shadow flew over. They all looked up. Falahad shielded his eyes. "It's Dors. Now what?"

They circled to land. Dursdan felt the tickle in his mind. *"Thought you might need some support. Besides, my Lord should hear all this."* The men backed up to make space in the already crowded courtyard. Trusumo dropped neatly to the ground.

Dorsadram jumped down from his Red's back. "I guess I shouldn't be surprised that he brought me here." He glanced over his shoulder then back at Dursdan. "Can you tell us what's going on?"

Dursdan looked at his father and Mergadan let go. He bowed to Lord Dorsadram then walked up to the large Red. "Good morning, Trusumo."

He could hear Lord Falahad laughing. Then Trusumo extended his claw and held it out to Dursdan. The men behind him gasped. Dursdan took one of the talons in his hand. "How shall we begin?"

* * *

Aramel had worked late into the night until the first rays of dawn began to paint the eastern horizon. Then he collapsed into his chair and dozed for a time. When he woke, he conjured something to quench his thirst and sate his hunger. He tossed the used platters and goblet back into oblivion.

The spell lay on the workbench, all the pieces carefully aligned and waiting. He opened a quick pool to see what was going on outside. It was still midmorning. He would have to wait. He closed the pool and reviewed the spell carefully. He'd made some modifications to it.

The original purpose was to gather herbs from distant places without actually going there, a useful thing for a Wizard, especially if the needed ingredient was found in a dangerous location. But reaching out and pulling back the egg was a little trickier. He'd have to undo the pouch and move the warmers aside. And he had placed special safeguards in the spell. He didn't want any harm coming to the egg during transport.

It was so simple. He smiled. Child's play. How many times in his youth had he been required to use this spell to stock the pantries of the other Wizards? Not that they had known he was using it instead of gathering the materials in person, but why bother to go out when you didn't have to. This was faster and less messy. He chided himself for not thinking of it before.

He wished he had a spell to make time go faster. But he would just have to wait. Soon enough, the egg would be in his hands. Aramel began to laugh.

Chapter 14

Falahad was either trying to hold back laughter or tears. Maybe both. Dursdan couldn't tell. He'd told them about the meeting during the night and some of the topics covered. He purposefully refrained from mentioning Timotha. Dorsadram at least kept a straight face. Mergadan kept pacing back and forth, stopping occasionally to stare at him and then up at Sinotio. But they had not interrupted. For that, he was grateful.

He turned to Trusumo. "What else should I tell them?"

The Red laid his head on Dursdan's shoulder and faced Dorsadram. "*Tell him I feel no remorse at sharing his fate. It has been good.*"

Dursdan translated Trusumo's words. Dorsadram nodded and gently rubbed the Red's nose. "Indeed, old friend, it has been good." A tear trickled down his cheek. Trusumo reached forward and caught it on his snout.

"*Would that I could truly cry. I would surely fill a lake.*"

Dorsadram hugged the Red's neck. "We shall always fly together." He wiped the tears from his eyes.

Falahad snorted. "This is crazy! Merg, maybe that troll bit your son and he's suffering from some strange illness that induces delusions."

Latofu growled and glared at Falahad. "*I will bite him and see what delusions he has.*"

Trusumo pulled his head back and looked eye to eye with the younger Red. "*You will do no such thing. A dragon does no harm to his rider.*"

Falahad stared up at them. "Now what was that all about?"

Dursdan shrugged. "There are some things that are better left unsaid." He looked meaningfully at Latofu. The dragon sighed and lowered his head.

"How do we know if the boy is telling the truth? You have to admit, Dors, this sounds awfully far fetched."

"*Just like his fish tales when he brings home a handsome catch claiming he is just skilled. Yes, skilled at taking fish from others. Ha!*" Latofu peered over Trusumo's neck.

Dursdan wasn't going to give away the Lord's secrets but it gave him an idea. "You talk to your dragons, I've heard Da do it many times. Ask me something that only your dragon would know."

Dorsadram nodded. "A true test indeed." He sat quietly for a moment staring up at his Red. Then his face brightened. "Last week I was thinking of an old friend who's actions were troubling me. Trusumo is sometimes the best confidant for such things. Whom was I thinking about?"

Trusumo growled. "*That rat, Soren. I wish you could tell Dors everything I know of what is really going on, but for now, his name will have to suffice.*"

Dursdan was puzzled. "Soren the woodsmith?" Both Trusumo and Dorsadram nodded. "But what has he done?"

"Things I'd rather not speak of right now."

"Trusumo wants to. He apparently knows more than you about it."

Dorsadram's eyebrows went up. "Really?" He looked up at the dragon. "Oh, that we could speak together."

"So this proves it then? You believe my son is telling the truth?"

Sinotio leaned over and looked at Mergadan. "*Tell him if he still does not believe you, I will tell you who he almost married instead of your mother, even after he had chosen her.*"

"Da was going to marry someone else?"

Mergadan's face went dark and he stared at the Silver. "Don't you dare! That was long ago and I have no regrets."

Dorsadram chuckled. "To be certain!" He stood. "I wish I had time for you to translate all that Trusumo would say to me but other Lords are concerned." He walked to his Red's side. "This will be hard for some of them to hear." He sighed. "Hopefully they will not pester you for constant translations." He mounted and Trusumo gathered himself and leapt into the sky.

They circled once. The dragon looked down. "*Have no fear of that. I will caution the others. You need to concentrate on your little one.*" Then they flew westward.

"What did he say to you?" Mergadan's voice was full of curiosity.

"He said I needed to concentrate on my egg."

Sinotio leaned over and nuzzled the pouch. "*I am worried. She is still hiding. She has not come out.*"

"I'm worried, too." Dursdan held the pouch protectively.

"Why? Is something wrong?"

Dursdan looked down. "I think I scared her. I'm still not sure what all happened. I think our minds touched or something. It frightened me so bad that I yelled at her." He rubbed the egg softly. "She's been hiding ever since."

Mergadan shook his head. "That egg's a pretty small space. I can't see that she's got any place to hide."

Falahad cleared his throat. "Well, I'll leave the two of you to figure all that out." He looked up at the Red. "I hope you don't mind me asking for a ride home." The dragon snorted and coughed. The Lord looked back at Dursdan. "What was all that about?"

Dursdan bit his lip. "Um, he was laughing."

Mergadan laughed. "I doubt this will change that much. After all, they've always understood what we're saying. We were the deaf ones."

After the Lord and Red had departed, Mergadan went and sat on the rock by Sinotio. He looked over at Dursdan, lost in thought. Dursdan shifted uncomfortably, uncertain what to say. The Silver looked down at his rider. "*He is not angry.*"

"I hope not."

Mergadan looked puzzled. "What did he say?"

"That you weren't angry."

"Of course I'm not." Mergadan motioned to the rock beside him. "Come sit a moment, Dur. There is something I wish to share with you."

Dursdan looked up at the dragon, swallowed hard, then joined his father on the rock. The sun had warmed it and the warmth was comforting in the cool morning air. He felt Sinotio chuckle in the back of his mind and looked up at him. "I understand why you like this rock now."

Mergadan seemed distracted and was surprised by the comment. "Yes, I've always found it rather comfortable once the sun has had time to seep into it." He looked up at the dragon then back at Dursdan. "Oh, he likes it, too. I'm glad to hear that." He sighed and pulled something out of his pocket and handed it to Dursdan.

Dursdan looked at it carefully. It was a small, finely crafted locket with a tiny latch. He opened it and found a painted portrait of a woman inside. The memories stirred on the edge of his mind. "This is Great Gran Korithiena, isn't it?"

Mergadan nodded. "She gave it to me before she left."

"Left?"

His father looked at him for a long moment. "Yes. She left after my Da was killed in the war. I think it was too much for her. She had argued against the conflict but the others wouldn't listen to her. She had wanted the dragons to leave before the war started but the Wizards Council had argued against it. I don't know all the details."

Dursdan's stomach turned cold. He thought about what he'd said to Gran. "Then it's true. If the Dragon Lords had left, there would have never been another war with the trolls?"

"I don't know. I'm not sure anyone could know. The Council believed that there were still a few Eastern Wizards who had escaped and that they were fueling the trolls. If the Dragon Lords left, there would be nothing to stop the trolls from destroying the human settlements beyond the mountains." Mergadan looked at Dursdan. "You know about them, don't you?"

Dursdan nodded. "Great Gran Armia's book tells of them." He looked up at Sinotio then back at his father.

Mergadan touched the locket. "She wanted me to give you this when you were ready. She knew you were different, even when you were a baby. She would hold you and you would look into her eyes, as quiet as could be, as if you knew what she was thinking."

Dursdan looked up at Sinotio. "Could she talk to dragons, too?"

"*Yes. I remember her.*"

"Oh. Do you suppose that's why I can hear you?"

The Silver leaned his head down and touched Dursdan's shoulder. "*You are special, like her.*"

Mergadan reached up and gently stroked the dragon's snout. "I still remember how excited I was when my Da gave me my egg. It was unlike any other in the Valley. I was so proud of him." He let his hand fall on Dursdan's shoulder. "You didn't want this, did you?"

Dursdan swallowed hard. "I'm sorry, Da." He looked down at the egg pouch resting against his stomach. "I was always hoping that somehow you could give the egg to Tola. I'm a better farmer."

Mergadan laughed. "Yes, without a doubt. But I think things may work out for your brother after all. There are some old traditions among our people. Cras is hoping Tola will choose Drasia and then he intends to adopt him formally and make him his heir. He intended to speak of this in the next meeting of the Circle."

Dursdan couldn't hide his grin. "I'm glad. It's what he wants most."

"And to think, I'll be the first Lord in generations to have both of my sons someday sitting together in the Circle." He looked over at the locket. "She knew you were destined for greatness. She told me that one day you would be First Lord."

Dursdan shuddered. He didn't want that kind of responsibility. He looked down at the locket, studying the painted face. "Where did she go?"

Mergadan shrugged. "I don't know. Eventually, all but Aramel left. And from what I have learned of him, I don't blame them for leaving him behind. I just hope he won't cause any more trouble."

"*The dragons will watch.*" Sinotio stretched his wings around them protectively. "*I will watch.*"

Mergadan looked over at Dursdan. "What's this all about?"

"He says he'll protect us."

Mergadan smiled up at the Silver. "Yes, my beautiful one, I know you will. How's the wing feeling today?" The Silver stretched it out for inspection. "When do you think you'll be ready to fly again?"

Dursdan listened. "Soon. He wants to know where you want to go."

Mergadan patted Sinotio's curved neck. "I have unanswered questions." He looked back up at his dragon. "Some things are best left unsaid."

Dursdan closed the locket and slipped it into the pocket of his shirt. He watched his father and the Silver for a moment then quietly retreated from the courtyard. He stood in the outer yard and surveyed the surrounding fields, then moved in the direction of the barn to check on the animals. Tolanar had obviously hurried through the chores. Dursdan put the tools away and scrubbed the water trough before refilling it. The cows poked their heads in to see if he was going to feed them but when no hay was forthcoming, they wandered off again.

He was just leaving the barn when Natalo flew over. Dursdan looked up and Tolanar waved back. Natalo swooped and made a daring turn. "*We fly!*"

Crastrom looked pale but Tolanar whooped for joy. *Yes, and you look well, but your Lord doesn't.*

The Red controlled his flight and brought them safely down in front of the barn. The chickens scattered in all directions. "I'm sorry about that, Tola. I don't know what's gotten into him." Natalo looked sheepishly at his younger passenger. But Tolanar stroked him on the nose. Crastrom grinned. "I'm grateful for your help. Will I see you again tomorrow?"

"Of course. It's Drasia's celebration day. I have something special for her."

The old Lord smiled. "Then I shall come for you in the morning."

"On Natalo? Oh, yes! Thank you, Sir."

Dursdan could hear the Red chuckling. "*I like him! He likes to fly! We fly well together, do we not?*"

"Very nice."

Tolanar turned to Dursdan. "Oh, don't worry, Dur, I'll do the chores early."

Dursdan shook his head. "It's all right, Tola." He bowed to Lord

Crastrom and Natalo. "It sounds like you have more important things to do tomorrow."

Mergadan came out of the courtyard and called to Crastrom. "Why don't you boys go get a steer for Sinotio."

Tolanar rolled his eyes and looked over at Dursdan. "Well, at least they're in the near pasture."

Crastrom hopped Natalo over the wall as Dursdan followed his brother out toward the field. Natalo looked back at him. "*Do not worry, I will tell you everything they say.*" It sounded like the Red was grinning.

Dursdan let his brother take the lead. He was distracted by Natalo's commentary. It was pretty much as he had suspected. Crastrom had spoken to Dorsadram about the union of Tolanar and Drasia and about naming Tolanar his heir. Dorsadram had checked his references and agreed that it was an acceptable solution.

Tolanar slapped him on the arm. "Hey, what now, fall asleep walking?"

Dursdan shook his head to clear Natalo's wispy voice out of his mind. "Sorry, just a lot on my mind."

"Anyway, Crastrom said Natalo was acting really weird this morning, like he didn't want to wake up. Cras was really worried. He was concerned that Natalo might be sick."

Dursdan looked back toward the house. He could see the Red peering over the courtyard wall. "All the dragons were like that. They were having a dream conference."

"How do you know that?"

"I was there."

Tolanar began to laugh. "That's a good joke. The one person in the whole Valley most afraid of dragons, going to some conference. How'd you get there? Were you dragged?"

"It's not like that, Tola. I don't know what it is." He wasn't ready to tell him what their father had said. "It has something to do with this egg. Ever since I got it, I've been dreaming dragons. And the other day, something really strange happened and I started hearing them."

"Just now?" Tolanar laughed again. "Everyone hears dragons. They growl, hiss, scream, purr, why, they make all kinds of sounds."

"But they also make sounds you can't hear. They talk."

Tolanar poked his arm. "Where's the funny line?"

"There isn't one."

They walked in silence until they reached the pasture gate. Dursdan looked out at the steers and groaned. He looked over at his brother. "Um, we'll have to separate the pullers out from the feed stock at some point. We want a few left to yoke to the wagon." Dursdan ducked under the gate.

Tolanar stopped. "You're serious about the dragon talk?"

Dursdan nodded. "I'm off for that dark one over there. I've been fattening him up for awhile. Why don't you wait here and work the gate."

Dursdan easily herded the steer up the pasture and Tolanar opened the gate to let it into the lane. They walked on either side of it. Dursdan was afraid to look at his brother. He didn't want to be laughed at again.

As they approached the house, the steer began to panic. Natalo was still peering over the wall. Tolanar turned to him. "All right, if you can talk to dragons in your head, tell Nata to duck so we can get this steer into the courtyard."

Dursdan sighed. *Natalo, could you please duck behind the wall, Sinotio's dinner is a little jittery.*

"*Of course.*" The dragon ducked his head and Tolanar gasped. "*Is that better?*"

Yes, thanks. "Come on. I think Crastrom wants to leave soon." He herded the steer through the gate.

The beast panicked on seeing the dragons and tried to bolt past the boys but Natalo grabbed it with a swift bite. He pulled the bawling animal through the air and set it in front of the Silver. "*I believe this is yours, and if I might say, you have a tasty meal to look forward to.*"

"*Thank you. I am guessing Dursdan picked this one. You will have to work on Tola. He just does not know how to pick a good steer.*" Sinotio bit down hard on the steer's neck and ended the noise.

Dursdan's stomach lurched. He had always avoided watching the dragon eat. Sinotio regarded him. "*I am sorry it bothers you.*" He dragged it around to the corner and hid his dinner behind his wings.

Crastrom laughed. "He doesn't eat in public?"

"It usually doesn't bother him." Mergadan looked over at Dursdan. "Son, you look a little pale. Why don't you go in and lie down."

Dursdan nodded. He bowed to Crastrom and Natalo and moved toward the door. Crastrom cleared his throat. "Excuse me, Dur, but your Da tells me you've developed a rather unique ability."

"Yes, sir."

Crastrom looked up at Natalo. "Perhaps you could help me with something. The other day Nata and I stopped at several different places and at one of them I misplaced my bag of leather ties." He shrugged. "I guess I'm getting old. Could you see if Nata remembers where I left them?"

Natalo chuckled. "*If he had not had so much of the spring wine Jasorad made, he would have remembered putting them down. He left them on a fence post near the barn of Jasorad.*"

Dursdan could hear Azu laughing in the background. "*They hang there still.*"

"Thanks. You'll find them at Jasorad's on a fence post."

Crastrom squinted his face them smiled. "Oh, of course. Thank you, Dur." He patted Natalo. "It's a good thing that one of us still remembers." He shook his head and climbed on. "Until the morrow!" Natalo jumped into the sky and headed south.

Tolanar was staring at Dursdan with his mouth open. Sinotio looked over his shoulder. "*Is he hungry? I could spare a bite.*"

Dursdan laughed so hard he cried. Sinotio snorted. Mergadan shook his head. "Does that fall under the category 'better left unsaid'?"

All Dursdan could do was grin. His sides ached. *You really are something, Sino, you know that.*

The Silver turned and grinned, then went back to eating.

A soft whisper nudged his mind. "*We come.*"

Dursdan forced himself to stop laughing and looked up. "Dozi is bringing Lord Humatsu."

Mergadan looked concerned. "I hope you will get some peace."

"No, I think this is something else. Do you want me to ask?"

His father grinned. "Why not. I'd rather be prepared."

Dursdan focused on his image of Dozi. *What is it?*

"*My Lord has some little creature in a bag. It smells like a gnome and by the way the bag wiggles, it still lives, although I would gladly change that.*"

Dursdan whistled. "Humatsu has a wood gnome!"

A few moments later the Bronze circled and landed gracefully in the courtyard. Humatsu jumped down with a leather bag in his hand and ran up to Mergadan. "You'll never guess what I've got!"

"A wood gnome."

Humatsu's jaw dropped and Tolanar burst out laughing. The Lord looked at Mergadan. "How did you know?"

The Bronze sneezed. Mergadan chuckled. "I'm afraid Dozi told Dursdan while you were on the way here."

Humatsu looked at his Bronze and then at Dursdan. "So it's true then. Dursdan can hear them."

Mergadan nodded. "So what were you planning on doing with that? I hear they don't make good pets."

"Huh? Oh, this thing. I'm not exactly sure. I was going to kill it but Norita made such a fuss. She wanted me to fly it far away and dump it somewhere. I just thought you'd like to see it first."

Dursdan was only half listening. He looked up at Dozi. *Can you understand wood gnomes?*

"*What is to understand? They are dirty little creatures that eat anything they can kill or steal. This one was in our grain bins. Nasty little brute.*"

Dursdan shuddered. Sinotio turned from his feeding. "*Dur, what is it?*"

Dursdan looked at the bag. *I can hear it.*

Sinotio sniffed in that direction. "*Yes, it is very noisy.*"

Dursdan shook his head. *No, I mean, I can understand it.*

Both dragons looked at each other and then at him. Dozi put her head down by his face. "*You can? What is it saying?*"

"Dursdan?"

He jumped at his father's voice. "What?"

Mergadan pointed at the dragons. "What is it?"

Dursdan sighed. "I can't really translate all that right now. Can I have the bag?"

Humatsu shrugged and handed it to him. "It's bound but I never could get a gag in its mouth. I wasn't getting anywhere near those little teeth."

Dursdan took the bag, undid the knot and looked inside. The gnome snarled up at him. "Dirty nasty human! Filthy pigs, all of you!"

Dursdan shook the bag. "Be quiet." The gnome looked up at him in silent shock. "That's better. Now Dozi said you were pilfering from Lord Humatsu's grain bins."

The gnome scowled. "It should be our grain. We protected it from the rats and other vermin."

"Hmm, that's all very well, but Lord Humatsu planted that grain and harvested it."

The gnome laughed coldly. "That old man doesn't work in the fields. We know. We watch."

Dursdan looked up at Lord Humatsu. "The gnome claims he's due a portion of the grain for protecting it from the rats."

"What? You can understand the little brute?" Humatsu looked at the creature in the bag. "Well, if it weren't for his kind, I'd still have cats to tend to the rats!"

The gnome rolled his little eyes and shook. "Ah, terrible ferocious beasts! They hunt our children and destroy our villages. We fight back to protect ourselves. But we protect grain from rats."

"Yes, I did get that part." He looked at Humatsu. "It seems the cats were attacking the gnome villages. I can understand how they feel. After all, the Lords protect the Valley from the trolls."

"I don't see how that is the same at all." The Lord shook his head. "We don't go off and steal from the masters of the trolls, if indeed they do have them at all."

Tolanar slid up behind Dursdan and peered over his shoulder into the bag. "Maybe you could work out a deal. If these little things are brave enough to fend off the rats in winter, I'd think that would be worth something. Don't we usually have some to spare?"

Dursdan turned and smiled at his brother. "That's a grand idea, Tola. We always seem to waste so much. What about it, Da, would the Circle be willing to work out a deal to end hostilities with the wood gnomes?"

Mergadan rubbed his chin. "Considering the damage they are capable of, I think it would be considered."

Dursdan looked back at the gnome. "Do you have a name?"

"Of course I do, do you think us uncivilized?"

"No, obviously not. I am Dursdan, son of Lord Mergadan of the Dragon Lords."

"I'd bow but I'm kind of tied up at the moment. And I'm afraid I don't have any fancy title. I'm just called Ferdj."

"Good to meet you. Since you are a civilized fellow, I see no reason to keep you bound. Please forgive past misunderstandings. I'm afraid there isn't anyone else among my people who can understand you." Dursdan reached in and carefully lifted the gnome out. "Tola, would you give me a hand with these bindings?"

Humatsu cleared his throat. "Are you sure it's safe to do that?"

Tolanar untied the lashings and the gnome brushed himself off. He bowed to Dursdan and then to Tolanar. "I'm glad to see there is some honor among your kind. Now, you spoke of a deal?"

"Tola, why don't you go through the winter barrels and see what we have to share." He set the gnome down on the small table near the courtyard wall. "How many do you need to feed?"

"There are only two villages left, maybe 100 folk in all. We try to stock up enough to last but this winter was bad. A raven found some of our stockpiles. And the spring greens aren't quite ready yet."

Dursdan nodded. "And I'm sure our people are competing for the few things that are." He thought of Gran's berry cobbler. "I have some corn still in the bin. The grass is green enough for the cows. I can spare a good sack full."

Ferdj bowed. "You are generous. Be certain that my people will protect your lands well. It will be far for us to travel but we will make the trip on your behalf."

Tolanar returned from the cellar carrying a large bulging sack. "I think this should keep them quite well."

Humatsu eyed the bag. "Are you giving him your pantry?"

Tolanar laughed. "Dursdan is a great gardener. We always have more than we can use. If they are going to keep the rats away, they're going to need all their strength." He turned to the gnome. "Where do you need this delivered?"

Ferdj stood staring at the sack then turned to Dursdan. "Who is that?"

"That's my brother, Tolanar."

"What a grand family you have. I am honored. I am certain all of my kin would pledge loyalty to you and your family."

"That's good of you. I'll grab a sack of corn from the barn and Tola and I will walk you home."

Mergadan shook his head. "I'd feel better if you didn't go off like that."

"Da, if I have a problem, every dragon in the Valley will know about it." He went down to the barn and got the corn. When he returned, Tolanar was sitting next to the table, drawing on a board.

The gnome laughed. "He is good!"

Dursdan looked over to see the sketch. It was a remarkable likeness of the gnome. "Wow, I didn't know you could draw so well."

Tolanar smiled. "Just something I do in my spare time."

Dursdan held out his hand and Ferdj jumped on. He brought his hand to his shoulder. "Have a seat. The view is better." He waved at Mergadan and Humatsu. "We'll be back before dark."

Following the gnome's directions, the boys headed south through the fields and eventually came to the lane that separated Humatsu's farm from Conor's place. Dursdan whistled. "So that's why you visited Conor's grain bins. You must live nearby."

"Indeed, just over that hill in the forest." Ferdj pointed. "I'd better let them know we're coming." He whistled loudly.

"That sounds just like a meadow thrush." Tolanar tried his best imitation.

The woods rang with tiny laughter. Ferdj tried not to join in. "Tell him to keep practicing." He shouted down to the forest floor. "It's all right. The Big Ones are with me."

Another gnome stepped out of hiding. "Did you capture them all by yourself?"

Ferdj slapped his forehead and pointed at the gnome. "And this is what she gave me for a firstborn. Can you imagine that?" He looked back down at his son. "Datru, you're a fool. This is Lord Dursdan and his brother Tolanar. They have made a peace pact with our people and they bring food. Run ahead and tell your muth we are coming."

"Aye, Fud, I go." The little gnome took off running through the undergrowth and was quickly lost to sight.

"Well, they are fast. No wonder they do so well against rats." Tolanar shifted the sack. "I hope we're almost there. This is getting heavy."

"Oh yes, not far now. This way." Ferdj pointed toward the hill.

Dursdan topped the hill in a matter of steps and stopped. The ground was covered with small gnomes running everywhere. He was afraid to move. Ferdj pointed to a stump near a small stream. "That is our home. If you could put the bags here, my people will take care of the rest."

Dursdan looked back at Tolanar, who was staring at the smallest gnomes climbing up his boots and sliding off. "This is the place."

His brother looked up. "How'd you guess?" He unslung the sack and looked down. "Everyone look out!"

The gnomes ran for cover as he set the sack down. He dumped it over so that some of the food spilled out. A little female gnome rushed forward and ran her hands along the surface of an apple. "Oh, Ferdj. How did you manage it? I haven't seen an apple in seasons!"

Dursdan grinned. "And here's some corn. If I would have thought of it, I'd have brought along some already ground so you could make fritters."

She smiled up at him. "Bless my soul. Do you understand me?"

Ferdj put his hands on his hips and looked down at her. "Don't be daffy. Of course he can hear you." He looked up at Dursdan. "Beg pardon, my Lord. She's a bit of a ninny. That's my mate, Pufta. A hollow head but at least she can cook."

Dursdan gently put the gnome down next to his wife. "Good day to you, madam. I hope this food is to your liking."

She curtsied and giggled shyly. "Well I'll be. A fine gentleman." She patted the bag of corn. "This will more than do." She looked off behind him. "Camtri, stop that. These are guests."

Dursdan looked back at a small gnome digging a hole under Tolanar's shoe. He looked up at his brother and grinned. "I think we should carefully take our leave. I promised Da we'd be home before dark." He pointed down to alert him to the little gnome.

Tolanar looked down. "Now what's that about?"

Dursdan shrugged and turned back to Ferdj. "Until we meet again." He bowed and carefully backed away from the gnomes. As Tolanar backed up, Dursdan noticed a small fire in the hole. He decided not to say anything to his brother. He winked at the little gnome holding the blazing twig. Then followed Tolanar out of the woods.

They walked down the lane, enjoying the warmth of the afternoon. Tolanar glanced back. "You have to admit, he does have a bunch to feed."

"Indeed he does." Dursdan caught the snatch of a song and looked around.

Conor was working a team of steers at a plow in the field next to the lane. He waved and called to Dursdan. "Hey Dur, come about!"

Dursdan looked at his brother. "I hope he's not still angry with me."

"Why would he be?"

"We had a bit of a disagreement."

Dursdan felt a tickle. "*Merg is worried about you.*"

"Da is worried but I'd really like to make things up with Conor."

Tola looked up at the sky and pointed to several dragons crossing the Valley. "We should be fine. There are dragons everywhere. Let's go see what he wants."

"All right." He focused his thoughts toward Sinotio. *All is well. The dragons watch the Valley around us. Tola and I are by Humatsu's farm.*

"*I hear them. They feel no danger. See your friend.*"

The boys jumped the fence and jogged over to Conor. He stopped the team as they approached. "Hey, Dur. What did you take out to the woods?"

"Just some peace offerings. We won't have any more problems with wood gnomes." Dursdan looked at the team, trying to find a way to settle his concerns. He slapped the rump of a steer. "I see you have Stinger leading the plow. How's he working?"

Conor grinned. "Like a charm! He's kept old Rumble in line. And this field is almost done and ready to plant." He tapped Tolanar on the shoulder. "Hey, Tola, I saw you up on Crastrom's Red today."

"Natalo is awesome! And Crastrom is coming to get me in the morning, too."

"Going to Drasia's party, no doubt." He winked at Dursdan. "And how do things go with you?"

Dursdan swallowed hard. "Con, I just wanted to say I was sorry."

"For what?"

He glanced over at Tolanar. "For what happened with Mirana."

Conor laughed. "Are you still carrying that around? Don't be silly. It's past. You need to let things like that go, Dur. We all go forward in life." He pointed to the field. "When I plow, the dirt builds up on the spars. I have to kick them every now and then to dump it off. If I didn't, the plow would eventually become to heavy for the steers to pull."

Dursdan shook his head. "I don't understand."

"Things like that, our disappointments and such, are like dirt that gets piled up on us. If we don't let them go, out lives get too heavy. I learn a lot from my broken wishes and I'll keep the lessons, but I let go of the disappointment. You shouldn't let it weight you, either. I hope it works out between you and Mirana. She's far better than any of those empty headed Lord's daughters." He looked over at Tolanar. "No offence meant to you. I'm sure Drasia is wonderful."

Tolanar's cheeks reddened. "Well, I should let Da know all is well. While you can talk all you want to Sinotio, he can't have a chat with Da." Tolanar waved to them and jogged off across the field.

Conor laughed and slapped his knee. "Did you see that? He's gone on her for sure!" He made an odd expression. "What did he mean by that, anyway?"

Dursdan leaned on the rump of the steer. "It's a long story. Something happened yesterday." He looked down at the egg pouch.

"Heard you had a run in with a troll. Imagine that! My Pa says there haven't been marsh trolls in the Valley for a long time. Since the last war, I reckon."

Dursdan shook his head. "I guess the Valley does need to be protected." He looked up at the dragons with their riders patrolling the sky. "But it's more than that, Con. This egg is different." He sighed. "I'm different. Somehow, I'm changing."

Conor wrinkled his brow. "You don't look any different to me."

"The changes are on the inside. I can hear them. And not just the dragons, the wood gnomes, too."

Conor stared at him. He looked up at the dragons. "You can hear them?"

Dursdan nodded. "She woke up, or something. I don't know. But it changed me. It's like I'm becoming something else."

"We all become something else, Dur. We grow up. I'm getting

stronger. There was a time when I couldn't run a team alone; they'd pull me off my feet. But now I do all the plowing."

Dursdan smiled. "Thanks, Con. You truly are a good friend."

Conor held out his hand. "I always will be."

Dursdan shook it. "I hope you'll come to my Day Natal."

"You'll be at mine, right?"

"Of course. It's the night before mine." Dursdan looked up as Osiral flew over. "I'd better get going before my Da comes looking for me. I have something I've been saving for your Day Natal. I'll see you then."

Conor grinned and called the team forward. "Can't wait! I only have a few rows to go and I want to get this done before dark. Be well, Dur."

He left Conor and walked to the Village. He noticed Tolanar by the mercantile door and walked over. Marx handed Tolanar a bottle. "This is what she asked for. Send her my best and thank her for the butter."

"That I'll do, Marx. Hey, Dur. You ready to head back?"

"Wow, you're quick. Have you been home already?"

Tolanar held up the bottle. "I have. Gran needed something so Rad dropped me off in town."

They walked together across the bridge and down the road back toward home. As they passed Aber's farm, Dursdan noticed Mirana headed out to the barn. "I need to go have a quick chat with Aber. He had a couple of tired cows he wanted to trade. The way Sino is eating, we might need them."

Tolanar nodded. "I'll tell Da you'll be along shortly."

Aber was finishing evening milking as Dursdan entered the barn. The farmer looked up and grinned. "Well, you've managed to make quite a stir yet again."

"How so?" Dursdan lidded a milk can and carried it to the creamery.

Aber lifted his into the cooler box and grabbed the one Dursdan had carried. "It's all over town. Everyone is talking about the fact that you can talk to dragons."

Dursdan laughed. "Anyone can talk to a dragon, Aber. It's just that

I can hear them." He looked down at the egg. "This has really changed my life. I'm not sure I like that."

"Change happens. It's the one thing you can really count on. What makes us who we are is the way we handle those changes. It seems to me, you've done quite well." He shook his head. "Mirana had a hard day of it though. I think she's up in the loft crying."

"Why?"

"She and her Ma were in town today. I don't know what all transpired. Kalista didn't tell me everything. Just something about how stuffy some of the wives of Dragon Lords had become and that the daughters weren't much better."

Dursdan felt a tightness in his throat. "I'll find her." He headed for the ladder but paused at the door. "By the way, if you still have any old nags you want to dump, I'll gladly consider a trade. I was down in the fields with the steers today and I'm getting worried that we might run short."

Aber nodded. "I've got a couple that I was considering butchering but they're so old we couldn't do much more than stew the meat."

"I've got a large bull in the breeding stock that I was going to take down. He's just two and quite fat. Would he make a good trade?"

Aber smiled. "That he would but he's worth more than a couple ragged dry milk cows. I'll help with the butchering and make sure that Carala has a nice fatty roast out of the deal."

"Consider it done."

Dursdan climbed the ladder into the loft. In the gloom, he was guided more by her sobs than by sight. He found her curled up in a pile with the book on her lap. "Mirana? Are you all right?" He sank down beside her.

She tried to dry her eyes. "I didn't expect to see you. From all the talk in town, I thought you'd be too busy to bother with a simple farm girl like me."

"What in the world are you talking about?"

She looked up at him. Her face was tear streaked and drawn. "Your Mum and a cluster of other Lords' wives were all going about working on decorations for your Day Natal, and such. And their daughters were all taking bets on which one of them you'd choose."

"Oh, Mirana." As best he could with the egg pouch always in the way, he took her into his arms. "There is only one girl that I have ever had an interest in and she's right here." He laid his forehead on hers. "Let the wives and daughter scheme, but when it comes down to it, I'll be the one making the choice, whether my Ma likes it or not."

She curled around the egg as if it were a part of him. "Is it okay?"

"I'm worried about her. I'm afraid I frightened her and she's been hiding. And with all this other confusion all around us, trolls and gnomes, and what not…"

"I heard about the troll, but the gnomes?"

Dursdan laughed. "It's the strangest thing. I don't get it. I can understand what they are saying. And I understand why they've been borrowing from several grain bins on the south side of the Valley. They have a village over there and lots of hungry little mouths to feed."

"Pa always said that they were pests to be gotten rid of, like rats or moles."

"The gnomes keep the rats and moles from the crops. They always have, I guess, but they're so small we've never noticed. And they figure since they help, they are due a share of the harvest."

"I suppose that's fair." She laid her hand on the egg pouch and rubbed it softly.

Dursdan could feel a warmth in the back of his mind. "Mirana, keep doing that. She's always liked you." He closed his eyes and concentrated on the warm glow. *Come out little one, it's all right. I'm not angry with you.* The warmth seemed to grow.

Another presence interrupted. "*I hate to bother but I thought you would like an early warning. Merg just left heading out to find you and he does not seem happy.*"

Dursdan groaned. "Oh, bother." The glow seemed to retreat again.

"What's wrong?"

"My Da is coming looking for me. Ever since the troll incident, he become over protective."

"With good reason. What if the trolls want to steal the egg?"

"Shells! I never thought of that. I'll tell you something. All of the other eggs in the Gold's clutch were smashed. Maybe it was the work of trolls."

"Everyone puts them down as being mindless brutes. But then, that's how most people think of gnomes, too." She put the book away and went down the ladder. "The trolls went to war against us several times. What if they know about your egg and are afraid you might become a serious threat to them. They could be trying to squash the threat before it becomes too big."

"Or it could be an Eastern Wizard."

"What?"

"It's possible that not all of them were destroyed in the war."

Mirana gasped. "Oh Dursdan! What if it's true and he knows about the egg?"

Another thought came to him. "I've heard the Lords speak of Aramel as if he wasn't a very strong Wizard, but the way he attacked me in the forest, what if he's working with an Eastern Wizard?"

Mirana buried her face in his shoulder. He could feel her trembling. He felt Sinotio in the back of his mind and knew his Da was almost there. "I have to go." He stood a moment longer in the darkness of the lower barn and held her. Then he kissed her forehead and cradled her face in his hands. "You will be there on my Day Natal." He kissed her lightly. He felt Sinotio's warning again and let her go. "Be well."

He turned and left the barn, almost running into his father. Aber leaned out of the creamery. "Will those do then?"

Dursdan sighed. "They will do, Aber. I'll see you on the morrow."

Mergadan raised his eyebrows. "What will do?"

"Aber is thinning out some milk cows and I'm trading a butchered bull for them. At the rate Sinotio is eating, we won't have any steers left if I don't supplement his food supply."

"Oh." Mergadan waved to Aber. "Thanks." He guided Dursdan down the lane toward the road. "I was beginning to worry. Who knows what's lurking around and Tola said you were right behind him."

Dursdan paused in the road and looked at his father. "Do you think the trolls might have had something to do with the other broken eggs?"

"I had considered that. The Circle discussed it at some length when I first reported it to Dorsadram. They are thinking on it."

Dursdan bit his lip, almost afraid to suggest what he was thinking. "Could one of the Eastern Wizards have survived?"

Mergadan's face darkened. "Their fortress in the Eastern Mountains was totally destroyed. My Da passed on in that battle, as did many others. It was a terrible price to pay for that victory." He sighed and patted Dursdan on the shoulder. "Tola said the gnomes seemed most appreciative of your gifts."

Dursdan decided not to press for more information and followed the change of topic. "It seems they plan on giving us extra protection from now on."

"I can't decide if that's good or bad."

A dark shadow glided overhead. Mergadan moved to protect his son. Dursdan reached out and touched the dragon. *Good eventide. Is all well?*

The dragon circled. "*My apologies for missing the meeting last night, but my Lord Gilhadas was steamed about missing the battle with the troll and desperately wanted to find his own to kill.*" Eziki laughed. "*I smell nothing for miles but he still has to search.*"

"Dursdan?" Mergadan shook his arm. "Are you all right?"

"Sorry, Da. I was listening to Eziki. There are no trolls about so you can rest easy."

"That's a relief." He waved up at the Black's rider. The dragon circled one more time then headed off to the west. "This is going to take some getting used to. Well, your Ma will be in a state if we miss this fine feast she has concocted."

Dursdan silently thanked the dragon for his vigilance then walked home with his father. Sinotio greeted then in the courtyard. He turned to Dursdan. "*Sleep well. I watch.*"

Dursdan rubbed the Silver's nose. *Thanks. Will I see you later in the Mists?*

"*Perhaps. I doubt all will come again like that. It scared the Lords. That is not good. But perhaps you can tell Timotha that I will see her soon.*" His crystal blue eyes seemed to glow by themselves.

Dursdan grinned. *I'll do that.* He gave the dragon a final pat and went in.

Dachia was putting a large roasting pan on the table. "I was beginning to worry."

Mergadan encircled her waist. "We're fine, dear." He kissed her on the cheek.

"That the roast would burn." She batted him on the arm with a towel then grinned. "Well, wash up quickly. Food should be eaten while it's warm."

Mergadan laughed and followed Dursdan to the washroom. He pumped the water for the basin. "Your Ma can really be something sometimes." He winked. "I just can't figure what!"

Dursdan looked at their faces in the glass. Was his beginning to look more like his Da's? There was a loose straw caught in his hair. No, he still looked like himself.

The dinner was grand. Dursdan polished off a second plate, matching Tolanar's appetite for a change. They joked and laughed, as they had never done before. Tolanar had great fun telling everyone about their adventure with the gnomes. Dachia and Carala were both slightly disturbed. They'd both killed them in the pantry at one time or another.

Dursdan rolled into bed feeling full and satisfied. It was rare and he treasured it. He left his shutters open so the sun would wake him then rolled over and went to sleep.

* * *

Aramel watched the boy nestle under his covers. He slumbered deeply. Everyone else in the house went to sleep. The timing was perfect. He carefully began the chant and pushed each piece into place. The haze began to form. Soon he could see the sleeping boy within its shadowy boundaries.

The boy was mumbling in his dreams. The egg pouch still rested on the boy's stomach. Aramel didn't want any mistakes this time. He double checked the spell then carefully pushed his hands through the haze and reached down to undo the latch of the pouch.

The boy turned in his sleep, a frown crossing his face. Aramel drew back, fearing the boy might wake. He watched him for several moments. He still slept but his dream was obviously troubling him.

He reached once again for the pouch. The dragon outside began to bugle. What was the cursed beast doing? Something stung his hands and they began to burn! The boy was beginning to stir. He heard pounding footsteps coming down the hall. The boy began to scream!

Aramel frantically made a final grab for the pouch but he couldn't touch it! He pulled his arms back quickly as someone brought a lantern into the room. He broke the spell. Panting, he collapsed into his chair. What had happened? All of his careful planning had failed again!

He looked down at his hands. They smoldered. Now, what had gone wrong? He reviewed everything. It was if the egg itself had attacked him!

Chapter 15

Dursdan lay panting, trying to figure out what had just happened. Mergadan was demanding answers and he could hear the concerned whispers of dragons all over the Valley. He closed his eyes and tried to block out all the confusion and noise. His father shook him. Dursdan opened his eyes and glared at him. "Just a moment! I'm trying to sort everything out!"

Mergadan backed away from the bed. "I just want to know if you're all right."

Dursdan looked around the room. All was as it should be. *Sinotio, do you see anything outside?*

"No, and Dormaro sees nothing from his vantage above. What ever that was, it moved quickly away."

Dursdan shook his head. "It's gone. Dormaro watches the house and fields from above and it sounds like others are also rising to search."

"What was it?"

Dursdan sat up. "I don't know. I don't think I actually saw it. Trusumo and I were talking and suddenly…" He looked down at the pouch and swallowed. He opened the lid and moved aside the warmers. The swirling golden patterns swarmed across the surface in agitation. "She felt it. And I think she did something to it."

"The egg?"

Dursdan readjusted the warmer pads and closed the lid. "In the Mists, I saw her run past me and attack something. It was like a thick black shadow that was trying to cover me." He looked around the room again. "I thought I saw something when I first opened my eyes but now I'm not sure. It looked like a hand."

"The Mists?" Mergadan frowned. "What is that?"

Dursdan didn't get the chance to answer. Tolanar pushed passed the curtain. "Lord Dorsadram is here."

Dursdan could feel Trusumo in the back of his mind. *Are you all right, Dur?*

I think so. What was that? He closed his eyes again and tried to remember what had happened. They'd been sitting on cloud chairs discussing the age issue when a darkness had begun to creep into the Mists. Dursdan had tried to get up and move away from it but it had reached out and grabbed him. Then she had come out of nowhere, run passed him, and stuck a burning golden sword into the darkness. The Mists had flung apart and he had woken. Not much of it made sense. He opened his eyes.

Dorsadram was at his side. "Dur, what can you tell me? Every dragon is the Valley is on edge."

Dursdan shook his head. "No one can find it. It moved fast." He glanced at his father then back at the Head of the Circle. "What ever it was, it wanted the egg. But she fought back. I think she did it some damage."

Mergadan leaned over Dorsadram's shoulder. "Who is she?"

Dursdan looked down at his egg. "I don't know her name." He reached out trying to find her but she'd sunk back deep into hiding again. "She's very frightened."

"No doubt." Dorsadram sighed and stood up. "This is not a good thing. Attacked in his own room in his own house." He looked at Mergadan. "It smells of magic."

"How can we be sure that the Eastern Wizards were really all destroyed? Maybe one survived and is coming back to take revenge. Dursdan and I had just spoken of this before dinner." Mergadan looked down at his son. "Golds hold powerful magic that a Wizard could use to increase his own."

Dursdan was thinking about a different Wizard. "Aramel."

Dorsadram frowned. "That old buffoon? He can't even get his parlor tricks to work right. I know he approached you in town but how could he be up to this level of magic? Besides, he's a Western Wizard. They're on our side."

"Are you sure? What if he's working with an Eastern Wizard?" Dursdan wrapped his arms around the pouch. "He wanted the egg. He tried to get me to trade it for another but I turned him down. And then he attacked me in the forest when I went after the steer. If it weren't for Terarimi, he might have succeeded."

"I seem to be missing a piece of this story."

"Oh! I had almost forgotten about that." Mergadan looked over at Dorsadram. "I was so focused on Tera that I let it slip."

Dorsadram put a hand on Mergadan's arm. "I'll be interested in the details. I'm just not sure what we could have done anyway. I don't know where Aramel hides. There's an old stronghold up in the mountains somewhere but who knows where." He looked down at Dursdan. "Don't worry. If we see the old beggar around, we'll corner him."

Mergadan laughed coldly. "I don't think it will be that easy. If he can slip in here past a watching dragon, what makes you think you'll be able to corner him?"

Dorsadram shook his head. "I hear what you're saying."

Other voices echoed in the outer rooms. Dursdan felt the dragons. "It's Humatsu and Sorazan. Dozi says she and Mithra have crossed the entire Valley and found nothing."

Dorsadram nodded. "I apologize, Merg. I didn't mean for your home to become a message center." He looked back at Dursdan. "Do you think you'll be able to get back to sleep?"

Dursdan shook his head. But Sinotio rumbled. "*I will help you sleep. You are tired. Tell them to go.*"

"What's up with Sino?" Merg looked ready to go to battle.

"He wants me to sleep." Dursdan shrugged. "I'm too tired to argue with him."

Dorsadram chuckled. "Wise boy. Come Merg, I'll give you a ride. I'll post Sangan and Nalfram with their Blacks nearby. I want all the Lords called to Circle."

Mergadan looked down at him. "Will you be all right, Dur?"

"I will."

Dorsadram nodded. "Good lad. Sinotio is right. You should get some sleep. If your little one did do that thing some damage, it's probably off licking its wounds and won't bother us again tonight." He took the lantern and pulled Mergadan out of the room.

Dursdan leaned back and pulled up the covers. The pads felt warm. The egg was safe. *Sinotio, can you feel her? Is she all right?*

"*I feel her fear but her love of you is greater. Now, sleep. Feel the Mists gathering around you. All is well.*"

Dursdan closed his eyes. *She loves me?* He could feel Sinotio humming in the background. It was a very comforting sound. Soon the Mists were gathering around him. Timotha was there, and ran to his side. "Dursdan! I was so worried. I was just coming to join you when the darkness appeared. What was that?"

"Everyone thinks it was magic. I think Aramel the Wizard is probably up to something. I wouldn't trade him the egg, or give it to him, so now he's trying to take it."

Timotha put her arms around his shoulders and called up a cloud. She pulled him down next to her. "That was Sinotio singing you to the Mists, was it not?"

"Yes. I don't think I could have fallen asleep without his help." He looked around. "I doubt we'll see any of the other dragons tonight. The Circle has been called and many of the younger riders are on watch. I don't know if they would be much good against magic."

"Probably not, but it makes them all feel as if they are really doing something." She shook her head. "I still remember the first war in the Valley. The Wizards came down to help us fight. They smelled funny and carried all manner of strange things in their pockets. I remember Altimon." Her eyes seemed to glow. "He was the leader of the Western Wizards, reportedly one of the greatest that had ever lived." She looked down at Dursdan. "It is said that he personally trained Zaradan. Did you know that the daughter of Altimon asked a wild Gold for an egg and gave it to your ancestor? Malthia was the largest and most powerful of all the dragons."

"What happened to her?"

Timotha covered her face with her hands and began to weep. "Oh,

Dursdan! She sacrificed herself for me!" She curled into a ball and sobbed for some time.

Dursdan didn't know what to do. He put his arms around her and held her until she finally quieted. "Please tell me what happened."

Timotha sniffed and tried to smile. She pulled out a hanky and wiped her face. "I am sorry, I just have not thought of all that in a long time." She seemed to regain most of her composure. "Do you know anything about the war?"

"Just a little. Armia, my Great Gran, wrote a book about the history of the Valley. Mirana has been reading it and giving me the highlights." He looked down at the dull glow. "I've been kind of busy."

"Well, it would be interesting to see what she wrote. I was there. I remember. The first dragons taught all of us about the war beyond. They passed down their memories to us so that we would never forget where we came from or why." She sighed. "But perhaps they did not know the whole truth either."

"Trusumo and I were speaking of that tonight. Is that why so many dragons died in the first war?"

"It was a terrible battle that lasted for months. The trolls had attacked during a late winter blizzard and caught everyone unprepared. But the fighting lasted almost until midsummer." Her voice broke. "Voramato was struck down just days before the end. I brought him back but I knew his injury was fatal. Zamisha had lost everyone else and it nearly drove her to madness that she would also lose her twin brother. So she climbed on my back. I could feel her anger and it fueled my own. We were off before anyone else knew it."

"They didn't see you go?"

She shook her head. "We left in the dark of night. I was so sooty from the battle fires that I was more gray than white." She sighed. "But Mertrodan knew. Like his grandmother, he could hear us. He was just a tiny lad at the time. He ran and told his grandfather what was happening and Zaradan and Malthia came to help us. I know we would have never succeeded without their aid."

"What were you attacking, a fortress?"

"No, a troll unlike any other. He was huge. He towered over me like a tree. Our only advantage was surprise. The Lords had only battled during the day and those were defensive stands, not attacks. The trolls thought they were safe at night. We flew into their main camp without anyone noticing. It was not until we made our first run that the alarm was raised."

He took her hand. It looked as if she was about to start crying again. "That was all long ago, Timotha. It's been over for many years."

She looked at him and smiled. "When you have lived as long as I have, you will discover that older memories seem sharper."

"What did Zaradan and Malthia do?"

"They followed us in. After the other trolls realized we were attacking their leader, they started gathering to protect him. Zaradan realized that if we did not take him down fast, we would fail. Malthia got right in front of him and conjured a light spell to blind him."

Dursdan gasped. "She could do magic?"

"Of course, she was a Gold. Anyway, Zamisha made full use of that distraction and landed on the back of the neck of the troll. I dug in my claws and held on and she used her spear over and over again to stab the vile thing. It flung around wildly, unable to reach us. It stuck Zaradan and Malthia out of the air."

"What happened after the troll died?"

"All of his horde ran in panic. Zamisha found Zaradan on the ground. I went to Malthia. She was in bad shape. Even with all of her magic, she could not save herself or Zaradan. Zamisha held him as he died, there on that field covered in blood. And as he passed on, so did Malthia." Timotha began to weep again.

Dursdan shook his head remembering all the names of the riders and dragons that had perished in that terrible war. And the sacrifice of the Gold and his ancestor that had allowed Timotha and Zamisha to end it. "It was a valiant thing you both did."

Timotha sneezed. "I doubt Zamisha expected to survive anymore than I did. I could feel Voramato dying. But I could not leave Zamisha there so I held to her and survived."

"And you bonded to her son?"

"Yes, he was born in the fishing village we found. She named him Norimato. And when he was 16, he became my rider. Then he had a son, Larimato, who became my rider when he turned 16. And it was so with his son, Karimato. And early this spring, on the eve of his sixteenth year, Varimato became my rider."

"By the way, how is he doing? Is he past the illness?"

Timotha smiled. "He is much better. I was glad to leave the dark green forest behind. Now we fly over vast lands of grasses. We can see great cities in the distance and I wonder if Menatash lives in one of those. But today, for the first time, we saw mountains on the horizon."

Dursdan laughed. "Then you're almost here!"

She shook her head. "It still feels very far away. I am not flying the same route Zamisha and I took. That was very here-and-there. It took us months to find the village. I am trying to find a more direct route home."

"I wish I could see those cities. I've never thought about anything beyond this Valley until I began dreaming you and Menatash."

"I will show you what I see." She opened a cloud window. "But we keep away so as not to be seen. The First dragons remembered that the men of those cities feared us and wanted to harm us. That is why the first Lords left the Kingdoms of Men and came to the Valley."

Dursdan was listening to her but his attention was drawn to the magical places he saw in the window. He could never have imagined such places existed. One caught his attention and he made the image stop. The city was vast with many tall spires rising between other large structures. Sunlight gleamed off of polished dome roofs. "It's so beautiful."

Timotha chucked. "Vari had a similar response. It was certainly bigger than the fishing village we lived in."

"What was that like?"

The view in the window changed to a small village with houses built on posts near the edge of a vast expanse of water. People of all ages moved though the lower poles, working on boats, mending nets, preparing food, or tending younger children. "It looks very peaceful."

"It has been for many years. But it was not the case when we first arrived." Timotha closed the window. "They lived in constant fear of pirates who raided their village and killed or enslaved their people. Zamisha and I changed that." Timotha looked smug.

"What did you do?"

"Oh, we did not hurt anyone, just flew over their boat." She laughed. "They were so terrified that they turned and ran. And that is all we ever had to do. We would fly out when ever a sail was sighted on the horizon. If they looked friendly, we would go back to the village and tell them who was coming. But if not…" She grinned. "We would dive down and frighten them so badly that many of them would jump right out of their ships. It was great fun!"

Dursdan had to laugh. He could only imagine what those men must have thought. Then he remembered that he was once afraid of dragons, too. He looked down at his stomach. The glow was very faint. "I think I saw her today."

"Really?"

"She attacked the darkness with a golden sword."

Timotha touched his stomach gently. "She is still very afraid." She rubbed the glow softly. "Come out, dear one. You are safe here. Do not be afraid."

The glow seemed to brighten a little.

Trusumo came through the mist. "Ah, Timotha, so good to see you." He bowed to Dursdan. "Grave tidings, my Lord. The Circle is most concerned about you. They are placing a watch around you night and day."

"Great." Dursdan sighed. "There goes the last of my freedom."

"They will not impede you from movement, simply follow you around so they are near if trouble should arise."

"But I can talk to every dragon in the Valley. It's not like they have to stand over me like an infant."

Trusumo shook his head. "I understand their concern. If this is Wizard's Work, it will be hard enough to respond to the threat. We want to be close by to come your aid quickly."

Timotha smiled at him. "I agree with Trusumo in this. I have seen what Wizards can do. It is best to have others close by."

Dursdan laid back and the cloud adjusted to support his weight. "My Day Natal is coming up. I get the feeling that everyone expects me to choose the daughter of a Lord. But I've already made my choice."

Trusumo chuckled. "So Sinotio has told me. Personally, I approve. Noladon was a great Lord and a close friend of Dors. It was a terrible loss when both he and Lenadon fell in the last Great War. It is fitting that you choose the granddaughter of Lord Noladon as your mate."

"Is she pretty?" Timotha smiled. "Vari was suppose to mate with a girl from the village, too, but he thought they were all ugly. I think he was glad to leave the girl his parents chose."

"And that's my biggest fear." Dursdan stood up and began pacing. "That my parents will try to force the girl they think is right on me and not accept my choice."

Trusumo nodded. "Perhaps we can help with that. I will speak with Sinotio on the matter. Dragons have been known to influence such decisions in the past."

Dursdan felt a tug. The Mists were beginning to fade. "I must go now. Good day to you both and safe journey, Timotha."

They both bowed to him as the Mists vanished. The tug grew persistent. "Dursdan, can you hear me?"

Dursdan yawned and looked up at his father. "I'm sorry, Da. I'm awake." He looked around and noticed that they weren't alone. Humatsu, Sorazan, and Petolam stood crowded in the doorway.

Sorazan wiped his brow. "Lad, you gave us a start when your Da couldn't rouse you. We feared we were too late."

"I'm sorry I worried you. I was dreaming with the dragons. It's harder for me to wake up when I'm in the Mists."

The Lords exchanged glances. Humatsu frowned. "Are you sure that's safe? You were attacked in your sleep last night."

"Would you prefer that I go share the rock with Sinotio out in the courtyard?" Dursdan pulled himself out of bed. "I'm sorry. But I don't know how to keep away from the Mists. They just happen when I go to sleep."

"Why don't we let the lad get up and change. The house is surrounded by dragons. I can't imagine anything getting past them in broad daylight." Sorazan bowed to Dursdan and backed out of the room. The others followed his example.

Mergadan sighed. "Be sure and call if you need anything. We're not far."

"Da, I'll be fine, honest." His father shrugged and left. Dursdan felt the dragons in the back of his mind. Surrounded indeed! Half the Circle must be at his house.

He heard Samita chuckle. *"We are here. Your animals are not happy."*

Dursdan groaned. He hoped the cows would be all right with so many dragons around.

Dozi laughed. "*We would not eat your cows. Besides, when I saw what a fright we were causing, I made sure everyone stayed on the other side of the house. Our Lords are not happy about this. But we would not budge.*"

That explained why he couldn't see any dragons from his window. *Thank you all. I'm sorry this has caused you so much grief.*

He could hear a multitude of chuckles. Lamiga shushed them. "*It is all right, Lord Dursdan. It gives us a chance to see Sinotio.*"

"*And it has been so boring without company. It is just no fun when you cannot fly. Do hurry and come out. Everyone wants to see you.*"

Dursdan dressed quickly and put the egg pouch back on. The pads felt cool. He went toward the kitchen but found the house was packed. The assembled Lords and Riders parted to let him pass. The kitchen was full of women. Dachia and Carala worked around their helpful guests and good smells issued from the oven and big roasting pot. Avanta came over and gave him a hug. "Sorry about the mess. Do you need fresh warmers?"

Dursdan hugged his aunt back. "I do. It's quite a party in here."

"Don't worry. I'm sure things will thin out soon. The Circle has been up all night. They'll need to sleep. It sounds like they're setting up a watch. Rad wanted to be in on the first row but it will be underlords for the day." She winked. "He's so young, he sometimes forgets he's a Lord."

Loimitia brought the pads and helped Dursdan arrange them. "Huma said it was a beautiful egg." She smiled at him. "You are very lucky." She went back to cutting vegetables with Jadala.

It was hard for him to picture the wives of Humatsu and Sorazan peeling potatoes, but everyone had to eat. He shook his head and slipped out through the crowd and into the courtyard.

Unfortunately, it was no less crowded. Mithra was lounging on the rock with Sinotio, Azu and Moroto were a gleaming red pair in one corner, Kazar and Radafi added a blue contrast to the scene, and Osiral was curled up trying to stay out of everyone's way. Dozi's head rested on the wall. "*Oh this is nothing. There are nine more of us out here.*"

Other heads popped over the wall and a general murmur ran through the dragons. They were all staring at him. Then they bowed.

The Lords had grown silent. Lord Kalafri cleared his throat. "Well, that's highly irregular."

Radafi rolled his eyes. "*I am sorry, Lord Dursdan. Please forgive my Lord but he has been up all night and he tends to get rude and cranky.*"

The dragons chuckled. Lamiga looked up at Sinotio. "*All Lords are that way, are they not, Sino?*"

A shadow flew overhead and dragons and humans alike looked up. Dursdan felt Natalo. "It's all right. It's just Crastrom." He looked around. "Oh, where is Tola?"

Itogan pointed toward the barn. "He's trying to convince one of your cows to give milk." The Lord shook his head. "He's all thumbs."

A few others chuckled. Dursdan shook his head and pushed out of the gate. Tamini made to follow him. Dursdan looked back at the Yellow. *I'm sorry, but the cows are jumpy as it is. I'll call if I need you, honest.*

The Yellow stopped. "*As you request. I wait for your command.*"

Dursdan was at a loss. *Why would you wait on my command? Shouldn't your commands come from your rider?*

"*While it is true that Lord Osiris is my rider, you are Lord of the Golden. All dragons will look to you.*"

Dursdan shook his head. *But Dorsadram is the Head of the Circle. He's the one who commands your Lords. I'd think you'd look to him before me.*

"While you're just standing there staring at Tamini, could you hold the milk? Cras is here, and I don't want to keep him waiting."

Dursdan jumped. "Tola, you scared me half to death."

His brother laughed coldly. "First you're scared of dragons, then suddenly you can hear them, and now you're scared of me. What's next?"

Natalo came up and put his head down between them. "*Why does he have such anger in him?*"

Dursdan patted the Red's neck. *Because he loves dragons and he doesn't understand what I've done for him yet.* He looked over the dragon's head. "You should go. Don't want to keep Drasia waiting on her celebration day. I know she'll like the gift."

Tolanar stared at him a moment then scratched Natalo's eye ridges. The dragon purred. "*Oh, I like that.*"

Dursdan smiled. "You always did have a way with them. Here's Cras. Have a good time."

Lord Crastrom and Tolanar mounted and Natalo jumped into the sky. "*I will make sure he has a good time, do not worry.*" They turned west and flew off.

True to Avanta's prediction, things quieted down in the afternoon and most of the dragons left. Soon, only Green Fari and White Nasila shared the courtyard with Sinotio. Maloras and Molahad followed Dursdan around, occasionally helping him with chores, but more often telling stories of their adventures with their dragons. Their dragons would laugh and correct the exaggerations. He began weeding the garden, making sure not to harm the tender shoots. Dursdan was growing accustom to their constant chatter.

He was startled when they stopped talking. "Can I help you?"

He looked up at Molahad's derisive tone and found Mirana standing at the edge of the plot. She looked bewildered. "Dursdan, is everything okay?"

Before the riders could say anything else, Dursdan put down his hoe and quickly stepped across the rows. "Mirana, I'm glad you're here. I want you to look at the gray cow. I'm afraid she took a fright this morning when my yard was full of dragons." He emphasized the words carefully and wished he could speak to her in his mind the way he could with the dragons. He turned to the riders. "It's hot. Why don't you go see if my Ma has something cool for you to drink? We'll just be out in the barn. The dragons will know if there's trouble."

Maloras shrugged. "He's right, it is hot out here." He turned to Dursdan. "You be sure and shout if any thing comes up."

"I will." He pulled Mirana in the direction of the barn before they could change their minds.

"What was that all about? What happened?"

He put a finger to his lips and looked back over his shoulder. The riders had gone into the courtyard. The gate clicked shut behind them. He breathed a sigh of relief and pulled her into the shadows of the barn. "I'm so glad to see you." He pulled her close and kissed her.

She smiled then looked around. "But the cows are out in the field."

"Yes, but they don't know that." He could see the concern growing in the soft edges of her face. He gently tried to smooth it away. "Don't worry. Every dragon in the Valley is watching out for me."

"Please tell me what happened."

He pulled her toward the hay pile in the back of the barn. "It's not as nice as your loft." He sat, pulling her down with him. As quickly as possible, he filled her in on the events of the night. "Now the Circle has assigned a watch to me, night and day."

"But if this thing got passed Sinotio, will a couple of extra dragons make a difference?"

Dursdan shook his head. "I've been thinking about this. Gran said the other night that she'd never heard of a marsh troll coming anywhere near the Valley."

She gasped. "Do you think the Wizard might have had something to do with it?"

"It's a possibility. I remembered the strange metallic taste when I encountered both him and the troll. I didn't make the connection until later. He keeps trying different things and when one thing fails, he tries something else. The egg fought back when he tried to touch her. I don't think he'll try the same approach again."

"But you think he'll try again." She buried her head in his shoulder. "Oh, Dursdan, I just want you to be safe."

He held her close, the sweet smell of her hair, the soft touch of her skin; it was a tonic on his raw nerves. "Don't fret, love. All will be well in the end."

He felt Fari in the back of his mind. "*Malo is looking for you. He comes to the barn.*"

Dursdan sighed. Would he ever have peace again? He would be glad when his Day Natal came and he could officially choose Mirana. Then it wouldn't matter who saw then together. "One of the riders is coming."

She sat up and wiped her eyes on her sleeve. "I should be getting back to help my Mum. She's finished a project on the loom and we'll have to set the ends."

He pulled her to her feet. "I was supposed to help Aber butcher a bull today."

"I heard him talking to your Pa early this morning. It's been postponed for a few days. That's why I got worried. I was afraid that you were hurt or sick."

He smiled. "I'm fine. I'll be going to Conor's Day Natal tomorrow. Are you coming?"

"I'm not sure. I've been helping my Mum with birthings lately and there are several women due any day. I'll be there if I can."

"I'll save a dance for you." He winked then saw the shadow cross the barn threshold. "Well, tell your Da that we'll butcher that bull as soon as I'm allowed to." He chuckled. "My Day Natal is the day after tomorrow. Maybe things will calm down after that."

He reluctantly let Mirana go, watching her walk toward her father's farm. He looked around. This would be their farm if Crastrom formally adopted Tolanar.

Maloras tapped him on the shoulder. "So, how's the cow?"

"Huh? Oh, she's out grazing now. I guess she'll be all right. Hopefully we won't get curds and whey for the next couple of days."

The rider's brows went up. "Cows can do that?"

* * *

Aramel slammed the book shut and tossed it on the stack. He'd been through every volume he had on dragons. He was still puzzled as to what had gone wrong with the spell. Maybe it was the Gold's magic that prevented the transport. He slumped into his chair. It could be a worse scenario. The dragonling could have bonded with the boy already. This would pose a problem.

He scanned the shelves of his workshop looking for ideas. The egg belonged to him but if it had already bonded, he couldn't just take it. He'd have to use deeper magic, and soon! But then he needed the boy as well. He sighed. All these complications. What a bother.

He got up and studied the corner of the room. It would do. He pulled some items from the shelf and set them on the floor then began the chant. These wouldn't be ordinary walls; they would be bound in magic, to prevent the Gold dragonling from escaping, if it had such abilities.

He worked at it far into the night then rested, admiring his handiwork. Two stout walls with a thick steel gate penned in the narrow corner. He supposed he'd have to find a way to keep the boy alive until he could separate the egg. He didn't want any harm to come to his precious Golden dragonling. Afterwards, the boy wouldn't matter. The Gold dragon would be his.

Chapter 16

Mergadan woke in time to join them for dinner. Tolanar was still at the party. Conversation at the table was subdued. Dursdan was relieved that the riders had gone home to their own families. Mergadan kept watching him and it made Dursdan nervous. He was relieved when the meal was over.

His father cleared his throat. "I'm concerned that your room might not be safe. I'd rather you slept in the parlor, where we can keep an eye on you."

Dachia shook her head. "That's ridiculous, Merg. How is he suppose to get any sleep if people are constantly brooding over him?"

"I'm sure I'll be fine, Da. I really don't think he'll try the same thing twice. I might be safer in my room." He felt the dragons. "And it seems the house will be well protected. Ma, maybe you should make another pot of tea for Itogan and Gilhadas. I'm guessing they'll be up all night."

She shook her head. "Will things ever be quiet around here again?"

Mergadan laughed. "Have you forgotten what it's like to have a hatchling in the house? A few of months from now it will be even worse."

Dursdan ran his hands over the egg pouch. A few months. At first it had seemed like an eternity, now it seemed like too short a time. He looked up as the Lords entered.

Gilhadas patted him on the shoulder. "Don't worry, Dur. My Eziki and Ito's Samita won't let anything get in this house."

Eziki chuckled. "*Just let anything try!*"

Samita laughed. "*Listen to him. He was startled by a rat in his sleep and took a fright. But do not worry, Lord Dursdan. We will watch. Dream well.*"

"My thanks to both of you."

Itogan smiled. "It's all right, lad. The Circle will protect you. Oh, I almost forgot." He reached into his pack and withdrew a leather bound volume. "Dors asked me to give this to you."

"Thank you." Dursdan took the book. "Well, I'll see you all in the morning then." He took a candle and retreated to his room. He could hear the Lords talking quietly in the dining room. They had slept most of the day; no doubt they'd talk most of the night.

Sinotio was chatting with the two Blacks. Dursdan had learned to tune out the sound so it didn't bother him. He changed, readjusted the pouch, and slid into bed with the book.

It was old, obviously written a long time ago. He turned to the cover page. It was written by Lord Sorendram of the First Circle. Dursdan whistled softly. He remembered the name from Armia's book. He was the first Lord of the house of Dram. The events seemed to begin when an elf courier came to his father's house seeking him. Apparently his skill with the sword was well known.

Dursdan read of Sorendram's initiation into the Dragon Lords, of his training, and his feelings over receiving his egg. It surprised Dursdan that this great Lord had many of the same uncertainties that Dursdan himself felt. He looked down at the pouch resting warmly on his stomach. It didn't seem like such a burden anymore.

His eyes were growing heavy. He closed the book, set it on the table, and blew out the candle. The voices had quieted to just barely audible. In a way, it was comforting to know he wasn't alone.

Sinotio softly whispered in his mind. "*You are never alone. We are with you. Now sleep. I will walk with you in the Mists tonight. The Blacks watch over us both. We are safe.*"

Dursdan closed his eyes and let the Mists swirl around him. It felt as natural as breathing. The Mists became draperies that parted. Sinotio was waiting for him. He bowed formally. Dursdan started at him. "Is everyone treating me this way because of the egg?"

"No, my Lord. They recognize something much greater in you."

"I don't understand."

"That is not surprising." Trusumo emerged from the Mists. "You are young and do not hold the memories of all of your predecessors for humans have no such capacity to do so."

Dursdan shook his head. "In a way we do. We write books. I was reading tonight about the First Lord of the House of Dram, Sorendram, and how he was chosen by the Wizards because of his bravery and ability with a sword."

Trusumo smiled. "Ah, Sorendram, rider of Silver Ralitha. He was truly a great man. Did you know that he was Second of the First Circle?"

"I guess I haven't gotten that far yet. I'm up to the part where he's waiting for his egg to hatch. He didn't know what color it was going to be. Apparently, the queen had been a White."

"Really? I did not know that. Perhaps there is something to the way humans record their memories. Dragons remember what has been. They can not see what has been before."

"And Sorendram spent a lot of time thinking on paper. I like that. He's been dead since the First Great War but I can still read his thoughts."

Trusumo shook his head. "What a marvelous thing. There are many times that I wished I knew what Dors was thinking. I can hear his words and see his actions, but sometimes they make no sense to me."

Dursdan laughed. "I had a similar thought this afternoon." He looked at the Silver and Red. "I'm grateful to share thoughts with you."

Sinotio smiled and patted Dursdan on the shoulder. "As we are with you, my Lord."

The Mists shimmered and Timotha stepped through. Sinotio immediately went to her side and she sank into him. Dursdan was concerned by her appearance. He ran to her side. "Timotha, what has happened? Are you ill?"

"We were attacked."

"What?" Trusumo took her other arm and formed a cloud chair for her. "By whom?"

"By men with arrows. We had skirted some farmlands in the morning, trying to stay out of sight but the humans have cultivated vast stretches of the grassland here and we could not find a way around them. We made it to some trees along a stream so that Vari could rest and we could drink. They set on us there."

Sinotio gasped. "My love, you are wounded!"

Dursdan could see the red spreading across her hip. He wanted to cry.

"I took an arrow deep in my flank before we could get airborne. We got away as fast as we could. At least Vari is all right."

Dursdan felt the pain as if it was his own. He reached out and touched her leg. The red began to recede. He could feel the pain draining away. Timotha's gasp startled him. He looked up at her.

She was looking down at him, a look of wonder on her face. "How are you doing that?"

"I don't know." He continued to watch the red disappear. Soon it was gone, as was the pain. He removed his hand. "Is it better?"

She was staring at him. She mouthed a word that Dursdan couldn't hear. Trusumo and Sinotio were also staring at him. Trusumo shook his head as if waking from a daze. "Could it be?"

Sinotio shrugged. "Only time will tell." He looked down at Dursdan and smiled. "Some things are better left unsaid." He looked up. "Bother, now what?" He sighed. "I am being called." He kissed Timotha lightly on the forehead. "Be well." Then turned to Dursdan. "Remain yet, it may be nothing." He slipped back through the Mists and was gone.

Timotha stood, testing her leg. "It is healed." She hugged Dursdan. "I know we will succeed. The mountains are still distant on the horizon but I can feel that we are drawing closer. My greatest concern is the cultivated areas we must fly over."

"Why don't you fly at night? The moon is nearly new and doesn't come up until the early hours. Even though you are white, you'd still be hard to see. When dawn comes, you could find a place to hide for the day."

She looked at Trusumo then back to Dursdan. "Why had I not thought of that?"

Trusumo chuckled. "Because you are a White and accustomed to day rather than darkness. But you should be all right. Granted, your night vision is not that of a Black but if you are high in the air, it hardly matters. There is nothing to run into. And you can use the stars to set a course."

"Yes! That may solve much." She sighed. "Now how do I get Vari to understand?"

"That's simple enough. You were injured, right?" Dursdan pointed at her leg. "Lay low all day and stir once night falls. He'll just assume that you needed the day to rest. And maybe he's bright enough to figure out that it's safer to fly under cover of night."

"Let us hope so."

Dursdan felt something tugging on him. "I have to go. Be well, my friend, and safe journey."

Trusumo grumbled. "I too am being called. Something must be up. I will speak with you shortly."

Dursdan opened his eyes. His mother's face was a mask of fear in the flickering candlelight. "Dursdan, something terrible has happened. Lord Crastrom has fallen."

Dursdan sat up. "What happened?"

"I'm not sure. Tola is all right but he's staying with Natalo. Lord Jasorad came to bring us the news."

Dursdan reached out to touch Natalo. *Are you all right? Is Tola hurt? How is Lord Crastrom?*

Natalo whimpered. "*He wanted to fly Tola home. It was not good. I could smell the wine. Sometimes he drinks too much of it. I tried to be careful.*" Natalo sobbed. "*He fell! I could not stop him. Tola tried but lost his grip. I caught Tola. He is unharmed. Crastrom is not.*" The Red continued to sob.

"Dursdan?" Mergadan shook him. "Maybe the shock was too much for him."

Dursdan looked up at his father. "Tola is all right but it sounds like Lord Crastrom is hurt pretty bad."

Mergadan's eyebrows went up. "How did you know that?"

"Natalo just told me what happened."

"Oh. I keep forgetting. Well." He cleared his throat. "I'm going to ask Jas to bring Tola home. No use having him under foot."

"No!" Dursdan grabbed his father's arm. "Natalo needs Tola. Let him stay." He reached out to the weeping Red. *Natalo, lean on Tola. He'll support you until Cras gets better. Don't worry.*

"Dursdan, your brother is good with dragons but he's no healer."

"Ma, Natalo wasn't hurt, just Crastrom, but the Red is scared. He knows Tola and Tola knows him. They need to be together."

He felt Trusumo. "*I am here now. Natalo is not hurt. Tolanar is not hurt. Crastrom is all broken. He is old. Yamitra is here; we brought her. She will tend Cras.*"

Make sure Tola stays with Natalo. Dursdan looked up at his father. "Please, let Tola stay."

Mergadan shrugged. "Very well. But I want to go and help. Jasorad has come for Carala. She's good at bone setting." He kissed Dachia and ducked through the drape.

His mother stared at him. "Do you think that's fair to Tola? If Crastrom dies, Natalo will die, too. That would be so hard on your brother."

"Natalo might not die if Tola is there."

"What do you mean?"

"There are things about the dragons the Wizards never told the Lords. I don't know if it will work in this case. Crastrom and Natalo have been together a long time. But if Tola can bond with Natalo before Crastrom dies, the dragon will survive."

Dachia gasped. "Are you certain of this?"

"I know a very old dragon that still lives because she has been passed from one generation to the next. So it is possible. I'm just hoping Tola and Natalo are strong enough."

There was a soft tap at the door. Itogan pushed back the curtain and peered in. "I'm sorry to disturb you. Gil and I are going to help with the carry. Lord Wasoras and Thorazan have arrived to take over the watch."

Dursdan got up. "Thank you, sir. I will greet them. Tell Tola to hang on to Natalo. Don't let them be separated."

The Lord gave him a puzzled looked. "To what end?"

"If Crastrom dies, Tola may be Natalo's only hope."

"I don't understand but I can't hear them as you can. I will convey the message." He bowed and let the curtain fall back.

Dursdan managed to shoo his mother out of the room so he could dress. He found the Lord and Rider at the table. Their dragons were restless in the courtyard. He could hear Kazar grumbling. "*And this is what comes of foolish humans who insist on poisoning themselves. You would think they would know better. Can they not smell the danger?*"

Tasia chided him. "*They are only humans. They have no sense of smell.*"

Dursdan shook his head and joined the men. "Good morning, sirs. I'm grateful of your company. How fare you?"

"Well enough, thanks." Wasoras drained his tankard of mulled cider. "Your family seems to have taken quite a streak lately." He eyed the pouch. "Who's to say if any of it's good."

Thorazan stared at the Lord then cleared his throat. "Sorry that they woke you. I'd imagine you haven't been getting very good sleep as it is."

"As if the rest of us have." Wasoras put the empty cup down. "I think I'll go check on the dragons." He got up and went out the door.

Thorazan shook his head. "It's not you. That's just the way he is."

Dursdan chuckled. "Now I know where his dragon gets it."

"Have a seat. Your Ma said something about a sweet bread almost being done. I seem to recall her cooking is outstanding."

"It is." He felt the pouch. "I have to change the pads first."

Dachia came from the kitchen with the warmer basket in one hand and a plate of fresh bread in the other. "I'll be glad when that egg hatches and the warmers don't take up half my night oven."

Thorazan laughed. "Yes, but then you'll have to put up with a voracious hatchling waking the house up at all hours. I know. We have one!"

She smiled. "How is Mora getting on?"

"Not bad. Shatsu is getting too big for the house though. He'll have to be moved outside soon. I don't think Mora is happy about that. He claims he'll go sleep outside with his hatchling if we kick it out!"

She shook her head. "I'd almost forgotten how much fun that is."

She looked down at Dursdan and smiled. "Well, in a few months, I'll be reminded."

Dursdan opened the lid and pulled out the cooled pads. The rider leaned over. "Can I see it?"

"Sure." He let Thorazan help him with the warm pads.

"It's beautiful. When I'd heard that Merg had managed to find a Golden queen, I was a little jealous. I'd only managed to find a Red. I had hoped maybe she'd found a Bronze to her liking but Mora seems quite happy with Shatsu."

Dursdan remembered seeing him at school. "As long as he's not stuck on a roof." He heard Tasia chuckling in the background. "Does he do that a lot?"

Thorazan rolled his eyes. "I've lost count of how many times I've had to rescue him. Still can't figure how he gets up and then can't get down."

Tasia laughed. *"Shatsu thinks he is scared of heights."*

"What?" Dursdan noticed the surprised expression on the rider's face. "Sorry, Tasia says the hatching is afraid of heights."

"How can a dragon be afraid of heights? They fly."

"Yes, that could be a problem. Mora isn't afraid of heights, is he?"

Thorazan thought for a moment. "I wonder if he is. Last week when Sha ended up in the tree, it would have only been a short easy climb. But he couldn't do it." He shook his head. "Why didn't I notice that before?"

"I think dragons tend to exhibit many of the same characteristics that their riders do. Lord Wasoras is a bit grumpy and so is Kazar."

The rider laughed. "You would be the one to know." Then his face grew serious. "Could you ask Tasia something for me?"

Dursdan groaned. This was the one thing he'd feared most when everyone found out that he could hear the dragons. "As long as it's not too personal."

Thorazan shook his head. "I've noticed that she seems uncomfortable on her rock. If I knew why, I might be able to change something to make it better."

"I can ask." Dursdan gently felt for the dragons. They were deep in conversation and he didn't want to be rude. *Tasia?*

"There you are. Is my Lord boring you?"

Not really. He is actually quite concerned about you. He says you don't look happy on your rock and he wants to know how to make it better.

"*How thoughtful.*" She seemed quite pleased. "*Ever since they cut down the old tree, I do not have shade from the sun or a break from the wind. I miss it. I know he can not put it back, but some kind of shelter would be nice.*"

It gave Dursdan an idea. *You wouldn't mind sharing it with Shatsu, would you?*

She laughed. "*Of course not. I like the little brat.*"

Dursdan had to refocus on the dining room. "Well I've discovered the problem and I may have a solution to both issues. Tasia is missing the protection an old tree used to provide. I guess Greens don't like direct sun."

"Really? I didn't know that. My poor girl. I hope she'll forgive me."

"Well, you have the other problem of Shatsu getting too big for the house. Maybe you could make them a shed. Tasia says she wouldn't mind sharing it with him. Then if Mora really was serious about sleeping outside with his hatchling, at least he wouldn't be exposed to the elements."

"*And I would keep them both warm and protected.*" Tasia chuckled. "*And I am not mad at Thor. I love him dearly. I knew he just did not understand.*"

Dursdan was trying to find a polite way of restating that idea when Trusumo interrupted. "*Forgive but the matter is urgent. The Lords have successfully moved Cras but he grows weak.*"

Thorazan was puzzled but Dursdan held up his hand. "A moment and I will explain." *How is Natalo doing?*

"*He clings to Tola. I have made sure that no one interferes. We all watch. If Natalo lives beyond Cras, this may impact all of us. Though I for one will pass on when Dors does. We have shared too much together in this life. I will walk with him into death.*"

Dursdan felt tears burning his eyes. *I don't look forward to that day.* He tried to focus on Thorazan but he had to blink the tears out first. "I'm sorry. Things aren't going well with Lord Crastrom. They've moved him but his condition is failing."

Thorazan shook his head. "What a sad affair. Do you know he'd asked the Circle to formally adopt your brother as his heir?"

"I had hoped that would happen. In a way, I sort of set all this in motion. But Tola may end up with a dragon after all."

"How so? If Crastrom dies, I doubt the Circle will confirm the line unless Tola already has an egg."

"But he may have Natalo."

"That's not possible. Natalo will die when Crastrom does." He looked at Dursdan. "Won't he?"

Dursdan shrugged. "That remains to be seen." He reached out his mind and felt for Natalo. He could feel the grief and regret, a sense of shame and remorse. *Hang on to Tola, Natalo.*

The Red moaned. "*But I would be giving up on Crastrom.*"

Dursdan had a thought. *No, you'd be saving him by saving his house. Tola will become your rider and he and Drasia will rebuild the house of Trom.* He looked up at Thorazan. "I should be there."

The rider rose. "Then Tasia and I will take you."

Dursdan followed Thorazan out into the courtyard. Wasoras had been sitting at the little table against the wall. He rose as they left the door. "Something is up with the dragons. They've been acting odd."

Dursdan looked over at them. "Do you agree with this?"

They all bowed. Sinotio swung his head to look at him. The first colors of dawn reflected off his eye-ridges. "*You see beyond what we can. I know what Timotha has said. It can be as you believe. If you feel this is right, than I agree.*"

Other dragons echoed his approval. Tasia and Kazar nodded.

"What's all this? What are they doing?" Wasoras turned to Dursdan with a questioning look.

"I will tell you as we fly. I believe time is short."

Sinotio sighed. "*I wish that I could carry you myself but my wing still aches. I know Tasia will bear you well.*"

"*I am honored, my Lord.*" She advanced and bowed her leg.

Dursdan looked at Thorazan and the rider of the Green grinned. "Well, let's go then. Up you go, Dur. Mount up, Was."

"Where are we going?" The Lord was having some trouble getting on Kazar. "Will you stand still a moment? Are you trying to crush me under your feet?"

The smaller Blue pulled up apologetically next to the larger Green and let his Lord mount but his body still quivered with excitement. *"We fly!"* He jumped into the air and Wasoras cursed as he grabbed on.

Kaz! Be careful. We're already loosing one Lord tonight. Let's not make it two. Dursdan held on as Tasia sprung into flight.

Dursdan managed to tell Wasoras where they were headed before Tasia took the lead. The ground passed below at an alarming speed.

He felt the tickle of Tasia in his mind. *"Do not fear. I will not let you fall."*

Dursdan closed his eyes and felt the powerful muscles of the Green pushing forward. A moment later, Thorazan tapped him on the shoulder. They were circling Crastrom's homestead. The yard was already packed with dragons. They all backed up to make room for them to land. Dursdan could hear the anticipation in their thoughts.

Dorsadram was there to meet them as they landed. "Dursdan. What are you doing here? I was hoping they'd have let you get some sleep."

"Other things are more important. I believe Crastrom is dying." The Head of the Circle nodded sadly. Dursdan took him by the arm. "Thorazan said the Circle was considering Crastrom's request to assign Tolanar as heir."

"We were. We have lost so many houses. To loose another when it could be prevented, would be unthinkable. But without an egg."

"What if Tola has a dragon?"

"What? What dragon?"

"Natalo."

Lord Wasoras joined them. "I still don't understand."

"There isn't time to explain. Just please answer me, Dors. Would the Circle approve Tola as Crastrom's heir?"

Dorsadram shrugged. "I suppose. But Crastrom would have to make the marriage contract official between Tola and Drasia."

"Then let's do that. By the look of things, all the Lords are here, anyway."

Dorsadram looked over at Wasoras. "They are now. Come then. I agree that time is short."

Dursdan followed the Head into Crastrom's home. He could hear women weeping and hoped they weren't too late. He cursed the silly traditions that required all of this. As they approached the main room, people parted to let them pass. Murmurs began to run through the group.

Crastrom was propped up on a makeshift bed. Carala and Yamitra looked up. Dursdan could see that the old Lord was still breathing. He looked at his grandmother. "Can he talk?"

She nodded. "For a little while yet." She stood up and touched his arm as she walked past. "He is near the end. I will do what I can to comfort Madrea."

Dorsadram motioned all the others to leave except the Lords. "Crastrom brought before the Circle a proposal just a day past. Is there anyone present who would protest it?"

The room was silent. Dursdan knelt beside Crastrom and the Lord opened his eyes. "I'm an old foolish man. Look what I've done. And my poor Natalo must share my fate."

Dursdan wiped the Lord's brow. "I wish I could mend what ails you but I don't know how. I tell you that there may still be a chance for Natalo."

Crastrom gripped his arm tightly. "Save my beautiful Red if you can." Tears welled in his eyes. "I will pay for my foolishness. But if you know of some deeper magic that will preserve Nata, I beg you to use it."

"It's nothing I do. It's up to Tola and Natalo. They must be strong enough to hold each other when you pass."

"Dors!"

The Head came forward. "Rest easy, Cras, save your strength."

"No. I want you to bring me to the yard where Natalo is. I fear he would not fit in the house. And there are things I must say to him."

Dorsadram looked back at the other Lords. Mergadan, Radachi, Dormato, and Balashir came forward and gently lifted Crastrom. Dursdan followed the procession out into the courtyard where Tolanar was wrapped in Natalo's wings. The Red lifted his head as his Lord was brought forward.

All of the other dragons came forward as well and formed a protective circle around the humans. Under other circumstances, Dursdan would have been terrified but he was focused on the dying Lord, his faithful dragon, and Tolanar.

Crastrom called out to Drasia and she came running. "I'm here, Da."

Crastrom looked over at her. "Do you care for this boy? Would you accept him as a husband?"

She looked up at Tolanar then back at her father. "He's a good man. He'd be a wonderful husband." Her voice choked and tears stained her cheeks.

Crastrom called Tolanar forward. "I ask a great deal of you, lad, more than is my right. But would you consent to marry my daughter and take my family name?"

There was a mixed reaction from the crowd, approval from the Lords who already knew and sounds of surprise from others. Tolanar looked up at his father and Mergadan nodded.

Tolanar was choked with tears but found his voice. "I do so with honor, sir."

Crastrom reached out and took his hand. "From this day forward, you are my heir. Let it be recorded so. You are Tolatrom." The Lord looked toward his Red and Natalo laid his head on his Lord's shoulder.

Crastrom looked back at Tolatrom. "I have one last thing to ask of you. I pay the price for my foolishness but it is not right that Natalo pay it. He tried his best to save me, as did you." He laid Tolatrom's hand on Natalo's head. "There is a deeper magic that I do not know but the dragons do. Take Natalo and save him. Hold him as I go." His voice faltered.

The entire assembly was silent, even the dragons. Natalo looked up at Dursdan. "*He wants me to stay. This will save his family?*"

Dursdan nodded. *It will. The one who was my brother is now your Lord.*

Natalo looked back at Crastrom. "*He passes but I remain. My Lord is Tolatrom.*"

All the dragons began to bugle. The people stood staring at them but Dursdan saw Crastrom take his last breath and lay still. Dorsadram knelt and closed the fallen Lord's eyes. He looked up at the boy and dragon. The Red curled his neck around his rider while the boy wept.

Dorsadram looked up at Radachi. "It's been awhile since we've had such a young lord within the Circle but I've learned that the young bring new ideas and new energy." He stood and addressed the assembly. "This is a sad day as we gather to remember Lord Crastrom but within this sadness there is a new hope." He looked over at the Red. "This day we greet Lord Tolatrom and his Red Natalo."

It was a speech as old as the Dragon Lords themselves. The crowd began to cheer through their tears. Dursdan went forward and embraced his brother the best he could. The egg was in the way. Drasia came to the other side and clung to him. Tolatrom reached up and pulled her close. Natalo enclosed them with a wing.

The other dragons leaned over and one by one, gently touched Natalo. Dursdan could hear their encouragement and reassurance. He patted Natalo's neck and got up. Natalo nodded to him then drew his other wing around to enclose the grieving couple.

Dorsadram shook his head. "So it's true. How did you know?"

"Timotha told me. She yet lives because she was passed from one rider to another."

The Head of the Circle gasped. "Timotha the White still lives? Where is she?"

Dursdan looked up at Trusumo. "Is it time we told your Lord everything?"

Trusumo bent his head down and rested it gently on Dorsadram's shoulder. "*It is time. There is much he needs to know.*"

Dursdan nodded and guided Dorsadram and his Red away from the gathering. They found a quiet spot near a small stream and Dursdan told the Lord everything that he knew. He also reinforced Trusumo's desire to remain with Dorsadram rather than choose a new rider. The old Lord embraced his dragon and wept.

Dursdan bowed and left them together. He found his father sitting under a tree not far from the protective Red. Mergadan looked up at him. "I want to see him but I don't want to disturb Natalo."

Dursdan could see that his father had been crying. He sat down beside him. "He is still your son. That will never change, even though Crastrom named him heir."

Mergadan smiled. "I know. How often does a man get to sit next to his son as an equal Lord within the Circle? I should feel honored."

He looked over at Dursdan. "Not only that, but my firstborn is gifted and carries a Golden egg."

"That you risked everything to obtain." Dursdan put an arm around his father's shoulders. "I don't think I've properly thanked you for that."

Mergadan hugged him, unable to speak.

After awhile, Dursdan gently released his father. "I can ask Natalo how Tola is, if you'd like." Mergadan nodded. Dursdan softly touched the Red's mind. *How are you?*

The Red turned and looked at him. "*We are well.*"

Mergadan was hoping to see Tola before he left.

Natalo nodded and opened a wing. Tolatrom looked up. "Da?"

Mergadan rose and went to him. They embraced. "I'm proud of you." He looked at Drasia. "I'm honored to call you daughter."

She managed a teary smile. "Thank you, Da."

Mergadan shrugged. "I have no idea how I'm going to explain all this to your Ma." He looked up at Natalo. "Any of this."

Radachi found Dursdan under the tree. He sat down next to him and they watched the sun rise in silence. Then his uncle put a hand on his shoulder. "And how do you fare?"

Dursdan didn't know what to say. "So much has happened tonight. Have I done the right thing?"

Radachi chuckled. "You have saved the house of Trom and perhaps changed forever the idea that a dragon is doomed to die with his rider." He looked over at Osiral. "I know he's young; I can feel it. He doesn't age like I do. I would hate to think that my life would shorten his. It doesn't seem fair."

Osiral looked in their direction. "*He speaks of me, does he not?*"

Dursdan nodded at the dragon. He looked at Radachi as Osiral came toward them. "Is it true that some Lords are having trouble finding eggs for their sons?"

"Yes. Vortrax, Klastromos, and Balashir have all been out searching. None of them have even sighted a dragon in months. Your Da was very lucky to find you one." He shook his head. "What will we do if there are no more wild dragons?"

Dursdan bit his lip, remembering that it wasn't long ago that he had wished for that very thing. He looked down at his egg, wrapping his arms around it and rocking gently. He looked up at Osiral. "There may yet be hope."

"How so?"

Dorsadram whistled as he approached and Dursdan rose to greet him. Radachi jumped to his feet as well. Osiral bowed. Dorsadram looked older in the early morning light. "We will take our leave. The family wants to prepare for the passing ceremony, which will take place three days hence." He looked at Dursdan. "I believe you have a big day coming tomorrow, my boy. I look forward to welcoming you into your place as a young man." He looked back toward the Red who still sheltered Drasia and Tolatrom. "And I'd imagine we'll have a wedding to look forward to soon." He smiled then sighed. "So much in so little time."

Dursdan shook his head. "I feel as if I should be apologizing."

"Nonsense. Were it not for you, our future would look dark indeed. Don't fret. Change happens. It's just harder for the old to accept." He patted Dursdan on his shoulder. "You must be tired. I'd say we aren't letting you get much sleep."

Radachi looked around. "Would you like a ride home, Dur? I'm guessing Merg will be a bit yet."

Dursdan brushed off a few clinging pieces of grass. "Thanks, Rad. There are chores waiting back at home and by the look of things, I'll be the only one around to do them." He gave a final glance back toward his father and brother.

Dorsadram held out his hand. "Until tomorrow."

Dursdan shook it firmly then followed his uncle toward the waiting White.

Osiral flew high over the Valley and Dursdan managed to keep his eyes open. It was a beautiful place. He looked down on the patterns of fields and houses that he had only seen before from the ground. It was a different perspective. Osiral circled their own hill a few times to give Dur the chance to look at the fields. Then he brought them gracefully down into the courtyard.

Sinotio bugled a greeting. "*You return!*"

The house was still. Dursdan went inside but there was no sign of Dachia. He found a note on the table. She'd gone into town and would be back shortly. He returned to the courtyard. "Ma's not here."

Radachi laughed. "Has she got a shock coming!"

Dursdan looked up at the Silver. "Did she mention where she was going?"

Sinotio shook his head. "*She left as the sun rose. Rayina came. They talked of colors. I did not understand. Then they left in the cart that brought Rayina. I did see that it was one of your pullers attached to it.*" Sinotio grinned.

Dursdan sighed. "Ma's gone back to town. I guess they were working on decorations yesterday."

Radachi shook his head. "It's just the way women are." He winked. "Well, I best be getting home myself. Avanta hasn't been feeling well."

"Is she still sick?"

His uncle grinned. "Only in the morning." He jumped up on Osiral. "Come my handsome lad, home we go."

Osiral sprang into the sky and circled once. "*You did it, Dur! All will be well.*" Then they turned south for home.

Sinotio looked over at him. "*I wish I could have been there. I listened. Natalo will live and Tola is a Lord. Osiral is right, you have accomplished much. But you still seem sad.*"

Dursdan sat in the chair. "I'm worried about her." He looked down at the egg. "In the Mists, her glow is so dim. It frightens me. What if I've done something wrong and hurt her?"

The Silver reached out and nuzzled the pouch. "*I feel her. She sleeps but I do not sense any pain. A tinge of fear but not nearly as much as before.*"

Dursdan rubbed the pouch. "The pads are cooling. I'd better change them before I do the chores."

"*Be silent in the house. Jasorad brought Carala home not long ago. She looked tired. She sleeps now.*"

Dursdan smiled up at the dragon then went in, changed the pads and went out to the barn. Three hungry cows greeted him with complaints. He got to work right away.

Dursdan put the hayrack back on its hooks and picked up a milk bucket. Only the gray cow needed to be milked. The black and white cow was heavy with calf and the reddish brown was almost dry. His careful planning meant that his mother always had a fresh supply of milk.

Dursdan patted the gray on the rump, reached for the stool, and was about to sit down when a shadow crossed the doorway.

"Dursdan, are you here?"

He smiled. "Back in the gray's stall, Mirana." He sat, cleaned off the udder, positioned the pail, and began milking.

"I heard what happened with Lord Crastrom." She leaned over the cow's bony hips and looked down at him. "Is Tola okay?"

"I guess that depends on how you define okay." The streams of milk made a comforting rhythmic patter on the inside of the bucket. "He's just been made the official heir of the house of Trom, pledged in marriage to Drasia, taken over Natalo, and been made a Lord all in the matter of a few minutes."

Mirana leaned back against the rough walls of the stall and sank down into the fresh straw. "All that? Oh my goodness!" She grabbed up a handful of stems and began braiding it. "Have you been up all night? You must be done in."

"Not at all. Just let me finish this up and turn the cows out. I want to see how the garden is doing."

Another shadow crossed the doorway. "Dursdan, are you out here?"

He looked around the animal's rump in surprise. "I'm here, Ma. I'm just finishing up the milking."

"Wonderful! Fresh milk is just what we need."

He was puzzled over the tone of her voice and even more surprised that she had returned so soon. "Something up, Ma?"

"Oh, we just have some guests."

Dursdan leaned farther out of the stall and stared. Instead of her everyday linen dress, she wore a long blue lacy affair. He'd only seen her wear it a few times.

She smiled at him. "Please bring it up as soon as you're done."

"I'll do that." He watched her go then readjusted his position on the seat. Mirana turned back from the crack she'd been peeping through. Dursdan shook his head. "Wow! She's taking everything quite well. Maybe Tola brought Drasia over."

"So soon? I'd think they'd both be resting."

"It must be something important."

Mirana shooed away a nosy fly from the milk bucket. "Why do you say that?"

"Just the way she was dressed. She hardly ever wears that unless there's something really special. Gran told me once that the dress was made by Ma's Gran. It's very old." He finished and lifted the full bucket out of the stall.

Mirana got up and took it from him. "I'll lid it for you."

"Thanks." Dursdan opened the stall collars and the three cows backed out and made their way toward the field door. The black and white cow paused to sniff at the egg pouch.

Mirana laughed. "Maybe she sees something in common."

He shooed the cows out the door and frowned. "Maybe she's afraid mine will grow up to eat hers."

"Dursdan! You're awful!" She laughed and threw a handful of straw at him. He threw some back. She came over and gently rubbed the egg pouch and looked up into his eyes. "This one will be beautiful. The first thing this baby dragon will see is you. It will always love you, like any child loves its parent."

There was a softness to her voice. The sunlight gleamed off her deep auburn hair, not like the fiery red of his mother's, but a deep rich hue like a late summer sunset. She smelled of loam and sweet grass. Her eyes reminded him of a reflected forest on a still pond. He wanted to forget the world and take her in his arms.

"Dursdan! Are you coming soon?"

His mother's distant voice startled him. He swallowed. "I'll be right there."

Mirana turned away, gazing out into the fields where the cows were gradually finding a comfortable place to graze. He wanted that moment back but it was gone. "Well, I'd better get this milk up to my Ma."

She nodded and followed him from the barn. The chickens gathered around their feet, hoping for a dropped morsel. Dursdan clucked at them and they clucked back. Even the old rooster crowed.

Mirana laughed. "You certainly have a way with animals."

He felt better seeing her smile. He watched her whirl around, the chickens trying to catch the hem of her skirt. She lost her balance and he reached out with his free hand and caught her. They were both laughing and she was out of breath.

Dachia opened the courtyard gate and frowned. "There you are, Dursdan. I was wondering what was taking so long." She took the milk pail. "Good morning, Mirana."

"Good day to you, Dachia. I hope you're well."

"Well enough. Is your Da going to be haying these fields today? It does stir up such dust."

"These fields won't be ready to hay for a few weeks at least."

Dursdan tried to peer around his mother's shoulder into the courtyard but he couldn't see beyond her puffed sleeves. "I asked Mirana to come up and help me finish the weeding. I got distracted yesterday and the egg kind of slows me down."

"Actually, we have guests. I'm sorry Mirana, what with everything only a day away, there's just so much planning to be done."

"Planning?" Was Tolanar going to marry Drasia already?

Someone came up behind his mother. "Hi, Dursdan."

He gasped. "Ashandra! What are you doing here?"

She came out and slipped a slender arm around his. "Oh, I just came by with my Ma. She's helping your Ma with your Day Natal decorations."

"Well, maybe Mirana can stop by latter this afternoon and help you work on the garden." Dachia smiled but Dursdan could hear the disapproval in her voice.

Ashandra pouted. "Oh, but I was hoping Dursdan and I might go on a picnic this afternoon."

Dursdan turned and stared at Ashandra, realized she still had a hold of his arm, and shook free. "What's gotten into you all of the sudden? Did you and Rashir have a little spat?"

Her face wrinkled into a frown. "Just because Rashir thinks I'm his girl doesn't mean that I agree."

"Funny, I heard you agreed just fine at Steban's wedding dance."

Dachia cleared her throat. "Dursdan, why don't you and Ashandra come and have some tea." She motioned in the direction of the courtyard.

He gave a final glance at Mirana. *Wait for me by the tree.* He hoped she could read his mouthed words. She nodded and turned down the hill. Dursdan sighed and reluctantly went through the gate. Sinotio sat watching from his perch on the rock. *I could use a little help.*

The Silver grinned. "*I do not like this one. She smells funny.*"

His mother had brought out some extra chairs and had arranged a beautiful spread of delicacies on the courtyard table. Normally, Dursdan would have been thrilled.

Rayina waved to him from one of the chairs. "Good morning, Dursdan."

He nodded politely but didn't sit. "It's been quite an eventful morning." He glanced over at his mother. "I don't suppose Da has come home yet?"

"Not yet, Dur. I'm sure they're off tending to Lord Crastrom. I was relieved to see that you had come home. Time is so short and there's so much yet to be done."

Rayina poured some tea. "Let's talk about colors. What will Dursdan be wearing?"

Dachia smiled and sat down. "Oh, I've spent some time working on this outfit." She opened a cloth bag and produced a beautiful golden yellow tunic and trousers with accents of red and silvery gray. "It took me some time to get the colors right. The golden yellow for Dursdan's dragon, the silver for Mergadan's and the red for his granddad's."

"It's very stylish. I'm sure I can find something for Ashandra that will match."

Dursdan stared at Rayina. "Match?"

"Why, yes, of course. You should look grand when you stand next to each other. Why Lodaki and I had beautifully matched sets."

Dursdan felt the heat rising. "And why would Ashandra and I stand next to each other?"

There was a moment of uncomfortable silence. "Now, Dursdan." His mother got up and put her arms around his shoulders. "There are only a few Lord's daughters your age. It was a simple process of elimination to figure out who your choice was going to be. After all, you were on your way to her house when that nasty troll attacked you."

Dursdan pulled away from his mother. "I was walking with Steban who was delivering a flute. I wasn't going there to visit anyone."

Dachia looked uncomfortable. Sinotio leaned forward and sniffed Ashandra's hair and sneezed.

Ashandra jumped out of the chair. "Oh, how disgusting!" She started wiping at her dress.

Dursdan bit his lip to keep from grinning. *Not bad, Sino.*

"*I told you she smelled funny.*"

"Sorry about that. Da's Silver is on the mend and he's very sensitive to certain smells. It must be something you put in your hair." He turned to his mother. "I've got work to do today. I don't have time for tea." He looked at the clothes. "It's a very nice outfit and I know you spent a lot of time working on it, but I think you have more important things to be planning."

"Yes, there are choices of food and decorations."

He shook his head. "Tolatrom has just been made a Lord this morning and has been pledged to be married. He'll need all kinds of things planned for him. As for me, I've already made my choice and you'll just have to accept that." He looked at Ashandra. "I'm sorry, but I could never marry someone who my Da's dragon is allergic to."

He looked at his stunned mother. "I'm sure Da will be home soon to tell you all the rest. You'll have to excuse me, I have something to attend to."

Ashandra started to move toward him but Sinotio huffed in as if he might sneeze again. Her eyes grew wide. She went around the back side of the table and hid behind her mother.

Dursdan bowed, and went out the gate. It clicked shut behind him. He let out his breath. That was close. *Thanks, Sinotio.*

The Silver chuckled. "*It was fun. I will listen. Find your girl.*"

Dursdan ran off down the hill toward the tree. He crossed the field and came to a stop. There was no one there. "Mirana?"

"I suppose you can't climb anymore with the egg pouch and all." She was sitting in the upper branches. "That was a short party." She climbed down.

He caught her on the last step and turned her around. "It wasn't my party. It was my mother's fantasy. She and Rayina have been friends since they were children. I think they used to pretend that they would grow up, marry, and have their children marry. That is what little girls do, don't they?"

"That's maybe what Lords' daughters do but farm girls are usually to busy helping the family survive to have that much time for folly."

"Good. That means a farm girl's head isn't stuffed with fluff and she knows that when a man has chosen her, it's not because it was his Ma's fantasy, or his Da's ambition, or it had anything to do with position or status." He took her face in his hands. "It's because when he looks in her eyes, all is right in the world and nothing else matters." He kissed her.

Mirana formed herself around the egg and returned his kiss. In the back of his mind, he could feel the glow brightening. She was happy! He picked Mirana up off her feet and swung her around. She and the glow laughed.

* * *

Aramel watched them through the pool on his workbench. Imagine that. The farmer's daughter! This was too easy. She would be the perfect bait. He smiled and wiped the pool away.

He turned to his shelves and began sorting ingredients. Some of the important things were running short. It was time for a visit to the farmer, anyway. He wasn't going to make any mistakes this time. He took everything that he could possibly think of. He mentally ran though a long list of spells.

Once his bag was packed, he walked over to examine the cell. The walls were sound. He tested the bars of the door. They were firm. He stepped inside and felt the dulled sense of power. He tried a basic light spell. Nothing. He laughed gleefully. As magical as the Gold may be, it would not escape his prison.

He went back to his chair and conjured a good meal. No sense working on an empty stomach. As he ate, he planned the details in his mind. He'd watched the peasants. They had been having a series of festivals and celebrations. It certainly looked like more were coming. Tomorrow he'd watch the farmer and the boy. Maybe he could determine the best time to strike.

He finished his meal and whisked the table away. Useless clutter. He decided to sleep in his bed and get a good night's rest. He would need to be fully alert for tomorrow's events. He even walked along the ramparts of the stronghold for a while, something he'd not done in months. He enjoyed the sharp contrast of the straight white walls to the dark volcanic rock they sank into. He looked down over the wall and felt the giddiness of height. It was a straight drop on all sides.

The ancient Wizards, who had built this keep, had used the entire top of a mountain. It was the perfect stronghold. Their magic had woven shields around it to protect them from attack. No human eyes had ever seen this place. He felt safe.

Aramel went back inside and looked over his preparations one more time. His past defeats had taught him caution. This time, he'd have his egg, even if he had to put up with the boy until he found the right spell. There were other books of magic deep in the vaults. There he would find an answer. And the Gold dragon would finally be his!

Chapter 17

Dursdan wove through the crowd with Damitri on one side and Lorad on the other. He was far more comfortable being with the winglings who were closer to him in age. They were enjoying the event as well. Yellow Cari rested on the roof of the blacksmith shop while Blue Miniki curled around the bell tower of the meeting hall. In the back of his mind, he listened to their comments about the crowd. He was grateful the rest of the people couldn't hear the young dragons.

He felt the pouches of seeds tucked in his pocket. One was for Conor as his Day Natal gift. He scanned the crowd looking for Samal. He'd promised the man a bag of seed to repay the damage the gnomes had done to his grain stores. He briefly wondered how Ferdj and his little tribe were getting along.

Damitri tapped him on the shoulder. "Looks like Andomy has a stand set up. Lets go see what wonders he's put together tonight."

"I remember my Day Natal, Andomy built a dragon out of sweet pastry." Lorad looked toward the booth. "I think I ate too much of it, though."

"That's evident!" Damitri patted his friend's stomach.

Dursdan smiled at their banter. He remembered when they were in school with him. They had always been a pair, like he and Conor. He looked around for his friend. He spied Conor with a cluster of girls around him. Every eligible farm girl was here tonight. All except one. Mirana had not been able to come tonight. Her mother had needed her help.

Lorad shoved a fancy pastry into his hand. "You've got try this! It's as light as air." It was evident by the smudges of soft sugar around his mouth, that he'd already sampled a few.

Damitri laughed. "If you keep eating like that, Miniki will never be able to get you home!" The Blue echoed the thought.

Dursdan covered his laugh by popping the fresh dainty into his mouth. It was sweet and melted on his tongue. He smiled at the baker. "That's quite a treat, Andomy. How did you come up with that idea?"

"Oh, you think this is something? Wait until you see what I've got for your Day Natal tomorrow!" Andomy winked. "I've been working on it for the past couple of days. It's a good thing your cows make such fine cream and your chickens lay such good eggs."

The sweet pastry curdled in his stomach. He didn't want to think about tomorrow. He glanced around, still searching for Samal.

Someone tapped him on the shoulder. Dursdan turned around and found Jacobi grinning at him. "I know it's Conor's Day Natal but I have something for you. I know I should wait until tomorrow and all, but I wanted you to be able to wear it." He held out a small box.

Dursdan took it. "Are you sure you want me to open it now?"

"Oh, please do. I've been waiting forever to give it to you. I'd like to see your expression when you see it."

"Well, all right." Dursdan opened the box and gasped. "The stone!" He remembered the day he and Jacobi had found it. They'd gone up the river to go fishing and turned up a small side creek. A glitter in the pebbles of the creek bed had caught his eye and he'd waded in to retrieve it. "But where has it been all these years?"

Jacobi laughed. "Remember, you gave it to me to carry because your pocket had a hole. I tore the trousers I was wearing and tossed them into the rag pile when I took them off. A few months ago, my Pa asked me to fetch a rag, and what should I grab, but those very trousers. And the stone was still in the pocket. I had Arazan set it. Do you like it?"

Dursdan held up the fine chain so that he could admire the binding the blacksmith had used to hold the stone. Cari whispered in his mind. *"What do you have, Lord Dursdan? I can see it from here. It glows!"*

Dursdan frowned and looked at the rock. It was shiny from being tossed by the stream. Small golden flecks seemed to float just below the surface. That was what had originally caught his eye. But it still looked like an ordinary rock.

"Don't you like it?"

"Oh, Jacobi, it's splendid! I was just remembering that day, that's all."

Jacobi grinned. "Well, you can't catch a fish everyday. Just because I came home with a full string and you came home with naught." He laughed.

Lorad put his hand on Dursdan's shoulder. "Something is up with the dragons."

Dursdan paid attention to the whispers in the back of his mind. Cari and Miniki were both commenting on the stone. He looked up at the Blue. *What do you see?*

"I see a glow. Not like light. Something else." Miniki paused. *"Something deep."*

Dursdan shook his head. "It looks like an ordinary stone to me."

Jacobi's face fell. "I'm sorry. I just thought it would remind you of the good times we used to have."

"No, I love the gift. You don't understand. The dragons see something in it." He put the stone back in the box and took his friend's hand. "I'm grateful that you remembered. Those were grand days, weren't they?"

Jacobi shrugged but smiled. "They were." He looked down at the egg and sighed. "I guess we won't be off fishing anymore."

"Don't be silly. We'll still have a chance to do some fishing. Why, I even found out that my Da likes to fish."

"Really? We'll have to show him our favorite spot sometime."

The people around them grew silent and looked up. A man nearby shook his head. "They've got their own party coming tomorrow. What are they up to dropping in on ours tonight?"

Trusumo invaded his thoughts. *"Dursdan, are you here somewhere?"*

Dursdan shook Jacobi's hand. "I don't know what's up but that was Lord Dorsadram that just flew over. I think we'd better go see."

"I'm sorry I'll miss your party tomorrow. It's a shame that it's during the day. I never understood that. Why do only the Lords have their sons' Day Natals during the day while everyone else has theirs at night?"

Dursdan shrugged. "I don't know. Maybe it's because of all the dragons that show up. The Lords don't want them blundering into each other in the dark."

"That must be it. The rest of us are sensible and party after we've finished the day's work." Jacobi grinned. "Good Day Natal, Dursdan."

Damitri pulled on Dursdan's arm. "Come on. Lord Dors landed by the smithy."

Dursdan followed Damitri through the mass of people with Lorad coming behind him. *What does Dors want, Tru?*

"He has no idea why we are here. I brought him. I was listening to the young ones talk about the stone. You must show it to him."

Dursdan shook his head. "Well, this should be interesting."

They found Dorsadram talking to Arazan near the door of the blacksmith shop. The Head of the Circle looked up as they approached. "Oh good, Dursdan. Maybe you can tell me what's gotten into him. He got all agitated and when I went to see what the problem was, he nearly shoved me on his back. And we came here. What is going on?"

Dursdan lifted the stone out of the box by the chain and held it up. "It's because of this." He handed it to Dorsadram. "The winglings said it glowed."

Trusumo leaned over from the shadows and looked down at the stone his rider held. Dorsadram shook his head. "It's beautiful but I don't see any glow. It looks like a sparkly rock. Could they have been seeing the light reflected off the surface? It is shiny."

Dursdan looked up at the Red. He was staring at the stone. "What do you see?"

"Power. This is no ordinary stone. Where did it come from?"

"I found it in a creek a couple of years ago while Jacobi and I were out fishing. I gave it to him to carry and we both forgot about it. He found it a couple of months ago."

Arazan touched the chain. "I remember this. Jacobi brought it in and asked me to set it. I thought it was interesting because I couldn't get a firm set on the stone without using gold for the band. The silver seemed to melt away."

Dorsadram looked at it closely. "It couldn't be!" He looked around. "Ara, may we step into the shop where there's more light?"

"Of course." He looked up at the dragon. "But I don't think he'll fit through the door."

"He'll probably just poke his head in. I want a closer look. If this is what I think it is, it's quite a find." He looked over at Dursdan. "How long ago did you find this?"

Dursdan shrugged. "I don't know, maybe two years ago. Why?"

"Hm. There's more to you than meets the eye, lad. Come in and see."

They stepped into the smithy and Arazan brought a bright torch. "I use it for fine work when I really need to see the detail. It's actually a type of metal that's burning. My Pa invented it."

"A good invention." Dorsadram held the stone up in the light. Tiny motes seemed to dance around the room. "Amazing!" He looked at Dursdan. "Do you know what you've found?"

"I get the feeling it's more than a pretty rock."

The old Lord nodded. "In a way, it belongs to you anyway. I believe that this is the Eye that was given to Zaradan by Altimon the White. It was a wedding present when the First Head married the Wizard's daughter, Korithiena."

Dursdan thought back to the sketch on the page of Armia's book and gasped. "He used to wear it around his neck in a tight band!"

"How did you know that?"

"From a picture that Korithiena drew of him." Dursdan looked at the stone. "I just remember seeing the glitter in the bottom of the stream. I was curious and picked it up."

Dorsadram nodded. "No one knows what became of it. That may have been near the very place where he died. The trolls had advanced well into the northern end of the valley by the end of the war." He held the stone out to him. "Take the stone and hold it in your hands."

Dursdan took the chain and looked at all the faces, human and dragon, that were watching. What were they expecting? He shrugged and took the stone in his hand.

The room changed. He could see every angle of every plane in acute detail. The forge glowed with heat even though the coals had been turned for the night. The lamp Arazan had brought over glowed a bright blue. The people also glowed, as did Trusumo's head. But most of all, the strongest glow came from the egg in his pouch. It radiated a brilliant golden light that enveloped him where he stood.

He could hear Trusumo, not just in the back of his mind, but as if they stood in the Mists together. "*What do you see?*"

"Don't you see it, too?"

"*All I see is you glowing.*" The dragon turned his head and looked at him. "*You spoke in the elder tongue. I did not know you knew that language.*"

"I'm speaking as I always have spoken."

"*To you, perhaps, but to all other ears, they can not understand what you say. I know it because I remember. It was taught to the First dragons by the Wizards of the West. It is ancient and steeped with magic.*"

Dursdan let go of the stone and turned to the Red. "I don't like magic."

The people around him were all staring. Finally Dorsadram spoke. "What words did you say?"

Dursdan shook his head and looked at the stone. "Trusumo claims it's some elder tongue. I don't know. I didn't hear it any differently than how I normally talk."

Arazan shook his head. "I've never heard words like that before."

"Put it on around your neck. See if it has the same effect."

Dursdan looked at the stone. If it was magical, he'd rather not have it around his neck. But the Head of the Circle was adamant. So he put it on. Nothing happened. "Does my speech sound odd?"

They shook their heads and Dorsadram nodded. "And this may have been why Zaradan wore it around his neck. It must be only effective when held in the hand." Dursdan moved to take it off but the Lord stopped him. "No, Dur. Keep it on. Under the circumstances, it may very well protect you."

Dursdan slipped the stone under his tunic. It felt warm against his skin. He felt her reach out to touch it and wanted to cry. She had truly come out of hiding. He looked up at Trusumo. The Red had a soft smile on his face. "*She stirs. All is well.*" The Red withdrew his head from the shop.

"Well, I should go out and find Conor. It is his Day Natal."

Dorsadram nodded and looked at the wingling riders. "Stay close to Dur but let the lad have some privacy. You don't have to dance with him."

Damitri and Lorad exchanged glances. Damitri bowed. "We'll keep an eye on him, sir."

Dursdan left with the two riders in his wake. The party was in full swing now. He noticed that Steban and his father had a good-sized ensemble playing. He liked the tune. He noticed Conor near the steps of the gazebo and headed in that direction. Several girls were still gathered around Conor. Dursdan looked at his friend's face. He had a good idea who would stand beside him on the platform soon.

Ragan appeared in front of him, blocking his path. "What are you doing here? This is a farmers' celebration." He looked at the two wingling riders behind him. "Stick to your own."

Dursdan shook his head. He thought back to what Mirana had discovered about their families. "It's a shame that blood relation should carry such an old feud for so long."

"What are you talking about? What feud?"

"Didn't your Da ever tell you why he disliked my family so much? Didn't you ever wonder?"

Ragan looked back into the crowd. Doran stood near Conor's father in animated conversation. "He hates your Pa because of some cattle he had to give up."

"Is that what he told you? But we have our own herd. We don't take cattle from anyone except in fair exchange. This has nothing to do with your Da or mine. It goes back several generations. Why should we fight over something that is long past?"

Ragan looked confused. "You seem to know what it's all about. So tell me."

"Your great granddad was Aradan, the brother of Sitrodan, my two Greats granddad. Aradan was angry when the rules where changed concerning the dragons. He wanted to be a Lord but because he was still young and hadn't received his egg yet, his nephew, Mertrodan, received the egg instead."

"Do you mean we are family?" He started to laugh. "What dung!"

"Is it? Have you ever seen your Da and mine together? They look a lot alike. We are distant cousins, whether you like it our not. And I won't fight with you. I've always been taught that family stands together."

Ragan stared at him. "Our family fought over a dragon egg? Can you prove this?"

Dursdan looked around and noticed Frecha sitting in the shadows of the platform with a book in her lap. "I bet she could." He pointed in her direction. "If I'm not mistaken, she's looking up family ties right now for Conor so his Choice can be approved. Ask her to show you the House of Dan. You will see your family and mine are both the same."

Ragan had an odd expression on his face. Dursdan couldn't imagine what was going through his mind. Ragan took a final look back at his father then started off toward Frecha.

Lorad sighed. "If it's not as you say, he's liable to come back and pound you."

"But it is the truth. Armia kept track of all the families in her book." He looked around at the happy people dancing and laughing together. "We all came from the same roots. Good roots."

A shout went up from the gazebo. Shanan, Conor's father, stood holding up his hands to get everyone's attention. "Thanks to all of you for joining us this night on my son's Day Natal. It's an important event for every boy as he steps into adulthood and takes up the responsibilities of a man." He turned and looked at Conor. "A man has to have a good partner to walk with him through life. Conor, whom do you choose to ask?"

Conor walked forward and looked across the crowd. There was a silent anticipation in the assembly. He smiled and held out his hand. "I choose Daltrica, daughter of Mondasal."

The crowd broke into wild applause and cheers. Daltrica took his hand and joined him on the platform. Her face was radiant in the subdued light. Dursdan glanced over at the potter. Both Mondasal and his father, Salamond, had broad grins on their faces. It would be a good match. Both families were happy. He noticed that Frecha was nodding. She approved it as well. He also saw that Ragan had found his way to her side. Perhaps there was hope after all.

The dancing began in earnest. Dursdan passed up any requests.

He finally got to Conor's side. Conor had Daltrica on his lap and they were both laughing. Dursdan patted him on the shoulder. "Good luck to you, Con."

His friend looked up and smiled. "Glad you could make it. And thank you." He looked behind Dursdan and waved. "I see Dimi and Lo came with you."

Dursdan frowned. "Not by choice, I'm sure. I think they've been bored most of the night. I'm afraid I'll have to leave soon but I have something for you." Dursdan pulled out a small leather bag. "It's for your first crop."

Conor smiled. "Some of your best seed, no doubt. I'm honored. You always have the best yields on your crops. I hope you'll show me some of your tricks."

"Come by this fall and I'll show you what I look for." Dursdan held out his hand and Conor shook it. "As always, my friend." Dursdan bowed and backed away so others could come forward to congratulate the young man.

He began moving away from the center of the group toward the edge. Ragan stopped him. "You were right. She showed me in the book." His voice was very quiet. "I'm sorry I've been such a pud about it all."

Dursdan shook his head. "You didn't know. And I'm honestly wondering if your Da even knows or if he's just carrying what his Da may have told him. But we aren't our ancestors." He smiled remembering Trusumo's words. "And we can change." He held his hand out to Ragan.

Ragan looked at him for a moment then shook his hand. "Cousin." He smiled shyly and for a moment, his face looked a lot like Tolanar's.

Dursdan grinned. "Cousin." He looked back at Conor. "I gave Con some of my best reserve seed as a gift. I still have some extra corn seed. Would you like to try it?"

Ragan's face brightened. "I've always admired your fields and wondered how you got such good crops. Our corn didn't do well last year."

"What did you rotate it with?"

"Rotate it?"

Dursdan fished out the bag he had intended to give to Samal and handed it to Ragan. "Try this. Plant it where you had beans grow last year. See how it does."

Ragan took the pouch. "Thanks, I will." He looked back at the party. "Looks like things are really moving now." He turned back and grinned. "I bet your Day Natal tomorrow will be grand, too. Good luck."

Dursdan nodded and watched Ragan fade into the crowd. He sighed. Wait until Mirana heard about this. She'd regret not having been able to come tonight. He started walking toward the bridge. Lorad tapped him on the shoulder. "Do you want a ride? Miniki could carry us both. He's gotten quite strong."

Dursdan looked back to where the Blue sat on the smithy roof, next to Yellow Cari. *Please take no offense.* "I appreciate your offer but I don't want to cause any harm to your dragon. I think you may be a challenge for him as it is."

Damitri and the dragons laughed but Lorad looked disappointed. "I know we're suppose to watch over you."

A large form flew overhead. Lorad looked up, startled. Dursdan felt Sinotio in his mind. "*I will carry you home.*"

Dursdan shook his head. "Sino, does Da know you're here?"

The Silver landed and pranced up lightly. He was grinning. "*I am testing my wing. It is much better now. Come. We will fly!*"

Dursdan sighed and looked back at the wingling riders. They both stood staring at the large Silver. Damitri shook his head. "Where's Merg? Dragons don't fly without their riders."

"So I've been told." Dursdan laughed. "Well, you'd better call your dragons if you want to keep up with us." He looked up at Sinotio. "He's been perched too long." He carefully mounted the Silver and waited for the Blue and Yellow to land and accept their riders.

The three dragons jumped into the sky, almost as one. Dursdan remembered to keep his eyes open. The darkened Valley below was covered with tiny lights. These were the souls of the Valley; the descendants of those who had made this place their home. He laid his head along side of the strong silver neck.

Sinotio purred. "*It is good. I feel her. She is well. She likes to fly.*"

Dursdan put a hand on the egg pouch. He could feel a soft tingle where they touched. A very quiet giggle echoed in the back of his mind. Dursdan smiled.

Sinotio circled the house on the hill and landed gently in the courtyard. Mergadan stood in the doorway. "I was wondering where he'd gone off to." He walked up and helped Dursdan dismount. "Are you all right?"

"I'm fine, Da." He looked up as Cari and Miniki circled. He waved. "My thanks to both of you for your company this evening."

"They can't hear you from here, Dur."

The Yellow and Blue dipped and turned toward their respective homes. "The dragons could." He looked at his father and smiled. "Conor had a great Day Natal. He chose Daltrica, daughter of Mondasal the Potter. They'll be a good couple."

Mergadan grinned. "Your Ma is still fretting over your choice. She had been hoping that you'd pick Ashandra."

"I hadn't missed all the hints but I've already made my choice, and I'm afraid Ma will be disappointed. Ashandra and I have nothing in common."

Mergadan shrugged. "She's pretty."

"She is also empty-headed. I've known her all my life. She knows nothing of farming and hates dirt." He pointed at the walls of the courtyard. "We have land and fields to tend and I'm going to be busy with a dragon soon. I'm going to need a wife who's not just pretty, but useful and smart."

Sinotio chuckled. *"And she is all of those things. She is a good choice for you."*

"Thanks, Sino. I just hope Ma agrees with you."

Mergadan looked up at his Silver. "I don't suppose you could give me a hint." The dragon snorted. "What's that all about?"

Dursdan looked at his father. "He's laughing at you." He smiled. "How's Tola getting on?"

"Well enough. He's staying with Natalo. That Red won't let him out of his sight." He shook his head. "I think he's sleeping outside with him."

Dursdan softly reached out to touch Natalo. *Is all well?*

"We are. You should sleep. I will walk with you in the Mists."

Dursdan nodded. "They're both fine. Well, I'd better get some sleep. Tomorrow's a big day."

Mergadan smiled and put an arm around his son's shoulders. "Yes it is."

Dursdan lit a candle and took it into his room. He noticed that the clothes his mother had made were neatly draped over his chair. He touched the fabric. It was soft to the touch. He wondered who had made it. The colors were unique. He'd never seen gold or silver cloth before. Maybe Tresel had something to do with it.

Dursdan blew out the light, changed, and sunk into bed. He closed his eyes and drifted into the Mists. Timotha and Sinotio were already there. They sat together, arms around each other, talking softly. Dursdan didn't want to disturb them.

He was surprised to see Menatash. "How are you? You've been gone for some time."

Menatash looked up and smiled. "I've been in the library most nights. I dare not go there in the day. My father would want to know what I'm looking at. For some reason, my grandmother said I should keep it a secret."

"Did you find anything interesting?" Dursdan pulled up a cloud and sat down.

"I did." Menatash opened a window. A scene from an old book appeared. It looked familiar.

Dursdan gasped. "The very first war that the Dragon Lords fought!"

Menatash looked at him. "You've seen the picture before?"

"Yes, in Great Gran Armia's book." He called up a window of his own and pulled the image from his memory. It looked much like the image in Menatash's window.

Menatash shook his head. "It wasn't our war, and it wasn't even the first. The elves and trolls had been fighting for centuries. I'm not sure how the Wizards got involved. It took me forever to figure out who the Wizards were. They looked human in all the pictures."

"Weren't they human?"

"Partly. It seems that back then, some elves and humans got together and had children. It wasn't accepted by either side but love knows no boundaries. Their children were unusual. They appeared human but had the ability to control magic, like the elves. They became the Wizards."

"Maybe their elven relatives asked for help with the battle."

"I'm afraid it's worse than that." He flipped through the pages. "The Wizards were forced to live in exile but not all of them were happy about it. They were angry with their parents for making them outcasts. They kind of formed their own group high in the eastern mountains."

"The Eastern Wizards."

"Yes. The other Wizards lived in the western mountains near your Valley. They were the ones who helped the elves. The got involved because the Eastern Wizards had started helping the trolls. That's when the war began affecting the Kingdoms of Men. The Eastern Wizards wanted revenge on their human and elven ancestors."

Dursdan shook his head. "It always seems to come down to something that happened long ago. It's the same here in the Valley. Old animosities are passed along from one generation to the next until the real cause is long forgotten. Only the anger remains."

Menatash nodded. "It's the same everywhere, I'd imagine. It's just the way humans are. It took my family forever to reunite the Three Kingdoms. I'm sure it was something stupid that broke them apart in the beginning and no one remembers what it was. They were just set in their ways. My father had to marry my mother to bring the Kingdom of Zarimundi together with Eldramith and Falendor. And I've learned that there was some fighting along the way. Change is never easy."

Dursdan looked down at his brightly glowing stomach. He was changing, too, and it certainly wasn't easy. He looked up as the Mists parted and Natalo joined them. He bowed. Dursdan smiled at the Red. "Good Dreams, how fair you?"

"We are well." He looked over at Menatash and bowed politely.

Dursdan grinned over at Menatash. "You missed a grand occasion. All of the dragons in the Valley were in the Mists at one time. This is Natalo, the Red of Lord Tolatrom." The name still sounded odd to him.

Menatash rose and bowed formally. "I am honored to meet you, sir, and most disappointed that I missed your full company. Will you join us?"

Natalo smiled and created a cloud couch to his liking. "I see our baby Gold is better tonight." He looked at Dursdan and tilted his head. "And there is something different about you." He reached out a hand and gently touched Dursdan's neck. "I feel a strong power that has not been there before."

Dursdan touched the spot. He could feel the warmth through his fingertips. "It's a stone. Dors called it an Eye. I guess it belonged to Zaradan long ago."

Natalo gasped. "You found the Eye?"

"A couple of years ago, actually." He told them about the fishing adventure and the recent gift from Jacobi.

Natalo nodded. "It was lost during the battle. Some believe that is why he died. Many searched for it but it was never found. Perhaps it was because they searched for the wrong reason, or maybe because it needed a special touch."

Menatash looked up and stood. "Lady Timotha, Lord Sinotio. I'm glad you joined us."

Sinotio winked at Dursdan and sat next to Timotha on a cloud she formed. "Forgive us for not doing so sooner but we had much to catch up on." He ran his hand through her long white hair. "I will be so glad when you finally arrive."

She shook her head. "I have had a terrible time with Vari. I just cannot seem to get him to understand that we need to fly at night. We did not start out until late afternoon but he wanted to stop again when it got too dark to see the ground. I am not sure the place we are in is safe."

Dursdan shook his head. "It's a shame we don't know where you are." He looked at Menatash. "Wait a minute. Timotha, you showed me an image of a city. Can you show it to Menatash? He might recognize it."

She formed a window and they all leaned forward. Menatash gasped. "That's Ranquin, on the boundaries of Falendor! I've been there a few times with my parents." He readjusted his own window to show a map. He pointed to a large city. "Here it is." He made the window bigger and the map smaller. "And if I'm not mistaken, your Valley is somewhere in these mountains."

There was a collective groan as they all realized how far apart the two places were. Timotha sighed. "There is still so much land to cover. We still fly over cultivated lands. When will they end?"

Menatash studied the map. "You must be here, the great farmlands of Falendor. Much of the food for the Three Kingdoms is grown there." He studied the route and bit his lip. "You still have a long way to go north and east. If you went farther east first, you'd eventually come to the end of the farms but there is a desert beyond. The farmers must irrigate these outer fields. They bring the water all the way from this river."

Timotha shook her head. "I can do without water for a few days but Vari cannot. There are more large cities to the west. We dare not go that way. We will have to stay with the fields."

"It should only be a few more days, if I understand correctly where you are. Then you will be in the foothills. There are very few settlements in that area and there are more wooded spots for you to hide in. Can't you just refuse to fly until nightfall and then refuse to land?"

"Refuse my rider? That is unthinkable. He has had a great deal of patience with me as it is. He still has no idea why we are traveling or where we are going. But he is very brave and comes with me anyway. But I could never refused him."

Menatash looked at her. "What if he asked you to turn back?"

Timotha looked at Sinotio and tears welled in her eyes. "Every day I feel the burning growing hotter. I fear what will happen if I do not reach the Valley in time."

Sinotio held her. "Then I would come to you."

"You would leave your rider?"

He shrugged. "If it must be."

Dursdan had listened quietly. "Why don't I tell Da what's going on? He knows that I can hear you. That way, if you have to go, you can take him with you and he could help Vari the rest of the way."

All the dragons stared at him. Menatash grinned. "Sometimes I think they forget we aren't dragons."

Sinotio glanced back at the Mists. "He stirs early today. I must go, my love. Do not lose hope. I will come if you call." He reluctantly let her go and got up. He looked down at Dursdan. "Speak to him of Timotha. Tell Merg that I honor our bond but I love her and if she needs me, I must go to her."

Dursdan nodded. "I will." He watched the Silver disappear through the Mists. He looked at the others. "Then I too should go. Is Tola planning to come, Natalo?"

The Red chuckled. "As if he would miss your Day Natal." He rose and bowed. "I will see you there."

Timotha smiled at the boys. "Thank you both for your help. We shall all succeed. Good luck to you on this day, Lord Dursdan. May you choose well and wisely."

Dursdan nodded. "Don't worry. I've found the right one." He looked over at Menatash. "Until we dream together again."

Menatash rose and held out his hand. "Until then."

Dursdan turned and parted the Mists. He opened his eyes. Dawn was just breaking. He could hear voices in the hall. "You don't have to whisper. I'm awake."

There was a slight tapping on his doorframe and Carala peered around the drape. "Am I disturbing you?"

"No, Gran, come in." He pulled himself up slightly in bed, readjusting the weight of the egg. He would need to get fresh pads soon.

She sat down beside him. "I wanted to show you the finished blanket. It's for your girl."

He ran his hand across the even tight stitches. It was an intricate pattern of golden dragons on a sky blue field. "You used the yarn I brought you from town."

Carala smiled. "Yes, it was much better quality than anything I had in storage." She took his hand gently in hers. "How are you feeling today?"

He looked at her and noticed the deep lines of her face, highlighted by the shadows of the early morning sunlight streaming in through the open windows. Had she forgiven him? "I'm sorry about the other night."

She shook her head. "Sometimes the truth is hard to hear." She looked down at their hands. "You are young but you have a deeper wisdom that far surpasses your years. Korenthiena was right." She looked up at Dursdan. "You are destined for greatness."

He felt uncomfortable and touched the egg pouch. "She's a little cool. I'd better hurry and get up. These pads need to be changed."

Carala let go of his hand and patted his arm. "Oh, of course, well, get yourself up and get dressed. Don't worry about things. Merg did the morning chores. I'll bring the blanket along to town."

"Thanks, Gran." He kissed her on the cheek and she got up and left. He dressed in the new clothes his mother had made and tucked the stone under the shirt. He'd wear it to please Jacobi. He also discovered a new matching egg pouch under the other things. He carefully moved the egg from the old pouch to the new one. The patterns swirled around his fingers as if teasing them. Dursdan chuckled. "Sorry, we don't have time to play right now. Let's get you some warm pads."

Dursdan headed for the kitchen. Dachia was busy packing a large basket of baked goods. She glanced over at him as he scooped up a new warming pad and dropped the used one into the basket. "You look nice." Her voice was tense.

Dursdan sighed. He'd almost forgotten about the spoiled tea party. Evidently, his mother hadn't. "The new egg pouch fits well."

"Aber brought it over last night while you were gone. It seems Kalista has a new loom and she made it for you." Her voice was harsh.

"It goes with the clothes you made. Were you talking colors with her, too?"

Dachia shook her head. "She just seemed to know. Maybe Mirana mentioned it." She finished the basket and pushed the edges of a towel down inside to trap the food. "Do you suppose they will come to your Day Natal?"

"I hope so." He took a sweet roll from the tray.

She stood staring at the packaged food, wringing her hands. "You're not going to ask Ashandra, are you?"

"No, Ma." Dursdan watched her for a moment. He couldn't be certain but he thought she might be crying. "I'm sorry, but this is my choice."

"Yes, of course."

"Have you seen Da?"

"He's out in the courtyard with Sinotio."

Dursdan hugged his mother. She felt stiff in his arms. He shrugged and left the house. Mergadan was brushing the Sliver with a long handled broom. Sinotio nearly jumped off the rock when he saw Dursdan. "*You will tell him?*"

Dursdan laughed. "Yes, Sinotio. I'll tell him."

"Good! He's nearly trampled me several times this morning. What's on his mind?" Mergadan put down the broom and stared at the dragon. "I'd swear it was his Day Natal instead of yours."

"Hmm, your not far off the mark. Maybe you'd better come sit down." Dursdan motioned to the small table and chairs by the wall. Mergadan frowned but followed his son. Dursdan looked up at the Silver. "Sinotio has a girl on his mind."

Mergadan's brows went up. "Who?"

"Her name is Timotha. It's a very long story. She's coming to this Valley from a long ways to the south. Her rider's name is Varimato."

"I've never heard of him but the dragon's name is somehow familiar."

"That's not surprising. She left the Valley a long time ago. You'll find her story in Armia's book. I can show you later."

"How can she be so old and still be alive?" Then he stared at Dursdan. "This has something to do with Natalo and Tola, doesn't it?"

Dursdan nodded. "Timotha has been passed from one generation to the next. Varimato is her sixth rider, counting Voramato and his sister, Zamisha."

"Those names I remember. Zamisha took Voramato's dragon and killed the Troll King in the first Great War. But that was a long time ago."

"Dragons aren't supposed to age the way humans do." Dursdan paused to let his father consider this. "The Wizards who gave the dragons to the Lords didn't want the dragons to live to maturity."

"Why? That's horrible." He looked over at Sinotio. "I would want my dragon to live to his full potential."

"I'm not sure how long that is. A female dragon doesn't become fertile until she's 80 years old." Dursdan sighed. "And the Wizards did have their reasons. Consider how many eggs a dragon lays. I've wondered for some time now why there aren't more wild dragons."

Sinotio shrugged. "*Maybe something eats their eggs. We found all those other ones crushed.*"

Dursdan shook his head. "No, I'm certain now that it was Aramel who destroyed those other eggs. He wanted this one."

"I thought it was odd that so many males were chasing that Golden queen. Usually only a few males go after a female."

"Maybe with fewer males, there are fewer eggs."

"That's a possibility. I've never seen another nest." He grinned. "I only have one firstborn son."

Dursdan looked up at Sinotio. "Well, we may be the first to find out. She's coming here because she wants to mate with Sinotio. I guess you could say he's made a choice, too."

Mergadan gasped. "Sinotio?"

The dragon smiled and stretched out his wings proudly. *"She has chosen me!"*

"Well, I'll be."

"There's more to it than that, Da. She's having a hard time getting here, with the difficult lands they have to pass through and her rider not really understanding. She has to mate or she might die. And her time may be running out. Sinotio wants you to understand, if he has to leave to meet her."

"I will come with you." Mergadan got up and went to his dragon. Sinotio lowered his head and rested it on his rider's shoulder. The Lord stroked it gently. "We have been through much together, you and I. We have battled angry Wizards and fierce trolls. If you must go to your new mate so that she can survive, then I will come with you." He hugged the Silver's neck.

Dachia came out the door with Carala and stopped. "Did we miss something?"

Dursdan grinned and wiped a tear from the corner of his eye. His father looked at him. "It seems both our boys should be celebrating today." He patted Sinotio. "You will let me know, yes?"

The dragon nodded. He looked at Dursdan. *"He understands!"*

"Yes, he does." He took the basket from his mother. "Would you like me to drive you and Gran into town?"

"I can manage the wagon. I thought you might like to fly in with your Da. It's tradition, you know."

He didn't miss the tone in her voice. Dursdan looked over at Mergadan and Sinotio. "Ah, tradition." He sighed. "Well, can't go breaking with tradition now, can we." He felt a very tiny giggle in the back of his mind and laughed. "It seems she wants to fly, too."

Sinotio jumped down from his rock and Mergadan mounted, holding out a hand for his son. "Climb up then. Mustn't disappoint her." He made Dursdan comfortable in front of him and waved to his wife and mother. "We'll see you in town."

They launched into the sky. Sinotio was singing! "*What a grand day to be aloft. Look at the sky, Dur. Have you every seen it so blue?*"

Dursdan felt his own excitement blend with that of the Silver's. "It is grand!" He looked down over the fields. He could see his mother and grandmother moving down the lane. He followed the road. Aber was standing at the head of his lane waving his arms frantically. A dark heaviness tightened his stomach. "Something is wrong." He pointed at Aber and Sinotio dove toward the farmer. The Silver pulled up at the last moment and made a perfect landing before the startled man.

The minute the dragon was still, Aber rushed forward. "Dur, something's happened to Mirana. I can't find her anywhere."

Dursdan jumped down. "Did you try the loft?"

"Aye, it was the first place I looked. I'm worried sick and so is her Mum. We were all going to ride into town together for your Day Natal celebration."

Something in the distance caught his attention. He looked toward the tree. Was she standing there? He looked at Sinotio. "You have better sight than I do, Sino. Is that her?"

The dragon looked. "*She stands under the tree.*" The dragon snorted. "*Something is wrong.*"

Dursdan started running. He heard his father and Aber calling. He felt Sinotio gain the air and fly with him. Other dragons echoed concern. Trusumo called, "*We are coming.*"

Because of the branches, the large dragon had to circle around before he could land. Dursdan reached her first. "Mirana!"

She remained still. Dursdan's stomach became a burning rock. His skin tingled and he tasted a strange metallic tinge on his tongue. "Aramel!" Dursdan whirled around looking for the Wizard.

Sinotio paced around the tree sniffing. "*He is here. I smell him.*"

Dursdan came back to Mirana. He reached out and gently touched her. He could see that she was breathing. He tried to shake her. "Mirana, wake up."

"It's no use, boy. You can't wake her."

Dursdan spun around and faced the Wizard. "What have you done to her?"

"Oh, I've done nothing drastic, just a little sleep spell. She'll wake from it in short order."

"If I were you, I'd leave this Valley and never return. The dragons will tear you shreds, just like the troll you sent."

Aramel's brows went up. "How did you know that?"

"Release her from this spell!" Dursdan advanced on him.

The Wizard laughed. "Foolish boy. As if you would understand the ways of Wizards. This has nothing to do with the pale insignificant daughters of farmers." Aramel grabbed Dursdan's shoulder. "It is you I want!"

Dursdan tried to pull away but his arm screamed in pain. He could hear all the dragons of the Valley echo their battle cry. Sinotio crashed through the branches of the tree, reaching for the Wizard. "*I come!*"

Aramel screamed. "You won't cheat me again!"

Before Dursdan could do anything, the world seemed to slip away around him. It was as if everything was growing smaller. Looking down, he realized he was somehow being pulled away. He watched in silent frustration as Sinotio snapped at empty air, Mirana awoke, and Mergadan screamed his name. He wanted to call back. Then the world slipped into utter darkness.

* * *

Aramel pulled the next book off the stack and began flipping through the pages. He had tried every spell he could think of. The egg would not let him touch it. He looked over at the crumpled form of the boy, still unconscious, clutching the egg. It was bound to him in a deeper way than any egg should have been. Aramel growled in frustration. Perhaps it was the deep magic of the golden dragon. But then there must be a spell to unbind it.

He shoved the volume aside and grabbed another. More of the same. There were plenty of references to caring for the eggs and raising the hatchlings, tips on training the winglings, and flight techniques for the grown dragons but nothing spoke of how to break the bond. He slammed the book closed.

He collapsed into his chair and reached for his staff, strengthening the light spell. He was going to have to dig deeper and that meant a trip down to the vault. Aramel groaned. All those steps. He wished for the thousandth time that he could just portal down there. But the protection spells prevented that. Meant to keep out other rival Wizards, no doubt. Aramel snorted. Not as if he had that problem. Curse the Others for abandoning him in this pit!

But he would have his way out soon. With a golden dragon, he'd have the power to open the portal. The Keeper the Western Gate would knock it down!

The boy stirred in the cell. He would be waking soon. Aramel briefly wondered if he could just kill the boy but wasn't sure of the results. He didn't want to risk harming the precious golden dragonling. No, that meant he'd have to feed the captive as well. Bother. He got up and went to his pantry. What do you feed a captive? Stale bread and bones. No. Must keep the little dragon happy. He took down some powders from his shelves and sprinkled them on his workbench. He chanted a few words and conjured a plate of food fit to eat. For the boy, anyway. Aramel would dine on better food later.

The Wizard left the plate on the floor where the boy could reach it and moved a bucket of water there as well. He contemplated eating before his descent but decided to wait. It would be a victory dinner.

Chapter 18

Dursdan woke with a start. Every part of his body ached. He opened his eyes to utter darkness and panicked. He touched the pouch. The egg was still there. He felted around with his hands and discovered the dimensions of his prison. It was smaller than his bed back home.

His head rang with a strange buzz. He reached out for the dragons. *Sinotio? Trusumo? Where are you?*

But there was no reply. Just the buzz. He sat up, leaned against a wall, and curled into a protective circle around the egg. He could barely feel her. She must be terrified and gone back into hiding. He began to cry.

He eventually drifted off into a troubled sleep. The Mists were dark, not the airy white clouds that he was used to. Something was terribly wrong. He searched through them, shouting everyone's name he could think of but there were no replies.

He jumped with the clanging sound. There was light. His eyes blinked away the tear sand.

"Well, are you going to eat or starve? It doesn't matter to me. I don't care about you, only the egg."

Dursdan looked up at the Wizard. "What have you done? Where am I?"

Aramel cackled. "Bold questions for a prisoner. Why don't you just give me the egg and I will let you out."

"Never! She would never serve you. When the Lords find you, their dragons will tear you to shreds."

Aramel really laughed then. "Find me? Ha! No one has ever found this fortress. The Ancient Ones wove such spells around it that only a trained mage would stand a chance. And your puny Lords, with their weak little dragons, have no chance at all!" He looked down at Dursdan and seemed to grow in size. "Give me the egg!"

Dursdan looked at the Wizard. Why hadn't the old man just taken it? Unless he couldn't! That was it! He'd tried in Dursdan's room but she had fought back. That was his one hope. "She doesn't want you. She never will."

"Bah, what do you know of dragons, boy? Nothing! The first dragons were bound by magic therefore that binding can be undone by magic." Dursdan shrunk back against the wall. Aramel leaned closer. "But you don't like magic, do you." The Wizard produced a small bent stick and pointed it at him. "Give me the egg or I'll turn you into a rat!"

Dursdan hugged the egg protectively. "You won't do anything that might endanger the egg."

"Who says it will harm the egg." He thrust the stick out and said a few strange words. A golden glow appeared around him but nothing else.

The Wizard went into a rage. "Ah, you stupid beast! Why do you protect him? He's nothing but a useless human. I am a powerful Wizard. I could increase your potential! Let go of that whelp and join me. Together our power will be greater than any Wizard or dragon that has ever lived."

But the glow continued. He could feel her touching his mind, like tiny fingers gently exploring. Dursdan reached out and touched her. Her fingers encircled his within his mind. He looked up at the Wizard. "I will never let you harm her. Let us go now, while you still have a chance."

The Wizard shook his head. "It is you who are running out of time,

Little Lord." He picked up a book from a large stack. "I will find a way to undo this and then, you will die." Aramel turned away and ignored him.

Dursdan sank down against the wall of the cell and let his mind drift into the Mists. He knew she was there. He could see her form running through the dark shadowy tendrils, tinted gold by her presence. He sighed, pulled up a cloud chair and sank into it. He called up a window with his favorite memory of Mirana. "I hope you're all right." He tried to reach out and touch her but the image dissipated under his fingers.

Dursdan tucked his face in his arms and began to cry. Tiny fingers touched his arm and he looked up. A small girl with bright golden hair and shining yellow eyes stood in front of him. She had a look of uncertainty on her face. "You want Biyoni?"

Dursdan immediately reached down and enfolded her in his arms and pulled her into his lap. "Of course I do." He cried into her hair. "I've been so worried about you. Are you all right?"

"Biyoni is here."

"I know, little one." He hummed softly and rocked them both to sleep.

Dursdan lost track of time. There was no night or day in this place, only the light from the Wizard's staff when he was about. Aramel would occasionally stomp toward him, chant some strange words, and sometimes even throw odd smelling powders on him. But the effect was always the same. The golden glow shimmered around him. He could feel her with him. Afterward he'd sink into the Mists and she would be there waiting.

Hunger drove him to finally eat the food and, when no side affects manifested, accepted his daily rations without comment. Aramel made sure that the pads were always warm. Dursdan watched the Wizard carefully. Most of the time he was consumed by his books and paid no attention to him.

Sometimes he would disappear for extended periods. Dursdan was afraid that the Wizard would not return and he would starve to death in the tiny cell. But Aramel always returned, arms loaded with more dusty volumes.

Occasionally the Wizard would rant and rave, cursing some long gone predecessors. He'd go into a passionate furry and bang his staff on the floor, sending cascades of sparks sizzling to the ground. Dursdan huddled in the corner of his cell during these episodes, trying to stay as far away from the rampaging magic as possible.

There were always more books. Dursdan had never dreamed that so many volumes on anything existed, much less magic. Aramel would spend hours painstakingly reading each volume only to slam it shut in frustration.

The latest trip had produced only a single thick volume. Aramel had spent hours mumbling, while reading the tiny script. Dursdan had given up trying to make any sense of the strange words the Wizard used. He was more concerned that Aramel hadn't produced another warming pad in some time and the current one was getting cool.

He cleared his throat. "Excuse me."

"Huh? What do you want?" Aramel turned away from his book and stared at him.

"The egg is getting cold."

Aramel grumbled but got up and pulled a warmer from a basket. He spoke a few words in a different language, and held out the steaming pad.

Dursdan opened the sack and removed the cool one. Aramel leaned closer. "What does it see in you, boy? Why does it cling to you?" He shook his head and dropped the warmer on the egg. Then turned back to his book.

Something tickled Dursdan's mind. He could hear her whispery voice. "*Bad.*"

"She's afraid of you."

"What?"

A flash of memory, an old dream image, came back to Dursdan. "She knows what you did to the other eggs."

"How do you know about that?" Aramel left his book and came back toward the cell.

Dursdan stared at him. "She knows."

The Wizard's brow wrinkled and his eyes squinted. "And what would a young whelp like you know of dragons. You hate magic. You know nothing!"

"I know you smashed all the other eggs."

Aramel sneered at him. "Proves you know nothing. They were all insignificant. No Golds among them. The revealing spell shattered them because they weren't pure."

"But they were baby dragons."

"Ha! They were lesser colors, mostly blues, a few yellows, a red or two." He pointed at the egg sack. "That was the only Gold among them. And it should have been mine!"

Dursdan felt a rage unlike anything he had ever experienced. He pushed away from the wall and grabbed the bars of his cell. "How dare you judge those dragons! You had no right!"

"I had every right. I called those males to her. If it were not for my spell, there would have been no eggs at all. Therefore the eggs are mine, to do with as I choose."

"Not this egg."

The Wizard grabbed up his staff and whirled it over his head. "I'll turn you to dust!"

"She won't let you."

Aramel screamed and brought his staff down on the floor with a smack. The very stone seemed to cry out but nothing harmed Dursdan. The Wizard glared at him. "Be thankful I haven't found the unbinding spell yet, for when I do, you will wish I had just killed you!" He whirled away, ignoring Dursdan, and went back to his book.

Dursdan sank back down into the corner of the cell, utterly exhausted. He fell into a deep sleep. The darkened Mists swirled around him. At first he didn't notice the difference. He looked around expectantly. It was very gray and dismal. "Biyoni?"

Silence. His chest tightened. Where was she? He began to run through the Mists, searching for her. The gray tendrils seemed heavy as he pushed them aside. A brighter area appeared ahead and he rushed toward it.

Biyoni was lying on a pile of clouds, her normally bright glow very dim. Dursdan rushed to her side. "Biyoni! What's wrong?"

She looked up at him. "Out?"

"What?" Dursdan looked around trying to decide what she meant. Then a thought struck him. How long had they been in this place? He looked back at her. "Do you mean you need to hatch?"

She nodded weakly. "Out? Soon?"

"Not yet!" He gathered her into his arms. "Hang on a little longer.

I've got to find a way to get you out of here. It's no telling what Aramel would do to you if you hatched here."

"Bad."

"Yes, little one, he's bad."

Her fingers brushed across his chest and it glowed briefly. He looked down at himself. "What did you do?"

Biyoni shook her head. "Eye."

Dursdan gasped. He'd completely forgotten about the stone! He touched his chest and felt a warmth there. It began to spread outward and encompassed Biyoni. A little color returned to her fading cheeks. He looked down at her. "Don't worry. I'll get us out of here."

She reached to touch his face.

A loud shout shattered the Mists.

"Yes! This is it!"

Dursdan jerked awake. He could still feel the tentative touch. He had to get her out of here. He looked over at Aramel who was tapping a bony finger on a book. The Wizard's smile sent shivers through Dursdan's body. What had the Wizard found?

Aramel went to his shelves and began sorting out jars and boxes. He stacked some on the table and left others on the shelf in disarray. Every once in a while he would refer back to the book. Soon the pile on his table had grown considerably. He mumbled to himself as he worked. The words sounded strange.

Dursdan remembered the Mists and looked down at his stained shirt. He groaned. His mother had worked so hard on these beautiful clothes and now they were dirty and torn. He slipped his hand inside the shirt and felt the chain. He let his fingers slide down the metal until they touched the stone.

The room abruptly changed. It glowed strange colors. The walls and bars of his cell flickered a cold metallic blue. Aramel's words came into sharp focus. "And to unbind the bond they share, a wiry thread of tiger hair." The Wizard dumped a glowing thread into the pile.

Dursdan stood and looked over at the table. The Wizard ignored him and continued his search for ingredients, coming back to the book and reading from the list. Dursdan focused on the book. He could read it! The letters were a fine script. Experimentally, he let go of the stone. The room dulled and the page of the book appeared to be a mass of strange squiggles. It must be written in a different language. What had Trusumo called it? The elder tongue?

The Wizard stamped. "Bat's breath! I have no weasel toes." Dursdan shrank back and slid down in his cell, masking his growing understanding with a cloak of very real fear. The Wizard came over to the cell. "It won't be long, you know." He looked at the egg pouch then back at Dursdan. "I might have let you live if you'd given me the egg. Shame to waste but you're existence is unnecessary. The egg will be mine soon."

He dragged the basket of warmers over and chanted. Then pulled the plate out of the cell, sprinkled something on it, and chanted again. "That should keep you while I'm gone." Aramel went back to his table and spread some ingredients around, chanted a few words, and disappeared.

Dursdan was left in darkness. Where had the Wizard gone? He felt the egg pouch. It was still warm. He'd learned that Wizard's spell would stay until it was touched, and then the pads would begin to cool. "Now what do I do?"

Dursdan was startled by the sound of his own voice. It had been sometime since he used it, and it sounded strange. He shook his head. He felt Biyoni in the back of his mind. "*Out?*"

He sighed. "Soon. Hang on, little one."

He examined the lock and shook his head. It was something magical. He'd never seen Aramel open it. Experimentally he grabbed the stone.

The room came alive with glowing color. The lock looked different, too. Dursdan studied it carefully and figured out how it worked. He could see in his mind what needed to turn to open the lock. There was a soft click. The mechanism released.

Dursdan pushed open the door of his cell and moved out into the strangely glowing room. Each item seemed to have a hue or shade of its own. It was like walking through a rainbow. He went to the book that Aramel had been reading. "Oh no. I think he may have found a way to undo us."

Dursdan spent some time studying the different volumes on the table. He quickly recognized most of the ingredients. The containers had been conveniently labeled. He was drawn to a spell laid out on the corner of the workbench. He'd seen Aramel use is on several occasions but had no idea what it was for. He thought back to what the Wizard had done and poured a small amount of the silver liquid into the middle of the circled twigs.

Nothing seemed to happen. He touched it. An image came into focus. "It's like a window." He thought of Mirana. She was bending over a garden plot, harvesting vegetables. He stared at the image. It was his garden! But was it fall already? He quickly thought of Trusumo. The Red swam into view. He sat over Dorsadram's chair in a large room. Dursdan had never seen the chamber of the Inner Circle. He sighed. The way things were going, maybe he never would. He looked down at the dragon. "I wish I could tell you where I am."

The Red looked up in confusion and swung his head around. Dursdan could hear a very faint whisper, like a distant echo, in the back of his mind. "*Dursdan? Where are you?*"

His heart skipped a beat. "Tru, can you hear me?"

The Red was agitated, as were all the other dragons in the circle. He could feel them all now. All except one. Trusumo reached out to him. "*Dur, tell us where you are!*"

"I don't know. In Aramel's stronghold somewhere in the mountains."

"*We have been searching for months. The Lords fear you are dead. They think your Da has gone mad with grief and deserted the Valley.*"

"Da? But where is Sinotio? I can't feel him." Dursdan felt the panic rise from the pit of his stomach.

"*We still touch him in the Mists. He has gone to Timotha. Her time was upon her. She could not wait.*"

Dursdan felt a buzz in the back of his mind. "I think the Wizard is returning. I will find some way to escape this place. She needs to hatch soon." The buzz grew louder. "I have to go!" He quickly closed the pool and rushed back to his cell, closing the door. At the last moment, he grabbed the plate of food and let go of the stone.

Aramel reappeared with his lighted staff. He looked wet and ragged. "Curse this damp weather!" He looked up at Dursdan and smiled. "But I have everything I need now thanks to my good friend." He patted a small leather bag. "Humans are so frail. I'm amazed how far they will go to extend a worthless life."

He strolled over and looked down at Dursdan. "Eat up, boy. It will be your last meal."

The food went sour in his mouth. He was running out of time. He could hear Biyoni in the back of his mind. She was whimpering.

Hang on, little one. I'll think of something. He watched Aramel go back to work. He slipped his hand around the stone so he could listen to what the Wizard was saying. At first, little of it made sense. But gradually, he began to understand what the Wizard was doing. It must be a complicated spell that it required so much preparation.

He stood up and looked over at the large wooden table scattered with books. Many had been left open. He ignored the Wizard and began to read. There were many different kinds of spells, each with its list of ingredients and chants. Some had explicit directions on timing and placement. Dursdan read as fast as he could. None of them offered any help in his escape.

Finally the Wizard was silent. Dursdan let go of the stone and looked at the old man. His eyes had dark circles around them and his face seemed to droop. He almost felt sorry for Aramel. "Why do you want this dragon so badly?"

Aramel scowled. "Because it's mine. I will harness its power to open the Western Portal and be free of this wretched place for once and for all." He made a few small adjustments to the items on the table then looked up at Dursdan. "It's done. But I'm too tired to begin it now. You're lucky. You have a few more hours to live."

Dursdan touched the egg pouch. He would do anything to save her. "What if we helped you open this portal when my dragon was old enough. You could let us go and we'd come back and help you."

Aramel laughed weakly. "You? You know nothing of the magic required to open a portal. The dragon must be bound to a Wizard to generate the required energy. Your dragon won't bond with me while you still live."

Dursdan felt weak. He released the bars and sunk into the corner of his cell. He'd have to find a way to get them out of the Wizard's keep.

The Wizard pushed away from the table and collapsed in his chair. He chanted a quick spell. A steaming cup appeared on the small table beside him. Aramel drank deeply. He looked over at Dursdan. "Best prepare yourself for your end, in what ever way your kind does. It is coming tomorrow." The Wizard put the cup down and closed his eyes.

Dursdan reached under his shirt. With the stone in his hand, he could see the effects of the sleep spell take hold. The Wizard was soon snoring softly. He got up, quietly opened the door of the cell and crept out, pushing it shut until it clicked. He surveyed the spell laid out on the table and looked at the directions in the book. As he read the text, he began to realize what the spell would do. The Wizard didn't want to be the baby dragon's partner; he wanted to be her master! Dursdan shook his head.

He glanced over at one of the other books he'd been reading and began flipping the pages. He found a spell that had similar ingredients but a much different effect. He walked into the storage room and found a roll of silver thread. He made a few alterations to the spell on the table then placed one end of the thread in the center and tied the other end to the butt of Aramel's staff.

Dursdan grabbed a few of the books from the table and noticed a book on a shelf not far away. The binding glowed brightly. It read in fine script, 'Basic Spells'. Dursdan shrugged and grabbed that volume as well. He took a sack from the storage room and pulled things off the shelves, not really knowing which ingredients might be useful. He made sure to grab the things he'd need to reheat the pads.

Aramel shifted in his sleep and Dursdan held his breath. The Wizard settled into a different position and began to snore loudly. Dursdan sighed and looked around the room. There were several doors that he'd seen Aramel use on different occasions. He bit his lower lip and clutched the stone tightly.

He looked carefully at each door and chose one. It opened with a slight push and he slipped through, closing it behind him. The walls glowed faintly. They must be impregnated with magic. No wonder the dragons couldn't hear him.

He made his way along the passage until it came to an intersection. Now which way? Dursdan sighed. This wasn't going to be as easy as he'd hoped. He studied the walls and noted that one seemed slightly brighter than the others. He shrugged and took the passageway. He wanted to put as much distance between himself and the Wizard as he could.

He followed corridors that twisted and turned, occasionally pausing to test doors and peer behind them into dark and dusty rooms. No one had entered them in a long time. There were no windows in any of them nor did any of the doors open to the outside world.

He could feel Biyoni twisting. *"Out soon?"*

Hang on, Biyoni. I'm trying. Dursdan picked up his pace, jogging through the hallways, lit in the mysterious glow of the stone's Eye. He rounded a corner and found yet another dead-end. He closed his eyes and leaned his back against the wall. It felt cold. It must be an outside wall.

Dursdan swallowed. What if there was no door? Aramel had used a spell to leave and return. He opened his eyes and began shuffling through the sack. He found the book he'd grabbed off the shelf. Basic Spells. He paged through it, looking for something mentioning a portal. A word caught his attention. He began to read quickly.

* * *

Aramel woke slowly. The sleep spell always had that effect. He sighed. At least he was refreshed. He opened his eyes. The boy wasn't visible. He must be curled up on the floor of the cell again. Oh well. At least the dragon would be well rested. He knew it was close to hatching. Such a simple solution. How could it have eluded him for so long?

The texts spoke of the binding and unbinding many times. The Wizards themselves had experimented with dragons of their own but had discovered that it took more time to tend a dragon then they wished to spend. They had nurtured the first eggs, binding them to themselves at first but as the eggs got close to hatching, they had unbound them and rebound them to the First Dragon Lords. It was so simple. Of course he'd made a few modification of his own. No use having a powerful dragon quarreling with you.

Aramel smiled. The first thing he would do when he had his own Golden dragon, would be to create a powerful unbinding spell and set it loose across the valley. What fun it would be to watch the bewildered faces of the Lords as all of their dragons reverted to the wild state and flew away. Then he would call up a horde of trolls to lay waste to that miserable settlement. And finally, when his Gold was strong enough, he'd open the Portal and take his revenge on the Others.

He grinned with satisfaction and pulled his staff toward him to help him up. The room was suddenly filled with a blinding light and a mighty scream that threatened to burst his eardrums. He couldn't hear himself talk. He covered his eyes with his arm and brought his staff down with a bang. The room became still and dark.

Aramel relit his staff and looked around. The spell that had taken so much of his time and energy to lay out was ruined! He was furious. He stalked to the cell, ready to bring his anger down on the boy, and stopped. The boy and the egg were gone! Had another Wizard somehow intruded in his stronghold and interfered? He whirled around the room, chanting a spell, searching for the trail of magic. Finally, he found it. He opened the door and ran down the hall.

Chapter 19

Dursdan heard the distant bang. The Wizard must have activated the spell he'd set. He was out of time. He could feel Biyoni's quiet groans and his heart ached. She needed to hatch soon! He dumped out the sack and quickly sorted the contents. He read the spell again and found the things he needed and dumped the rest back in the sack.

He laid out the ingredients against the wall and began the chant. He could hear the running footsteps of the Wizard in the halls. He focused on the spell. A light gray spot formed on the wall in front of him. The footsteps were getting closer.

Dursdan continued to chant, the sound of his voice echoing oddly in the elder tongue. The edges expanded and began to shimmer. A spiral formed in the center and became a vortex that expanded to meet the shimmering ring. A faint glow of mage light turned the corner at the far end of the corridor.

Dursdan could feel the breeze now. It was cold on his sweating face. He glanced briefly toward the growing form of Aramel. He could hear the Wizard beginning to chant. The portal began to close.

"No!" Dursdan grabbed up the sack and put his foot through the vortex. He felt gravel beneath his toes. He swallowed hard and pushed through the swirling gray. A world of clouds and sharp spires of rock greeted him. He started to take another step but could feel nothing to step on so he moved sideways. He heard the Wizard scream his name. The portal continued to shrink. Dursdan remembered the closing line and spoke the word. The vortex snapped shut with a small popping sound.

He made the mistake of looking down. His stomach heaved and he almost lost his balance. He leaned back into the wall and closed his eyes. A gust of howling cold wind tried to tear him from the rock. Dursdan willed his heart to beat slower, controlled his breath, and opened his eyes again.

The world was a palette of gray. Clouds oozed around the rock spires and swirled into one another. Glancing up, he could see the wall at his back extending upward to be swallowed by more clouds. The wall was smooth and unnatural with only the barest hint of texture. It continued on either side of him until it bent around to be swallowed by the billowing Mists.

Dursdan looked down carefully and discovered why his foot had not found purchase. The narrow ledge at the base of the wall ended abruptly. As he moved his feet, a shower of pebbles dropped into the expanse and disappeared, not even leaving behind a sound. Somewhere below the ledge, another layer of clouds formed a misty mat that stretched out, broken only occasionally by the tip of a spire.

Dursdan felt his insides rolling again. He swallowed and felt an odd sensation. It wasn't his insides that were rolling. He gripped the egg pouch. "Biyoni, are you all right?"

Dizziness and disorientation clouded his mind. The little golden girl was crying. He rocked her gently. She clung to him, nuzzling into his mind's embrace and gradually relaxed.

The wind struck him, an angry predator, trying to loosen his fragile grip on the ledge. He slowly brought himself back into focus so he wouldn't upset her. "Don't worry, little one. I'll get you out of here." He looked again at the bleak skyscape. "Somehow."

He reached out his mind for the dragons but felt nothing. The magical shield must extend beyond the physical walls of the keep. Well, he couldn't stand here forever.

He studied the ledge with redefined intent. It appeared to widen a short ways to his right. He pressed his back into the wall and slowly moved in that direction. Dursdan wished that he had time to learn a few more spells.

The ledge broadened as it curved around a bend in the wall and then ended. He sighed. It seemed the only direction now was down. He studied the rocks below the ledge and began picking out a possible route. Marking in his mind a rough trail that seemed to drop into the cloud carpet below, he eased himself over the edge, found his footing, and began the decent.

It was a treacherous endeavor. The wind continued to stalk him. Often he had to balance at awkward angles to protect the egg from sharp protrusions. The rock face tore at his hands, already numb from the cold wind, and long unused muscles burned in complaint. Occasionally, he would find rotten patches that would crumble under his searching toes.

The gray clouds began to darken and a swirl of light snowflakes danced around him. The sun must be near to setting. It was going to get cold. Dursdan paused under a slight overhang to recharge the warming pad. That had been one of the first spells he had learned. He felt Biyoni stir just briefly then she slipped into a restless sleep. The smell of the magic made him queasy. He looked at the meager bundle of ingredients and tried to calculate how long they would last. He rolled them up and tucked them back into the sack. And how long would it take the Wizard to find him?

A strong gust of wind stirred up the dust under the overhang. He shielded his eyes from the fragments. The wind funneled down on him again, stronger this time and accompanied by a familiar sound. Dragon wings! Dursdan turned in time to see it coming and ducked. The claws closed on empty air. Strong downdrafts shoved him against the rock as the dragon back winged to avoid slamming into the jutting overhang.

Dursdan's mind filled with raging fury and frustration. The wild Red screamed in defiance and turned for another attempt. Dursdan tucked himself as far under the overhang as possible. He tied the sack around his waist and pulled the egg pouch close, covering it with his own body. The Red attacked again, missing by a hand's width but the back surge from his powerful wings loosened the rock. Dursdan felt it giving under his feet and scrambled to find his footing. The solid surface crumbled and Dursdan slid along with the avalanche toward the drop. Flaying out his arms, he managed to find a handhold but his feet continued to slip on the fragments.

The Red screamed. Dursdan looked up to discover that he was no longer protected. He reached out to touch the wild mind. It was full of strange images and touched by magic. Aramel must have called it to find him!

The Red dove. There was no place for Dursdan to go. The claws extended to grab him. He tried to dodge the attack but lost his precious hold on the rock. The Red missed but Dursdan spun out of control, off the mountainside and began to fall.

The cloud cover rushed to meet him, hiding his fate. Dursdan held the egg close, glad that she was sleeping and unaware. He was overcome by a deep sadness that she would never see the world beyond her shell.

His mind exploded with wild energy and pain ripped into his left shoulder as the Red sunk its claws into Dursdan. The heavy downbeat of wings lurched him upward and he screamed in agony. The sound echoed off the mountainside and the dragon rebounded, jerking Dursdan in a new direction. He could feel the warm blood oozing around the dragon's talons. Sheer waves of pain surged through his body with every beat of the dragon's wings.

She was awake now. He could feel her slender arms warp around his mind. His golden girl was terrified. He fought to control the pain so it would not pass to her.

Another scream rent his mind one of defiance and fierce protectiveness. There was a flash of dull gold. It blurred with the red above. The Red roared a challenge and jerked his prize closer.

The pain overwhelmed Dursdan. He began falling. For some reason the Red had let them go. He could vaguely hear a battle above then the clouds swallowed him. He was dimly aware of Biyoni. She was crying. They broke through the clouds and Dursdan surveyed the valley below as they rushed toward the ground.

He was grabbed around the waist, the sharp gold talons just missing the egg pouch on either side. The sack around his waist made his girth too large for the claw to close fully but Dursdan still struggled to breathe in her crushing grip. They were moving parallel to the valley floor where the river roared between narrow walls.

The egg lurched. The stitching was beginning to give at the seams. He clung to the egg with his good arm. He could feel Biyoni clinging to him as well.

The Gold dove, slipping out of the cloudy valley, and glided over a darkening forest. The sun was sinking at the horizon. She banked and swooped toward a rocky ledge.

Dursdan was aware of the ground quickly rushing to meet them. He felt one toe touch then twisted in her grasp. She let go and he curled protectively around Biyoni's egg and tumbled across the ledge, coming to rest against a sun-warmed wall of rock.

The wild Gold closed in on him. Her thoughts resounded through his mind, anger and desire for the egg. She reached toward the pouch.

Biyoni clung to him. Dursdan could feel his little golden girl shivering in her shell. He looked up at the Gold, seeing the fierce beauty of the wild dragon. He remembered that reflection all too well. Dursdan held Biyoni close and swallowed. "Biyoni, she's your Ma."

The little Gold snuggled closer to his mind. "*No, She frightens me.*"

The Gold queen reached powerful talons for the egg.

Biyoni panicked. "*Leave me alone!*"

A spear came out of nowhere and pierced the Gold's shoulder. She reared back in pain and shock. It echoed in Dursdan's mind. He and the dragon turned in unison to see the man standing on the edge of the cliff.

"Run, you fool, while she's distracted!"

The Gold reached out for him. Dursdan grabbed the stone. "NO!"

The Gold pulled back, shaking her head. The heavy eye ridges seemed to wrinkle. Dursdan could feel her confusion. She turned and looked at him. "*He harms me!*"

Dursdan pushed himself up and came forward. He could see the angry wound where the spear protruded. He remembered Timotha. He carefully grabbed the spear with his other hand, pulled it from her body and tossed it on the ground. Then he covered the wound with his hand and closed his eyes. He could feel the power of the stone move through his hand to the wound and her pain diminish.

She touched his mind. "*You help me? Why?*"

For a moment, he was in a cave with broken shells oozing colorful slime. Only one egg remained intact. Her egg. He recognized the place. Tears overflowed from his eyes. Then a smoldering ember of anger flared. Dursdan wanted to squash the Wizard who had done this. He felt the anger rise and burst. The Gold screamed with him. It echoed across the canyon.

"By the shell! What are you doing?"

Dursdan opened his eyes and looked at the dragonless man. "I am sharing her grief and loss. Like you, she has lost what she cared for most."

The Gold turned to look at the old man. "*Who is he?*"

"His name is Terarimi. He once rode a dragon into battle and he grieves because he survived and his dragon did not."

The Gold slowly reached down and nuzzled the pouch. Biyoni wailed. "*No! I want Dursdan!*"

He was overcome. His love and protectiveness encircled his little golden girl. The Gold dragon pulled back. Dursdan could feel the mother dragon crying. He gently reached out and touched her face. "Don't worry. I will take good care of her." The Gold met his eyes. He looked over at Terarimi and she followed his gaze. "There is a place together for those who have felt loss."

She nodded, and then sniffed at his torn shoulder. The blood had clotted into a dark clump. She reached out and licked it. The new scab tore loose and Dursdan gritted his teeth. But she continued her ministrations and the pain gradually faded. He glanced down at his shoulder. The wound was closed. All that remained was a jagged white scar. He moved his fingers and raised the arm. There was only a slight tinge, a lingering memory of the pain.

The Gold turned toward the dragonless man. "*You will ask him for me?*"

Dursdan looked at him. He was still staring, wide mouthed at the Gold queen. "She has lost her clutch and is all alone. She wants to know if you would fly with her."

"She wants me?" His voice was an awed whisper.

The Gold moved forward and extended her head. He slowly reached out and touched her. Tears trickled from the corners of his eyes. She moved closer and nuzzled him. He wrapped his arms around her neck and began to sob.

Dursdan shook his head. Somehow he had just bound a mature wild dragon to a man. He looked down at the stone in his hand. It reflected the first star of evening in its shiny surface. He felt a familiar tickle in the back of his mind and looked around. "Sinotio?"

The large Silver dove around a rock spire and pulled up tight to land on the rock ledge. The Gold backed up to give him room. He bowed formally and she bowed back. Another dragon circled the ledge, a white blur against the darkening sky. "Timotha!"

She too managed to find space on the ledge. She grinned at Dursdan. "*We have come! I see you in the light of day!*"

Dursdan looked up to the man on the Silver's back and began running. "Da!"

Mergadan slid off the Silver and met him half way. He enclosed Dursdan in his arms, the moisture of his tears running down on the recently healed shoulder. "My son, you're alive." He buried his face in his son's hair and sobbed.

Dursdan accepted the embrace for a moment but he could feel Biyoni trembling. He gently pushed his father away. "Time enough for this later. I've got to get Biyoni to a safe place. She needs to hatch."

Mergadan nodded. "You can fly with me." He looked over at Sinotio.

The three dragons were making introductions. A boy clung to the White's back, staring at everything. Dursdan whistled to get his attention. "And you must be Varimato."

The boy's eyebrows went up and his jaw dropped. "How does everyone know my name?"

Though the words had a strange accent, Dursdan understood them. He shook his head. "I'll tell you about it later." He approached the dragons and bowed to the Gold queen. "There's an angry Wizard after us. Biyoni is about to hatch. I must get her to safety.

The Gold nodded. "*We go now.*" She nuzzled the pouch one more time and looked concerned. "*She is not well.*"

"I know." He touched her face once more. "Be well, Gold of Terarimi."

"*Be well, human of my daughter.*" She looked toward Terarimi. The old man jumped on her back and she launched off the ledge. She turned out of her dive, circled, and swept back over them.

The Silver and White bugled. Sinotio raised his head. "*We will watch over her. Have no fear.*" His eyes twinkled. "*And you will dream with us, yes?*"

She nodded then turned away and vanished into the clouds.

Mergadan shook his head. "I've seen so many unusual things in the past few days, but this tops them all." Sinotio nudged him. "Yes, you're right. Get on, Dur. Let's get going."

Varimato groaned. "I hate flying at night."

Timotha turned and looked at him. "*I will not drop him.*"

"I know you won't drop him." Dursdan climbed into the harness in front of his father. "I'm ready."

Sinotio chuckled. "*We fly!*" Silver and White launched off the ledge into the near darkness. The moon was rising, nearly full and the forest below was draped in long silvery shadows.

Dursdan felt a cold metallic taste in his mouth. Magic! "Be on the lookout. Aramel is up to something!"

The sky erupted in heaving clouds that quickly swallowed the stars. Lightening flared and thunder shrieked across the sky. The wind rose to a beastly howl and rain began to pelt them. Mergadan leaned over Dursdan, trying to protect him from the worst of it. "I've never seen a storm come up like this!"

The dragons fought against the on slaughter of the wind. Varimato struggled to keep his balance on the smaller White. He looked over a Dursdan, the whites of his eyes visible in a flash of lightening. "We should land!"

Mergadan guided them down the valley. Dursdan could see the river cutting through the trees. Mergadan yelled in his ear. "We might have a chance if we can get to the river and fly below the tree tops. They should shield us from the worst of the wind."

As the turned to dive, a strong gust threw Sinotio completely over. Dursdan felt himself go pitching into space. In a bolt of lightening, he could see white caps on the river below. It would be a wet landing. He glanced around looking for his father. Mergadan was headed for the forest. *Sinotio, grab Da!*

The Silver regained his balance, tilted in the air, and plucked up his rider in his claws, sweeping upward, just brushing the treetops.

Dursdan fell into the cold water. He clung to the egg and forced his way to the surface. The sack around his waist resisted his movements but he didn't want to lose the ingredients. He broke the surface of the water and took a breath. He looked up and saw the outline of the Silver flying beside the river. He was relived to see Mergadan scramble back into the harness.

The turbulence buffeted him about and slammed his back into a rock. He tried to grab at the slippery cold surface but his fingers found no purchase. He spun around in the current, bobbing through the eddies, and grabbing small gulps of air when he could. Sinotio flew over him. "*Dur, where are you?*"

He could hear other dragons stirring in his mind. They must finally be outside of the shield! "Here, in the river!"

There was no way his physical voice could have carried over the roar of the water but Trusumo shouted in the back of his mind, "*We come!*"

The pull of the river grew and the roar was getting louder. He looked up at the dragon overhead. *Sinotio, what do you see?*

"*The river drops away into a gorge.*"

Dursdan gasped. He was coming up to the waterfall! He could feel the mist on his face. Lightening flared and he could see the jagged rocks that clung to the edge. The current pulled him faster.

A white form flew over his head. "*Here, I have found him!*" Timotha turned for another pass.

Sinotio cautioned her. "*He will be heavy with water. Allow me, my love.*"

Timotha flew beside him. "*Together we will bear him, dear one.*"

Dursdan looked up and saw the dragons coming toward him. He could hear the water rushing over the edge. Sinotio and Timotha dove as one. Dursdan reached up and grabbed the Silver's claws. The dragon carefully closed his talons around Dursdan's arm. "*Hang on!*"

Dursdan's stomach lurched as his dangling toes tried to follow the water over the edge. Timotha grabbed him gently around the waist.

He looked down into the dark mists below and clung to the egg pouch with his free arm. The egg felt cold.

Dursdan reached out with his mind but he couldn't feel her. "We have to find a safe place to put me down. I'm worried about Biyoni."

The dragons turned and headed for the lowlands. They flew over a clearing. Timotha carefully let him go so that he dangled below the Silver. Sinotio circled and back-winged so Dursdan could get his feet down and let go. Both dragons landed a few paces away and Mergadan was quickly at his side.

Dursdan was focused on the egg. "Biyoni!" He took the egg out of the soaked pouch and opened his shirt, holding it next to his skin. He struggled to untie the knot that bound the sack to him. Mergadan helped. Dursdan dumped it out. All the ingredients were wet. There was no way to charge a warming pad. Dursdan sobbed.

Mergadan touched his son's shoulder. "How does she fair?"

"She's dying!"

A large Red landed nearby. More arms surrounded him. "Oh, Dur, you're alive. We'd given up hope. We searched everywhere."

Dursdan embraced his brother. "Tola!"

"What can I do?"

"We need to get her warm." Dursdan thought of a warm dry place and an image came to mind. He grabbed Tolatrom's arm. "Fly ahead to Aber's farm and find Mirana. Tell her to warm blankets and bring them to the loft."

Tolatrom slapped his brother's shoulder and jumped up on Natalo's back and they were gone. Dursdan looked up at Sinotio. "Can you fly?"

The Silver smiled. "*We will fly!*"

His father helped him to his feet. Sinotio knelt to make it easier for Dursdan to mount. Mergadan pushed him up and got on behind. "With your best speed, Sinotio!"

The Silver launched back into the stormy night. Timotha, with her terrified rider clinging to her back, joined them. But they were no longer alone. Other dragons flocked around them. A great Bronze guarded one side and a mighty Red the other. Dozi looked over at him. "*We are here.*"

The Silver flew straight to Aber's barn, circled once to be sure it was safe, then lightly dropped down. Mirana came running up. "Oh, Dursdan! Tola said you were alive." She touched his arm. "You're like ice!"

Kalista came out with a bundle of warm blankets. "Here, drape this around him."

Dursdan accepted the blanket as his father helped him down. "We have to get her up to loft. She's cold and it's warm there."

"In the barn?" Mergadan looked at the structure.

Aber came up beside him. "Aye, the cows below keep the loft warm above. Come, I've a lantern."

Mergadan and Tolatrom helped Dursdan up the steps and into the loft. Mirana laid down warm blankets in the hay and he sank down onto them. She covered him with more. He closed his eyes. "This will do." He stroked the egg. It felt cold to the touch. He frantically reached out with his mind. *Biyoni? Are you okay?*

He felt a wave of cold sweep over him. His teeth chattered and his body shook. "She's too cold."

Mirana lay down next to him and added her warmth. Dursdan leaned his head on her shoulder and wept. "Oh, Biyoni! What have I done?" He felt just the briefest tingling in his mind.

Mirana took a quick peek under the blanket. "Dursdan, the egg doesn't look right. The colors aren't swirling."

Dursdan's eyes were filled with tears. "She's dying. She's too cold."

Mirana put her hands on the egg. "You said she's ready to hatch, right?"

"Yes, she's been holding back."

Mirana looked up at Mergadan. "Then we have to break her out. It'll be much easier to warm her."

Mergadan started at her and shook his head. "Break the shell?"

"Well, that is how things hatch from eggs."

Dursdan looked down at the egg resting on his stomach. "*Biyoni? Can you come out? I'll help you.*" There was only the slightest tingle in his mind. His little honey -haired girl was fading. He looked up at Mirana. "Can you find me something to break it?"

Aber called up to them from the bottom of the ladder. Mirana got up. "Pa has brought more blankets. I'll go down and get them and bring a hammer." She slipped down the ladder.

Dursdan cradled the egg close. Tears streamed down his face. Mergadan tried to comfort him. Tolatrom laid a hand on his shoulder.

Dursdan felt lost. What if it had all been for nothing? He wished that the Wizard had killed him. He could feel Sinotio and the other dragons on the edge of his mind. It was more of a feeling than an actual thought, as though they had all curled around him to comfort him somehow.

Mirana reappeared with an armload of blankets. She handed Dursdan the hammer. He took it and hesitantly tapped on the shell. He felt a tingle in his mind. "She's still alive!" He hit harder and the shell fractured. Afraid he might hurt Biyoni, he laid the hammer down and tore at the pieces. A large section pealed away revealing small golden scales. It was her back.

Mirana sank down beside him. "Oh, Dursdan. I hope it's not too late."

Tolatrom helped him peel the sections away until they finally found her head. She wasn't moving. "Biyoni!" Dursdan pulled her out of the rest of the shell. He nestled into the hay and laid Biyoni on his chest. Mirana wrapped warm blankets around both of them.

Biyoni struggled to breathe. Dursdan could feel the faint puffs on his chin. Her heart fluttered against his chest. She cried weakly. He wrapped his mind around hers and held on. He could feel her slipping away.

In desperation, Dursdan grabbed the stone. Its golden light exploded around the barn for his eyes alone. He focused completely on the tiny Gold. He could feel the hum of the magic; the metallic taste burned his tongue. The power made his skin crawl. Part of him wanted to drop the stone. He hated magic. But he would not give up his beautiful golden girl.

He could feel the strength returned to her. She opened one eye and looked up at him. "*You want Biyoni?*"

Yes! The power surged around him and rebounded off the walls of the hayloft in rainbows of dazzling color. The dragons outside bugled in chorus.

Biyoni opened the other eye and lifted her head slightly. "*Then I stay with Dursdan.*"

Dursdan enfolded her tightly within his arms. "My beautiful Biyoni." His tears washed the remnants of egg sack from her golden scales. Dursdan let go of the stone and the colors faded.

Mergadan wiped the tears from his eyes and sat with his arm around Tolatrom. Aber and Kalista came up into the loft. The Lord looked over and smiled. "I think all will be well."

Biyoni laid her head under Dursdan's chin and sighed. She closed her eyes.

Mirana was crying. Dursdan reached a hand out to her and pulled her close. "It's all right. She'll be okay." He pulled another blanket around Mirana's shoulders and snuggled deeper into the hay. He could feel Biyoni's shallow breaths on his chest. She was getting warmer.

She tilted her head and opened an eye. For a moment Dursdan was disoriented. He looked up at his own face! Not the face of a young schoolboy, but a strong weathered face, much more like his father's. Biyoni closed her eye and snuggled closer.

Dursdan finally closed his eyes. He could feel her drift off into sleep. She was hungry but too tired to think about food. He briefly puzzled over what she would eat. Mirana snuggled closer. Dursdan felt the warmth sinking into his tired limbs and drifted off into the Mists.

* * *

Aramel stood at his workbench fuming. First the Red had bungled the job and now he'd lost the boy in the storm! His own spell had backfired on him! He raged around the room, stomping his feet. He had to find the egg before it hatched!

Aramel grumbled as he looked around the room. It would take him days to sort through the mess the boy had made of his workshop. He shuffled around the scattered remnants trying to locate the ingredients for a search spell.

He had to substitute lesser ingredients; the boy had run off with some. But he would find him. There was no doubt. He phrased the opening words and the space inside the twigs became alive with color and movement.

The pool focused on a barn. It was the barn of that bothersome farmer! But of course the boy would have run back to see if the girl still lived. He tried to focus the spell tighter but with the lesser ingredients it was harder to control. And the golden egg might still be blocking him.

Aramel finally released the search spell and sagged into his chair. He couldn't even find the ingredients for a basic portal spell! He shook his head. How much time did he have? He got out of his chair and began assembling a basic grab spell. He'd have to pull the plants himself. There was no time to spare. The egg might hatch any day.

Chapter 20

The Mists were crowded. All the dragons of the Valley wanted to meet the newest member. Dursdan sat with Biyoni on his lap as all of the admirers stopped to chat. Obodo brought little Jatema, Sormato's new baby Red, over to meet them. "She is quite a handful." He patted her head and smiled down at her. Jatema and Biyoni sat giggling at each other.

Nasila, with Durdansi in tow, also came over to meet the new Gold. The little Bronze peered around Nasila's long white gown. "Can she play?"

Dursdan shook his head. "Not yet." He looked down at his honey-haired girl and smiled. "She's had quite a long day. Maybe another time."

Trusumo and Natalo came and joined him. The elder Red seemed tired and weak. Dursdan was concerned. "Are you all right, Tru?"

He smiled but shook his head. "I am afraid it has been a difficult fall for Dors. He took ill a few weeks ago and just has not been the same. We are growing old."

Dursdan shook his head. "You don't have to, you know."

"No, I have already made my decision to pass on with Dorsadram.

We have been together too long." He looked over at Natalo. "Some may choose to take another rider, but I will keep only one."

Natalo grinned. "I have no regrets. I do miss Cras but Tola is grand. He has such energy! I have never felt so fine, even in my younger days."

Dursdan smiled. "I noticed Tola sat in the Circle the other day. I'm glad he was accepted."

"We accepted him." Trusumo rose. "And that is what counts." He turned as the Mists parted. "I believe we have a guest." He bowed to the beautiful Golden lady as she stepped through.

Dursdan stared and Biyoni turned and hid in his arms. Dursdan slowly rose. "I'm glad you decided to join us." He bowed.

She looked around then back at him. "I knew you were different. I thank you for introducing me to Tera. He is a good man. I have never known a good man before, beside you, of course." She bowed to him and looked at her daughter. "And how does she fare?"

Dursdan turned his little Gold around. "It's all right, Biyoni. She won't hurt you."

Biyoni peered at her mother. "Stay with Dur."

"Yes, dear. I know." The Gold smiled. "He will take good care of you." She looked around at the other dragons. "Ah, the White and the Silver are here."

Sinotio led Timotha forward. Timotha looked a little pale. Dursdan reached out and touched her hand. "Are you all right?"

She shook her head. "I will have to lay my brood in the morning. The eggs are ready." She looked at Sinotio. "I'm just not sure where."

Dursdan considered her size. That might be a challenge. Mithra and Tasia came up and joined them. "You will be needing a place then." The Green nudged her companion.

Mithra cleared her throat. "Yes, indeed. It seems Thor built a large shed for Shatsu and Tasia. He actually built it for all of us but I prefer to be outside. Come by and make use of my corner. We will make sure Shatsu does not bother you."

Timotha frowned. "But how would your riders feel? I would not want to offend them."

The Bronze snorted. "Nonsense. We invite you. They will just have to accept that." She turned to Dursdan. "You could explain things to Sora and Thor, could you not?"

"I'd be happy to help."

Sinotio put an arm around the White. "Do not fret, my love, all will be well." He looked over at the Bronze. "I hope it would not offend you if I stopped by."

"Of course not! You should be there." She looked at the Gold queen. "Should he not? I have always seen our riders attend the birthing of their children. It seems logical that it would be the same for us. Why, I myself attended the birth of Thorazan."

The Gold smiled. "I do not know. This was my first brood. And they came and were gone." She shrugged and looked over at Sinotio. "Had I such a mate, I would have wanted him by my side."

Dursdan felt sorry for her. What Aramel had done was cruel. "I'm sorry that Wizard put you through so much grief. It was wrong."

She came over and gently touched his face. "But you made it right."

Dursdan looked around the Mists. "Has anyone seen Menatash?"

Timotha and Trusumo exchanged glances. The Red sighed. "It has been difficult for him to join us lately. He has spent many late hours exploring some library he discovered. He claimed to have found books concerning the early wars. I am sure that he will join us soon with many new revelations."

The Gold queen shook her head. "I remember the conflicts that I have seen in my few years. Why do they happen?"

Dursdan sighed. "I wish I knew. I'm hoping that Mirana has had time to read more of the book. I'm sure there must be answers."

Dursdan felt someone calling his name. "I'm sorry to leave you so soon. A good day to you all." He opened his eyes and blinked in the lantern light. His mother knelt by his side, tears in her eyes. He touched her hand lightly. "Don't cry, Ma. Everything is all right now." He looked down at the still sleeping baby Gold and smiled.

"I've just been so worried." She lay down on the other side of him and buried her face in his shoulder and sobbed. "Oh, Dursdan, I'm so sorry."

He felt Mirana stir. She lifted her head. "Oh, your Mum is here. Are you warm enough?"

"I'm fine. But Biyoni will be hungry when she wakes."

"My Mum mentioned that. I recall she said something about cooking up some breakfast for her. I'll go down and see if it's done."

Mergadan came up after she left. "I'm a little concerned about the White. She's flown off without Vari. Poor boy's quite shocked."

"She has to lay her eggs. I think you'll find her over at Lord Sorazan's place. It seems Thor's built a fine big shed for the dragons and Mithra invited Timotha to use her corner."

Mergadan chuckled. "Well, that will be something. I'd better let them know what's going on. Only a few people know about her. Is that where I'll find, Sino, too?"

"Most likely."

His mother sat up and dried her eyes. "May I see her?"

"Sure." He pulled back the blanket to expose the small golden head. Biyoni opened one eye, tilted her head slightly to observe the people around her, then went back to sleep. Dursdan chuckled. "She'll probably sleep most of the day."

"No doubt." His father pulled the blanket back up. "I hope we've given you enough sleep."

"I'll be fine, Da. Don't worry about me."

Biyoni raised her head, fighting with the blanket. Her nostrils were flaring. She looked at Dursdan, her yellow eyes wide. *"I smell food! I am hungry!"*

Dursdan laughed. "Mirana must be coming with something good."

She appeared at the top of the ladder carrying a large bowl of steaming ground meat. She bowed to Mergadan and Dachia and came to Dursdan's side. "Mum said this will make her happy."

"All for me?"

"Yes, little one, all for you. But let me feed you so you don't choke yourself trying to eat it all at once." Dursdan carefully broke off small bites of the warm meat and fed the hungry Gold. A strange sound started in the back of his mind. Timotha was singing her birthing song. Biyoni cocked her head to listen, too. She giggled. Then looked at Dursdan. *"More?"*

Dursdan spent most of the early hours of the morning tending to Biyoni. Aber brought a bucket of warm water and Mirana helped him give the little Gold her first bath. His parents finally left, although Mergadan had to pull Dachia away. "Let him be, he's not going anywhere. He needs rest after his ordeal."

Sometime after midmorning, Timotha finished her song. Dursdan looked at Mirana. "Would you like to go see what White dragon eggs look like?"

"Are you sure we should disturb her?"

Dursdan felt for Timotha with his mind. *Would we bother you if we slipped in and had a peek?*

"Of course not! There are plenty of people here already. Besides, I think Sinotio would be very proud if you came."

Dursdan looked down at his stained and torn clothes. "I'm afraid I'm not dressed to go visiting."

Mirana laughed. "I doubt anyone will care." She leaned forward and kissed him. "I'm just glad you're home."

Dursdan smiled and helped her to her feet. He picked up the sack and tied it back around his waist. Mirana looked puzzled. "It's some things I borrowed from Aramel. I'm hoping your Da can tell me how he prepared the plants. I'm afraid the ones I have are a little damp."

Dursdan and Mirana climbed down from the loft. Kalista met them at the bottom of the ladder. "I know you've been carrying her egg around for all this time but it will be some while before she gets around on her own." She held out a new pouch. "This one will fit her fine and she'll be able to peek her head out and see the world."

"Thank you, Kalista." Dursdan kissed her on the cheek and the woman blushed. "Oh, go on you two. I'm guessing you're off to see the eggs. It's the talk of the town. Can you imagine that! A White from long ago come back and laid a brood." She shook her head.

Dursdan and Mirana made their way over to Sorazan's place. A sizable crowd was gathered, both people and dragons. Trusumo looked over and smiled at him. *"Welcome, Dur."*

All the other dragons turned and bowed. Biyoni popped her head up out of the pouch and hiccupped. The people laughed. Dorsadram came forward to admire the new baby Gold. "She's beautiful, Dur. We're glad to have you home safe."

"Thank you, sir. I hope Lord Sorazan wasn't too put out that Mithra invited Timotha to clutch in her space."

"Not at all. I think he's quite honored. Come along and see them."

Dursdan took Mirana's hand and followed the Head of the Circle into the shed. The crowd parted to let them through. Timotha and Sinotio sat together looking down on five gleaming eggs. The surface of the eggs swirled with white and silver patterns. Sinotio looked at Dursdan. "*Is she not grand?*"

Dursdan smiled back. "Yes, she is."

Humatsu came over and stood next to him. "This is quite unique. What do we do now? I don't know that there are five Lords sons ready for an egg."

"Maybe it's time to let go of old traditions." He looked up at Timotha. "Do you want your children to have riders?"

Humatsu gasped but the White nodded. "*Oh, yes!*" She looked over where Varimato sat staring at the newly laid eggs. "*I love my rider and I know that my children will also love their riders.*"

"Then perhaps you should choose who they will be. There are many young boys in the Valley, not just Lords sons, but also the sons of farmers, and millers, and black smiths. We are all descendants of the First Lords. All should have the right to make a choice to be a rider or not." He looked at Humatsu. "There are many times I wished that I had a choice." He looked down at Biyoni and she looked back at him. "I'm glad I have Biyoni, I don't regret her. I just wish I could have made the choice myself." He scratched her eye-ridges and she purred.

The Lord nodded and looked up at the White. "And what does she say?"

"*Bring them to see the eggs. I will see who each egg chooses.*"

Dursdan had never considered that. Maybe the baby dragon would like a choice, too. "She says anyone can come but the egg will have to choose them."

Humatsu's eyebrows went up. "Well, isn't that a twist!" He laughed. "As it should be." He bowed to the White queen and left.

Dursdan felt something tugging at his trousers and looked down. To his surprise, Ferdj stood looking up at him. Biyoni looked down, too. "*Food?*"

"No, little one. This is our friend, Ferdj." Dursdan reached down and opened his hand and the wood gnome stepped on. Dursdan picked him up. "How have you been? Is your family well?"

The gnome bowed. "Well indeed, my Lord. We were overjoyed to hear that you returned safe. All the woods gnomes searched after you disappeared but our short little legs never got very far."

Dursdan bit his lip to keep from laughing. "I'm honored that you made the attempt."

Mirana looked over his shoulder. "Dur, what are you talking to?"

Dursdan turned around so Mirana could see the little gnome. "Forgive me for not making proper introductions. Ferdj, this is Mirana, my intended. Mirana, this is Ferdj, king of the wood gnomes."

Ferdj bowed formally. "I'm honored to meet you, my lady. My family and I would be delighted if the two of you would join us for harvest festival."

Dursdan looked over at Mirana. She had a quizzical expression on her face. He'd forgotten that he was the only one who could understand the gnome. He quickly translated what Ferdj had said then added. "As guests at such an occasion, it would only be proper that we bring a dish to pass, don't you think? I'm betting the garden did well."

She blinked. "Oh, yes. It did splendid." She looked up at Dursdan. "We are going to a feast with gnomes?"

"Yes, dear. It will be grand. They have a lovely home. Wait until you see it." He turned back to Ferdj. "We shall come and bring something to share. Please tell your wife I'll be honored to see her again."

Ferdj bowed and Dursdan put him down. The gnome looked between the feet toward the eggs. "Don't worry, we'll keep the rats away."

Dursdan smiled. "Thank you, I'm sure Timotha will be pleased to know that. I'll tell her on your behalf."

"Oh, it's our little gnome friend. Hi, Ferdj." Tolatrom waved at the gnome. The gnome waved back. He looked toward a moving pile of hay, hoisted his spear, and went to stalk his prey.

Dursdan turned and hugged his brother. "Tola!" Biyoni squawked, caught in the squeeze. Dursdan looked down. "I'm sorry, little one, did you want to greet Tola, too?"

She turned her head and studied him. Tolatrom laughed. "I'm just so glad you're home. Drasia and I are getting married, you know. We've decided to wed at midwinter."

"That's grand." He looked over at Mirana. "I guess I missed my Day Natal."

Tolatrom chuckled. "Well, at least you don't have to worry about Ashandra. It seems she's too closely related to marry you. When Frecha wrote out our family line for our wedding, she noticed the ties between our house and the House of Aki."

Dursdan smiled. "I wasn't planning on asking her anyway." A blush had come to Mirana's cheeks and Dursdan was certain it had nothing to do with the warmth of the shed. He looked up at Timotha, briefed her on the gnomes, then pulled Tolatrom and Mirana away.

"What are you up to, Dur?"

Dursdan turned to his brother. "I want to show you something." He sat down in the shade of the barn and untied the knot that held the sack. He dumped out the books and ruined ingredients.

Tolatrom whistled. "What's all this stuff?"

Dursdan picked up one of the books. "These are spell books. I used some of them to escape."

Mirana was examining the ingredients. "I recognize some of the pouches. My Mum made them. They must contain the special plants that Pa grows."

Dursdan nodded. I'm hoping your Da can teach me how to prepare more."

"You're going to do magic?" Mirana looked uncertain.

Tolatrom grinned. "You're not going to turn me into a toad, are you?"

Dursdan shook his head. "I don't think Aramel is about to give up. I want to learn how to protect us from him."

Mirana paged through one of the books. "What are these strange symbols?"

"They are wizard's script. I can read them when I hold the stone." He pulled it out so Mirana could see it.

"Where did that come from?"

"Jacobi gave it to me the night of Conor's Day Natal. It was suppose to be a gift for mine. He knew he wouldn't be there so he gave it to me early."

Mirana touched it. "It's beautiful."

"Can anyone use it?"

"I don't know. Gran said that magic runs in our bloodlines. If anyone else could use it, it should be you. Hold it in your hand and look at the book."

His brother took the stone and held it. "I don't see any difference."

Dursdan took the stone back. He frowned and looked down at Biyoni. "Maybe it has something to do with having a Gold."

Sinotio tickled in the back of his mind. "*You have always dreamed with us. You are different.*"

Dursdan sighed. "I suppose so."

Mergadan and Dorsadram wandered over. The old Lord smiled. "Ah, there you are, Dur. Your Da and I have just been talking about your missed celebration. If you're feeling up to it, we could reschedule the day."

Dursdan shrugged. "Why not." He looked down at his clothes and groaned. "But I'm afraid my Ma will be disappointed."

Mergadan laughed. "Don't be silly. I doubt she'll care what you wear and long as you actually show up this time."

Dachia did care what he wore and spent the next few days fussing over his new clothes. Dursdan spent most of his time feeding Biyoni and visiting with Mirana. She baked an amazing sweet potato pie for the gnomes' harvest festival and Dursdan snuck in a huge sack of garden vegetables. Timotha liked the gnomes. They fiercely protected her eggs from the rats.

Dursdan stopped in to see how things were going the day before his rescheduled celebration. Timotha was peering at Rashir. Dursdan stayed in the shadows.

Dorsadram sat on a box near the White queen and shook his head. "I'm sorry, Rash."

Rashir shrugged. "It doesn't matter. My Da will bring me a better egg anyway." He turned and strutted out of the barn.

Dorsadram sighed, looked up, and noticed Dursdan. The Head beckoned him forward. Timotha grinned at him as he approached. "*What a nasty boy. None of my eggs would want someone like that.*"

"It seems Rashir didn't make a good impression on any of the baby dragons."

"So it would seem." Dorsadram glanced up at the White then back at Dursdan. "And how fairs the baby Gold."

Dursdan looked down at the pouch where Biyoni was curled up sleeping. "She's recovering." He noticed a shadow in the doorway of the barn. "Who's there?"

Ragan came into the light. "I was just wondering what they looked like."

Dursdan smiled at his cousin. "Come have a look."

Ragan slowly approached. He looked up at the White. His body trembled. He stopped at the edge of the hay pile and looked at the eggs. "They are beautiful."

Timotha leaned forward. "*Ask him to come closer.*"

"It's all right. She wants you to look at them."

Ragan moved into the hay and knelt near the eggs. Timotha smelled his hair. He held very still but his eyes flinched. She rolled one of the eggs closer to him. He looked up at her. She touched him lightly with her snout. He slowly reached out and touched the egg.

"*He is good. The baby likes him!*"

Dursdan didn't know what to say. He knelt beside Ragan and put a hand on his shoulder. "That's your egg."

Ragan gasped and looked up. "For certain?"

Dursdan could only nod. He smiled up at Timotha. Dorsadram shook his head. "Well, I'll be." He stood up and extended his hand to Ragan. "Welcome, eggling carrier."

Ragan stood up and took the old man's hand. "Thank you, sir." He looked up at Timotha. "And thank you."

Timotha smiled. "*Tell him I like him.*"

Dursdan relayed her comment. Ragan seemed to blush. Dorsadram clapped him on the arm. "Tell your family, collect your things, and return here. Your new place is with your egg."

Another figure appeared in the doorway. Dursdan turned. Framos stood waiting with a bag in each hand. Dorsadram smiled. "Ah, and here is another. Are you ready to take on your new responsibilities?"

The boy nodded. He came in and set his things near a row of cots that had been set up along one wall. He pulled an egg pouch out of a bag. "My Ma made this."

"Then come forward and accept your eggling."

Framos walked up to the nest and Timotha pushed his egg toward him. Dorsadram carefully picked it up and placed it in the pouch. Dursdan helped tied it on. He looked up at Timotha. "Does the baby have a name?"

The White nodded. "*Her name is Lazana.*"

Dursdan told Framos and the boy smiled and began talking to his egg. He wandered off through the large open door.

Ragan looked up at Timotha. "Does my baby dragon have a name already?"

She nodded. "*His name is Santoth.*"

Dursdan walked with his cousin until their paths parted. They paused at the crossroad. Ragan looked down the road in the direction of his house. "I don't know how my Pa will take this. He wasn't happy when I told him our families were kin."

"What matters most is what you feel. I don't know how my family will feel about my choice tomorrow but I know in my heart that she's the right one."

Ragan nodded and held out his hand. "Good Day Natal tomorrow, Dur."

Carala met him at the courtyard gate. Dursdan took the egg basket and carried it in for her. Mergadan was washing Sinotio with a long handled broom. He paused a moment to watch. Biyoni woke up and poked her head out of the pouch. Carala chuckled. "Do you want a bath, too?"

Biyoni chirped and looked up at Dursdan. "*Play in water?*"

Dursdan laughed. "I guess she does."

He followed her into the house. The warmth wrapped around him after the chill of the late autumn afternoon. Rich smells made his stomach rumble. "Ma must be cooking something good for dinner."

"Most of it is for tomorrow but I'm sure she won't let you starve tonight." She paused at the dining room door. "Why don't you use the main table? The kitchen has very little space right now. I'll bring you a bowl of water."

Dursdan went into the dining room. He could hear voices in the kitchen. He recognized Rayina's and groaned. What would she say to him? He was glad he hadn't gone in.

Carala, with towels draped over her arms, brought a large pot of steaming water in and set it on the table. Biyoni scrambled out of the pouch and almost fell. Dursdan caught her and plopped her into the pot. She giggled and splashed. *"Play in water!"*

"If you splash all the water out of the bowl, you won't have any left for your bath." Dursdan hid a laugh behind a towel. He mopped up the water that continued to escape the pot.

Carala smiled. "She's such a sweet baby." She reached out to stroke Biyoni's head. "I knew you would come to accept her with time."

Dursdan studied his grandmother for a moment. He hadn't seen much of her since his return. She seemed to have aged far beyond the time he'd been gone. "Gran, did Armia ever tell you anything about the Eye?" He pulled it out from beneath his shirt.

Carala looked up and gasped. "Where did you get that?"

"It's a long story. I don't know if there are any references to it in the book. I haven't had a chance to look yet."

She came closer and touched the stone lightly. "The Eye of Zaradan. I thought it was lost when he died."

"I found it in a stream a few years ago. Jacobi carried it home for me and we both forgot about it. He found it before my Day Natal and gave it to me as a gift."

She sat down in a chair and shook her head. "Armia and Korithiena had discussed it a time or two but I don't think she ever wrote about it." She looked up at him. "Can you use it?"

Dursdan nodded. "I can read and speak the elder tongue when I hold it and everything looks different."

"The Eye was given to Zaradan by the Greatest Wizard of the West as a wedding present. Korithiena said that it gave him the ability to focus the power of his Gold dragon. But you are different. Their blood flows through you. Wizard's blood. Elven blood. Torg had some unusual abilities." She reached up and touched his face. "Somehow, I always knew that you did, too."

The outer door slammed and the hallway filled with noisy happy voices. Dursdan slipped the stone back under his shirt and took his grandmother's hand. "I think it best that this be kept in silence for the time being."

She nodded. "I'll let you finish up here and go help your Ma with dinner. It sounds like we'll have a houseful tonight."

Carala left the dining room. Radachi and Avanta, followed by their children, entered. Radachi grinned. "There you are! As the Da does, so does the son, I see."

Biyoni ducked under the water and blew bubbles through her nostrils. The children laughed with delight and volunteered to help finish washing her. Dursdan agreed and soon the little Gold, all neat and clean, was tucked back in her sack.

The dinner table was indeed packed that night. Tolatrom and Drasia also joined them, making it cozy but joyful. Dursdan spent most of the meal watching and listening. He hadn't realized how much he had missed them. He eventually excused himself and went to his room. A new pair of clothes was folder neatly on his chair.

He spent only a short time in the Mists and woke early, did the chores, and came back in to change. Dachia fussed over the new clothes. She seemed sad. When she disappeared into the kitchen, Dursdan looked over at his father. "What is it?"

"I think she wanted you to choose Ashandra but she's already taken. I guess your Ma is a little disappointed, that's all."

Dursdan sighed. Would she accept Mirana? He hoped so. He rode with his father on Sinotio. Biyoni laughed the whole way. Other dragons flew along side. No one wanted to risk loosing him a second time.

The village was overflowing. It seemed the barriers between Lords and farmers were falling away. Conor rushed up and hugged him followed by Jacobi and Steban. Steban held out a new flute. "It's a gift for you on your Day Natal." He laughed. "A few months late, but they say better late than never."

"It's beautiful, Steb. I can't wait to try it. And how are things with you and your wife?"

Steban grinned. "It seems we're expecting our first come spring."

Dursdan laughed and shook his hand. He looked around and finally found Mirana in the crowd. Biyoni chirped and she looked up and waved. Steban chuckled. "I guess it's no surprise who you're choosing."

Dursdan smiled. He noticed Ragan in the crowd. Conor looked over and whistled. "Will you look at that! He's carrying an egg."

Jacobi shook his head. "I heard he had a rough time of it with his Pa. It's no secret that Doran has no love of dragons or their Lords."

"I'm hoping my cousin will do well, in spite of his family."

"Cousin?" Steban's brow wrinkled. "How did that happen?"

Dursdan grinned. "I'll tell you about it sometime."

Mergadan began his speech and called Dursdan to the platform. He felt a little awkward climbing the steps but he turned and stood next to his father. Mergadan's voice boomed out over the crowd. "It's an important event for every boy as he steps into adulthood and takes up the responsibilities of a man." He turned and looked at his son. "A man has to have a good partner to walk with him through life. Dursdan, who do you choose to ask?"

Dursdan looked across the sea of faces but only one drew his attention. "I choose Mirana, daughter of Aber." There were gasps from some of the crowd and approving murmurs from others. He held out his hand to her and she took it, allowing him to pull her gently up onto the platform.

Frecha closed the book. "It's a good match."

Mergadan sighed and turned to them. He smiled at Mirana. "I hope you'll allow me to call you daughter."

"Thank you, Da."

Dursdan wanted to cry. He took her in his arms and kissed her. The crowd broke into a wild applause. Mergadan climbed down from the platform and went to his wife. She was smiling though her tears. Aber made his way up to them and the Lord and farmer shook hands.

Biyoni was the first to notice the green dragon circling the square. *"She comes!"* She laughed.

It took Dursdan a moment to realize what she was seeing. "It's Balashir!"

"Where?" Mirana shaded her eyes and looked up.

Dursdan whistled to his father and pointed at the incoming dragon. Mergadan motioned people to back away from the large grassy patch in front of the gazebo.

Biyoni crawled out of the pouch and climbed onto Dursdan's shoulder, dug her talons in, and wiggled her tail in delight. Her giggles echoed in Dursdan's mind. "Ow! Watch the sharp claws, little one!" Biyoni pouted sheepishly then rubbed her head against his cheek.

Mirana laughed. "Is that her way of asking for forgiveness? I should try that."

Dursdan pulled her closer so that he could rub his head on her neck. Mirana and Biyoni both laughed.

The strong beating of wings echoed across the square as the green dragon collapsed in the clearing. "Balashir looks exhausted and Chatia is bleeding!" He slowly reached out his mind to touch hers. He felt the echoes of pain, biting teeth and raking claws. Dursdan stumbled.

Mirana caught him before he fell out of the gazebo. "Are you all right?"

He steadied himself on one of the supports. "I'll be okay but Chatia needs care."

"Balashir doesn't look so good himself."

Mergadan helped Balashir off the dragon and supported his weight as he led him toward the steps. "What grabbed you?" He gently eased him down.

Rashir pushed his way through the crowd and approached his father with a goblet of wine. He extended it in shaking hands. Balashir took the cup and drained it. Then he set it down and pulled a sack from his vest. He reached inside and withdrew a shimmering blue egg. Rashir stood staring at it.

Dursdan remembered the first time he had seen Biyoni's egg and reached up to stroke her neck. She snuggled against him, purring softly.

Balashir held the egg out to Rashir. The boy looked up at his father. "It's blue," he whispered.

Balashir nodded. "The biggest of the entire brood. It will probably be a large male."

Rashir still didn't take the egg. Mirana nudged Dursdan and leaned closer. "What's wrong with him? Why doesn't he take the egg?"

Dursdan shook his head. "None of Timotha's eggs wanted him. He was bragging that his Da would bring him a better one. Somehow I don't think this is what he had in mind."

A deep rumble invaded his thoughts. He glanced up and met Sinotio's eyes. "*I pity the egg!*" He snorted.

Biyoni giggled and flickered her tongue. Dursdan stroked her neck. "Be polite, little one."

Rashir finally reached out and took the egg. There was a collective sigh from the onlookers and then a general round of applause and whistles. Mergadan clapped Rashir on the shoulder and looked up at Dursdan, a smile wrinkling his weathered features. "It looks like were celebrating for two of our young men today."

The crowd cheered and the musicians began to play. Biyoni bounced in time to the music and flipped her tail.

"Looks as though Biyoni likes music." Mirana grabbed Dursdan's hand. "Come on, let's teach her how to dance!"

Dursdan let Mirana pull him into the dance line. As they whirled, he watched her laughing face and flying hair that reflected the hues of the changing leaves. He began to whistle along with the music. Maybe tonight he would try the tune out on his new flute.

Epilogue

Aramel pushed open one of the great hay doors and stared at the town. Somewhere, in that dancing mass of people, was his baby dragon with that whelp of a boy. He considered various spells but ruled them out one by one, too much commotion. He didn't want to draw attention to himself; he still might need these simple-minded peasants.

They were all there, ignorant of their fate. To think that a foolish lad had even the slightest chance of controlling a golden dragon, why, it was laughable. Oh, they would soon discover the error of this mockery. Only a real Wizard had the ability to control such ancient magic.

But he would have his dragon. He patted the moldy leather volume tucked in his satchel. There were other ways. He turned away from the festivities and shuffled across the floor of the hayloft. Gathering up the sack of ingredients, he climbed into the hay. There he laid everything out and cast the spell. He extended his hand over the mixture and, as he chanted, a soft glow appeared in his palm.

He moved toward the piles of hay and the glow became brighter. He let the power of illumination guide him. Soon it became very bright. With his other hand, he gently sifted through the loose straws.

Something below began to glow in response. Aramel shifted a few more loose strands and the entire hayloft exploded into an array of magnificent rainbows. He carefully reached down and extracted a tiny shard of eggshell. Aramel smiled.